Von Ryan's Express

by David Westheimer

VON RYAN'S EXPRESS
SUMMER ON THE WATER
THE MAGIC FALLACY
WATCHING OUT FOR DULIE

Paperbound

J P MILLER'S DAYS OF WINE AND ROSES
THIS TIME NEXT YEAR

–Von Ryan's Express–

——David Westheimer——

Doubleday & Company, Inc., Garden City, New York

Library of Congress Catalog Card Number 63–20513
Copyright © 1964 by David Westheimer
All Rights Reserved
Printed in the United States of America

W

To Larry Kennedy

Von Ryan's Express

—I—

The small Italian sentry was lounging placidly in the plum-colored shade of the prison camp wall, his toylike carbine propped near his leg, when the new prisoner was brought in. The sentry had seen many American and British officers enter Campo Concentramento Prigionieri di Guerra 202 and had long since lost interest in them. He never noticed faces any more, only boots. The new one was Americano, the sentry noted through half-closed eyes. Americane boots, the kind the Americani called GI. He would gladly have given a month's wine and tobacco ration for such a pair.

Then a scalding voice pinned him against the wall. The sentry shrank back, his elbows and shoulder blades grinding into the warm dun brick, his little carbine clattering to the baked earth. He did not understand the words but their tone was unmistakable.

"Don't you salute officers in your army, soldier?" the newcomer demanded in a hard voice. "And pick up that popgun before you trip over it."

The sentry gaped at the American officer, his eyes abulge and furtive.

"Jump to it, soldier!" the American snapped.

"Colonnello," stammered the boyish Italian second lieutenant escorting him, "he is not understand."

"Then explain it to him," the American ordered.

The lieutenant shouted at the sentry, taking refuge in anger from the insecurity instilled by the American colonel. The sentry fumbled for his carbine, came rigidly to attention and, shaking, presented arms.

The American responded with a crisp salute, then studied the dusty weapon.

"Disgraceful," he said.

He turned to the lieutenant.

"Have him clean that piece."

The lieutenant stared with brown fawn's eyes, a look of anxious concentration on his smooth face.

"Have him clean that carbine," the American said. "Not that I'm trying to help you run your war but I wouldn't want anybody shot by a filthy carbine."

"Si, colonnello," the lieutenant said hastily, wondering why he was taking orders when he should be giving them but unable to withstand the prisoner's cold assurance. "Domani. Tomorrow."

"Domani," the American said. "God knows how many times I've heard that word in the last six hours."

He returned to his scrutiny of the squirming sentry.

"Ask him when he shaved last," he demanded, without taking his eyes from the man.

The lieutenant asked. The man answered sullenly and hung his head. The lieutenant snapped at him. The sentry snapped back. They argued with increasing heat.

"As you were!" the American ordered.

They stopped immediately and looked at him as if awaiting instructions.

"Lieutenant," the American said with patient irony, "no wonder you people are losing a war. An officer does not argue with an enlisted man. He *tells* him."

"I know, Colonnello," the lieutenant said apologetically. "But these imbecilli . . . Those who guard the prigionieri are, how you say, the dregess."

He searched the colonel's face for sympathy.

"Dregs," the American corrected. "You're assigned to this prison camp, aren't you, Lieutenant?"

The lieutenant looked betrayed. He was perhaps twenty-two, with a sensitive, handsome face. His hair was dark and curly, his jaw firm, his lips full.

"While I'm on the subject," said the American, "when was the last time you had a shave, Lieutenant?"

"Only this morning," the lieutenant said eagerly, thrusting his face forward for closer inspection.

The American drew back distastefully.

"What do you use for after shave lotion?" he demanded. "Chanel No. 5?"

Without another glance at the lieutenant or the sentry, he turned and strode toward the barricade of timbers and barbed wire separating the forecourt from the prison compound, where a jostling throng of prisoners waited. The lieutenant hurried after him.

The colonel was tall and conspicuously erect. His dark blond hair was short and bristling, with a scatter of gray at the temples. His face was deeply tanned except for two ovals around the unblinking gray eyes where the skin had been shielded by sunglasses. His eyes were finely wrinkled at the corners and squinted a little from looking into the sun for enemy fighters. His was a tough face, grim almost, with no vestige of softness of any kind. It was, from a distance, a young face, but viewed closely was older than its thirty-six years.

There was a soiled lump of bloodstained bandage on the side of his head, held there by dirty adhesive tape which came down over one ear and within an inch of a heavy dark eyebrow. His flying suit was oilstained and rusty with dried blood. On his shoulders, stamped on squares of brown leather, perched the silver eagles of a colonel. On his left breast the wreathed wings of a command pilot glinted in the beetling sun.

When the colonel had first come through the prison camp

gate a prisoner who had been amusing himself making faces at the indolent sentry had shouted, "Fresh meat!"

It had quickly brought to the wire a crowd of fellow prisoners who had been taking the sun or were otherwise engaged in meaningless outdoor preoccupations. They were joined in turn by a horde of prisoners who came tumbling out of every barracks exit, thick as ants around a stickthrust.

The man who had cried out was sun blackened and ribby. He was barefoot and one-eyed. His only garment, a pair of dirty desert shorts, hung low on his bony hips revealing a black glass eye staring fixedly from his enormous navel. Except for the eye in his belly, he was not particularly conspicuous among his fellows. Though not so thin or deeply tanned, they were similarly dressed. Their hair was long and unkempt and many of them had inventive beards and mustaches. Some wore eyeshades made of cardboard and twine and a man in the forefront had a tin plate on his head, held there with a black shoelace tied beneath his chin.

The prisoners jeered and applauded, a holiday crowd at a ragpickers' carnival, while the colonel toyed with the sentry. When the colonel approached them, they pressed closer, forcing the men in front against the barbed wire and filling the air with greetings and cries of pain.

"Hey, Colonnello, welcome to P. G. Doochentydooey."

"We got Messina yet?"

"Have we landed up north?"

"Where'd they get you?"

"You ain't gonna like it here, Colonel."

The newcomer did not answer or smile. He surveyed the mob with a look of distaste on his hard brown face, his eyes frosty in their pale ovals of untanned skin. The prisoners, unabashed, continued their clamor. The sentry at the barricade, having witnessed the scene at the camp entrance, threw open his gate and came to attention. The colonel returned his salute and stepped through, followed by the lieutenant.

"I bring you a new companion," said the lieutenant, smiling.

"You're a good kid, Bobby," a prisoner called out.

"Thank you," the lieutenant replied.

"We'll leave your name off our shite list when our chaps get here," cried a British voice.

"Thank you," the lieutenant said again, "but it is not necessary."

"That's what you think."

A sturdy man in a broad-brimmed Australian hat came shoving through the press toward the newcomer.

"Stand aside, you buggers," he said in a deep, good-natured voice.

He had a black mustache like the horns of a Cape buffalo, immensely thick in the middle and curving out and up in a noble sweep of luxuriant jet. His eyes were blue, his chin and jaw heavy. His skin was more pink than tanned. He wore greasy British battle dress trousers hacked off at the knee, and broken desert boots. His big toe protruded through a gap in the left one.

"Who's the senior officer here?" the colonel demanded.

The sturdy man shoved aside the prisoners nearest the colonel and stepped forward holding out a broad hand.

"Fincham here," he said. "Eric Fincham, leftenant colonel, Royal Army. Welcome to P. G. Two-oh-bloody-two, Colonel."

The colonel seemed not to see the proffered hand, his eyes fastening instead on the Britisher's arching mustache. Fincham's face went a shade pinker.

"A light colonel," said the American. "I'm a bird colonel."

He shook the Englishman's hand at last, then turned to face the center of the noisy throng.

"I am Col. Joseph Ryan," he announced. "Your new senior officer."

"Iron-ass Ryan," exclaimed a burly man with a big peeling nose who had just rushed from the barracks to join the mob at the gate. "I had him at advanced. Only he was a captain then."

If Ryan heard him he gave no indication of it.

"I'll want a talk with you after a while, Colonel," Ryan said to Fincham.

The Italian lieutenant cleared his throat and said apologetically, "I must report now to the settore office. With the colonnello's permission . . ."

"Carry on, Lieutenant," said Ryan.

"Good afternoon, gentlemen," said the lieutenant.

"So long, Bobby," the prisoners chorused.

Ryan turned to the prisoners.

"Break up this high school pep rally and go back to your quarters until further orders," he said.

He did not speak in a particularly loud voice but his words carried to the rearmost ranks. The prisoners stared at him in uncomprehending silence.

"I gave an order!" Ryan snapped. "Move."

He looked at the skinny man with the glass eye in his navel.

"Except you," he said. "You stand by."

Muttering, the prisoners began moving slowly toward the surrounding barracks.

"A pretty raunchy bunch, Colonel," Ryan said, turning to Fincham.

Fincham's pink deepened again and his lips parted as if in retort, but instead of answering he pressed them together so firmly the tips of his mustache vibrated.

Ryan's eyes dropped to the skinny man's belly.

"You're staring," he said.

"Sir?" the man blurted. "No, *sir!*"

"Put that eye where it belongs."

"Yes, *sir!*"

He plucked the glass eye from his navel, popped it into his mouth to moisten it, and inserted it in his empty socket. His good eye, lighter in color than the artificial one, roved nervously.

"That's better," said Ryan. "But not much. Hitch up those shorts."

The man raised his shorts above his hips but they slipped back down immediately.

"Get yourself a belt," Ryan ordered. "What's your name?"

"Frankie . . . I mean, Orde, sir. Orde, Franklin. Second lieutenant."

"Colonel," Ryan said to Fincham, "why hasn't this man been repatriated?"

"I suggest you take that up with Colonel Battaglia," Fincham replied angrily.

"I will," said Ryan. "Lieutenant, carry on."

"Sir?"

"Taxi after the others."

"Yes, sir."

Orde left at a trot, his thin arms pumping, his calloused feet slapping on the hardpacked earth of the courtyard.

"Now," said Ryan. "Where can we talk?"

"My quarters . . . sir," Fincham said with savage courtesy.

"Lead on."

Fincham led him across the courtyard and up ironbound cement steps to the top floor of the two-story U-shaped barracks. Socks and less identifiable articles of clothing hung on the iron guardrails like the banners of some ragged but dauntless army. When they reached the second floor, Fincham thrust his hands into the frayed pockets of his shorts and sauntered along the porch. The porch was a six-foot strip of dirt-scabbed cement cluttered with pots and boxes of reddish earth from which protruded random spears of onion and straggly garlands of radish.

"This supposed to be a garden?" Ryan asked.

"Tunnel dirt," said Fincham. "Must get rid of it somehow."

"How far along are you?"

"New one's just begun. The one before was almost to the wall before the Ites found it."

The prisoners were noisy in their quarters. When Ryan and Fincham passed the doorless entrance to a living bay the occupants fell silent, stared at Ryan, and resumed their yammer when he passed. Midway along the porch they reached a small, shallow room.

Fincham paused, bowed mockingly and, with a flourish of his hand, said, "My humble quarters are at your disposal, sir."

"Thank you," said Ryan, ignoring the irony.

The room was dim and cool after the penetrating glare of the untempered sun. The floor and walls were dark brown tile, the ceiling light plaster. The room was six feet wide, eight deep, and eight high. It gave an impression both of bareness and clutter. The only furniture was a heavy four-sided stool of solid unpainted wood and a rickety two-deck bunk, also of unpainted wood. On the top bunk was a thin paillasse and a flat pillow. The frame of the bottom bunk formed a little pen containing a pair of British boots and two cardboard boxes full of tin cans. A pair of woolen socks, some underdrawers, and a small soiled towel hung on a string stretched between the bunkposts.

Fincham placed his palms flat on the top bunk, sprang into the air, twisted lithely and landed in a sitting position as the bunk shuddered in imminent collapse. He sat grinning down at Ryan, his teeth white in the gloom.

"This is one of our posh suites, sir," he said. "Guinea a night, bed and breakfast. We have less dear accommodations for subalterns. But I expect the colonel will be wanting our very best. Flying pay and all that."

Ryan ran a finger along an inchwide wall projection and looked casually at the grime he collected.

"I used to do this wearing white gloves," he said. "And gigged a man when I found a speck on 'em. When was the last time this room was policed?"

"Policed? Oh. What month is this, July? Yes, so it is, July. June, I believe it was. Or was it May? You know how time flies when you're on holiday. Sit down, sit down, sir. Try the easy chair there."

Ryan remained standing. He rubbed a hand across his chin.

"I need a shave," he said. "Is there some tackle I can borrow until I get my issue?"

Fincham's grin broadened.

"Your issue, did you say? I expect that might be a bit, Colonel. Unless you've arranged to have it parachuted in."

"I see."

Fincham dropped to the floor and rummaged through the litter in the lower bunk. He straightened, holding a small tin of soap, a molting brush, and a battered safety razor.

"I'll sharpen the blade," he said.

"That won't be necessary."

"Bold words, Colonel. But reckless."

Fincham took out the blade and rubbed it rapidly around the inside of an earthenware mug.

"There," he said. "That should do it."

The brush fell to the floor as he was handing it to Ryan and both men stooped to retrieve it. Ryan's legs buckled. Fincham grabbed him before he hit the floor.

"Are you all right?" he asked.

"Damn," Ryan said angrily. "I must have lost more blood than I . . . I'm all right, Colonel. Let go of me. You've got an arm like an anaconda."

Fincham released him and went to the door.

"Bonzer!" he shouted. "Quick time!"

Heads popped out of every door in the two-story warren, looked toward Fincham's room, then popped back inside again.

"What're you up to?" Ryan demanded.

"My runner. Want to lie down?"

"I told you I'm fine. I don't guess there's any hot water for shaving?"

"Not unless you brought it with you."

Hobnailed boots pounded along the porch and a squat man knocked, burst into the room, and flung out a massive arm in an exaggerated British salute. His only garment was a kilt made of coarse gray blanket. He had a short stubble of red hair and a thick red mustache running across his ruddy cheeks and turning into sideburns.

"Sir!" he bellowed, standing at straining attention, his deep voice reverberating in the tiled room.

"Fetch Captain Stein," said Fincham.

"Sir!" Bonzer shouted again, saluting, whirling, and racing off with a clatter of hobnails.

"Who's Captain Stein?" Ryan asked.

"One of yours. Still keen on shaving?"

"I said I was all right. Got a mirror?"

Fincham dived into his cache again and emerged with a jagged triangle of glass.

"The mirror's sharper than the razor, I expect," he said.

He poured water into a tin can from a wine bottle hanging by a string from the bunkpost.

"You'll have to go outside to shave," he said, nodding toward the small dusty bulb screwed into the ceiling. "No lights until dark and then bloody little."

Out on the porch, Ryan made a thin lather and spread it on his face. He showed no further sign of weakness. He had finished shaving one cheek, the cold, dull blade dragging at his whiskers, when Bonzer returned with Captain Stein.

Stein was a spare man of medium height with a shock of wiry brown hair, alert brown eyes, and a brown mustache which looked as if it had just been clipped and combed. He wore a neat khaki uniform with the shirt sleeves buttoned at the wrists. His GI shoes were glossy. Ryan looked at him approvingly.

"That's more like it," he said. "What can I do for you, Captain?"

"It's what I can do for you, sir," Stein replied.

"What did you have in mind?" Ryan demanded.

"I'd like a look at that scalp of yours."

"Why?"

"I'm a doctor."

"A doctor? What's a doctor doing in a prisoner of war compound?"

"Colonel, sir, you have no idea how many hours I've lain in my lumpy sack asking myself that question."

"Captain Stein refused repatriation, Colonel," said Fincham.

"Nobody shoots at me here as long as I behave myself," Stein explained.

Prisoners had gathered at the bay entrances to watch the

tableau on the second floor. It was seldom they had such diversions. Bonzer was standing at attention.

"Sir?" he boomed.

"Oh," said Fincham. "You still hanging about? Muck off."

"Sir!" cried Bonzer, sprinting off.

His hobnails struck sparks on the cement.

"Soldierly type," said Ryan. "First one I've seen around here."

"He's 'round the bend," said Fincham, grinning.

" 'Round the bend?"

"Daft," Fincham explained.

"Nutty as a fruitcake, to put it in precise medical terminology," Stein said. "Would you mind sitting down while I have a look at that wound? Finch, you want to move the stool out here where I can see?"

Ryan resumed shaving while Stein removed the bandage. He did not wince when Stein pulled the adhesive tape away and worked the bandage free of the crusted wound.

"Ugh," Stein grunted. "Doctor who did this should have stitched you up. Hurt?"

"Only when you fumble around with it."

"My experience with this end of the patient is comparatively recent," Stein said placidly. "In civilian life I'm an obstetrician. I'll just run down and get my tool kit out of hock and see if I can't clean you up a little. Your tetanus current?"

"Yes. Also cholera, yellow fever, typhus, typhoid, and smallpox. I'm inoculated against everything but flak."

"Good," said Stein. "Since I don't have any anti-tetanus serum. I just asked out of curiosity. Be right back."

He left carrying the bloody bandage dangling from his hand.

"What'd he mean, get his tool kit out of hock?" Ryan asked.

"The Ites keep his medical kit locked up in the dispensary. Brought it in with him. The Ites bagged him with full kit. Got himself lost behind their lines looking for his billet with a green driver."

"So that's why he's got a clean uniform. Does he wear it all the time or did he put it on in my honor?"

"He put it on for you but I dare say not in your honor," Fincham said dryly. "He wears his clean uniform when he visits any patient. Even an OR."

"OR? Oh, Other Rank. Enlisted man. Tell me something, Colonel. If Captain Stein can keep himself presentable in here why can't the other officers?"

"We weren't all fortunate enough to be put in the bag with full kit, Colonel."

"I'm not referring to his uniform, Colonel. He's clean and his hair's cut. Which is more than I can say for anyone else I've seen so far."

"You tell me something, Colonel, if you please."

"Yes?"

"What do you hope to gain with this headmaster manner?"

Ryan saw the prisoners grinning from doorways.

"Let's step inside, Colonel," he said. "I'm not putting on a floor show."

Inside the room, his manner grew icy.

"You can call my manner what you want to, Colonel," he said. "Maybe if you had some of it this place wouldn't be in such miserable shape. I've seen some hellholes in my time but this has got anything I've seen in North Africa beat. The wogs have an excuse. They don't know any better. But you're supposed to be officers."

Fincham's eyes glinted in a mask of red.

"You're bloody right, there," he snapped. "We're officers. Not chars."

"You will be before I'm through with you. And a lot more. This camp is a disgrace. It's filthy. And you've let the men get raunchy, childish, and undisciplined. They've forgotten what it means to be soldiers, if they ever knew."

Fincham thrust his face close to Ryan's.

"See here, you bloody Yank! You stroll in from bacon and egg breakfasts and a cushy billet and expect to find things the same here. This is no bloody picnic and you'll find that out if you don't get your bloody head bashed in first."

Ryan's expression of cold distaste did not change.

"In the British Army is it customary to address a superior officer in such an unmilitary manner?" he asked.

"Ballocks!"

"Do you acknowledge that I am in command here?"

"Worse luck for all of us."

"If you keep that in mind it'll save you a lot of grief. Now, I've got some questions to ask you."

Before he could continue, Stein came in carrying a medical field pack.

"These second-floor house calls are a pain in the neck," Stein said. "Those stairs are steep. If you'll just come back out in the light I'll get to work."

"Colonel, I'll get back to you after Captain Stein gets through with me," Ryan said.

Fincham leaned against his bunk, scowling, his arms folded across his thick chest. Outside, Stein cleared a place with his foot and set out a square of rough white cloth on which he placed a bottle of alcohol, cotton, and swab sticks.

"You may find this a little uncomfortable," he said conversationally as he began cleaning the wound.

The prisoners gathered in their doorways again to watch the show. Ryan endured Stein's ministrations stoically though he grunted when Stein took the first stitch.

"Felt that, did you?" Stein asked cheerfully.

"What are you doing up there, brain surgery?"

"That was my dear old mother's dream back in St. Louis," Stein said, tying off the stitch. " 'My son the brain surgeon.' That was her dream. She never learned to pronounce obstetrician. She says 'baby doctor.' Doesn't sound the same, does it? 'My son the baby doctor.' But that's life. Sometimes it comes up heads, sometimes it comes up tails. There. A neat job if I say so myself. Too bad it's where you can't admire it, Colonel."

"Thanks, Captain," said Ryan. "I've had barbers who talked less."

Stein smiled pleasantly.

"It may ache a little but you'll live," he said. "Keep it clean and dry and stay out of the sun as much as possible. And if I were you I wouldn't do any swimming or dive-bombing the next few days."

He stored his instruments in the field pack and left. Ryan went back into Fincham's room.

"Now, Colonel," he said, "I want some answers."

"The first thing I want is an explanation of why you've permitted discipline to deteriorate so shockingly," said Ryan.

Fincham planted himself firmly on his thick legs, thrust his hands deeper into the pockets of his greasy shorts, and stared into Ryan's face with feigned guilelessness.

"Simple enough, actually, Colonel," he said blandly. "First I brought all these sods into the bag with nothing except the uniforms they stood in. Then I built this bloody great wall around them. Then I put them on short rations and closed down the NAAFI. Yours call it the PX," he explained.

"And then I put the pubs and cinemas out of bounds and sent away the wives and sweethearts," he went on in the same reasonable tone. "Shall I continue?"

Ryan showed neither anger nor amusement.

"When you've finished playing games I'd like a straight answer," he said. "If you're capable of giving one."

"I'll give you a straight answer, then. If you're capable of understanding one."

"Try me."

"There happens to be a bit of a war on, Colonel. We're fighting our share of it as best we can. The bloody little buggers are still the enemy and we've damn well let them know it."

Ryan listened silently.

"They make it hard for us but we make it harder for them and no mistake," Fincham continued with growing vehemence. "If we played their game we'd have hot showers and flicks and full parcels and the lot. But we prefer it our way."

He took his right hand out of his pocket and poked a broad tobacco-stained finger under Ryan's nose.

"Now do you understand?" he demanded. "Or would you prefer daily dress parade and high tea?"

He awaited Ryan's answer with an anticipatory smile of vindication and triumph. Ryan looked distastefully at Fincham's finger until it was removed.

"Colonel Fincham," he said with calculated restraint. "Aren't you aware there are certain standards of conduct for officers? Regardless of the circumstances?"

"You still don't understand this is a war we're in!" Fincham cried in frustration. "Not a bloody baseball match!"

"Game," said Ryan. "Not match. I think I know there's a war on, Colonel. I didn't get this head from a pitched ball. But this is no time for there-I-wuz stories."

His tone grew more cutting.

"I fail to see how filth and shaggy hair and a complete breakdown in discipline indicate a signal victory over the Italians. And tell me something. How many casualties have you inflicted and how many escapes have you effected with this victory-or-death policy of yours?"

Fincham's face knotted with fury.

"None!" he spat. "But . . ."

Ryan cut him short.

"I don't intend to debate tactics with you, Colonel. I intend to give orders. Which I expect to be obeyed. Is that clear?"

Regaining some of his composure, Fincham clicked his heels together in obvious imitation of Bonzer and snapped, "Sir!"

"We'll discuss your insubordinate manner when there's time for fun and games," Ryan said. "But now I want a look around to see just how bad things really are. Shall we go?"

When Ryan appeared on the porch the prisoners began shout-

ing and banging tin cups against the walls. They wedged themselves into doorways, faces grim with resentment at being kept
indoors. A roving guard stopped his patrol and stared anxiously
at the demonstrators from the courtyard. The guard at the barricade unslung his carbine and an Italian officer burst out of the
guard office in the forecourt and hurried toward the inner gate,
his eyes fixed on the barracks.

"Oriani," Fincham said. "A proper swine."

"What's his rank and what's he do?"

"Major. Battaglia's executive and the worst of a bad lot."

Ryan nodded.

"As you were!" he shouted, his voice crackling across the
courtyard.

The roving guard and the soldier at the barricade turned to
look at him and Major Oriani halted in mid-stride. The prisoners quit banging their cups but a sullen murmur persisted.

"I said knock it off," Ryan ordered in a quieter but no less
compelling voice. "Back inside. Move!"

They moved.

The roving guard resumed his casual stroll, the barricade
guard returned to his contemplation of the baking earth at his
feet, and Major Oriani, after a long scrutiny of Ryan and the
empty compound, returned to the guard office.

"There's no reason for keeping them inside," Fincham said.

"That's for me to decide, Colonel. We'll start with the bottom
floor."

As they walked down the sharply pitched stairs, Ryan said,
"I'm not doing this capriciously, Colonel Fincham. I want everybody in place during my inspection. And Colonel. Don't consider this an explanation. Consider it instruction."

"I'm sure I've much to learn from the colonel," Fincham replied.

In the center of the courtyard Ryan stood with his hands
clasped loosely behind him and made a searching, unhurried
survey of the compound. The barracks was an angular U, the
arms two stories high and the back a single story with a higher

roof than the first floor of the arms. Where it could not be reached by the hands or feet of the prisoners the dun stucco of the barracks walls was clean and variously toned in the sun.

The gaunt lines of the building were bladesharp in the impenetrable blue of the low sky and the brittle sunlight picked at the heavy glaze of a row of dark brown tiles set along the edge of the flat roof in an ineffectual attempt at ornamentation.

The reflection dazzled Ryan for a moment and he blinked, then grimaced as if in impatient rejection of this display of frailty. His head throbbed but his expression offered no clue to his pain, nor did he once raise his hand to the bandage covering his wound. Though his flying coveralls enveloped him in heat he was not perspiring except lightly at groin and armpits.

The earth of the courtyard was like brown stone and nowhere was there a blade of grass or hint of color except for a few reddish pebbles imbedded in the brown and polished by many feet. The prison compound was separated from the forecourt by a double fence of wooden trestles and barbed wire seven feet high. The space between the fences was heaped with loose coils of barbed wire. In one corner of the forecourt was a small square building bordered by a wide bed bursting with the colors of closely planted flowers, at the moment being tended by a sweating Italian soldier with a mattock as long as himself. In the other corner was a similar building, but small-windowed and flowerless.

Enclosing all was a fourteen-foot brick wall, its top encrusted with shards of broken glass which sparkled in the sun. At each corner of the wall was a small, cagelike sentry box of wood in which a guard leaned with his elbows on a rail and looked without interest into the compound.

After a while Ryan said, "Brief me on the layout before we go inside."

Fincham's manner changed when he described the camp to Ryan. He was precise and knowing and showed no trace of his previous truculence. He was giving a military report and he did it in correct military fashion.

The commandant, Col. Basilio Battaglia, had little direct contact with the prisoners, leaving most of the operation of the camp to the executive officer, Maj. Vittorio Oriani. Lt. Roberto Falvi, who had escorted Ryan into the compound, was responsible for the American sector of the camp, Settore I, and a Capt. Pietro Alessandro for the British sector, Settore II. There were other officers involved in the administration of the camp but the prisoners seldom saw them.

"Battaglia's a stick, Oriani's a swine, Falvi's a friendly ass, and Alessandro's mad for another pip," Fincham said.

"I assume that means he's bucking for a promotion," Ryan said agreeably.

The flower-bordered building in the forecourt was the guard office and quarters for the on-duty sentries. The companion building on the other side of the court, which Fincham called "the cooler," was a prison within the prison. Prisoners who broke rules were kept there in solitary confinement for varying periods.

"You haven't won your spurs until you've had a go at the cooler," Fincham said.

There were five sentry boxes on the wall in addition to the two visible from the center courtyard, one on each back corner and others midway on both sides and at the back.

"The sentries bang away at every shadow during the night but they're bloody awful shots," Fincham said. "When they shoot at a shadow, it's best to be in it."

A seven-foot barbed-wire fence separated the prison compound from the wall.

"It began with a trip wire and orders not to cross it but so many of our chaps had a try at the wall Battaglia had to put in a proper fence," Fincham said proudly.

There were 911 officers in P. G. 202, 602 British and 309 American. In addition, there were 53 British Other Ranks who worked in the kitchen and did other camp chores. Officers were not permitted to work except as supervisors of functions directly related to their own welfare.

"Not that we'd do anything to help the clots even if we could," Fincham added.

In addition to a Red Cross parcel issue, the prisoners received Italian rations which were cooked in the communal kitchen at the back of the U and served in two mess halls flanking it.

"That's the gen," Fincham said. "Yours call it the poop," he added in answer to Ryan's unspoken question. "I expect you'll want to know a good deal more but I can fill it in while you're having your shuftee."

"Shuftee?"

"Look 'round. Yours call it running a reccy. We've a bit of a communications problem at times."

"I've noticed."

Ryan began with the ground floor of Settore I, the American side. The front portion of the first wing was a dusty storeroom with a long counter and wooden shelves, empty now except for a few torn cardboard boxes.

"We draw Red Cross parcels here," said Fincham. "One per week per two-man section. Should be one per week per man but that sod Oriani says he hasn't staff to deal with a thousand parcels every week. Actually, it's because I offered a guard a parcel for his carbine and the little perisher reported it. The next week we went on half parcels."

"Then Oriani's claim he's shorthanded is just an excuse for reprisals," Ryan said.

"I expect he could find a way to move the bloody parcels if he gave a bloody damn about feeding us. But I'll grant the swine that. He is short on staff."

"What did you hope to gain by getting a carbine?"

"I'd find a proper use for it and no mistake," Fincham answered, bristling.

He had become less antagonistic during Ryan's attentive reception of his briefing but now the rancor was returning.

"There is no proper use for a single carbine among almost a thousand men," Ryan said.

He took a pencil and a small notepad from the knee pocket of his coveralls and made a note.

The ORs lived behind a wooden partition at the rear of the storage wing. They were away at their duties but a jumble of triple-deck bunks, boxes, tin cans, and clothing and a thick, fusty smell gave ample evidence of crowded occupancy.

"Is this the way you permit your enlisted men to live?" Ryan demanded.

"I expect they live rather better than the officers, Colonel. They receive working rations. Officers are on garrison rations."

The center wing housed a dispensary and primitive hospital. It was divided into two rooms. In the first, two tiny Italians in white smocks were smoking pungent cigarettes and playing cards at a porcelain topped metal table. They looked up carelessly when Ryan and Fincham entered the room and returned to their cards but only momentarily. One of the corpsmen gave a sharp cry and the two of them sprang to attention in a clatter of metal stools. Ryan's reputation had preceded him.

Ryan ignored them while he surveyed the room. There was little to indicate its function except an eye chart and a locked glassfront cabinet containing Captain Stein's medical kit and a few vials and bottles. A wooden stool and an iron cot completed the appointments.

"At ease," Ryan said at last.

One corpsman, understanding the command, relaxed warily, followed by the other. They watched Ryan out of the corners of their eyes.

Four iron beds occupied the narrow emptiness of the back room. There were men in two of them. One patient, spotted with measles, was snoring. The other was moaning, his fists clutching sweaty wads of the rough sheet on which he lay.

"What's the matter with this man?" Ryan asked in a low voice.

"Stein thinks a kidney stone. But there's damn all he can do for it."

"What's his name?"

"Carter. Leftenant. He's one of yours."

"His first name?"

Fincham shrugged.

"He's one of yours."

Ryan went to Carter's bedside.

"Pretty bad?" he asked.

"Christ, yes!"

"I'm Colonel Ryan. New senior officer. Hang on, Lieutenant. I'll see what can be done."

"Oh, Christ! Will you, sir?"

"That was rum, putting his hopes up," Fincham said when they were in the front room again. "There's damn all you can do."

Ryan turned to the corpsmen, who had not moved.

"You know where to find Captain Stein?"

"Si, colonnello," said the man who understood English.

"Bring him to me. I'll be somewhere around."

The corpsman saluted and ran out.

"Stein runs a good shop," said Ryan.

"He *likes* these little buggers," Fincham said disapprovingly.

The wooden doors of the next, and last, wing of Settore I were locked. Ryan looked questioningly at Fincham.

"Showers,"Fincham said. "Oriani announced there was no water or fuel to heat it—two hours after he found our tunnel in the shower room. No showers since. Except the day the Protecting Power made his visit."

"Protecting Power?"

"Every three months a Swiss pops in to see if the Ites are playing the game properly. Geneva Convention, you know."

"From the looks of this place he doesn't seem to be doing his job very well."

"He makes his report, right enough. But the Ites do damn all about it. It might interest you to know P. G. 202 has been denounced in the House of Lords as the worst officers' camp in Italy," Fincham added with a trace of pride.

"I'm not sure the Italians are entirely to blame for that, Colonel. I'll want to see your copy of the Geneva Convention as pertains to prisoners of war."

"My copy? I've never seen the bloody thing."

"Par for the course," said Ryan.

He made more notes on his pad, not bothering to explain the American expression to Fincham.

The mess hall at the back of the U was jammed with food-stained trestle tables of grainy, unfinished wood and long, rump-polished backless benches. Ryan gave a grunt of distaste.

"The serving girls and chars are on holiday," Fincham said cheerfully, enjoying Ryan's reaction to P. G. 202's squalor.

The kitchen was a huge sooty room with a gritty flagstone floor. In the center was a vast black stove, fifteen feet on a side, with four round openings in the top like some obsolete and grossly exaggerated kitchen range. Great kettles nestled in three of the holes and from a fourth flames spewed, sending billows of cinders to float against the blackened ceiling and sift back to the floor. Clamped to one side of the stove was a towering metal crane from which a blackened kettle hung by chains and a hook. Nearby was a heavy iron tripod on rollers, from which dangled a similar arrangement of hook and chains.

A dozen or so sweating men in soot-crusted battle dress trousers cut off at the knee were busy in the kitchen cutting up pumpkins on a long dripping trestle table or carrying wood from a pile in the corner to hurl into the stove's maw, leaping back to avoid the sparks cascading into the air. A man in a desert shirt and shorts, wearing a strip of blanket across his shoulders to protect his uniform from the drifting soot, was sitting at a small wooden table in a far corner.

"I say, Roger," Fincham called.

The man pushed back a copybook in which he had been making entries and came toward them. He was tall, gaunt, and fair with a blond brush mustache. His pale face was freckled with flakes of soot which he brushed away as he approached. He wore a preoccupied expression, as if doing sums in his head.

"Colonel Ryan," Fincham said, "Captain Beresford, OC messing. Roger, put out another bowl tonight. Colonel Ryan has joined our merry little band."

Beresford bowed.

"Roger had a posh restaurant on civvy street," Fincham said.

"I want something done about this soot," Ryan said. "It's getting in the food. What's in those kettles, anyway?"

"The potage du jour," Beresford said, unsmiling. "Pumpkin soup."

"Pumpkin soup?" said Ryan. "I've never heard of pumpkin soup."

"I had not either, sir," Beresford replied. "But since I've been in the bag I've seen rather a lot of it."

"Rather," said Fincham.

Just then Stein came in accompanied by the little corpsman, who saluted Ryan and left quickly.

"You wanted to see me, sir?" Stein asked, flicking soot from his khaki sleeve.

"I just saw that man in the dispensary. Carter. Is he in any real danger?"

"I'm not sure, Colonel. Not without an X ray. I don't think so. But the pain is severe."

"Captain, I want you to go to the front gate and raise hell until they give you something to fix him up or send an ambulance to take him to a real hospital."

"Colonel, I spent so much time learning my bedside manner I never learned how to raise hell."

"Then start learning. As of now."

"Yes, sir."

When Stein had gone, Ryan turned to Beresford.

"Captain," he said, "bring me a ladle."

Beresford called to one of the kitchen orderlies, who brought a long iron spoon. Braving the heat, Ryan plunged it into one of the kettles and raised it to his lips. Fincham watched him expectantly. Ryan gagged, then swallowed with an effort. He saw Fincham's eyes on him.

"Needs salt," he said unemotionally. "This part of dinner?"

"This *is* dinner," Fincham said gleefully. "With a bit of fruit. As for salt, we take what we can get when we can get it."

Ryan added to the notes on his pad and led Fincham outside. Stein was at the barricade arguing with a growing cluster of Italian soldiers, his voice loud and insistent.

"He's learning," said Ryan.

"There's another dining hall on the other side of the kitchen," Fincham said. "Precisely the same as the first. Or do you want to see for yourself?"

"I'll take your word for it."

"Thank you, I'm sure. That accounts for our public rooms. I expect you'll find the bedroom suites just as smashing."

When they looked down from the second-floor porch, Stein was walking toward the outer gate with Captain Alessandro, both of them shouting and waving their arms.

"This is A Bay, Settore Uno," Fincham said at the entrance to the front wing.

Ryan stopped short a foot inside the door.

"Phew!" he said. "How can they stand the smell?"

"What smell?" Fincham replied, genuinely puzzled.

"That overripe odor of jockey straps and armpits."

"Had you expected a boudoir, Colonel?"

The bay was long and narrow, lined on either side with double-deck wooden bunks a foot apart. The glass of the side windows had been painted over in white and what had been a large window at the rear, overlooking the wall, was sealed off with mortar-splotched brick. It was dark inside the bay and Ryan, entering from the brilliant sunlight, could see little at first.

He stood just inside the doorway letting his eyes adjust to the gloom. The bay was crowded as a hive and the buzz of conversations was beelike. The buzz subsided as awareness of Ryan's presence spread through the bay. Soon the occupants were looking his way in sullen silence.

"The next time I enter this bay the first man to see me will call the room to attention," Ryan said. "And you will remain at attention until given at ease."

He turned and walked out, motioning to Fincham to follow. The glare outside burst against Ryan's eyeballs like a fist and he closed his eyes. He opened them with an effort.

"Why've the windows been sealed off?" he asked.

"Oriani had the side windows painted because he said we were signaling from bay to bay. He bricked up the rear window after your chaps tried to stretch a ladder to the wall. Bloody fools. It's ten yards or more to the wall."

"Let's try again," said Ryan, walking back into the bay.

"Ten-hut!" bawled the first man to see him.

Caught by surprise, the men leaped up, jostling one another in the narrow aisle and dropping from top bunks in a shower of elbows and feet. Ryan threaded his way through the crush, pausing to examine bunks at random. They were festooned with odd bits of clothing hanging from ropes stretched between the posts, a flotilla of boats in some beggars' regatta. Each bunk had a narrow wooden shelf between the posts at both ends and on each shelf was a Red Cross carton filled with open tin cans.

"What's this?" Ryan demanded, pointing at a carton. "Garbage?"

"The larder," Fincham said. "The fridge is bust."

"Doesn't food spoil in this heat?"

"Doesn't get a ruddy chance."

Ryan paused before the big man who had recognized him earlier. He had a thick chest, thick waist, and broad hips, not a handsome physique but one of great power and stamina. His matted hair, a tarnished gold, was kinky and his eyebrows, also tarnished gold, were shaggy. His brows were heavy, projecting above his pale eyes in great bony ridges. Golden stubble covered his heavy jaw. Despite the craggy strength of his features and the resentment which now possessed him, his face was a good-natured one, almost clownish.

"Emil Bostick, isn't it?" said Ryan. "Goon Bostick."

"Yes, sir," the big man said with undisguised hostility.

His voice was incongruously light and high.

"If I'd washed you out on that check ride you wouldn't be in this fix, would you, Lieutenant Bostick?"

"No, sir. And it's Captain Bostick."

"My apologies, Captain. And congratulations."

Ryan picked his way back to the door.

"Carry on, gentlemen," he said, just before stepping out on the porch.

A wave of angry sound lashed after him. Fincham grinned. Ryan gave no sign he had heard the remarks.

Next to the living bay was a washroom. A long wing like the living bay, it was divided into two parts. In the front half one wall was lined with washbasins, the other with low troughs filled with scummy water.

"What are those?" Ryan asked.

"Dhobi troughs," said Fincham.

"Dhobi troughs?"

"Washtroughs, yours call them. We've water two hours in the morning, one at midday, and one in the afternoon."

"Why only then?"

"Water's short, Oriani maintains."

"Is it?"

Fincham shrugged.

"I expect so," he said grudgingly.

The back half of the washroom was occupied by a latrine with vile smelling urinals on one side and on the other a series of shallow square depressions in the tile floor. In the center of each depression was a round hole flanked by two raised tiles.

Fincham studied Ryan's perplexed expression.

"Captain Stein informs us the squatting position is most natural and healthful," he said.

"Let's get out of here," said Ryan.

On the porch, he made more notes.

"You wish to see more, Colonel?" Fincham asked. "I expect you'll find the other bays a slice off the same joint."

"I want to see them all."

Before Fincham could conduct him farther a bugler in the forecourt sounded a call.

"Evening parade," Fincham explained. "We form in the courtyard to be counted. Or does the colonel wish Colonel Battaglia informed we're confined to quarters and can't oblige?"

"Order the men to fall out, Colonel."

"Very good, sir," Fincham said mockingly.

He went to the rail and shouted an order. The prisoners poured out into the courtyard, catcalling and roughhousing, and formed wavering lines around its perimeter. Major Oriani, Captain Alessandro, and Lieutenant Falvi came through the barricade gate followed by a detail of tiny soldiers who had to trot to keep up with the long-limbed major.

"Mine are across the way," Fincham said before leaving Ryan in the courtyard. "I expect Major Wimberly will direct you to your place."

"Major Wimberly?"

"SAO. Senior American Officer. Rather, he was until today."

Falvi saluted when he caught sight of Ryan. Ryan returned the salute and stared at Oriani. Oriani stared back, a faint smile of malice and amusement on his thin lips. He was as tall as Ryan, but slender, with cat-yellow eyes in his dark, patrician face. His tailored uniform fit beautifully and his boots had a high gloss.

"Don't you salute superior officers, Major?" Ryan asked.

"If it amuses you, Colonel," Oriani replied, still smiling.

His English was flawless and British in accent.

Oriani gave a mocking Fascist salute, holding his slim, well-manicured right hand briefly aloft.

"You're a little behind the times, aren't you, Major?" said Ryan. "Or didn't you know Il Duce's been canned?"

Ryan turned abruptly and called out, "Major Wimberly, front and center."

A soft-looking youth with slightly protruding eyes and wavy chestnut hair stepped out of the ranks. He wore a threadbare khaki shirt on which pilot wings were picked out in white thread. Below the wings were hand-fashioned Distinguished Flying Cross and Air Medal ribbons.

"Here, sir," he said, taking a black, gap-toothed comb from the waistband of his shorts and running it through his waves.

"I appreciate your efforts to be well groomed under such trying circumstances, Major," said Ryan, "but an officer does not comb his hair in public."

"But, sir . . ." Wimberly began, breaking off and staring at the comb as if surprised to find it in his hand. "I didn't even realize I was . . ."

"Where's my place?" Ryan interrupted.

"We line up by bays, sir. There're some vacant bunks in B Bay so I guess you fall in with B Bay. The next one down."

"And where are your quarters, Major?"

"Oh, I'm in Room A, sir."

"Room A. Is that a room like Colonel Fincham's?"

"Yes, sir."

"Major, Room A is now mine. You will take a vacant bunk in B Bay. You will move your gear immediately after roll call. And I want it policed up."

Wimberly's lips formed a protest which went unuttered as Ryan added, "Any questions?"

"No, sir."

Crestfallen, he walked back to B Bay. Ryan took his place at the head of A Bay.

Oriani walked lynx-like to the center of the courtyard and stood with his knuckles on his trim flanks.

"If you are ready, gentlemen, we will proceed," he said with ironic courtesy.

Captain Alessandro bustled to a spot a few feet from Oriani and gave an order. Two soldiers marched to the back of the courtyard while other pairs took up positions at the center of both downstairs porches and between the formation and the barricade.

"We're surrounded," Frankie Orde cried in feigned terror.

No one laughed. Apparently it was a timeworn joke.

Falvi, trailed by a soldier with pencil and paper, began counting the Americans while Alessandro and another soldier counted
the British. Ryan stood quietly but the other prisoners talked
and moved about in ranks.

The officers counted aloud in Italian. At the end of each sub-
section they called out a total which was taken down by the
soldiers assisting them. When they had counted their sections
they returned to the center of the courtyard, Falvi first because
he had fewer men to count. The officers took the tally slips from
the soldiers and added the totals. They presented their count to
Oriani, who compared their figures with those in a small leather-
bound notebook.

Oriani thrust Falvi's tally sheet back at him. Falvi added the
figures again and shook his head apologetically. Oriani said
something cutting and, shamefaced, Falvi began counting the
Americans again.

"It didn't check," Orde shouted.

The prisoners cheered.

"Silence," Oriani cried.

The prisoners ignored the command.

"We will not continue until there is silence," Oriani shouted.

Ryan stepped out of ranks.

"This is a military formation," he cried. "Knock it off, you
men!"

Startled, the prisoners fell silent. Ryan stepped back to his
place.

Oriani smiled thinly and gave him a travesty of a salute,
which Ryan ignored. Falvi began over again, hurrying along the
ranks. Alessandro watched him with a self-satisfied smirk.

"What's up, Bobby?" a prisoner whispered.

"One few," Falvi whispered back, hurrying on.

He finished his recount and returned to stand abjectly before
Oriani. Oriani snapped out an order which sent Falvi and a
detail of soldiers hurrying up the stairs into the bays of Settore I.
Shortly after they disappeared from view there was a commotion at the front gate. The massive doors were flung open and

in strode an Italian medical officer ahead of Captain Stein and two white-smocked orderlies with a litter.

"It's Doc Stein," Orde cried.

Despite his one eye, he seemed always to be the first to see anything of interest.

Oriani charged to the barricade and confronted the new-comers. The medical officer handed Oriani a sheet of paper. Oriani read it and thrust it back angrily, waving the party on. Stein led the medical officer and the litter-bearers toward the dispensary. He winked when he passed Ryan. In a few moments the party emerged from the dispensary carrying Lieutenant Carter on the litter.

The prisoners watched in silence until the litter reached the barricade, then they started cheering.

"Good show!" a British voice bellowed above the din. "Oh, jolly good show!"

Stein waited at the barricade until the front gate was opened to let the litter out, then turned to the formation and clasped his hands above his head in a boxer's victory salute. He went to his place in the formation, shaking congratulatory hands along the way.

Oriani, who had regained his poise, watched the performance without expression.

"Now that we are all here, may we proceed, gentlemen?" he asked with mock weariness.

P. G. 202 *throbbed in the bluish night.* Standing in the doorway of his cell-like room, Ryan could hear the murmur of voices in the crowded bays washing over the compound, pierced now and again by laughter, a scrap of song, the shrill cries of an argument.

It was nine-thirty and all the prisoners were in their quarters for the night.

Over the door of each bay a weak amber light guarded the entrance dictating caution, though diffidently. Searchlights mounted in the guard boxes probed over the compound looking for company but when one beam encountered another they sprang quickly apart, as if startled. Ryan wondered if it were some sort of game the sentries played to while away the dull hours of their watch.

After roll call Ryan had been brought bedding, his share of a Red Cross parcel, dining utensils, and a few personal necessities. The personal items were to be charged against his pay, that of a colonel in the Italian Air Force.

In addition to the clothes he had worn into the camp Ryan now owned or had the use of a grass-filled paillasse; a knotty pillow; two abrasive grayish sheets; a blanket; a knife, fork, and spoon; small quantities of condensed milk, sugar, cheese, tea, English biscuits, margarine, something called meat roll and

something else called lobster paste, all in tins; a small towel; a
safety razor; one blade; a small cake of soap; a toothbrush; a
comb; and tooth powder. The razor, the blade, the toothbrush
and the tooth powder, though he did not know it, were concessions to his rank.

He had dined on pumpkin soup and a small brown roll and,
though it had been meager fare, was not hungry. Hunger, he
knew, would come later. The mess hall had been overcrowded
but the men on either side of him on his bench had given him
ample room and no one had spoken to him during the meal.

Now Ryan stretched, gingerly touched his sore scalp and permitted himself a sound which was half sigh, half groan. Peeling
off his coveralls, he hung them over the end of the bunk and
climbed into his narrow bed. Then he took off his shoes, stuffed
his socks into them, and hung them over the bunkpost by the
strings.

Ryan lay on his back, hands clasped behind his head, staring
up at the lonely little bulb screwed into the ceiling. He thought
briefly of his wife and three children in Santa Monica, hoping
it would not be too long before his wife received word he was
not killed in action but was only a prisoner, and of the problem
his capture would create back at group. But he had little time
to waste on such personal thoughts. He was responsible for the
welfare of almost a thousand officers and men. At ten the light
in his room went off but he continued to stare at the ceiling,
analyzing what he had seen and reviewing the notes he had
made. He could see them with his mind's eye as clearly as if he
were reading them on his notepad.

A sudden bird song in the night broke into his thoughts and
he wondered what a mocking bird was doing in Italy, realizing
almost at once it was a nightingale, not a mocking bird. There
had been mocking birds at Randolph Field.

It had been a long, full day and he was tired. He would sleep
now. Ryan shut off his thoughts as abruptly and totally as if in
response to an electric switch and in minutes was sleeping.

Joe Ryan would have graduated second highest academically in his class at the United States Military Academy had he not had almost twice as many demerits as the cadet next to him on the gig list. There was a story, accepted through the years by later classes but never authenticated, that with the exception of Ulysses S. Grant no West Point cadet had ever collected so many demerits and still graduated.

In his three years on the Academy boxing team, first as a middleweight and then as a light heavyweight fighting eleven pounds under his between-season one hundred eighty-six, he lost only two decisions, both close. Outside the ring he had lost more than two, and not always by close decision, but outside the ring there were no rules limiting the size or number of his opponents.

He had courted, but not so relentlessly as was his custom, the overweight daughter of his chemistry professor, chemistry being his one difficult subject. He had managed to make better than average marks in it not through any favoritism but through the professor's unwitting coaching. Ryan always called for the professor's daughter a half-hour earlier than expected and while waiting for her spent the thirty minutes discussing chemistry with her father.

Finding Army life dull after six months of duty as a second lieutenant, Ryan volunteered for pilot training. He was a troublesome student but a magnificent, though reckless, flyer. Had he been a flying cadet instead of a Regular Officer going through training in grade he would have been washed out for that recklessness. Despite this fault, or possibly because of it, he received special attention from Victor Runson, his squadron commander, a thirty-eight-year-old captain who had flown fighters in the World War.

Captain Runson, a bony, quiet, prematurely graying man, tried to make a reliable pilot out of him. Runson had a wife and two children and Ryan came to know them well. He often spent evenings with the Runson family, letting his friends in the Bachelor Officers Quarters assume he was out on one of his typical solitary quests in town.

Runson was cool, even cautious, in the air but despite this Ryan was never able to get on his tail in a dogfight, no matter how brilliantly or recklessly he flew. After a swirling rat race in which Ryan had almost flown into the ground trying to out-maneuver his instructor, Runson had walked to Ryan's plane immediately after landing and said quietly, "Joe, listen to me. I mean this. If you keep up that kind of flying you're going to kill yourself."

But Ryan did not kill himself.

He killed Captain Runson.

It was on a cross-country flight the two of them took to cele-brate Ryan's graduation from flying school. It was Ryan's first flight with wings on his chest. Determined to outfly his teacher, he pushed the throttle to the fire wall in a wracking maneuver and, boring in for a simulated deflection shot, chewed the right wing off Runson's trainer.

In horror he watched Runson's plane flop earthward in a ragged, accelerating spiral, waiting for the white blossoming of a parachute which never came. The plane exploded on impact, spreading a billow of flame and smoke over the wasteland north of Sonora, Texas. His propeller gone, Ryan made a jolting dead-stick landing which washed out his plane but left him unhurt. He climbed out of the shattered cockpit, sat on the barren ground with his head in his hands, and cried.

Then he got up and walked eight miles in the blistering sun to a ranch house and got a ride to the nearest telephone.

Runson's wife turned her head when he tried to speak to her at the funeral and herded the children to the other side of the chapel. A board of inquiry declared the accident 100 per cent pilot error on evidence volunteered by Ryan himself. He was found guilty of negligence, reprimanded, and moved down one hundred places on the promotion list. He found the sentence unbearably light.

For a while he considered resigning from the service but instead he asked for assignment to a flying school. Ryan's students were the most driven and resentful on the field. Despite this, after he became a squadron commander his squadron always won the blue ribbon at the Saturday morning parade, had the lowest percentage of washouts for flying deficiencies and the best flying safety record on the field.

As a check pilot he washed out more cadets than any two other instructors at the flying school. When another squadron commander, noting that Ryan washed out relatively few cadets from his own squadron, accused him of favoritism, the commandant of the school rejected the charge summarily.

"Ryan play favorites?" he snorted. "Ryan's got no favorites. He don't like anybody. He just happens to own the best squadron in flight training. Happens, hell. He hammers his cadets into shape like a Goddamn blacksmith."

Despite this professional opinion of Ryan, the commandant, like everyone else at the school, did not like Ryan personally. Ryan was the only lieutenant in his experience who could look at a major in such a way as to make the major wonder if he had something unbuttoned.

Shortly after making first lieutenant, Ryan married a girl he had grown up with in Santa Monica, California. If marriage mellowed him in any way it was not apparent to his students or colleagues. Ryan's students insisted he required his wife to lie at attention with her eyes fixed on a point while he made love to her, though some dissenters doubted that he was sexually interested in women at all.

"He gets his charge chewing out cadets," they explained. "If you want to know if a cadet belongs to Ryan's Regulars, just pull down his drawers and look. His poor old ass will be all chewed out."

When his first child, a daughter, was born, the legend was expanded to include the story that little Vicki was not permitted to go to the potty until the lieutenant gave his permission.

Ryan was aware of the stories about him and that cadets coming in from Basic received a complete, though wildly inaccurate, briefing about him from the upper class. He did nothing to stop the practice. Being a living legend made his job easier.

Where other officers had to persuade or threaten, he had only to direct a brief, cold glance. Though it amused him to see cadets tremble without cause when the circumstances of training brought them to his personal attention, he kept his sense of humor well hidden except with his family. In consequence, even when he smiled the cadets read into his expression a kind of chill ferocity.

When World War II broke out he was a captain with three children and commandant of cadets at an advanced flying school. He requested combat and went to the Middle East theater a major in command of a P-40 squadron. His squadron had the most kills in the group, the fewest aircraft shot down, and the best maintenance record. No one in the group inspired fiercer loyalty in the air or had fewer friends on the ground. Even the most capable officers felt uncomfortable in his presence.

Before Ryan completed his tour he was ordered back to the United States to become operations officer of a newly formed P-38 group. Again he made no friends, but the group was pronounced combat ready three weeks before the programmed date. He was promoted to lieutenant colonel and after the group had been in North Africa three months was made full colonel and group commander. Despite his unpopularity there were no murmurings that he had been unjustly promoted over the heads of more capable or senior officers.

Ryan's pilots complained among themselves but in the presence of members of other groups took fierce pride in being members of the "Galley Slave Group." On the breast of their leather flying jackets and coveralls they wore an unofficial emblem, a cartoon galley with slaves at the oars under the lash of an overseer. They had wanted to stencil the design on their planes but Ryan forbade it.

"These planes are weapons, not toys," he said coldly.

After the invasion of Sicily, Colonel Ryan's group was up

every day dive-bombing bridges and rail junctions and strafing transport in southern Italy. Ryan's plane was hit by ground fire as he led a formation in over a marshaling yard. He pulled up sharply but could not maintain altitude and made a smoking, wheels-up landing in a grove of young olive trees. Though the plane was demolished and burst into flames seconds after he scrambled clear, Ryan was uninjured except for a split scalp.

The owner of the grove, more incensed by the damage to his trees than by the presence of an enemy on his native soil, came at Ryan with a manure-encrusted pitchfork. Ryan had a .45 and could easily have killed the Italian but did not because he was a civilian and an old man. Instead, he loped toward a neighboring hill, leaving the old man screaming an alarm behind him.

Three carabinieri who had been hurrying toward the burning wreckage of Ryan's P-38 changed course and set out in pursuit, firing their small caliber carbines without effect. Ryan was contemplating stopping to ambush them when he saw, across a field of brown stubble, a gray-green detail of German soldiers fanning out toward him. Bold but not foolhardy, and certain escape was impossible at the moment, he let the carabinieri capture him as the lesser of two evils.

He hid his .45 under a rock to keep the carabinieri from getting a souvenir and walked toward them, his hands in his pockets, blinking away the blood dripping down into his left eye. The carabinieri shouted at him, indicating with their carbines he was to raise his hands. Ryan pretended not to understand. It seemed somehow undignified to raise his hands at the threat of such ineffectual weapons. He did, however, take his hands out of his pockets to show he was unarmed.

The carabinieri surrounded him, all talking at once. One of them looked at Ryan's bloody face and shook his head sympathetically, saying "Male, molto male." He took a dirty handkerchief from his tunic and reached out as if to dab Ryan's face. Ryan pulled away.

"I'll stick with my own germs," he said.

The German patrol arrived while he was being searched. The

German soldiers were sweating and scowling in the heat. They were armed with rifles and ugly machine pistols. The carabinieri quit searching Ryan and looked apprehensively at the Germans.

"Don't worry, men," said Ryan. "I'll protect you."

The leader of the German patrol motioned with his Luger for Ryan to follow him. Ryan shook his head. The German raised the pistol. Ryan shook his head again.

"You're a little late," he said. "I'm already taken."

"If the Herr Oberst does not come at once I will fire," said the German in careful English.

"You'll have to knock off your allies, too," Ryan said. "Or they'll report you for hijacking their prisoner. And I don't think you Krauts are any too popular in the neighborhood as it is."

The German was taken aback. He bit his lip and said angrily, "We are driving you into the sea in Sicily."

Ryan turned his back on him and said to the Italians, "Let's go."

He started walking toward the farmhouse. After a moment of confusion, and with a last apprehensive look at the scowling Germans, the carabinieri followed. The patrol leader looked after them irresolutely, then spat a command and led his men away. The carabinieri began laughing and slapping Ryan on the back. His wound throbbed painfully.

"Did I give you permission to touch me?" he barked.

The Italians, though they did not understand his words, stopped laughing and looked hurt. They continued toward the farmhouse in silence. The old man, who had been watching the Germans fearfully from inside the house, came out yelling and tried to attack Ryan again. The carabinieri restrained him and a shrill argument ensued. The throbbing of Ryan's scalp worsened.

"Knock it off!" he ordered.

The four Italians stared at him.

"Silence!" he said.

The old man went back to the house and the carabinieri resumed their search of Ryan's person. One of them tried to remove his wrist watch, a chronometer with two push-button stops. Ryan jerked his arm away and stood poised to resist further attempts. The carabiniere's two companions scolded their colleague and one of them, who wore the stripes of a non-commissioned officer, gestured an apology to Ryan. They continued the search, finding nothing else of interest except a pencil and a notepad in his knee pocket, which they permitted him to keep when they found it was blank, and half a pack of Camels in his breast pocket. This they appropriated with cries of joy. They lit up immediately, letting Ryan join them. The old man came running out of the house and was given a cigarette too. He went back smiling, smoking the cigarette clutched inside his hand between all four fingers and his thumb, the lighted end almost touching his horny palm.

The carabinieri marched Ryan half a mile to their post and turned him over to their officer, who saw the cigarette pack protruding from the non-com's tunic and took it from him.

The officer took a deep, grateful drag, peered at Ryan through the smoke and said, "For you the war is over."

"I doubt that," said Ryan. "What's your rank?"

"Che?" said the startled officer. "Tenente."

"Tenente," Ryan said conversationally, "where can I get a drink of water and wash my face?"

The lieutenant gave an order which sent a carabiniere scrambling for a bucket of water and a tin dipper. There was no soap. Another order dispatched a second carabiniere who hurried out and returned in ten minutes with a sour little civilian in a black suit with a Fascist party button in the lapel and a mourning band on the sleeve. The lieutenant did not speak to him. The civilian dressed Ryan's wound with bandage from a worn black bag, scowling and breathing heavily.

When he finished, he took a soiled paperbound English-Italian dictionary from his coat pocket, leafed through it looking up words and said, "Why does country so rich make war on country so poor?"

Ryan took the dictionary out of the man's hand and looked up two words.

"No commento," he said.

The civilian frowned. On leaving, he gave a Fascist salute to which the lieutenant responded with a grimace and a military salute. When he had gone, the lieutenant took Ryan into a little office and closed the door behind them. He poured drinks from an almost empty bottle into two small flawed glasses. He handed one glass to Ryan and raised the other in a silent toast.

"You are killing many Tedeschi, many German, in Sicilia?" he asked.

Ryan nodded and downed his drink. It was cognac but not very good cognac.

"Good," said the lieutenant. "Soon we kill Tedeschi together, yes?"

"Give me a five-minute start and I'll get back to doing my share right away," said Ryan.

The lieutenant shook his head regretfully.

"It no is possible," he said. "But I hope your wait is not long."

Six hours and two escape attempts after his crash landing Ryan reached P. G. 202.

—IV—

A *bugle awakened Ryan in the morning.* In the instant
before he opened his eyes he thought he was once again in his
quarters at the advanced flying school and when he realized he
was not, knew a fleeting moment of nostalgia. The moment
ended when he opened his eyes to the probing glow of the early
sun and his mind turned at once to the problems of the day.
His head hurt and he was aware of a host of new aches and
bruises but he ignored the discomfort.

In the washroom he joined a line waiting before one of the
basins. Though the washroom was noisy, he was surrounded by
a zone of silence. He washed himself thoroughly from face to
waist in the tepid water which came in a thin stream from the
spigot. He returned to his room without having exchanged a
word with anyone.

A man came down the second-floor porch shouting "Brew
up!"

Ryan took knife, fork, and spoon and his cardboard box of
tin cans and joined the throng of similarly laden men moving
toward the mess halls. There was nothing on the tables but tea
in large cracked bowls. The other prisoners had brought cups
made from meat roll tins but no one had bothered to inform
Ryan he was expected to provide his own container. Nor had
anyone informed him the small roll given him the evening be-

fore was intended to be eaten with both dinner and breakfast. The other prisoners were assiduously spreading half their loaf, saved from the previous evening, with a film of jam or food paste. Ryan looked at the steaming bowl of tea and began scraping out a can with his table knife.

A small dark man with mischievous black eyes and a bowl haircut approached Ryan and offered him a clean food tin with a wire handle.

"Ah've got another one, Cuhnel," he said.

His arms were like sticks and his body was matted with stiff black hairs all the way to his collarbone. He wore shorts and a reversed collar made of white paper. His self-possession was enormous.

Ryan stared at him, studying his strange garb.

"Thanks," he said belatedly.

"Colonel Ryan," said the swarthy man, "Ah'm Chaplain Gregory Costanzo. Ah guess you're one of mine."

"One of yours?"

"With a name like Joseph Ryan, what else could you be? Ah'm a Catholic chaplain."

"I don't like to disappoint you, Padre, but Grandfather Ryan was an Orangeman."

"Ah reckon it don't really matter, Cuhnel," Costanzo said with a grin. "In here you're all mine."

"I beg to differ with you, Padre. They're mine."

Costanzo's grin broadened.

"Renduh unto Caesuh . . ." he murmured.

"Padre, I appreciate the loan of the cup, but do you consider your costume appropriate for a chaplain in the United States Army?"

"This?" said Costanzo, touching the paper collar. "Ah just wear this to give the Ites a hard time. They don't approve of me at all, bein' an Italian and a J.B. and on the other side."

"That's very interesting, Padre, but I suggest you either get the rest of the rig to go with the collar or leave it off."

"Why sure, Cuhnel. Cuhnel, would you mind if Ah gave you a little advice?"

"I would."

"Ah'll give it to you anyway," said Costanzo, serious now. "Don't be too hard on the boys. They've come through some rough times."

"They're not boys," Ryan said curtly. "And things are rough all over."

"Ah'll pray for your enlightenment. See you in church, Cuhnel."

He went back to his own table.

At morning roll call, inhibited by Ryan's presence, the prisoners were less unruly than usual and the count was quickly taken. Alessandro was particularly fast, rushing along the British ranks with frequent furtive looks to check Falvi's progress. He seemed bent on proving that he could count his sector as fast as Falvi could count the other despite the fact there were twice as many British.

After the formation was dismissed, Ryan beckoned Fincham to join him.

"Let's take a walk, Colonel," he said. "We can do some business while we're getting our PT."

"PT?"

"Physical training. Exercise."

"God," said Fincham.

They walked up and down the courtyard, Ryan setting a brisk pace. The other prisoners gave them plenty of room.

"There's a lot of work to be done," said Ryan, holding his notepad by the end and tapping it against his palm. "I expect your complete co-operation."

"Your humble servant," Fincham said.

"We'll start by cleaning up the men and their quarters. How about mops, brooms, and buckets? We got any?"

"Twig brooms. Damn all mops and pails."

"They'll have to use twig brooms until I can promote something better. Those stools. They look like they ought to hold water. They can use those for buckets. I want those bays scrubbed down from front to rear and don't miss the walls. How about hair clippers and scissors?"

"There were some about. I don't know where they've got to."

"Find them. Every man is to have a haircut. And they'll shave every other day."

"Who's to provide razor blades?"

"We'll share what we have."

They neared Padre Costanzo, who was strolling along reading his office. He had removed his paper collar.

"Padre," said Ryan, breaking in on the priest's reading, "I assume you speak Italian?"

"Si, colonnello."

"I'll be needing you soon."

"For spiritual guidance, Ah hope."

"For that I go direct, Padre."

Ryan assumed his brisk pace, leaving Costanzo behind.

"I want the men to wear shirts at mess and in military formations," he said.

"That'll take a bit of doing. We've damn all shirts."

"Why? Isn't the detaining power required to provide adequate clothing for prisoners of war?"

"Don't complain to me, Colonel, I'm not the bloody Protecting Power. Actually, the sods have clothing for us. American khaki uniforms and British boots simply gathering dust in the warehouse across the road. But they won't release them."

"Why?"

"That bugger, Oriani. Says we'll dye them to resemble Ite uniforms and stroll out the bloody gate."

"That's ridiculous."

"I know. One of yours tried."

An OR passed them pushing a two-wheel cart on which four large wicker-covered bottles clanked.

"What's that?" Ryan asked.

"Wine ration."

"Wine ration? The Italians give us wine?"

"They consider it a necessity. Bloody awful swill. No one can stomach it but Q and the other Poona types."

"Would you mind explaining that last?"

"Q's the quartermaster, Bertie Grimes-Lemley. A Poona type's a tippler."

"You've got a lush for quartermaster?"

"There's not a better in the British Army," Fincham retorted, bristling.

"I'll reserve judgment on that until I know if it's a recommendation for Lemley or a criticism of your Quartermaster Corps."

"Grimes-Lemley," said Fincham.

"I want you to get me the names of the ten senior officers in Settore II. And have Wimberly get me the same for Settore I."

Ryan looked at his watch.

"That's enough PT," he said. "Fincham, have the men fall out in roll call formation right away. Call me when they're formed up. I'll be in my quarters."

"Sir!" said Fincham, imitating Bonzer.

In ten minutes he called to Ryan from the courtyard. Ryan brought his stool down the steps with him. The men, puzzled and restive, watched his progress from his room to a point at the front of the formation midway between the ranks. Ryan mounted the stool and stood looking at them in demanding silence until all talking and movement ceased. The guards assembled at the wire to see what was going on and Oriani watched from the open door of his office.

"Gentlemen," Ryan shouted, "effective as of now we will begin a number of changes in the conduct of P. G. 202. I am sure they will be accomplished cheerfully and efficiently."

A chorus of groans swept over the formation. Ryan waited for silence.

"Cheerfulness is not mandatory," he said. "But efficiency will be. The following orders are effective immediately. One. When the water comes on, bays will be scrubbed down beginning with A Bay, Settore I. Each bay will deliver its twig brooms to A

Bay. The men in A Bay will move all bunks, stools, and personal belongings to the porch. You will use your stools for water buckets and swamp out the bay and wash down the walls. Upon completion of this detail you will deliver the brooms to B Bay. B Bay will be policed in the same manner and the brooms delivered to A Bay, Settore II. And so on until every bay has been policed."

Ryan quieted the rebellious murmuring with a grim, sweeping survey of the ranks.

"Two. Every man is to have a haircut. All clippers and scissors will be delivered to D Bay, Settore II. The equipment will go from bay to bay in the same manner as the brooms. I do not expect a professional job but I do expect a military haircut."

"How about me, sir?" called a man in B Bay, Settore I, his bald head agleam.

Ryan waited for the laughter to subside.

"Three. No one is to waste any time with stupid jokes. Four. You will shave every other day. Mustaches are permitted if neat and military. There will be no beards."

"Sir?" a stubble-faced American second lieutenant called out in a worried voice.

"Yes?" Ryan answered, his tone unintimidating.

"Sir, some of us don't have any blades and no camp lira to buy 'em from the canteen."

"I see. I take it then that razor blades are available."

"Yes, sir," a large American in A Bay said nervously. "About a hundred."

He was heavy and the loose skin at his jowls suggested he had once been heavier. His face, neck, and the top of his bald head were burned a dull red and a long fringe of sandy hair hung over his sunburned ears.

"Who are you?" Ryan asked.

"Captain Smith, sir. Eunace Smith. E-u-n-a-c-e. Canteen officer. We've got these here blades but hardly nobody buys any. To tell the truth, they ain't much count."

"But they are available."

"Oh, yes, sir, if they've got the camp lira to pay. I'm carrying too many . . ."

"Captain Smith," Ryan interrupted, "you will extend credit to those unable to pay for razor blades."

He turned to the lieutenant who had first spoken up.

"Thank you for apprising me of the situation," he said.

"Thank you, sir," the lieutenant replied.

"Brown-noser," muttered an officer next to him.

The words, though not intended to, reached Ryan. His eyes sought out the man who spoke them and studied him briefly.

"Five," he said, returning his attention to the formation. "Enlisted men, Other Ranks, will salute all officers except when engaged in their duties. Company grade officers will salute field grade officers. This applies to both Allied and Italian personnel."

Bostick's high voice sounded clearly above the hush.

"Von Ryan, you're in the wrong army."

The prisoners waited for Ryan's reaction in challenging though apprehensive silence. He did nothing, giving no indication he had heard Bostick.

"You will receive further orders as I see a necessity for them," he said. "Either directly from me or from Colonel Fincham for the British or Major Wimberly for the Americans. They will be followed without question. Thank you, gentlemen."

The prisoners began complaining loudly among themselves and a few broke ranks.

"You have not been dismissed!" Ryan cried.

The noise stopped immediately.

Ryan stepped from his stool and strolled to A Bay on the American side.

"Anybody here got a pencil and paper?" he asked casually.

"I have, sir," blurted a youth in the second rank, blushing when he saw that his companions were glaring at him.

"Good. Will you step out of ranks?"

The young man came forward and stood before Ryan, his bare legs trembling. He was middle-sized and well knit, his baby face unmarked by the privations of prison camp life. His gray eyes were guileless and a wisp of downy golden mustache glistened on his full upper lip. A pink tongue came out to wet the lip and nervously explore the down.

"What's your name?" Ryan asked.

"Petersen, sir. Lt. Billy Petersen."

"First or second?"

"Second lieutenant, sir."

"It should not have been necessary for me to ask, Lieutenant Petersen. Lieutenant Petersen, get out your pencil and paper."

Petersen fumbled in the hip pocket of his shorts with a hand grown unmanageably large and at last produced a sweat-stained notepad and a stub of pencil.

Ryan pointed at Bostick.

"Lieutenant," he ordered, "take that man's name, rank, and serial number."

"Sir?" said Petersen, his face troubled.

"I gave you an order, Lieutenant."

Petersen took down Bostick's name, rank, and serial number, his hand trembling so it was almost illegible.

"Follow me," said Ryan.

He strode a few yards down the formation.

"Take down that man's name, rank, and serial number," he said, pointing at the officer who had muttered "brown-noser."

Petersen did so, his hand steadier.

Ryan continued down the line to the bald officer who had asked about haircuts. This time he said nothing, merely pointing. Petersen took the officer's name, rank, and serial number. Ryan went back to the head of the formation. Petersen, after a moment's hesitation, hurried after him.

"Lieutenant," Ryan asked, "do you have a shirt?"

"Yes, sir."

"Wear it. My aide must be in uniform at all times."

"Your aide, sir?" Petersen blurted, quailing.

"Are you suggesting I am not authorized an aide, Lieutenant?" Ryan demanded, his face impassive.

"Oh, no, sir."

"Very well. I'll send for you when I need you. You may return to the formation."

Petersen whirled to take refuge in the ranks. He took a step, froze, and turned to salute. Ryan returned the salute gravely.

When Petersen was back in place, Ryan said as if in afterthought, "The three officers on report are confined to quarters for twenty-four hours except for meals and official formations. Colonel Fincham. Dismiss the troops."

"Parade!" Fincham bawled. "Dismissed!"

The ensuing storm of resentful comment broke over Ryan without effect. He stood on his familiar stance, hands clasped behind him, as if inviting direct protest, but none of the men straggling back to their quarters accepted the invitation. Ryan watched them go. Fincham strolled up and stood before him, stroking his sweeping mustache with exaggerated care. They regarded each other in silence.

"It's taken me donkey's years to grow a proper mustache," Fincham said at last. "I don't intend altering it to suit the fancy of a Yank headmaster."

"I take it that means your mustache is not a product of P. G. 202," said Ryan.

"It is not!"

"I expect the British Army is more liberal about those things than mine is."

"I dare say."

"Colonel Fincham," said Ryan deliberately, "it is not my intention to impose unusual restrictions on the officers and men of P. G. 202. All I expect is a standard of conduct comparable with that of an operational unit. A disciplined operational unit. If it is the custom of your army to permit such grotesque facial hair you may keep it. You and such others as affect these growths. But I draw the line at beards. No one, British or American, is to have a beard. I'll trade you mustaches for beards. Is that agreeable?"

Taken off balance by Ryan's easy capitulation, which really

did not represent a defeat for the American, Fincham tugged at his mustache, hesitating between anger and acceptance.

"Very well," he said. "No beards."

"Thank you, Colonel," said Ryan. "I'm grateful for your co-operation."

Fincham looked closely at Ryan to see if he were being made fun of but Ryan's expression told him nothing.

Leaving Fincham still undecided, Ryan walked across the courtyard to Costanzo.

"Padre," he said, "have you got a shirt?"

"No, sir. Ah gave it away. Ah don't think it would fit you, anyhow, Cuhnel."

"Borrow it back and report to me immediately. Wearing it."

"Si, colonnello."

On the second floor, the men of A Bay were clearing their quarters, straining, and cursing "Von Ryan." Across the way, half a dozen Britishers were on the porch getting their hair cut and joining voices in an obscene song. When they saw Ryan watching them they fell silent.

When Costanzo returned with his bony shoulders draped in a faded khaki shirt, Ryan said, "Padre, how'd you like to pay a visit to Colonel Battaglia with me?"

"He sent for you, Cuhnel?"

Ryan shook his head.

"I decided not to wait for an invitation. I want you to come to the gate with me and tell the guard I want to see Colonel Battaglia. You did say you speak the language, didn't you?"

He started walking toward the barricade before Costanzo could answer. The priest hurried after him.

—V—

The guard, though intimidated by Ryan's presence, refused Padre Costanzo's request.

"He says it is not permitted," the chaplain translated. "He has no authority."

"Tell him to get somebody out here who does have authority. Major Oriani."

Despite Padre Costanzo's reassuring manner, the guard's agitation increased at the mention of Oriani.

"He's scared to death of Oriani," Costanzo explained. "All the Ites are."

"Isn't he afraid of me?"

"Yes, sir, but not as much as he is of Oriani."

"Padre," Ryan said with a tight-jawed smile, "this is a new experience for me. I've never been anywhere but at the head of the list in that department. I'll have to do something about that."

He turned to face the guard office and bellowed, "Major Oriani!"

The guard blanched. An Italian soldier watering Oriani's flowers jerked so that he drenched his trousers, and two guards came running up to reinforce the man on the gate. An inside guard, hearing the commotion, came pelting up from deep inside the prison compound. The prisoners on the porch suspended all activities and those inside rushed out to join them. Oriani looked out the door of the office, stared at Ryan, then went back inside.

"Major Oriani!" Ryan cried again.

Falvi came hurrying out of Oriani's office, a troubled expression on his friendly young face.

"What is it the colonnello wishes?" he asked, after saluting.

"I want to see Major Oriani."

"The maggiore wishes to know what is desired," Falvi replied uncomfortably.

"Go back and tell the maggiore not to send a boy on a man's job."

"Don't be so hard on the youngster," Costanzo whispered. "He's our friend."

"Padre," Ryan said coldly, "do I tell you how to pray?"

Costanzo shrugged, with the gesture appearing as Italian as the guard on the gate, though unintimidated.

"But, Colonnello . . ." Falvi stammered.

"Do I have to keep calling him?" Ryan demanded.

"At once, Colonnello," Falvi replied, resigned.

He returned to the office and came back with Oriani.

"May I be of service, Colonel Ryan?" Oriani asked silkily.

"That was the general idea, Major. I want to see Colonel Battaglia."

Oriani's eyebrows twitched in the only indication of his astonishment at the request.

"Perhaps if the colonel informed me of his purpose . . ." said Oriani.

"I'll tell Colonel Battaglia personally. I don't care to waste my time with subordinates."

Oriani's smile grew poisonous.

"It is not the prisoners who give orders here, my dear Colonel," he said.

The prisoners, who had been watching intently, could not hear the conversation but they could see from the way Oriani held himself that he was angry. They started jeering and Bostick cried out, "Up your rusty bucket, Oriani."

Ryan turned around and looked at him.

"Captain Bostick," he called. "I don't want to have to remind you again that you're confined to quarters."

Bostick shouldered his way through the crowd and disappeared inside the bay.

"Get to your quarters, all of you!" Oriani cried in a voice shrill with contempt and outrage.

"Stand fast!" Ryan ordered.

The prisoners did not move.

"You are placing your men in grave peril," Oriani said, taking pains to keep his voice level.

"That's what they're getting paid for, Major."

"And you are content to assume responsibility for actions which may be taken against them?" Oriani asked gently.

"That's what I'm getting paid for, Major."

Oriani pulled thoughtfully at the lobe of his finely shaped ear and smiled his lynx-like smile.

"Very well, Colonel," he said. "Because such public bickering is unbecoming for officers and gentlemen. But I assure you the matter is not closed."

He bowed ironically and motioned for Ryan to precede him. Ryan faced the prison compound.

"There will be no demonstration," he said. "Repeat. There will be no demonstration. Padre, come along."

The prisoners were quiet until the main gate closed behind Ryan, then they let loose with a jubilant roar.

"Your control over your men is rather imperfect, Colonel," Oriani murmured.

Colonel Battaglia's office was in a grim, two-story building of gray stone with windows and doorways edged in green-veined, pitted marble. On one side of it was the two-story guards' barracks, also of gray stone but unornamented, on the other, two long shedlike one-story buildings. The closed doors of the long buildings were under guard.

"Those the storerooms?" Ryan asked.

"Yes, Colonello," said Falvi.

Oriani spoke bitingly to Falvi in Italian. The young man hung his head, then saluted and left. Ryan returned the salute. Oriani ignored it.

Inside the building, Oriani left the two Americans under guard in an anteroom and went into Colonel Battaglia's office. The guard lounged against the wall, assuming a more military posture when he found Ryan's disapproving eyes on him. A noncom at a wooden desk pretended to be engrossed in a long list he was checking to hide his discomfort at Ryan's presence.

"Ah'm surprised Oriani gave in so easy," said Costanzo. "He never let anybody come see Battaglia before."

"Did anyone ever ask before?"

"No, Cuhnel," Costanzo answered, grinning.

"I've been intending to ask you, Padre. Where'd you get that corn-pone accent?"

"South Carolina, Cuhnel. And if you think Ah have one, you ought to hear my brothuh who never had the advantages of a seminary education."

Oriani emerged from Battaglia's office, smiling.

"Colonel Battaglia has consented to see you for a moment," he said. "He is most busy. And quite angry at your behavior."

"Thanks for paving the way, Major," said Ryan.

Colonel Battaglia was a spare, harassed, truculent man who held himself like a fighting cock poised to leap spurs first. His face was ruddy, his hair a beautiful silver. His nose was large, with a hook in it, and his eyes dark and deep under glistening black eyebrows like two fat caterpillars feeding on his forehead. Ryan had encountered him briefly the day before when the carabinieri delivered him to P. G. 202. Ryan had expected a searching interrogation but Battaglia, looking up from a mass of papers, had dismissed him with a brief and impatient, "For you the war is over," delivered almost enviously, and returned to his papers.

He was perched now at his broad desk regarding what appeared to be the same stack of papers. He looked angrily at the Americans and snapped something at Costanzo, who answered softly but with words which displeased Battaglia.

"We were discussing the bombing of churches by the barbaric Americans," Costanzo explained in a low voice. "He's against it."

"And you, Colonnello Ry-an," Battaglia said severely. "You are here one day only and already you create problems of gravity. Maggiore Oriani reports you have encourage-ed misbehavior among the prisoners."

"I take it then that everything was going smoothly before I arrived, Colonel," Ryan said calmly.

Battaglia glared.

Ryan looked deliberately around the office. Battaglia's desk, carved with a leaf and fruit design, was the only ornate object in the high-ceilinged room. The walls were lined with metal filing cabinets, several of them open and bulging with papers. Behind Battaglia on the wall was a portrait of King Victor Emmanuel and a rectangular area lighter than the rest of the wall where, Ryan surmised, Mussolini's picture had hung until his deposition a few days earlier.

"Colonel Battaglia," he said at last. "That's why I asked to see you. I've found conditions in P. G. 202 shocking and I am aware the prisoners have brought a lot of it on themselves with their attitude. I'm here to offer my co-operation."

Costanzo glared, shocked and unbelieving. Battaglia waited in wary silence for Ryan to continue.

"May we sit down?" Ryan asked.

"Sit, sit," Battaglia said quickly, anxious to hear more.

Ryan sat down, ignoring Costanzo's look of censure.

"Paper work," he said sympathetically, nodding toward the stack on Battaglia's desk. "The bane of our existence, isn't it, Colonel?"

Battaglia's face softened with agreement, then became stern again.

"This co-operation," he said. "What is propose-ed?"

Ryan took out his notes and studied them.

"First of all," he said, "I want to thank you for sending Lieutenant Carter to the hospital."

"Yes, yes," Battaglia said impatiently.

"Are you acquainted with the case of a Lt. Franklin Orde?"

"Tenente Orde?"

Battaglia shook his head.

"He's lost an eye. I'm surprised he hasn't been repatriated."

"Since Maggiore Oriani has not bring-ed the case to my attention it must be the tenente is not eligibile, eligible, for repatriation."

"I suppose that'll take care of itself anyhow," Ryan said, dismissing the issue and referring again to his notes.

"I have here a list of matters I'd like to assist you on," he said. "We are both equally interested in the welfare and discipline of the prisoners, are we not?"

Battaglia nodded warily.

"Good. I was shocked by the discourtesy the junior officers showed Major Oriani. I have ordered them to salute Major Oriani and otherwise behave in a correct military manner."

Battaglia nodded again.

"However, I think in the interest of good order Italian junior officers should salute American and British field grade officers. And Italian enlisted men should salute all officers before addressing them. Of course, the Other Ranks have been ordered to salute all Italian officers. Don't you agree?"

Trapped, Battaglia nodded. Costanzo's expression became less censorious.

"I find that much of the unruliness of the men stems from their lack of personal discipline," Ryan continued. "They are dirty, they are careless of their appearance, they dress in rags."

"True," said Battaglia. "Birboni."

"Ragamuffins," Costanzo translated.

"So I think if they took better care of themselves and their quarters, they would be much more manageable. For you and for me."

"That is so."

"Consequently I have ordered them to clean up their quarters, cut their hair, and shave regularly."

"Good, good."

"Of course I'll have to have a certain amount of co-operation from you, Colonel."

Battaglia's black eyebrows shot up. He was wary again.

"To make themselves presentable, the men need mops, water buckets, razors and blades, hot showers, new uniforms. I understand we have uniforms in storage over here."

"No uniforms," Battaglia said firmly. "Attempts have been made to render them into Italian uniforms for purposes of escape."

"I will give you my word no American uniforms will be used to aid in escape."

"I prefer to be guided by Maggiore Oriani in this matter."

"To hell with Oriani. Who's running this camp, you or Oriani?"

"Do not shout at me!" Battaglia shouted, striking his desk with his clenched fist and sending papers fluttering.

One of them fell to the floor and Costanzo bent to pick it up, taking advantage of the opportunity to release the grin he had been holding back.

"Mille grazie," Battaglia said mildly before turning on his anger against Ryan again. "Maggiore Oriani is not, as you say, running this camp. Nor are you, Colonnello. You are a prisoner of war. Do not forget your position."

"How could I, Colonel?" said Ryan, studiedly inspecting Battaglia's smart tunic and then his own flying suit. "But if you were my prisoner you'd have a clean uniform."

"The Italian people walk in filth and nakedness because of your bombs," Battaglia retorted. "And you destroy our churches."

With that he wagged a finger at Costanzo.

"That's propaganda," said Ryan. "Incidentally, are you aware we're being greeted as liberators in Sicily?"

Battaglia flushed but did not reply.

"All right," Ryan said. "We'll skip the uniforms for the time being. Colonel, I was surprised to learn Colonel Fincham didn't have a copy of the Geneva Convention covering the treatment of prisoners of war. I want one immediately."

"You have no need," Battaglia replied.

"What's the matter, Colonel, are you afraid I'll find out exactly how many rules you're breaking?"

"The manner of treatment is made necessary by the actions of your men," Battaglia said stiffly. "And Italy is a poor country. But the document will be obtain-ed for you."

"In English, if possible, Colonel."

"You ask much, Colonel Ry-an."

"Only what's coming to me, Colonel Battaglia," said Ryan.

He returned to his list, repeating his request for cleaning materials, razors, and hot showers and asking that the rear windows of the living bays be unblocked to give the prisoners more light and air, that the bunks be rebuilt into three-deckers to relieve the crowding, and that an increased issue of salt be substituted for the wine ration.

The last request astonished Battaglia.

"Salt for vino?" he demanded incredulously, adding shrewdly, "You have some plan to employ salt illicitly."

"I promise the salt will not be employed illicitly," Ryan said.

It was the only request Battaglia granted. Italy was poor, he said gravely, fighting a rich country, and there were neither water buckets, razor blades, nor fuel to heat hot water which could be spared for prisoners of war whose comrades even now were murdering civilians and destroying churches. The last was delivered with a severe look at Costanzo. Ryan listened patiently.

"One more thing," he said when Battaglia completed his little speech.

"Yes?" Battaglia said impatiently, his eyes straying to the litter of papers on his desk.

"I understand you're short of staff."

Battaglia sighed and sat back in his chair.

"Half the necessary troops I have," he said wearily, one colonel talking shop with another. "Half."

"I know, I know," Ryan answered sympathetically. "I've been in the same bind myself. The desk generals never seem to understand the problems on the operational level."

"True," said Battaglia. "True."

"I'd like to offer a little help," Ryan said.

Costanzo grew very attentive. Battaglia waited without comment.

"If you like, I'll select a detail of my men to come after the Red Cross parcels over here and handle the distribution," Ryan said, raising a hand to forestall the protest he saw forming on Battaglia's lips. "On parole, of course. I will be personally responsible for their behavior."

"They will not attempt escape?"

"I will personally order them not to."

Battaglia put his fingers together and leaned over them. Then he straightened and nodded.

"Very well. With that condition."

His eyes straightened again to the papers on his desk.

"Of course, with us providing the muscle there'll be no problem about moving enough parcels for a full issue," Ryan said easily. "One per man per week."

Costanzo looked from Ryan to Battaglia, holding his breath. Battaglia shook his head.

"When food is overabundant attempts are made to corrupt my soldati," he said.

"I'd hardly call one parcel a week overabundant. But if you wish I will order the men not to corrupt your soldiers with food."

Battaglia frowned. His words sounded unpleasant returning to him from Ryan.

"I give my word no Red Cross food will be used in any manner prejudicial to good order," Ryan said.

"What are you saying?" Battaglia demanded.

Costanzo quickly repeated Ryan's promise in Italian.

"So," said Battaglia. "In that case . . ." he continued thoughtfully.

"Good," Ryan interrupted. "Colonel Battaglia, my men and I are deeply grateful to you for your understanding of our problems."

Battaglia rubbed a palm across his silvery hair. He seemed embarrassed. He was shrewd enough to understand he had been virtually trapped into agreeing to full parcels. Suddenly and unexpectedly, a very human smile touched his tired face.

"I will instruct Maggiore Oriani to observe you most closely," he said. "You are most . . ." he snapped his fingers, . . . furbo, artful."

"I meant every word of it, Colonel," Ryan said. "I know you're a busy man. Do we have your permission to return to the compound?"

"Yes, yes," said Battaglia, once more the overworked administrator.

He seemed to have forgotten them before Ryan and Costanzo were out the door.

Oriani was waiting in the anteroom, sitting with his outstretched legs crossed and a cigarette between his lips. He was insolently graceful even in repose. He rose when Ryan emerged.

"I trust your conversation with Colonel Battaglia was most pleasant?" he said blandly.

"Very," said Ryan.

Oriani betrayed only a fraction of his surprise that the meeting had not left Ryan chastened.

"Really?" he said. "You found it so? Of what then did you speak?"

"We spoke of bombing churches," Ryan answered. "We promised to try not to do it any more."

"You are a troublemaker, Colonel Ryan. It can be most difficult for a troublemaker."

"True, Major Oriani. You're a troublemaker, too. You wouldn't have another cigarette, would you?"

Oriani laughed without warmth and offered a pack. Ryan took one.

"Padre?" he asked.

"Ah don't smoke," Costanzo said.

"That's not against your rules, too, is it?"

"Ah gave up smoking when Ah got in the bag," he explained. "Ah find that free cigarettes encourage some of my stray lambs to attend Mass."

"Light, Major?" Ryan asked, looking over his cigarette at Oriani.

Oriani measured him over the flame of his silver lighter.

"You are too sure of yourself, Colonel. But I am forced to admire you for it."

Ryan inhaled deeply, coughed, and regarded the cigarette with disgust.

"No wonder you people are losing a war," he said.

On the way back to the compound, Costanzo said, "Congratulations, Cuhnel. Ah think the men will change their attitude about you when they find out what you did for them today."

"They are not to know about full parcels until the parcels are in the camp," Ryan said sharply. "Battaglia could change his mind between now and then, after Oriani gets a chance to work on him. You are not to discuss anything that went on between Battaglia and me."

"Cuhnel, it would help you with the men."

"If and when I need help with the men I'll ask for it," Ryan snapped.

"You don't mind if Ah pray for you, do you, Cuhnel?" Costanzo asked slyly.

"I never interfere with an officer in the proper exercise of his duties, Padre," said Ryan.

—VI—

Orde, *as usual,* was the first to see the outer gate open and set up a cry when Ryan and Costanzo came through it. The prisoners in the courtyard surged toward the barricade to meet them, asking questions. Ryan ignored them. Costanzo spread his hands in apology and shrugged helplessly.

"Colonel Fincham," said Ryan, "I want to confer with you."

"Jolly decent of you, old chap," Fincham replied.

Seeing Petersen clad only in shorts, Ryan said, "Lieutenant, I thought I told you to wear a shirt."

"I'm sorry, sir," Petersen stammered. "I didn't know you meant . . ."

"Don't apologize to me," said Ryan, cutting him short. "Yes, sir, no, sir, and no excuse, sir, is all I ever want to hear."

"Yes, sir," Petersen said stiffly. "No excuse, sir."

"When you're in proper uniform report to my quarters. Colonel, come with me."

In Ryan's quarters, Fincham dropped his pose of indifference.

"What's the gen?" he demanded. "What did you see Battaglia about?"

"It had to do with Red Cross parcels," Ryan said. "Who on the camp staff is involved with parcels and Italian issue on the operational level?"

"Major Hawkins is OC Red Cross parcels. Then of course there's Q."

"Captain Beresford should be read in, too," said Ryan. "When Petersen gets here tell him to hunt them up and have them report here. And Major Wimberly. I'll be back in a few minutes."

"Closemouthed bugger, aren't you?" said Fincham.

"I see no reason for repeating myself. The staff members concerned will all get the poop at the same time. That goes for you, too."

Ryan left Fincham and went to A Bay. The tile floor was running with water and its occupants were moving bunks back inside.

"Ten-hut!" someone shouted when Ryan entered.

"Carry on," Ryan said. "Work details will not come to attention when in the performance of their duties."

He walked from one end of the bay to the other and on the way ran his finger over a streaked wall. It left a mark. The men, who had been watching him closely, exchanged anxious looks.

"I see you've rearranged the dirt," said Ryan. "If we ever get adequate equipment and soap I'll expect you to do much better. But under the circumstances, this'll do. Gentlemen, you pass inspection."

Despite their resentment of Ryan, the men were pleased with his approval. Ryan left without further comment.

Fincham, Wimberly, and Grimes-Lemley were waiting in his quarters. After a moment, Beresford came in, soot-speckled and flushed with heat from the kitchen. He was followed in a few minutes by Hawkins and Petersen. The six of them arranged themselves around the room and faced Ryan, who sat on his bunk.

"Well," said Fincham. "What's the gen?"

"Colonel Battaglia has agreed to co-operate with us on a few things," Ryan said. "This entails a certain amount of co-operation in return."

"Damned if I'll co-operate with the bugger," Fincham said defiantly.

"You'll do as you're ordered, Colonel. Effective immediately, we'll return to the military courtesy of saluting. Subordinates will salute superiors on all proper occasions. This applies to both Allied and Italian personnel. Colonel Battaglia has agreed."

"A fat lot you accomplished with your visit," Fincham said.

"The next concerns Major Grimes-Lemley and Captain Beresford particularly," Ryan said. "Effective with the next Italian issue, we will get additional salt."

"Good show!" Beresford exclaimed.

"As a substitute for the wine issue."

"For the wine issue?" Grimes-Lemley said, paling.

He was a large man with a prominent, heavily veined nose illuminated by the frightful red wine he drank so steadily. His mustache, though not so imposing as Fincham's, was large and wine-stained.

"For the wine issue," Ryan repeated.

Grimes-Lemley sighed and curled and uncurled the end of his mustache around a finger.

"The next item concerns Major Hawkins."

Hawkins was small, graying and old for a wartime major, with dewlaps and the soft, lugubrious eyes of a beagle off the scent. He straightened at Ryan's words and his sad hound's eyes showed interest.

"Effective with the next parcel issue, British and American personnel will be employed in transferring the parcels from the warehouse to our storeroom. On parole."

"So you've agreed to do the little buggers' work for them, have you?" Fincham said, disgusted. "You've been properly had, old boy."

"Major Hawkins," Ryan said, "I want you to make arrangements to handle approximately one thousand parcels."

"A thousand, sir?" Hawkins exclaimed.

"That's what I said."

The stiffness and resentment that had pervaded the room vanished in an instant.

"Bloody good, old cock!" Fincham cried. "My apologies for that ill-advised remark."

"Let's not congratulate ourselves, gentlemen," Ryan said. "We've still got a long way to go. I didn't get half of what I wanted. And a full parcel issue is not the main thing. The main thing is seeing that every man in this camp looks and acts like a soldier and an officer and that this place looks like a military post, not a pigsty. Fincham, half the troubles here you've brought on yourself with your bullheadedness. Battaglia's the kind of man who'll meet you halfway."

"Don't expect me to truckle to the sod," Fincham said.

"I don't intend for anyone to truckle. But in cases where we have a clear-cut obligation to co-operate I intend to see that we fulfill it."

"That's collaboration!" Fincham cried.

"That's an ugly word and I don't intend to hear it again," Ryan said. "Is it collaboration to salute superior officers and be saluted in return? Is it collaboration to stand firm in ranks at military formations? Or keep our persons and our living quarters clean?"

His voice grew less admonitory.

"Gentlemen, I don't want the news about parcels given out. Oriani may be able to talk Battaglia out of full parcels and I don't have to tell you the effect on morale if the men expected full parcels and didn't get them. Major Hawkins, I'll muster the work party after roll call on parcel day. You'd better augment your storeroom crew then, too."

"Right, sir."

"Fincham, I want you and Wimberly to stand by. The others may leave. You may go, too, Petersen. I won't need you for a while."

When the others had gone, Ryan turned to Fincham.

"I'd like those lists now," he said.

"What lists?" Fincham asked.

"The ten senior officers in each bay."

"You only mentioned it this morning," Fincham replied.

"When I ask for something I want it right away. Not tomorrow. Remember that. Major Wimberly, what I'm after is a list of the ten senior officers in every bay. I'll expect to have them in my hand by evening parade."

After they had gone, Ryan walked to the porch rail and looked down into the teeming courtyard. A group of men were gathered around Petersen questioning him about the meeting in Ryan's room. Petersen was shaking his head doggedly.

"Stooge," one of the questioners said angrily.

The word carried clearly to the porch. Ryan sighed.

At roll call, Fincham and Wimberly brought him their lists on sheets of brown paper folded small for concealment. Ryan sent Petersen around the mess halls at dinner to pass the word around that the senior men of each bay were to assemble at the back of A Bay, Settore I, fifteen minutes after the meal.

"They're to come in twos and threes," Ryan cautioned. "I don't want them arriving in a mob and attracting attention."

After dinner Ryan had Wimberly post lookouts to insure against discovery by the Italians.

When the prisoners had gathered around him—Fincham, Wimberly, and sixty curious and resentful officers—Ryan clasped his hands behind him and addressed them.

"Gentlemen," he said, "I have called you here to inform you that effective immediately I am organizing P. G. 202 into military units by bays. My experience has been with flights, squadrons, and groups but since ground personnel predominates here we will be organized into platoons, companies, and battalions."

Each wing was to be a battalion, each bay a company. Fincham and Wimberly were to command the battalions.

"Colonel Fincham will also be my deputy," Ryan said. "Major Wimberly, since you're Air Force, you better pick yourself a good Army man for your exec."

The senior man in each bay was to be its company commander, the other nine its platoon leaders.

"For the sake of convenience we'll divide the bays into platoons alphabetically. I want that done tonight. Every platoon leader will familiarize himself with the military duty and civilian occupation, if any, of every man in his platoon. Plus any special skills they may have such as foreign language, map making, mountain climbing, and so forth. Any questions so far?"

There were none.

"I'll give you two days to accomplish that. If I ask you for a commando who speaks Italian I want you to be able to identify him immediately if you have one. I don't think it's necessary to warn you the Italians aren't to know anything about this activity. I want absolute security. I have no further specific instructions at this time except to remind you that as platoon leaders and company commanders you are charged with transmitting all orders to your subordinates and seeing that they are executed promptly and efficiently."

There was a chorus of groans at this.

"It fills me with pride to see how you welcome an opportunity to perform as officers again, gentlemen," Ryan said. "To show my confidence and appreciation I am going to allow you to be personally responsible for any breach of discipline by any man under your command. When a man in your platoon goes on report, you go on it with him. Any questions?"

"Yes, sir," said Bostick, his clown's face stormy.

"Yes, Captain?"

"How do I transfer out of this chicken outfit?"

There was a sound of breath being drawn in sharply by Bostick's companions, followed by muffled snickers in the ranks.

Ryan regarded Bostick in frosty silence. The big man stood his ground.

"Captain," Ryan said at last, "this demonstrates how an officer's error in judgment can come back to haunt him. If I'd washed you out as I should have I wouldn't be obliged to play nursemaid to you now. I'd be delighted to transfer you out, Bostick, but there's nobody who'd have you. Not even the Italians. Though I think you'd be at home with their kind of discipline. Since you're still acting like a cadet I'll treat you like one. Beginning after morning parade tomorrow you will walk off ten daily tours of one hour counting cadence. Major Wimberly, you will see that Captain Bostick walks his tours in a military manner.

"When I dismiss this formation you will leave by twos and threes. The last man to leave will inform the lookouts that security is no longer required. Gentlemen, dismissed."

On parcel day the prisoners were as wildly playful as schoolboys whose girls were watching. They were so unruly at roll call that Ryan twice had to order them to quiet down. Anticipation crackled so noticeably in the ranks that Ryan believed someone had disobeyed him and spread the word about full parcels. Fincham assured him it was not so.

"They're always a bit giddy on parcel day," he said.

After roll call Ryan mounted his stool in the center of the courtyard.

"Gentlemen," he said, "I need 120 strong men for a work detail. Volunteers will step one pace forward."

Bonzer stepped out at once, saluting and shouting, "Sir!"

Everyone laughed.

Bonzer was followed by Fincham, Padre Costanzo, and Petersen. There were muffled jeers behind Petersen, who flushed. The other prisoners stood stolidly in place. Ryan was unperturbed. He leaped from his stool and made a circuit of the formation selecting the largest and strongest men.

"You, you, you," he said, pointing to the men he wanted.

Bostick was one of those he selected.

"You'll start walking your tours again tomorrow," he said.

When Ryan had enough men he mounted his stool again.

"Upon dismissal, all those not participating in the work detail or in other authorized duties will return to quarters until the parcel issue is in the storeroom. You will then draw parcels by bays as usual. You will stand by in quarters until called to draw parcels and you will return to quarters after drawing them and remain there until distribution is completed."

After Fincham dismissed the formation Ryan had the work detail move in close around him.

"Padre," he said, "I asked for strong men. I'm sure the spirit is willing . . ."

"Cuhnel, looks to me like spirit's what you've got the least of in this bunch," Costanzo said, looking at the sullen faces around him.

"Maybe you're right," said Ryan. "You can furnish moral support."

To the others he said, "Thank you for volunteering so cheerfully, gentlemen. I have agreed to provide Colonel Battaglia with assistance in moving the parcels from the warehouse to our storeroom."

The men stirred and murmured resentfully. Ryan heard the words "stooge" and "collaborator" as well as others reflecting on his parentage. His eyes narrowed and his face grew flinty.

"I haven't time to instruct you on conduct becoming an officer so I'll pretend I didn't hear that," he said. "But if there's any recurrence I'll take time."

The men grew still.

"We are being allowed outside the compound," Ryan continued. "I have given my word as your commanding officer and a colonel in the United States Army Air Force that no one will attempt to escape during the operation or create a disturbance of any nature. I am giving you a direct order. You will not attempt to escape. I promise anyone who does a court-martial when he returns to Allied control."

Ryan posted men four feet apart starting at the storeroom. When he reached the barricade, surrounded by his work detail, Oriani intervened.

"I will not permit so large a group to leave the compound simultaneously," Oriani said.

"It's not your decision to make," Ryan answered. "It's Colonel Battaglia's. And he seems to have made it. Have the guard open the gate."

Oriani grudgingly permitted Ryan to continue his line of men through the barricade and across the forecourt but balked again when Ryan told him to open the front gate and leave it open.

"And extend an invitation to everyone to leave at his pleasure?" Oriani asked sarcastically.

"I have ordered all personnel not in the work detail to remain in quarters," said Ryan.

"I cannot risk permitting the entrance to remain unclosed."

"Did or did not Colonel Battaglia inform you prisoners were to move the parcels?"

"He said nothing of the method you were to employ. Or that the entrance would remain unclosed."

"Then he obviously left it to my discretion, wouldn't you say, Major? Or do you intend to trot over and get instructions from Colonel Battaglia on every little detail?"

With a malevolent look at Ryan, Oriani ordered the guard to throw open the gate. He had the little man take his carbine off safety and hold the weapon ready for use. The soldier seemed embarrassed by this.

The prisoners bunched together outside the wall and stood gaping. None of them had been outside since arriving at P. G. 202. Ryan permitted them a moment of quiet contemplation before ordering them into position.

The line snaked from the storeroom to the door of the warehouse. Ryan had eleven men left when he reached the warehouse, just as he had planned. Ten were to unstack parcels and one was to count them. He assigned Costanzo to do the counting.

"What's the strength, Fincham?" he asked when his men were placed.

"Nine hundred sixty-four officers and Other Ranks."

"Nine hundred sixty-three," said Oriani.

"Nine hundred sixty-four," Fincham insisted.

"Do you intend sending Lieutenant Carter's Red Cross box to

Pescara?" Oriani asked cuttingly. "Or have you simply forgotten he was removed to the hospital there?"

Fincham shrugged.

"Well, I had a go at it," he said, unabashed.

Ryan took him aside, out of Oriani's hearing.

"Colonel," Ryan said, "I don't appreciate your jeopardizing Colonel Battaglia's concession with cheap tricks."

"Whose side are you on?" Fincham demanded. "What's the harm in doing the buggers out of a buckshee parcel?"

"Are you arguing with me, Colonel?"

Ryan turned abruptly to face his waiting men.

"All right," he said. "Let's get moving."

The parcels moved swiftly from hand to hand. Costanzo and an Italian noncom counted them as they were passed through the door. Oriani hovered over the noncom keeping a tally of his own. Inside the compound, the prisoners formed their customary gallery in the doorways and watched the stream of parcels entering the camp with as much interest as if it were a circus parade.

Ryan ranged along the line from warehouse to storeroom to keep the parcels moving in a steady flow. Inside the storeroom, Major Hawkins' crew worked at top speed stacking them. Colonel Battaglia, a clipboard in his hand, came out of his office to watch and, apparently satisfied with the way things were going, went back in again.

When the count reached 482, the men inside the warehouse straightened, stretched, groaned, and wiped their sweaty faces.

"That's bloody that," said a British lieutenant, sucking a blister on his finger. "I'd not fancy going through that again. Bloody black gang."

"Fall to, you buggers," Fincham bawled. "We're not done yet."

They looked at him blankly. When the significance of his words registered they began applauding.

"Thought you'd had throwing parcels about," Fincham said to the lieutenant who had complained.

"Suddenly I rather fancy it," the officer replied.

When the count went over half camp strength, word swept swiftly from the head of the line at the warehouse into the compound, preceding the parcels themselves.

"We've gone over half!"

The words went from man to man. Inside the compound, a passer shouted the news for all to hear. The prisoners in the barracks cheered and pushed their way to the porches to see for themselves. They began counting as the parcels came through the barricade, individually at first, then swelling into a chorus which became a steady roar. When 963 parcels had entered the compound, overflowing from the storeroom to the porch, and the long line of passers relaxed in place, there was a moment's hush. Then a great rolling shout surged over the compound.

Colonel Battaglia burst out of the headquarters building, alarmed, a sheaf of papers in his hand.

"They're cheering you, Colonel," said Ryan.

"Good, good," Battaglia said, smiling.

"While I have my men here we could move those uniforms without any trouble," Ryan said casually.

Battaglia's smile became a frown, then a different sort of smile. He shook his head and went back to his office.

"We'll take a breather before we go back," Ryan called to his men. "Smoke if you wish. Pass it along."

He was lighting a cigarette when he saw that several prisoners were looking disconsolately at those who were smoking. They had no cigarettes. Ryan looked at his cardboard box of Players, in which eight cigarettes remained, sighed, and called Petersen to him.

"Lieutenant," he said, "pass these around as far as they'll go. But don't let on they're not yours."

"Sir, I couldn't . . ."

Ryan's cold gaze stopped him.

"Yes, sir."

Before the men finished their cigarettes, Oriani shouted, "The work is completed. Everyone must return at once."

The prisoners answered derisively.

"Knock it off," Ryan ordered. "You heard the major. Move out."

Oriani hurried back to the gate to count the men in and seemed disappointed when none was missing. Ryan was the last man in. The prisoners cheered him from the porches. He walked to the center of the court and, turning slowly on his heel, scanned the crowded porches from one end of the barracks to the other.

"Who gave you permission to leave your quarters?" he demanded at last. "You will return to your bays until called to draw parcels."

Visibly resentful of this rebuff, the prisoners filed back inside their bays.

"You had 'em but you let 'em get away," said Costanzo, who had strolled up to join Ryan, the black hairs on his chest and belly still matted with sweat from the steamy warehouse.

"Padre," said Ryan, "I am not running for office here. I've already been elected for the duration."

Within two weeks, Ryan had transformed P. G. 202. The prisoners, clean shaven and with neatly cropped hair, maintained rigid discipline in ranks during roll call formations, coming to attention and saluting when Oriani entered the compound to conduct the count, obliging Oriani to return the courtesy. They gave their living quarters a thorough scrubbing once a week and the porches and stairs were swept every day. Ryan required them to keep their bunks tautly made up and no man who was not ill was permitted to lie in his bunk during the day except on Sundays. He made frequent surprise inspections to ensure compliance.

The courtyard was raked every morning. There was, of course, no problem with cigarette butts in the courtyard or on the floors of the bays. Butts were too valuable to discard.

When Ryan found that confinement to quarters and marching in the courtyard did not deter some of the more rebellious prisoners from acts of defiance, he assigned the transgressors to work details and had them scrub out latrines, flush the dhobi troughs, and carry wood to the kitchen, endearing himself to the ORs. When Bostick challenged him with the charge that it was against regulations for officers to be employed in menial tasks, Ryan blandly replied, "I'll forward your complaint to higher headquarters, Captain. When I establish lines of communication."

Because the prisoners were disciplined and orderly, Ryan was able to persuade Battaglia into one concession or another, seldom having to refer to Battaglia's obligations under terms of the Geneva Convention, with which Ryan had made himself thoroughly familiar. On Ryan's promise that no tunnels would be started in the shower room, Battaglia permitted the water to be turned on for an hour twice a week, though he refused to release fuel to heat it. Every prisoner, whether he desired to or not, took two cold showers a week.

On Ryan's assurance that the prisoners would not taunt the sentries in the guard boxes or try to communicate with civilians outside the wall, Battaglia had the rear windows of the upstairs bays unblocked and did not take reprisals when the prisoners scraped away the white paint on the side windows.

He permitted carpenters' tools and tin shears in the camp when Ryan guaranteed they would not be used in escape projects and would be returned when they had served their purpose. With them, the prisoners converted their bunks into tripledeckers and, using the tin from thousands of cans, manufactured a giant hood over the kitchen stove ducted to the window to carry off smoke and soot. The prisoners also made a variety of tin utensils to designs created by Beresford.

Ryan ordered all pay into a common pool for the benefit of the prisoners as a group. Second lieutenants were thus enabled to buy razor blades and the ORs, who received hardly any pay at all, were provided with blades, toothbrushes, and other luxuries. Battaglia permitted Grimes-Lemley to purchase mops, scrub brushes, onions, and fresh fruit with money from the pool.

The first week of full parcels Ryan allowed the men to use the food individually, as had been the practice before his arrival. The second week, however, he ordered that with certain exceptions all food was to be pooled and prepared in the kitchen. He made the announcement after morning roll call and for the first time encountered open rebellion. The air was filled with profane outcries against Von Ryan.

"At ease!" he shouted when some of the vehemence had spent itself.

By this time the prisoners were so conditioned to obedience that despite their fury they fell into burning silence.

"I did not invite suggestions," he said. "I gave an order. Except for such items as I specifically excluded, Red Cross parcels will not be distributed individually tomorrow."

The items which Ryan excluded were sugar, milk, chocolate, biscuits, jam, and sweets. These were all things which were normally used or traded according to individual tastes or which could not practically be converted to communal use. They also included the ingredients for the British officers' afternoon tea. Ryan was under no illusion that even he could interfere with that.

Ryan had meals served in two separate shifts, eliminating crowding in the mess halls. With the Red Cross food and a variety of utensils at his disposal, Beresford proved to be a culinary genius and gave the prisoners better meals than they had had in their officers' messes before capture. The prisoners did not, however, thank Ryan for this. Beresford got their undivided gratitude.

After the men had enjoyed a week of nourishing meals, Ryan decided they were ready for morning calisthenics. The announcement was greeted with as much anguish as the order placing Red Cross parcels in a common pool. Having learned from a platoon leader that Capt. Eunace Smith was a high school physical education teacher in civilian life, Ryan relieved him of his assignment as canteen officer and put him in charge of physical training. Smith, who had never felt adequate in the post, with its accounts and inventories, blossomed in his new role. Exercise was something he understood and believed in.

Every morning after roll call the prisoners spread out into open formation on Ryan's command and Smith came to the front of the group to lead them in side straddle hops, sit-ups, and deep knee bends.

No one was excused from calisthenics except for reasons of disability and then only on the recommendation of Captain Stein. Though Stein agreed with Ryan that the exercises were beneficial, he excused everyone who asked. The third day of calisthenics, dozens of apparently healthy men were lounging on the porches watching their friends sweat and grunt to the commands of the euphoric Smith.

After the exercise formation was dismissed Ryan sent Petersen to bring Stein to his quarters.

"Captain Stein," he said, "are we having some kind of epidemic here?"

"No, sir," Stein replied. "As a matter of fact, the camp population is remarkably healthy. If modesty permitted, I'd say healthier than a comparable group of civilians on the outside."

"Then what seems to be ailing the officers you've excused from PT?"

Stein smiled, unabashed.

"Colonel, when a man tells me his stomach's upset or his back aches I'm inclined to give him the benefit of the doubt."

"I see. Well, you're the medical man, not me. I wouldn't presume to tell you your business."

Stein was nonplused. He had expected severe criticism.

"However," Ryan continued after a pause, "just for the record, each man excused from calisthenics from now on will have an excuse in writing. From you. You will state the exact nature of the officer's disability and give your prognosis. I will require a new report daily. The canteen officer will be instructed to provide you with what writing materials you need."

Next day only a handful of genuinely ailing men sat out morning calisthenics and Ryan withdrew the requirement.

Fincham, as usual, refused to co-operate.

"I'm no bloody recruit to get down on my belly and grovel in the dust," he said when Ryan ordered morning exercise.

"You could use a little PT," Ryan said. "You're getting a gut on you. A couple of weeks of PT and you'll be back in shape."

Fincham looked involuntarily at his beltline.

"I'm bloody well pleased with my shape as it is," he said.

"I've been very lenient with you because of your rank and position, Colonel," Ryan said. "But don't think your insubordination won't be mentioned in my report."

"Bugger your report."

Every morning during calisthenics Fincham sat on the porch outside his room, his legs dangling in space, and watched the others exercise. The first morning he shouted false encouragement to his friends.

"I say, Bertie," Fincham called to Grimes-Lemley. "Do pick that great belly of yours off the ground. That's the drill, old cock. I can hear the vino sloshing about. Good show."

"Colonel," Ryan said, "you will either remain silent or go to your quarters."

With an insolent grin, Fincham got to his feet and went to his room. The next morning he was back at his observation post, silent but grinning eloquently. Ryan sent the lame and ill to sit with him but Fincham would not be shamed into coming down to join the formation.

Every morning after roll call Oriani would remain in the compound a few minutes to watch the prisoners exercise, a contemptuous smile on his lips.

"I am astonished you have not ordered Colonel Fincham to participate," he said to Ryan one morning. "Do you fear putting your authority to such a test?"

"Colonel Fincham," Ryan called out, "Major Oriani's asking about you."

Oriani strolled to a point just beneath Fincham and looked up at him.

"My congratulations, Colonel Fincham," he said in a voice loud enough for Ryan to hear. "I am delighted there is an officer here with too much dignity to participate in Colonel Ryan's childish activities."

Fincham stared down at him, his face blazing with hate.

"I see you've found a friend, Colonel," Ryan said dryly.

Without a word, Fincham pulled himself to his feet and came down the steps to take his place in the formation. After that, though he knew Ryan had used Oriani as a tool, he exercised every morning.

Ryan's next step was to order daily close-order drill. The men were marching and countermarching in the courtyard under command of their platoon leaders when Oriani came charging into the compound.

"Halt at once!" he cried. "Colonel Ryan, I insist you order your men to abandon this activity."

"Request denied," said Ryan.

"I must insist."

"I said request denied."

Oriani unaccountably became gently reasonable.

"Colonel Ryan, surely your study of the Geneva Convention has told you prisoners of war are not permitted to engage in activities of a military nature," he said.

"Who says this is a military activity?" Ryan demanded, on guard.

"I do. And I am quite sure, my dear Colonel, the Protecting Power will agree with my interpretation should I find it necessary to disperse the men by force."

Ryan looked at him thoughtfully. Oriani was sure of his position and aching for an excuse to show his power.

"Very well," Ryan said curtly. "Platoon leaders, dismiss your men."

The men broke ranks and cheered and for a few minutes Oriani knew the only popularity he had ever experienced at P. G. 202. Since he despised the prisoners as much as they despised him, it somewhat marred his triumph over Ryan.

The next day Oriani had his own men doing close-order drill in the forecourt under the supervision of Captain Alessandro. Afterward, targets were set up on sandbags piled against the wall and the soldiers spent an hour shooting at them. The prisoners gathered at the barricade to watch and they jeered until

Ryan came out and ordered them to stop. As days passed and the guards became increasingly proficient both at close-order drill and target practice, the prisoners grew thoughtful and did not need to be ordered to stop their jeering.

On the whole, Ryan was pleased with his men. They were neat and disciplined and their morale, though they would not admit it even to themselves, was high. But one thing continued to gall him. Every morning when they turned out for roll call they wore the same clothes they had when Ryan came to P. G. 202, clean and patched now, but still unsightly and inadequate. The thought of the new uniforms gathering dust in the storeroom across the road was never long out of Ryan's mind.

Though Battaglia had proved himself a reasonable man, he adamantly refused Ryan's regular requests for the uniforms. Ryan thought he understood why. The prisoners were now better fed and better disciplined than Battaglia's own troops and Ryan believed that if they were better dressed as well, Battaglia would consider it a final humiliation and a threat to the morale of his men. And Battaglia was greatly disturbed by the privations suffered by Italian civilians. It was only natural that he should resent sleek, well-fed, well-uniformed enemy officers in the prison camp when civilians outside the walls were hungry and threadbare.

One morning Petersen reported to Ryan with a discolored eye and a sleeve torn from his shirt. Ryan assumed he had been in a fight and that it probably had something to do with the other prisoners' disapproval of Petersen's loyalty to Von Ryan. Though Ryan liked the young officer and sympathized with him, he knew he could not show it because it would only make life more difficult for Petersen.

"Lieutenant Petersen," he said, "do you consider yourself in proper uniform?"

"No, sir."

"Then why did you report in this condition?"

"No excuse, sir."

"Tell me something, Lieutenant."

"Yes, sir?"

"Who won?"

"Who won, sir?" Petersen blurted, blushing.

Then he grinned.

"I guess I did, sir."

"Good. They give you a hard time, don't they, Lieutenant?"

"No, sir," Petersen said too quickly.

Seeing from Ryan's expression the colonel knew better, he said, "Well, yes, sir."

"Does it bother you?"

Petersen hesitated.

"Yes, sir," he said at last in a low voice.

"Would you like to be relieved of your assignment?"

"Oh, no, sir! I hope you don't think I don't appreciate being your aide, sir!"

"Your appreciation has nothing to do with it, Lieutenant. What matters is whether your personal problems with the other officers impair your effectiveness."

Petersen looked at the floor.

"Lieutenant, how is it you can take on a whole bay and then can't look one bird colonel in the eye?"

Petersen looked up, startled.

"As long as you're doing your job the best you can and in your considered judgment doing it right never be afraid to look anybody in the eye."

"Yes, sir," Petersen said, looking into Ryan's face.

"I take it that means in your considered judgment you're doing your job. And I concur. You've been a great help."

A grin stretched Petersen's face and shut his half-closed eye the rest of the way.

"Lieutenant," Ryan said abruptly. "I've decided to get you a new shirt. Tell Colonel Fincham I want the men on parade in fifteen minutes."

As was his custom, Ryan waited until the men were in formation before coming down from his quarters. He mounted the stool which Petersen had placed in the center of the courtyard and surveyed the formation with approval. The men were quiet and steady in ranks.

"Gentlemen," Ryan said. "You are about to participate in a strip tease."

The prisoners looked at one another in confusion. Fincham gaped at Ryan from across the courtyard and muttered, "What the bloody hell?"

"May I remind you you are at attention?" Ryan said. "Simmer down. Upon my command, you will take off your clothes. To the buff. You will then stand fast for the next command."

The ranks wavered as men turned to their companions asking for explanations.

"I said simmer down!" Ryan shouted.

He took hold of the zipper of his flying suit and cried, "Parade, strip!"

The prisoners were frozen in shocked uncertainty. Ryan paused with his zipper halfway down.

"I gave an order!" he shouted.

He pulled the zipper the rest of the way and the prisoners started peeling off their shorts. Ryan stood naked in front of them, almost repellent in his unrelieved muscularity. Every muscle was distinct, those on his belly as ridged as a turtle's shell. It was as if all fat had been rendered from his body over a slow fire. The other prisoners were naked in ranks, holding their clothes in their hands. The barricade guard stared, goggle-eyed.

Only Bonzer, in his kilt, and Padre Costanzo, in shirt and shorts, remained clothed. Fincham wore only his broad-brimmed hat and a blush extending halfway to his navel.

"Lieutenant MacLaughlin!" Ryan cried.

That was Bonzer's name.

"Sir!" Bonzer bellowed, saluting, his face anguished.

He had made the kilt himself from one of his two thin blankets and had slept under only one during the whole frigid winter. Ryan knew this from his discussion of Bonzer's case with Fincham.

"You may keep your kilt," Ryan said.

"Sir!" Bonzer cried, relieved.

Ryan turned next to Costanzo.

Before he could speak, Costanzo said apologetically, "Cuhnel, Ah take being a member of the cloth literally."

The formation exploded into laughter.

"Padre, I bow to your convictions."

The barricade guard found his tongue and gave a sharp, shocked cry.

"You will pass your clothing forward in file to the front rank," Ryan ordered. "Snap it up. Captain Bostick, take a detail of three men to the kitchen and bring back firebrands. On the double."

Guards were running up from all over the compound now, milling about and shouting. One of them ran toward the guard office.

There was a rustle of cloth as the prisoners passed their clothing forward. The front rank men stood waiting, their arms heaped with clothing.

"Front rank, front and center," Ryan shouted.

The guard office door opened and Falvi peered out. He reeled, then steadied himself and shouted a command which sent a soldier racing toward the front gate.

"All right, now, pile everything in the middle of the courtyard," Ryan said. "Snap it up."

The men surged forward and heaped the clothes in the center of the courtyard. Bostick and his men came running from the kitchen with lengths of blazing wood in each hand.

"Throw 'em on the pile and return to your places," Ryan ordered. "Everybody back in formation."

Oriani came through the front gate just as Bostick and his men flung their torches on the mound of clothes. He stood framed in the opening for half a minute, his slim body rigid. Then he charged toward the compound. He burst through the barricade gate clawing at his holster, his yellow eyes slits, his face wrathful and incredulous. Ryan, who had stepped down from his stool, turned to meet him. Oriani ran directly to him, his eyes fixed rigidly above shoulder level, and pointed his pistol at Ryan's head.

"What is the meaning . . ." he babbled, his lips flecked with spittle. "This obscene . . . Are you mad!"

"Careful with that weapon, Major," Ryan said coolly. "It might go off and hurt somebody. As you can see, I am not armed."

He made a sweeping gesture inviting inspection. Oriani refused to accept the invitation. Though greatly agitated, he regained a measure of control.

"What have you done?" he cried.

The clothing had caught and was now hissing and sending up a vile odor and spurts of black smoke.

"Extinguish the flames!" Oriani demanded. "At once!"

The pistol waved forgotten in his hand.

"With our bare hands?" Ryan asked civilly.

Oriani shouted orders and guards came running to kick at the smoldering pile. They managed only to spread the flames and blacken their boots and trousers. Livid, Oriani sent them running for water. They came back empty-handed. The water had been cut off at a valve in the forecourt after the two-hour morning wash-up time. Oriani sent a man to the forecourt to turn on the water. The guards were now scuttling about in confusion and screaming at each other hysterically.

The prisoners broke ranks, shrieking with laughter. Orde popped his glass eye into his navel and began doing a belly dance. The men around him clapped their hands rhythmically and yelled encouragement. Oriani looked uncertainly from Orde to the fire. He seemed ready to explode with outrage and embarrassment. A command from Ryan sent the men back into formation but did not halt their raucous merriment.

When the water came on, the guards scurried from the washrooms to the fire and back again carrying water in tin cans while Oriani paced in helpless fury. The only effect was to add random puffs of steam to the growing billow of black smoke. The stench became overpowering.

Battaglia came trotting through the gate, for once without papers in his hand.

"Parade, attention!" Ryan shouted.

The formation came to attention with a great rustle of calf against hairy calf. A thousand men stood mute and naked, their bellies, buttocks, and thighs a broad band of white across the ranks of brown bodies. Only an occasional burst of stifled laughter and the hiss of burning cloth broke the heavy silence.

Battaglia averted his face. He grew pale as the prisoners' buttocks and looked as if he were going to be ill.

"Maggiore," he called in a thin, strained voice, waving his hand in summons but not turning to face Oriani.

Oriani rushed to him.

"Padre Costanzo," Ryan called. "Front and center."

Costanzo came running.

"What are they saying?" Ryan asked.

"Colonel Battaglia's telling Oriani to make us clothe ourselves. Oriani says our clothes are burning up. Battaglia wants to know who's responsible. Oriani says you. He wants to shoot you."

"Go on," said Ryan.

"Battaglia's thinking it over. He says no, put you in the cooler. But get some clothes on you first. And the others. He's very emphatic. Oriani's getting sarcastic. He says how. Now Battaglia's as mad at Oriani as he is at you. He says he doesn't care how. Just do it."

"Thanks, Padre," Ryan said. "I'll take over now."

He walked quietly to Battaglia and touched him gently on the shoulder. Battaglia turned at the touch, saw Ryan's naked torso, and averted his face again.

"Now, Colonel Battaglia," Ryan said. "About those uniforms over there in the warehouse."

—VIII—

Ryan *went cheerfully to solitary confinement,* wearing a crisp new khaki uniform. He had the little two-cell building to himself except for his guards, who served in pairs and changed every eight hours around the clock. His cell contained only a cot and a stool. The single window was high and heavily barred and faced the camp wall. During the hours of darkness the guardbox searchlight picked regularly at his window.

Ryan was denied tobacco, letter forms for writing home, and communications with anyone except his guards. Twice a day he did arduous calisthenics, to the amusement and awe of his guards. They took turns peering through the barred grate in Ryan's cell as he shadowboxed for minutes at a time and did endless sit-ups and push-ups. Once, in a rare burst of mischief, Ryan walked to the door on his hands and, flipping nimbly to his feet with his face only inches from the grating, shouted, "Boo!"

Ryan amused himself by subjecting his guards to a rigid personal inspection every day, rising at midnight to include the third shift. Within a few days the cooler detail was noticeably smarter in appearance than any of the other guards at P. G. 202.

On the fourth day of his confinement Ryan had a visitor, Oriani. Ryan was lying on his cot, his hands behind his head, when Oriani entered the cell.

"Don't you knock, Major?" Ryan demanded, not changing his position.

"I beg your pardon, my dear Colonel. It was most impolite of me. But now that I am here, may I seat myself?"

"Help yourself."

Ryan swung himself to a sitting position and faced the major, his hands grasping the edge of the cot. The guard on watch at the grating, thinking Ryan was tensing to spring at Oriani, flipped his carbine off safety. He relaxed gratefully when he saw that Ryan was merely resting his weight on his hands. If Oriani shared the guard's apprehension he did not show it. He sat easily on the stool, his trimly clad legs outstretched, and took out a package of cigarettes.

"May I offer you a cigarette, Colonel?" he asked.

"I'd rather have one of my own. Even Players have those things beat."

"Unfortunately it is not permitted for prisoners in solitary confinement to have tobacco," he said. "I am afraid it is one of mine or nothing."

"Beggars can't be choosers," said Ryan.

He lit up and inhaled warily.

"I suppose a man could learn to smoke these if he had to," he said. "What's the purpose of this visit, Major?"

"I am concerned with the colonel's well-being, of course," Oriani replied, smiling. "Your welfare is my responsibility."

Ryan studied him without expression through a plume of cigarette smoke.

"And I wish to thank you for your attentions to my men," Oriani continued. "Since your confinement they have become, I believe the expression is, 'all spit and polish.' They rather put their comrades to shame."

"If you can't keep your troops on the ball that's not my problem, Major. As you can see, I'm a very busy man. If you've got something on your mind, let's hear it."

Oriani sighed.

"Colonel Ryan," he said, "you are obviously a man of some

education and attainment, yet you are quite rude in all your dealings with me. Even boorish. Why?"

"Because I don't like you, Major. Any more than you like me. And I don't waste my time pretending otherwise."

"I am distressed to learn you believe I dislike you, my dear Colonel," Oriani said, not appearing at all distressed.

He looked at his wrist watch, which he wore with the dial on the underside of his wrist, and rose gracefully to his feet.

"Thank you for giving me so much of your valuable time, Colonel," he said.

"Carry on, Major."

When Oriani reached the door he paused and turned around.

"By the way, Colonel Ryan," he said, "you might be amused by an incident in the compound today."

Though Ryan knew he was about to learn the true purpose of Oriani's visit he betrayed no interest.

"An effigy of straw is hanging from the railing of Settore Uno," Oriani said pleasantly. "Quite a droll figure, actually. With a placard upon its breast."

Ryan continued to regard him in silence.

"Lettered upon the placard is a rather droll inscription. 'Von Ryan.' Do you not find that amusing, my dear Colonel?"

"I'm in no position to judge, Major. I'd have to see for myself."

"Perhaps it will be there still when you return."

"Maybe. Major, inform Captain Stein I wish to see him."

"Unfortunately you are not permitted visitors."

"Am I to understand I am being refused medical attention?"

"Medical attention? I have never seen a person so bursting with strength, Colonel. And I have been informed you are most vigorous in your daily exercises."

"It's my scalp wound. Dr. Stein examines it once a week."

"It appears quite healed. But perhaps it only appears so to the untrained eye. I will send Captain Stein to you at once."

Ryan understood from Oriani's easy capitulation that the major wanted him to get news from the compound.

Stein arrived within a half hour, carrying his black bag.

"What seems to be the trouble, Colonel?" he asked.

"That's what I want to know," Ryan said. "Fool around with my head while you talk. That's why you're supposed to be here."

"It's healed nicely, Colonel," Stein said, inspecting his scalp. "Considering conditions here it's a tribute to my skill and your constitution."

"What's going on out there?"

"What do you mean, sir?"

"You know what I mean, Captain. Oriani couldn't wait for me to get a report. Why'd they hang me in effigy?"

"Oh. So you heard about that."

"Oriani told me. I don't give a damn that they did it. I want to know why they did it."

"It's mostly because of the parcels."

"The parcels?"

"Colonel Battaglia cut us back to half parcels because we burned our clothes. The men blame you."

"Naturally. I ordered it. What else? You said mostly."

"Let's see," said Stein, holding up his hand and ticking off items on his fingers. "No cigarettes. Four roll calls a day. No midday water. Lights out an hour earlier."

"What else?"

"Sir?"

"Don't 'sir' me, Captain. I know there must be more. Oriani was too pleased with himself."

"The men have sort of let themselves go."

"Let themselves go? Isn't Fincham keeping them on the ball?"

"Colonel, nobody's touched a mop or done a side straddle hop since you went to the cooler. Eunace Smith is out there every morning in his shorts but he can't get anybody to exercise with him."

Ryan paced the width of his cell and back, his eyes frosty. Stein maintained a cautious silence.

"Captain," Ryan said at last. "I want you to transmit an order

from me to Colonel Fincham. He is to resume quarters inspections and calisthenics at once. I am holding him personally responsible for the conduct of the men. When I get back to the
compound I expect to find conditions substantially as I left
them. And tell Major Oriani I want to see Colonel Battaglia."

Stein grinned.

"I'm not aware I said anything funny," Ryan snapped.

"I was just thinking," Stein said. "You're throwing me to the
lions and I'm not even a Christian."

"Under other circumstances I might find that amusing. But
what's going on out there isn't funny."

"Yes, sir."

"One more thing."

"Yes, Colonel?"

"That effigy. Is it a pretty good likeness?"

"No, sir. It looks like a pregnant woman."

"They can't do anything right, can they, Stein?"

Ryan waited half a day to be taken to Battaglia. When nothing happened he asked for Oriani. Oriani arrived in high good
humor.

"I trust you had a pleasant chat with Captain Stein, Colonel,"
he said amiably.

"Did Captain Stein tell you I wanted to see Colonel Battaglia?"

"Under the circumstances, do you not consider that request
rather presumptuous, Colonel?"

"I consider it presumptuous for you to interfere, Major. You
have a bad habit of assuming more authority than your rank
calls for."

"That is a matter of opinion, my dear Colonel. In any case,
the decision not to see you is Colonel Battaglia's, not mine. He
is most displeased with you."

"Major, you will inform the colonel I am formally protesting
his mass reprisals against the personnel detained in P. G. 202.
This is expressly forbidden by the Geneva Convention. He will
face serious charges when this camp is liberated."

"Come now, Colonel. You really do not expect Colonel Battaglia to be influenced by such threats?"

"I do not make threats, Major."

Ryan was released after only one week in solitary confinement though he had anticipated a longer sentence. He attributed his quick release not to any weakness on Battaglia's part but to the commandant's desire to restore order in the camp. The belief was confirmed when he walked through the barricade gate at morning roll call to find the men shirtless, unshaven, and disorderly.

"Von Ryan's back!" Orde shrilled.

The men booed. To their surprise, Ryan took no action. He walked to his place in silence.

"Welcome back, my dear Colonel," Oriani said in a loud voice. "I trust you enjoyed your holiday?"

"Very well, thank you," said Ryan.

"Have you observed the tribute your devoted men have paid you?" Oriani asked, nodding toward the second-floor porch, from which dangled a grotesque figure.

The effigy was fashioned from a paillasse tied off in each corner to make stubby arms and legs. The head was formed by a noose pulled tight near the top. Huge eagles cut from tin cans glinted on the shoulders and on the breast was a large Iron Cross. The "Von Ryan" placard was lettered with loving care.

"Better in effigy than in the flesh, wouldn't you say, Major?" said Ryan.

"Is that another of your threats, Colonel Ryan?"

"You flatter yourself, Major Oriani. Petty criminals are never hanged."

The prisoners close enough to hear laughed grudgingly.

After roll call Fincham came to Ryan, grinning savagely.

"Well now, Colonel," he said, "you've made a proper ballocks, haven't you?"

"Thanks for coming over, Colonel," Ryan said calmly. "Saved me a walk across the compound. Would you mind joining me in my quarters?"

Fincham was taken aback by Ryan's unexpected mildness. He stroked his mustache a moment before answering.

"Took a bit of ginger out of you, did they?" he said. "Thought you'd stand up to the cooler better than that."

In his room, Ryan ordered Fincham to sit on the stool and stood over him. Fincham refused to be stared down.

"Colonel," said Ryan, "in one week you've managed to undo everything I accomplished in a month. Congratulations."

"Thanks, awfully, old cock, but the credit's yours. Half parcels, no smokes, double parades. The lot."

"I am not referring to Colonel Battaglia's reprisals. For that I accept full responsibility. I'm talking about discipline. Did Captain Stein transmit my order that you were to resume inspections and calisthenics?"

"He did."

"And did you?"

"Ballocks."

Ryan's thick jaw muscles sprang into sharp relief as he gritted his teeth. When he spoke, his lips scarcely moved.

"Fincham, you are the most disrespectful, incompetent officer it has ever been my misfortune to serve with. Unfortunately I'm in no position to have you court-martialed. Consider yourself under arrest. You are confined to quarters except for meals and roll call and relieved of all duties."

Fincham sprang to his feet, red-faced.

"You're bloody well lucky I'm not more insubordinate, Yank!" he cried. "I'd break your bloody back for you."

"That's the most tempting offer I've had in years, Colonel. Under other circumstances I'd be delighted if you tried."

"Or could it be you've no stomach for it?"

Ryan eyed Fincham speculatively.

"Maybe we've both stored up a little too much adrenaline," he said.

He stepped to the porch and looked around. The porch was empty.

Back inside, he said, "Well, Fincham, my bloody back is at your disposal."

Fincham grinned in answer and crouched, his arms slightly flexed, his hands open. Ryan, who had some training in unarmed combat, saw that Fincham did not intend to make a fistfight of it. Nevertheless he took a stand-up fighter's stance and almost lazily started a left jab at Fincham's head. He jerked his hand back when Fincham reached for it and with the same motion that drew back the left crossed his hard right fist to Fincham's chin in a short, savage blow.

Fincham collapsed in a sitting position, his back against the wall, his head lolling. Ryan sat on the stool facing him. After almost a minute, Fincham opened his eyes and shook his head. His eyes focused on Ryan's shoes and traveled slowly upward to Ryan's face. He regarded Ryan in thoughtful silence.

"That was a smasher," he said quietly. "Caught me bang on."

"I've always argued that a major weakness of unarmed combat as taught by the military is the neglect of the feint, Colonel. Are you all right?"

"Quite, thank you."

"I'm sorry I indulged myself in a juvenile display of temper."

"I'm sorry you did too, rather," said Fincham, feeling his jaw. "Just what did you do?"

"Feinted with a left and crossed the right."

"Rather effective."

He got to his feet and dusted off his trousers. Ryan stood up, too.

"I suppose we should shake hands and that sort of thing," Fincham said.

"Naturally."

Gravely they shook hands.

"No hard feelings, as you Yanks say. Right?"

"Right. You're still confined to quarters, of course."

Fincham stiffened.

"Back in character, aren't we, headmaster?" he demanded.

But Ryan was not back in character. He was strangely indifferent to the anarchy into which the compound had relapsed. He made no rebuttal when Oriani commented ironically on his inability to control his men, and when Petersen was almost lynched while trying to take down the Von Ryan effigy, refused Oriani's offer to have it removed by Italian soldiers.

The men accepted this as a token of complete surrender and grew even more unruly and disrespectful. Still Ryan did nothing. Petersen was crushed. He would try to catch Ryan's eye, his face puzzled and pleading, silently begging the colonel to fight back. This, too, Ryan ignored.

Often, when he stood in roll call formation or walked in the courtyard, Ryan would find Costanzo or Stein studying him speculatively but he gave no indication that he had noticed. After three days Costanzo came to see him in his quarters.

"Are you all right, Cuhnel?" he asked.

"I assume you're inquiring about my spiritual well-being, Padre," Ryan replied. "Never better. And if Captain Stein is wondering about his department, tell him I never felt healthier."

"Cuhnel, it's not like you to stand for the kind of carrying on that's going on."

"You should be pleased, Padre. You're always telling me I'm too rough on the men."

"You worked wonders with them and for them. Now they're worse off than before you took over."

"Thanks for telling me. I'd never have suspected it."

Costanzo looked at him sharply.

"Is that what you want, Cuhnel?" he demanded. "To punish them by letting them fall apart?"

"Don't be an idiot."

"Why, then? Ah know you never do anything without a reason."

"You've heard what they say, Padre. Von Ryan left his guts in the cooler."

"Ah don't believe that, Cuhnel. There's nothing rugged about the cooler."

A look of revelation crossed his face.

"Cuhnel, Ah know why you're doing it. Ah don't know why Ah didn't figure it out before."

"Maybe you do at that, Padre. But keep it to yourself. That's an order."

Costanzo grinned.

"Yes, suh. Ah knew you had a reason."

After Costanzo left him, Ryan went to the porch and looked down into the courtyard. The swarming prisoners looked like mendicants. At the barricade, Orde, Bostick, and a handful of other men were taunting the guard. Oriani stood watching in the door of the settore office. At that distance Ryan could not see the expression on the Italian's face but Oriani's posture suggested a mood of tense fury. Ryan looked at the straw man dangling from its noose, the Von Ryan placard stirring in a small welcome breeze that swept in unexpectedly, smelling faintly of pines and sea. Ryan filled his lungs with the scent. Fincham came to the door of his room across the courtyard, stared over at Ryan, and went back inside. Ryan took a last look at the straw man and went into his room.

Next morning the compound was swept by a rumor that the Italians had received disturbing news. The rumor was reinforced by Oriani's unusually venomous sarcasm with the prisoners and his own men and by an air of apprehension and uncertainty which surrounded the Italian soldiers. Alessandro was nervous and Falvi was bursting with suppressed excitement. When the prisoners whispered questions Falvi shook his head and indicated with surreptitious gestures he could say nothing because of Oriani. After roll call he had a quick, furtive conference with Costanzo before hurrying from the compound, pulling away from the prisoners who plucked at his arm.

The prisoners turned their attention to Costanzo, who hurried to follow Ryan after telling them Falvi had pledged him to secrecy. Ryan was waiting for him in his room.

"We've crossed the straits at Messina and landed on the mainland," Costanzo said. "Bobby Falvi said they just got the gen this morning."

"I was afraid of that. A landing north of here would be a hell of a lot better for us."

"Ah think it's pretty good news, myself, Cuhnel."

"Oh, it is, Padre. It is. And maybe it's what we need to get Battaglia off his duff. I thought he'd be sending for me before now."

They were interrupted by shouts and the sound of running feet. Ryan and Costanzo went out on the porch. The men were massing at the barricade. It was evident they had heard of the landing from another source.

"Got your bags packed, Oriani?" Bostick yelled.

"Wanta give up now or wait until you got a rifle up your butt?" shouted another above the din of cheers and catcalls.

"Idiots," said Ryan. "We're almost three hundred miles from the action."

Oriani came striding from the settore office.

"Disperse at once," he cried.

He was answered with insults. He called out an order and in a few minutes a detail of armed soldiers came running out of the guard quarters. Oriani shouted another order and they lined up facing the prisoners and took aim.

"Don't you think you better do something, Cuhnel?" Costanzo asked anxiously.

"Oriani's doing all right," Ryan said calmly. "He knows his job."

"I will count to three," Oriani said. "If you have not dispersed my men will fire. One."

The shouting stopped and the prisoners looked uncertainly at the leveled rifles.

"Two."

The men began turning from the barricade and walking away slowly, pretending unconcern. Oriani, hands on hips, looked after them, smiling grimly. When the mob had dispersed he gave an order which sent the soldiers trotting back to their quarters.

The prisoners refused to maintain formation at the second morning roll call and Oriani stared pointedly at Ryan as if demanding the American do his duty and control his men. When Ryan did nothing, Oriani called out his troops again to enforce order. Half an hour after roll call, Falvi came to Ryan's quarters to inform him Colonel Battaglia wished to see him at once.

"Colonnello," Falvi said shyly, "the news is good today, is it not?"

"Just whose side are you on, Lieutenant?" Ryan demanded.

The young man's face fell at the rebuff, then grew resolute. "Of Italia, Colonnello. Not of the Tedeschi and Fascisti."

"I was pretty hard on you the day I came in, wasn't I, Lieutenant?"

Falvi shrugged uncomfortably.

"You're all right, Lieutenant."

Falvi stared at him with an expression of incredulous gratitude.

"Let's go," Ryan said sharply. "Colonel Battaglia's waiting."

Battaglia drummed his fingers on his paper-strewn desk and regarded Ryan severely.

"Colonnello Ry-an," he said, "did you not assure me of good behavior in reply for great concessions?"

"You didn't give us anything we weren't entitled to under the Geneva Convention. And now things are worse than ever."

"It is upon your own head, Colonnello Ry-an. You have betray-ed my trust. Firstly with the burning of clothing. And now by permitting disorder. I must warn you, with the nemichi, the enemy, on the soil of Italia, disorder will be punish-ed severely."

"Just what do you expect me to do about it, Colonel?"

"I insist you restore discipline and respect. For the safety of your men."

"Are you threatening me, Colonel Battaglia?"

"Yes," said Battaglia firmly. "I will maintain order however necessary. You understand? It is your duty as Senior Officer to assist in this."

"I'd like nothing better. But you've tied my hands."

Battaglia leaned forward, puzzled and angry.

"Che cosa dice? I have tied your hands?"

"You speak English so well I forgot myself. I mean . . ."

"Do not look to flatter me," Battaglia interrupted. "I do not pride myself on speaking Inglese. It is a painful necessity."

"Have it your own way, Colonel. What I mean was you've undermined my authority with the men."

"Undermine-ed? How have I done this, per favore?"

"You were justified in putting me in solitary. I grant that. But not in punishing my men. What it amounts to, you're punishing them for obeying my orders. It's only natural they hold me responsible for half parcels and the rest. Incidentally, I'd like to point out mess reprisals are specifically prohibited by the Geneva Convention."

"I do not require to be instructed in my duties," Battaglia said hotly.

"I just thought I'd mention it."

"You do not deceive me, Colonnello Ry-an. I am most aware you have purposely encourage-ed disorders so that you may bargain with me. I do not bargain."

"I'm not trying to bargain with you, Colonel. I'm just pointing out the unfairness of punishing the men for obeying my orders. I do think it would be a big help to me if you gave them back their cigarettes and full parcels but I wouldn't call that bargaining."

"Colonnello Ry-an. Not for one moment do I believe cigarettes and Red Cross packages are of necessity to you for controlling the men. I am not stupid. It is not for this I terminate retaliations."

"Does that mean we're going back to normal routine?"

"Please not to interrupt. There is to be no thought I do this as a means of gaining good behavior. I have other means of gaining good behavior. Maggiore Oriani would be delighted to employ such means."

"I know that, Colonel."

"This is a difficult time for my country and I impress on you order will be maintain-ed however necessary. You will impress this on the men. For their own safety. There will be no more demonstrations as this morning. Do you understand?"

"I don't see how you could make it any plainer, Colonel. I think we understand each other."

"Perhaps better than you know, Colonnello Ry-an. Perhaps better than you know. You may return to your duties."

Petersen was in the group waiting at the barricade. Ryan sent him to bring Fincham to his quarters.

"Colonel," Ryan said. "Have the men fall out in formation."

"Sorry, old cock. I'm confined to quarters."

"Your punishment is suspended until further notice, Colonel. We've got work to do."

"Whose, pray? Battaglia's?"

"Colonel Fincham. I gave you an order."

"Sir!" Fincham cried in his imitation of Bonzer.

Still bold and restless from the two-week remission of Ryan's iron discipline, the prisoners smoked and talked in ranks while Ryan eyed them from the vantage of his stool at the front of the formation. Prompted as much by curiosity as by his steady gaze, they gradually fell silent. When he had their complete attention, Ryan spoke.

"Gentlemen," he said, "the honeymoon is over."

—IX—

Because the return of strict discipline coincided with the ending of reprisals, Fincham accused Ryan of having capitulated to Battaglia.

"And just when the beggars are on the run," Fincham said.

He had been summoned, with Major Wimberly, to Ryan's quarters.

"As usual, you're exactly 180 degrees off," Ryan said. "The invasion's got the Italians so touchy somebody'd get shot if the men weren't under control. I knew that when I went in there and Battaglia knew I knew it. He put us on full parcels because he wanted to, not because he had to."

"Rot," said Fincham.

Wimberly shifted his weight uncomfortably and his bulging eyes bulged a little more. He did not like being present when Ryan and Fincham clashed. It was always possible he might be called upon to take sides.

"Battaglia doesn't know which way the cat will jump and neither do we," Ryan said. "We could be cut off by new landings north of us. On the other hand, there may not be any new landings and the Krauts might stall us down south and we'll be sitting here for weeks. Our big concern is whether the Italians will try to move us north if and when our troops get close. Don't you agree, Colonel?"

"I do not. What you're saying is we should sit on our bums and do damn all to help ourselves."

"Do you really think they'll try to move us, Colonel?" Wimberly said anxiously.

"Let the buggers try," said Fincham.

"I'd rather they didn't," Ryan said dryly. "But that's why you're here. To go into what to do about it. I've got some ideas of my own and I'm open to suggestions."

The last statement was directed at Fincham. Wimberly saw with relief that he had been summoned to listen, not to contribute.

"I propose we work out tactics, prang the Ites and get cracking for our lines," Fincham said.

"We'd have the Krauts on our necks before we got started. If the Italians show signs of pulling out we've got to leave without attracting attention."

"The tunnel," Fincham said.

"Right. I want the work speeded up. That'll mean more men working in the tunnel and more men on lookout. Wimberly, you'll furnish the Escape Committee with what men they need from your battalion. I want a map of the country south of here for every company commander. Both of you put every man you've got who can do maps to work making copies."

"Right," said Fincham.

Wimberly nodded.

"We'll need as much information as we can get about the way the fighting's going down south. I want a round-the-clock surveillance of the road. I want everything that moves in either direction noted."

"That could give us a clue," Fincham agreed. "I'll post men at a window in C Bay. A bit of the road's visible from there. Can't see troops on foot, though. Only vehicles."

"Good. Wimberly will split the duty with you. The two of you get together and work out what hours the American detail stands watch. We need a clue to what the Italians are thinking, too."

"The ORs sometimes get a bit of gen from the Ites," said Fincham.

"All we'll get from the Italian enlisted men is rumors. I'll get Padre Costanzo to work on Falvi."

"That young ass."

"Don't underestimate Lieutenant Falvi. I made that mistake myself."

"You made a mistake, Colonel? I'm shaken to the tits."

With work to be done, Fincham left the meeting in better humor than he had come to it. Ryan went looking for Costanzo.

"Padre," he said when he found him in the courtyard, "I need your help."

"Spiritual or temporal, Cuhnel?"

"Make yourself available to Falvi as much as you can. Get him to talking about the military situation and Colonel Battaglia's intentions. If they decide to move us we want as much advance warning as we can get."

"Ah'm a priest, Cuhnel," Costanzo said quietly.

"You're also a soldier—Captain. I'm not asking for secrets of the confessional. I want military intelligence."

Ryan next sought out Grimes-Lemley, the quartermaster.

"I want you to get together with Hawkins and Beresford," he said. "Have Hawkins turn over to you all the chocolate and half the sugar and Klim from the Red Cross parcels from now on. Tell Beresford to cut dried fruit and oatmeal from the menu. You and Beresford put together an emergency ration. Boil up oatmeal, dried fruit, chocolate, sugar, and Klim. Put the stuff in Scottish sugar tins and divide it up among the company commanders. They'll disperse it among the platoons. See that they keep a record of who has what."

That afternoon, Beresford hurried to him in distress.

"Colonel Ryan," he said, "about the sugar and fruit."

"What about it?"

"It means no plum duff for Sunday sweet, sir."

"I think we'll manage to struggle along without plum duff, Captain."

"Yes, sir," said Beresford sadly.

Surveillance of the road during the next few days indicated some movement of matériel but definitely not a rout. The road past P. G. 202 was not a main one and Ryan did not feel he could draw any definite conclusions from the amount of German traffic his men reported. Falvi described the action in the south to Costanzo as a German debacle but Ryan suspected Falvi's information was based more on wishful thinking than on fact. More important, however, Falvi had heard nothing of any plan to move the prisoners.

The tunnel went faster than before but progress was still painfully slow in the flinty soil. The head of the Escape Committee estimated it would be at least ten days before it would be outside the wall.

The prisoners were in an unremitting ferment, gathering in knots to exchange rumors and predictions and staying up at night for more talk. At roll call they attempted to taunt Oriani and the soldiers but Ryan kept them tightly in check. The morale of the guards deteriorated noticeably and some of them tried to make friends with the prisoners.

"Piece of cake to take over the lot," Fincham said.

"You've seen the stuff on the road," Ryan said. "There must be more where that came from. So far the Krauts haven't noticed us. I'd like to keep it that way. We'll sit tight."

Five days after the invasion of the mainland, a drawn and strangely monosyllabic Oriani came into the compound before morning roll call and summoned Ryan to Battaglia's office.

The commandant's eyes were dark pits of agony framed above in heavy black brows, below in black smudges of fatigue. Grief etched his face and there was little of the fighting cock in his bearing, only a great and somber dignity. He greeted Ryan solemnly, then peered outside as if making certain no one was eavesdropping and closed the door softly behind him. He did not speak to Ryan again for half a minute or so.

He stood looking out the window, his back to Ryan, his hands behind him, the thumb and forefinger of his right hand aimlessly turning a signet ring on the little finger of the left. He took a deep breath, raised and threw back his shoulders, and turned to face Ryan. He stood quite straight, his arms at his sides in an almost formal military posture.

"Colonnello Ry-an," he said in a low but firm voice, "it is my unhappy duty to inform you that Italia has capitulated."

Ryan leaned forward, clutching the arms of his chair, and stifled an urge to cheer. He rose deliberately to his feet.

"Colonel Battaglia," he said gravely, "I hope that now your country will be spared further sacrifices. And may I say I understand and respect your feelings."

"Thank you," Battaglia said, adding without bitterness, "congratulations, Colonnello Ry-an."

Ryan held out his hand and Battaglia shook it with melancholy ceremony.

"Now," Battaglia said with something of his former briskness, "we must talk."

He sat down and motioned Ryan to do the same.

"At this time only Maggiore Oriani is aware of that which I have inform-ed you. Within one hour it shall be announce-ed to the troops. You will please to inform your men at that time also and insure there will be no unhappy incidents."

"What happens after that?" Ryan asked. "What are your instructions about returning us to Allied control?"

Battaglia shook his head.

"I have receive-ed no instructions, only that I continue to be responsible for the safety of all until you are restore-ed to your own forces."

"Would this include intervening if the Germans try to take over?"

Battaglia spread his hands.

"I would resist such an attempt but unless I receive additional troops I promise nothing," he said.

"For the time being I think it will be best for you to continue your regular routine," Ryan said, assuming authority with the statement.

"Very well," said Battaglia, surrendering it.

"After I've had a meeting with my staff we can get together again and work out a plan for administering the camp jointly. We'll probably need your help."

Battaglia nodded.

"Colonel," said Ryan, "we've had our differences in the past but I realize you've always acted as you felt you must. I can't fault you for that. I can promise you fair treatment when Allied troops arrive."

"It is of no importance what becomes of me," Battaglia replied. "But I welcome any protection you may afford my men. There is great bitterness among some of your officers."

"I know. I'll keep them in line. Colonel, I'd better be getting back to the compound if I'm to time my announcement with yours. I'll get back to you later."

Ryan returned to the compound leaving Battaglia sitting motionless at a desk for once bare of papers. Oriani's agitation had been observed when he came for Ryan and several hundred prisoners were waiting at the barricade, Orde as usual in the vanguard and squirming with excitement. Ryan's expression revealed nothing and his voice betrayed no emotion when he singled out Fincham, Costanzo, and Wimberly in the crowd and told them to come to his quarters.

"You, too, Lieutenant Petersen," he said.

When they reached his room he ordered Petersen to stand watch outside.

"Don't let anybody get close enough to eavesdrop," he said. "If anybody gives you a hard time, sound off."

Ryan was hardly inside the door when Fincham said, "All right, out with it. What's the gen?"

"Gentlemen," Ryan said simply, "Italy has quit."

Fincham whistled and Wimberly cried, "Hot damn!" Costanzo's lips moved in silent prayer. In a moment they were shaking hands all around.

"Colonel Battaglia will be breaking the news to his troops in forty minutes," Ryan said. "I'll make the announcement to our men at the same time."

"Sir, did Colonel Battaglia say when we'd be leaving?" Wimberly asked, his lips wet.

"He had no details, Major. I don't want a word of this to leak out before I make the announcement. Fincham, you and Wimberly have each of your company commanders furnish a man to clear the tables out of Mess Hall Number One and move in benches from Number Two. I want every man in there and sitting down in thirty-five minutes."

"Question, Colonel," said Fincham.

"Yes?"

"I'd like to enter my bid for Oriani."

"What do you mean?"

"I'd like to have the sod for my very own. I've some scores to settle with him."

"There'll be no reprisals against Oriani or any other Italian. They're beaten, they've quit, and we're not going to disgrace ourselves with acts of violence."

"Then you'd best keep the clot where he won't be tempting us."

"After the announcement I'll call the staff together and we'll see where we go from here. Padre, when I finish the announcement I want you to lead us in a prayer of thanksgiving. A brief one."

Costanzo's smile of gratitude grew mischievous.

"Are you suddenly overwhelmed with piety, Cuhnel, or is it just that you think it's a good way of preventing a riot?"

"A little of each, Padre. When I first got here you said something about 'Render unto Caesar.' I think now's the appropriate time to implement the rest of the quotation. Gentlemen, if you have any questions I suggest you hold them until the staff meeting and we'll touch all the bases then. And remember, not a word about this. I've promised Colonel Battaglia our men will get the word the same time as his."

When they had gone, Ryan summoned Petersen inside.

"Did you hear, Lieutenant?" he asked.

"No, sir. There was too much noise out there."

"It's good news, Billy. Italy's surrendered."

Petersen grew pale. He put his hand against the wall to keep from falling. Ryan leaped to support him.

"What's the matter, Lieutenant? You all right?"

Petersen swallowed and wet his dry lips.

"Yes, sir. It's just that . . . I didn't know it was coming that fast."

"I didn't think that fainting spell was entirely due to my use of your first name, Lieutenant," Ryan said dryly.

"Sorry, sir. I've been sweating it out so long . . ."

"Get hold of yourself. We've all got work to do."

"Yes, sir."

Ryan waited in his room until the men had gathered in the mess hall. He went out on the porch and looked from the empty courtyard to the barricade, unguarded now, to the wall with its shards of glass fragmenting the sunlight into dazzle, to the buildings across the road.

Except for a murmur spreading out from the mess hall and the occasional clatter of a passing vehicle, P. G. 202 was engulfed in silence. If he listened carefully, holding his breath to still the sound of his own breathing, Ryan could hear a faint clatter of arms from the ranks of soldiers across the road. In the extreme distance the thin drone of an airplane turned to a muffled roar as it dived or changed propeller pitch. Ours or theirs, Ryan wondered. He looked at his watch and walked down the steps.

"Attention!" Fincham bawled when he entered the mess hall.

The prisoners, crammed shoulder to shoulder on the benches, sprang to struggling attention, on their faces a uniform expression of almost imploring curiosity. They had drawn the obvious conclusion from Ryan's summons but as men who had drawn too many false conclusions in the past and now feared if they allowed themselves hope they would somehow contrive their own disappointment, they did not dare accept the obvious.

Ryan looked at his watch, anxious to end their agony but

wanting to make his announcement as nearly simultaneously with Battaglia's as possible. In thirty seconds it would be a full hour since his conference with Battaglia.

"At ease, gentlemen," he said. "I know you will receive this information like officers and adults. One hour ago Colonel Battaglia informed me that Italy has capitulated."

For a moment there was no indication that anyone had understood. There was complete silence, utter blankness of expression. Then someone shouted a joyous, obscene word. It sparked an explosion of sound and movement. Men yelled incoherently and knocked one another over benches in laughing heaps. Here and there men wore the same dazed expression with which Petersen had responded to Ryan's news. From across the road came shots and wild cheering and bursts of exuberant operatic arias. The Italians were as jubilant as the prisoners.

Ryan watched in silence, permitting the men to enjoy their moment of triumph. Their reaction was too violent to be long-lived. Within a minute or two the celebration dwindled to low, emotional exclamations and self-conscious handshakes. Soon even that stopped and to a man the prisoners turned expectantly to Ryan.

"I'll go into detail in a minute," he said. "But first Padre Costanzo will lead us in prayer."

Costanzo came to the front of the mess hall, solemn now and separate from his fellow prisoners in a way none of them had seen before.

"Our Father," he said in a low, resonant voice, "we thank You for watching over Your children. We beg Your compassion for the Italian people and for all men, peace."

In the hush which followed, he said, "Will you please join me in the Twenty-third Psalm."

They bowed their heads and recited the psalm with Padre Costanzo. When the psalm was finished, Costanzo crossed himself. Stein grinned at him from the first row.

"Padre," he whispered, "I thought this was supposed to be non-denominational."

Costanzo winked and the spell was broken.

"Knock it off," Ryan called above the uproar, though with unwonted good nature. "Take your seats."

When the men were seated and quiet he said, "I know you are all anxious to get out of here as quick as you can and I wish I could give you an ETA for our troops."

"What's an ETA?" someone demanded in a carrying whisper.

"Estimated time of arrival!" Orde cried impatiently. "Quit interrupting Von Ryan."

"I trust everyone heard the translation," said Ryan, straight-faced.

He continued amid friendly laughter, for the moment a popular man.

"I'd like to be able to tell you exactly when, where, and how," he said. "Unfortunately, I have no specific information at this time. Colonel Battaglia has informed me his orders are to insure our safety until contact is made with our own troops. Beyond that he has no instructions. I'm confident the return of prisoners of war is spelled out in detail under terms of the surrender but they just haven't trickled down to the operational level yet. What the Germans intend to do now is still a big mystery. We will carry on as usual until we receive instructions from higher headquarters or circumstances dictate we initiate action of our own."

"I say let's get cracking now," Fincham said.

"I second the motion," cried Bostick.

"Hear, hear," an English voice cried and instantly the mess hall was in an uproar.

Ryan held up his hand for silence.

"I did not ask for a vote, gentlemen," he said. "I understand your feelings. Some of you have been in the bag a long time. But I don't want any of you getting yourselves killed just when the worst is over. No one is going to stay in P. G. 202 a minute longer than necessary. I will do everything possible to contact our forces for instructions. You will be kept informed at all times. That's all, gentlemen. When you're dismissed, leave the mess hall in an orderly manner and hold things down to a dull roar. Members of the staff and company commanders will remain. Colonel Fincham, you may dismiss the troops."

Fincham got to his feet but instead of dismissing the men cried, " 'God Save the King,' chaps."

The British prisoners rose and started singing. The Americans countered with "The Star-Spangled Banner" but they were outnumbered and drowned out.

" 'My country, 'tis of thee,' " Bostick yelled.

The anthem continued with the two groups singing their own words and finishing together. Fincham dismissed them and the men went racing into the courtyard, yelling, leaping, and doing handsprings.

Bonzer strolled up to Ryan, his thumbs tucked into the waistband of his kilt.

"Bloody good news, sir," he said.

Ryan stared. Bonzer had never before said anything but "Sir!" Stein rushed up and peered into Bonzer's eyes.

"Damnedest recovery I ever saw," he said incredulously. "Bonzer, how much do you remember?"

Bonzer's red side whiskers stirred in a tremendous grin.

"Took you in, too, did I, Doctor?" he said. "Pity the Ites didn't take your recommendation I be sent to Blighty."

"Well, I'll be damned!" said Stein. "Why'd you keep it up when it didn't work?"

"Bein' daft's no so bad. Saved me whiskers and kilt, did it not?"

"What a bloody tart you are!" Fincham exclaimed in admiration.

"Sir!" Bonzer cried, stamping his heel and saluting.

He stuck his thumbs in his kilt again and strolled out.

—X—

Though some staff members shared Fincham's desire
to leave without delay, most of them agreed with Ryan that it
would be foolhardy and precipitous. Despite the difference of
opinion, the meeting was conducted in an atmosphere of
amiable excitement.

"Fincham," said Ryan, "I want your best signal officer to get
over to Battaglia's headquarters and see if he can raise Allied
headquarters on the radio. But he's got to be damn careful he
doesn't alert the Krauts to the situation here. Wimberly, you
send a communications officer to work with him."

"Roger," Wimberly said.

"Major Grimes-Lemley," Ryan continued, "have the ORs get
hold of some carts and move all the Red Cross parcels from
across the road. If the ORs can't be spared from their other
duties, pick yourself a detail of officers. But if you use officers,
grab a couple of Italians to act as guards in case some passing
Kraut gets nosy."

Beresford cleared his throat and said, "Colonel Ryan?"

"Yes, Captain?"

"I think it's rather in order to lay on a bang-up bash to cele-
brate the occasion, don't you, sir? Just give the word and I
can promise a really wizard dinner."

"Hear, hear," said Fincham.

"Let's hold off until we see which way the cat jumps, Captain," Ryan said. "If we're stuck here for a while we may have to live off what's on hand."

"If it comes to that you won't find me sitting here on my bum," Fincham growled.

"We all hope it won't come to that," Ryan said, "but we can't consider ourselves out of the bag until those tanks on the road have stars on them instead of crosses."

"Stars, indeed," said Fincham. "You'd think the bloody Yanks were going it alone."

"My apologies, Colonel."

"I suppose there's no point in going on with the tunnel," said the head of the Escape Committee, a British captain.

"Keep the men digging," Ryan said. "A situation could arise where we need a back door. And maintain security. I don't want the Italians to know we have it. Captain Stein, you'll make a list of officers and men requiring medical attention. We'll want to get them out first when the time comes."

"Cuhnel?" said Costanzo.

"Yes, Padre?"

"Ah'd like permission to go up the road to Domira. Ah haven't been in a church in eleven months."

"Permission granted. But you better get yourself a habit somewhere. I don't want you leaving the compound in uniform. Have Falvi get you one. And Padre, while you're in town, see what you can pick up in the way of poop."

"Ah thought you gave in awfully easy, Cuhnel."

"I want all you company commanders to see your men stay in line. Some of 'em may get a wild hair about slipping into Domira or taking off on their own. I want a bed check made tonight. Any company commander who tries to cover up an AWOL will be in big trouble. But there better not be one. There'll be roll call as usual this afternoon but we'll conduct it ourselves. When this meeting's over I want each company commander to detail one man to move the tables back. Any questions before I go over to see Battaglia?"

"What about Ites in the compound?" Fincham demanded. "Damned if I fancy seeing them strutting about now they've packed in."

"I don't think they're doing much strutting, Colonel. I intend to have Battaglia remove the interior guards. But I want the sentry boxes manned for the Krauts' benefit."

"You seem awfully concerned about Jerry, Colonel."

"You're damned right I am."

When the meeting was over, Ryan and Fincham walked out together. Italian soldiers had gathered along the barricade in various states of intoxication and disarray. They had thrown canteens of wine over the fences and prisoners were tossing back cigarettes in return. A group of Italians at the barricade gate had thrust their hands between the planks and were shaking hands with all comers. Antagonisms were forgotten as the prisoners and their guards held laughing, one-sided conversations, neither understanding the others' words.

Ryan watched the scene tolerantly.

"Looks like there'll be no problem with reprisals," he said.

Almost as he spoke, Oriani came striding into the forecourt. Outraged by the spectacle of his men fraternizing with the prisoners, he shouted to them to come away. He was roundly ignored. Furious, he repeated the order. A soldier, his tunic unbuttoned and his eyes bright with wine, turned around and grasped the biceps of his crooked right arm with his left hand, his right forefinger and little finger extended.

Oriani turned white except for two rashlike patches of color on his cheekbones. He jerked out his pistol and in a choked voice ordered the insubordinate soldier to attention. The man sobered quickly and obeyed, taut with fear. At the sight of Oriani's implacable face, the other Italians broke off their loud chatter and watched him fearfully.

The prisoners, too, fell silent, but only for a moment. Then a low, ominous roar, chilling in its spontaneity, rose from the throng. They pressed against the barricade. Ryan and Fincham hurried toward them. When Oriani ordered his men from the compound the mood of the prisoners altered and the murderous drone broke into taunts.

"You'd look funny with that little pistol sticking out of your butt," Bostick yelled and an English officer, not to be outdone, cried, "Muck off before we have you for tea, you silly bastard."

The prisoners began competing to deliver the most colorful and crushing insult. They were enjoying it and if Oriani had left at that moment they would have been content with such a victory. Instead, he stood his ground and stared at them with supreme contempt. Their temper changed again and they surged against the barricade. Oriani did not flinch.

"Major," Ryan cried. "Don't you know better than to come in here?"

"I had assumed your men would behave as officers, not animals," Oriani spat.

"I'll show you how a bloody officer behaves, you clot," Fincham shouted, pushing his way to the forefront.

Ryan grabbed at his arm too late to stop him. Oriani pointed his pistol at Fincham. The prisoners cried their defiance.

"Think there's enough bullets for the lot of us, you filthy Ite?" Fincham demanded.

Oriani thrust the pistol back in its holster, snapped down the flap, and stared at Fincham, hands on hips, feet planted firmly apart. Then, with an abrupt move which caught everyone by surprise, he pushed aside the frightened sentry and stepped through the gate.

Fincham was the first to react. He leaped toward Oriani and took the Italian's throat in his two big hands. Oriani slipped his arms inside Fincham's and pressed his thumbs into the Englishman's neck in an unequal struggle. The other prisoners looked on in cruel rapture. Ryan burst through the crush, flinging men aside, and pulled Fincham away with an arm crooked around his neck from behind. Oriani looked on in silence, a faint smile on his face, his neck splotched red and white where Fincham had squeezed.

"That's enough, Colonel!" Ryan grated, spinning Fincham

around and sending him sprawling into the men behind him.

Without another look at Fincham he grabbed Oriani by the arm and hustled him out the barricade gate.

"You damned fool!" he said.

Oriani tried to shake himself free but Ryan's grip was too powerful. Still holding Oriani's arm, Ryan turned to face the prisoners, who were now pressed against the barricade yelling. Only Fincham, drained and numb, was silent.

"I'll have the first man who steps through that gate court-martialed," Ryan yelled.

The threat checked them for a moment though they continued to shout and press against the barricade.

"Now get out of here," Ryan ordered, releasing Oriani. "And don't come back."

Oriani brushed the spot where Ryan had grasped him, as if flicking away dust.

"Have you so little control over your men?" he asked calmly.

"You've made your point," Ryan replied with icy control. "You've proved you're a brave man. And a stupid one. It's not a question of whether I can control my men. It's whether I'll permit an egotistical maniac to create a disturbance."

As he spoke, he prodded Oriani toward the front gate.

"P. G. 202 has not yet been turned over to you, my dear Colonel," said Oriani.

"I have just assumed command, Major. And my first order is you're not to enter the compound again unless I send for you."

"We shall see."

"We damn well will. Open up," he ordered the guard.

The guard threw the gate open.

"Now get out!" Ryan ordered. "Move."

Oriani started walking with slow, insolent grace. Ryan gave him a shove which almost sent him sprawling.

"I said move," he said.

Back at the barricade, the prisoners were in better humor, mollified by his treatment of Oriani. Fincham was scowling, red-faced.

"I'll not forget that, Ryan," he promised.

"I can understand your feeling of gratitude," Ryan answered. "If I hadn't stopped you you'd have been court-martialed. For murder."

Raising his voice, he said, "You men came damn close to getting yourselves in real trouble. And fouling up orderly repatriation. I hope you've got all that out of your systems now. You better have. I'm going to forget this because I appreciate your feelings after the strain of the past months. But it's the last thing I am going to forget. Now break it up."

The crowd melted away from the barricade. Fincham was the last to leave. He glowered at Ryan long and bitterly, then shoved his hands in his pockets and walked slowly across the compound. Costanzo went to him, took his arm, and spoke to him earnestly. Fincham shook him off and continued on his way. Costanzo looked at Ryan across the courtyard and shrugged helplessly. Ryan lit a cigarette and took a deep drag. He saw that the lone Italian soldier on duty at the gate was watching him apprehensively. He released a lungful of smoke.

"For you the war is over," he said reassuringly.

He remembered how many times he had heard the phrase the day he was captured. And how wrong it had been.

At his second meeting of the day with Battaglia, Ryan arranged that camp routine would continue as before except that no Italians would be stationed inside the wall. Battaglia was to press his headquarters for specific orders regarding the return of prisoners. The communications men who had been sent to his office to contact Allied headquarters were having no success.

Costanzo, wearing a black habit and looking very Italian, returned from Domira late in the afternoon to report that the local civilians were friendly and sympathetic and that the area was swarming with German troops and equipment.

"Going or coming?" Ryan asked.

"Ah couldn't tell, Cuhnel. Looked like both. Ah'll tell you one thing, though, they didn't look like they were in any flap."

"I don't like that. Fincham, we better be damn sure we don't do anything to attract attention. And put more men on the tunnel detail."

Early in the evening Falvi came to Ryan, greatly agitated, to report the Germans had taken over Radio Roma and were exhorting Italians to repudiate the surrender.

"Never will we do this," he said. "Colonnello, do you think the Tedeschi will make of Italia a battleground?"

"I was going to ask you that, Lieutenant. I don't suppose any mention was made of prisoners of war."

"None, Colonnello."

"From what you've been able to see and hear, do you think the Germans can spare the transport to move us out of here, Lieutenant?"

"No, Colonnello. There is much bombing of the railways and much crowding of transport on the roads. The Tedeschi require all to save themselves."

"I hope you're right, Lieutenant."

Ryan arose early the next morning and went down into the center court before shaving to stretch his legs and breathe the cool morning air. Later the air in the courtyard would be humid and overbreathed. He was the only man awake except for a half dozen ORs who, passing hearty obscenities over the day's first cigarette and grinding crusted sleep from their eyes, straggled to the kitchen to start the fires for morning brew.

When they disappeared into the kitchen, there was a welcome stillness in the center court, at other hours so ringing with the restless babble and bustle of too many men with nerves stretched too tautly. Ryan looked about him. This could be the last morning he would spend in P. G. 202. It was strange that it was the first day since his arrival he was viewing a compound completely empty. There was not a human being in sight though the building surrounding him on three sides was as stuffed with flesh as a sausage. Even the Italians were gone, by his order. He strolled to the barricade and looked into the empty forecourt.

There were no guards in the sentry boxes on the wall.

The silence suddenly was ominous.

Ryan made a quick circuit of the perimeter. None of the sentry boxes was manned. He ran out the front gate and encountered Falvi hurrying across the road, unshaven, his wavy hair disarrayed, his tunic unbuttoned.

"Colonnello," he cried, "please to excuse my appearance but . . ."

"Forget it," Ryan interrupted. "What's happened to everybody?"

"This is what I was hastening to inform the colonnello. In the night, without warning, all have departed. Only I remain."

"Where's Colonel Battaglia?"

"At his quarters in Domira. It is too early yet for his arrival."

"Get on the phone and tell him to get here on the double."

"It is already done, Colonnello."

"Good work, Lieutenant."

Falvi beamed in boyish pride.

"What are we to do, sir?" he asked, buttoning his tunic and smoothing his hair in place.

The "we" was not lost on Ryan.

"You've been a big help, Lieutenant," he said. "It'll be in my report. Get on back to the office and wait for Colonel Battaglia. Tell him I'll see him there in a few minutes."

Ryan returned to the compound and awakened Fincham. Fincham swore when he heard the news.

"So the clots buggered off? I don't like it. Do you think they got some gen in the night that put them in a flap?"

"I don't see how they could get any poop Battaglia didn't have. I think they just got windy and went over the hill."

"Over the hill?"

"Deserted. Why should they hang around and take a chance on shooting it out with the Krauts? The war's over for them."

"I think they got some gen," Fincham said stubbornly. "And I'll give you another thought. I don't trust that perishing Battaglia. Why should he change about so suddenly after treating us like vermin?"

"I won't go into that now but that was as much your fault as his."

"Ballocks."

Fincham wanted to take the men out at once but Ryan was adamant.

"And put the Krauts in a position where they have to do something with us?" he demanded.

He made Fincham shave and accompany him across the road to Battaglia's office.

"If there was time for a shave there was time for my bloody tea," Fincham grumbled on the way.

"I've got some soluble coffee in Battaglia's office."

"Coffee!" Fincham cried.

Battaglia was as much embarrassed as concerned.

"Colonnello Ry-an," he said, distressed. "I know not how to apologize for the conduct of my men. To depart without orders. Shameful . . ."

He knew of no reason why his troops should leave so abruptly.

"Oriani heard the bloody radio and took them to join Jerry, that's where they've gone," Fincham said.

Battaglia shook his head.

"Maggiore Oriani was not like-ed by the men," he said. "And they have no sympathy for the Tedeschi. A few only, perhaps, who are Fascisti."

"If the Germans wanted to move us, do you think they have the means?" Ryan asked.

Battaglia was of the same opinion as Falvi, that the Germans could not spare the transport to move the prisoners even if they desired to do so.

"We can't be sure," said Ryan. "Colonel, see what you can find out. But don't let it be known you don't have the troops to control us. I'm going to put some of my people in Italian uniforms and put them in the sentry boxes. And a few over here to make it look like you're still staffed. If the Germans get nosy you can tell them you've kept a skeleton staff and sent the rest to help their German comrades down south. And that we're very docile.

"Are you around the bend?" Fincham demanded. "Putting our chaps on the wall?"

"Would you rather have Krauts there, Colonel?"

They returned to the compound to find the prisoners awake and milling about in the center court in great confusion, some of them taking comfort from the absence of guards, the more thoughtful of them disturbed by the defections. Ryan selected a group of men he considered reliable and sent them across the road to get into Italian uniforms. He placed them at the entrance and at the barricade gate as well as on the wall, with strict orders that no one was to leave the compound except Padre Costanzo.

"Shouldn't want any chaps missing when Jerry arrives, should we?" Fincham said angrily.

"For your information, and only yours, I intend to move the men out if we don't receive instructions from Allied headquarters in the next twenty-four hours," Ryan replied. "I've got a plan and if you've got a better idea sound off."

"Awake at last, are we, headmaster? What's the drill?"

"We'll move out in broad daylight. Under guard."

"Under guard?"

"We'll keep some of our men in Italian uniforms. I'll take Falvi with us. If he's questioned, he'll tell the Krauts he's moving us away from the front to a collection point farther back. I'll have Padre Costanzo recruit us a couple of guides in Domira who know the area. As soon as we're off the main road we'll head for the hills, split into platoons, and work our way south."

"Wizard," said Fincham. "Why not get cracking now?"

"I don't want to do it unless we have to. We could lose a lot of men. There's a lot of Krauts between us and the front lines."

In midafternoon, Bostick came to Ryan's quarters leading a delegation of four determined-looking officers. Bostick rapped on the wall outside the room.

"Sir," he said, struggling to mask his distaste at addressing Ryan so courteously, "we request permission to speak with the colonel."

"Permission granted. Come in."

Bostick stepped inside, followed by his four companions whose confidence seemed to drain away when they were actually face to face with Ryan.

"What can I do for you, Captain?" Ryan asked.

"Sir, we've got a plan to get through to our troops," Bostick said.

"All of us?"

"No, sir. I know we couldn't all do it. The five of us."

"I see. What about the other nine hundred and some odd?"

"We thought up the plan," Bostick said belligerently. "Anybody else that wants to go can figure out their own way."

"Tell me more."

"We've been saving chocolate, biscuits, and dried fruit a long time. Enough for five or six days each. We've got a map and we think we can make it."

"What if you get captured by the Germans?"

Bostick shrugged.

"That's our tough luck, I guess."

"Ours, too, Captain. If you got caught near this camp it would put every man here in jeopardy. Don't you realize the Germans would take over P. G. 202 so fast it would make your head swim? Permission denied."

"Damn it, Colonel . . ." Bostick cried, dropping his pose of civility.

"I said permission denied."

At the door, Bostick turned and said defiantly, "I'm leaving when I get ready and nobody's gonna stop me."

"Thanks for the warning, Captain. You're confined to quarters until further notice."

That night the prisoners went to their bunks with their own comrades standing guard on the wall with loaded carbines under orders to call Ryan immediately if anyone tried to leave the compound.

A touch on Ryan's shoulder awakened him. He sat up immediately, mind clear and alert.

"Who is it?" he demanded of the dim figure looming alongside his bunk.

"Dudley L. Hampton, sir. Major, OSS. Are you Col. Joseph G. Ryan, sir?"

"OSS? There's no Major Hampton in P. G. 202."

He dropped to the floor and thrust his face close to the other man's. He could see nothing but the shadowy outline of a face and the faint gleam of eyes and teeth.

"Who the hell are you?" Ryan asked.

"Major Hampton, sir," the man said evenly. "Are you Colonel Ryan, sir?"

"I know damned well there's no OSS man and no Major Hampton in P. G. 202. Who are you and how did you get here?"

The beam of a flashlight illuminated the man's face. It was blackened with burned cork. On his head was a knit cap and his upper body, all of it that was visible in the light, was covered by a camouflaged field jacket.

"I came over the wall, sir," he said.

He held up his free hand. It was wrapped in an olive drab handkerchief.

"Nobody told me about the glass."

"Say on," said Ryan.

"I'll have to know if you're Colonel Ryan, sir," the intruder said respectfully.

"I'm Colonel Ryan."

"What is your serial number, sir?"

Ryan told him.

"I guess you're Colonel Ryan, all right," the man said. "Sir, I have instructions from Allied headquarters."

"Just a minute, Major. How'd you know where to find me?"

"I woke somebody in the barracks, sir."

"Do you have identification?"

"Just this, sir."

The major reached inside his shirt and held out his dog tags on the end of a chain, shining a beam from the flashlight on them.

"These are easy to make," Ryan said. "Got anything better?"

The man grinned.

"Don't ask me about the World Series, sir. I don't follow baseball," he said. "But I'm from Nebraska. Ask me something about Nebraska, sir."

Ryan did not return the grin.

"What's the University of Nebraska football team called?" he asked.

"Cornhuskers, sir. And it's the University of Texas Longhorns, California Golden Bears, Wisconsin . . ."

"You've made your point, Major. Welcome to P. G. 202. What are the instructions you have for me?"

"Sir, could I have a drink of water and sit down? I've been scrambling through the boondocks half the night."

Silently Ryan handed him the straw-covered bottle he kept slung from the edge of his bunk. Hampton drank greedily and dropped to the stool near the bunk.

"That damn airplane driver dropped me at least five miles short of the target area," he explained. "Typical fly-boy operation. Oh. Excuse me, sir. You're Air Force yourself, aren't you, sir?"

"My instructions, Major. And you can turn off that light."

Hampton began reciting in a monotone, as if he had learned the message by rote.

"Intercepted German messages indicate the area surrounding Campo Concentramento Prigionieri di Guerra 202 will be free of hostile troops within three days."

"Three days of when?" Ryan asked. "Last night when you left, or today when you got here?"

"Today, sir . . . within three days," he continued. "British intelligence has learned the enemy is aware of the presence in the camp of approximately one thousand British and American officers and Other Ranks but plans no action unless they are found to represent a threat to the orderly withdrawal of German troops. You are therefore directed to remain within the confines of the camp at all times. No one is to be permitted outside or upon the wall where he might be seen by passing German troops, no one is to attempt to interfere with the German withdrawal, and no one is to commit any act of such nature as to direct unwelcome attention to P. G. 202 and the Allied personnel detained there. The latter includes particularly fraternizing with Italian civilians and addressing uncomplimentary remarks to the retreating enemy."

Ryan gave a short, harsh laugh.

Hampton paused in his recital.

"What rear area sprog thinks we'd be stupid enough to do that?" Ryan demanded.

"That shook me, too, sir," Hampton said. "But that's the way it says."

"Go on, Major."

"P. G. 202 is to be kept under constant ground and/or aerial surveillance and at such time as the area is free of uniformed German troops an advance detail of paratroopers will be dropped with food, medical supplies, and medics."

"How do they propose to keep us under ground surveillance, Major?"

"We've got a team in the hills, sir. They're in contact with an Eytie partisan in Domira."

"How do we contact him? I've got a man who can get in and out of Domira without attracting attention. A Catholic chaplain."

"I'm afraid you can't, sir. We can't afford to compromise him. Where was I, sir?"

". . . medical supplies and medics."

"Right. Thank you, sir. . . . medical supplies and medics. Those officers and men requiring medical attention will be flown out without delay. Remaining officers and men will be removed as expeditiously as possible to previously prepared quarters for physical examinations, interrogation, rest, and orientation before returning to the continental limits of the United States and/or England. Be of good cheer. You soon will be returned to Allied control. Your countries, the United States of America and Great Britain, deeply appreciate your sacrifices of the past difficult months."

"Is that last part of the message or just your own sentiments, Major?" Ryan asked dryly.

"Both, sir."

Ryan looked at the luminous dial of his watch. It was almost five.

"Lie down in my sack and get some sleep, Major," he said. "I've got things to do. I'll have a doctor in to take a look at your hand."

"It's not so bad, sir. I was in too big a hurry to get over the wall. I didn't know if the guards were Krauts or Eyties."

"They're American and British."

"Sir?"

"Your intelligence is about twenty-four hours behind the times. The Italians went over the hill night before last. I put my own people in the guard boxes for the benefit of the Krauts."

"Good stroke, sir. That should keep 'em from looking too close."

"Let's hope so, Major. Now that we've been ordered to stay put."

Ryan dressed quickly and slipped into Petersen's bay. He awakened Petersen with a touch and put his hand over the young officer's mouth when he gave a startled cry. In a low voice he ordered Petersen to get dressed and meet him on the porch. Outside, Ryan told him to awaken Stein and send the doctor to his room to treat a man for a cut hand.

"After you've got Captain Stein up, wake Major Wimberly and have him get dressed and meet me in Colonel Fincham's room right away," he continued, ignoring the question in Petersen's eyes.

Ryan went across the courtyard to Fincham's room, returning the salute of the sleepy Englishman in Italian uniform on duty at the barricade gate.

Fincham awakened with a start, reaching for a sidearm which was not there.

"It's Ryan," Ryan whispered.

Fincham shook his head to clear it.

"Dreamed I was on outpost duty," he said. "Never waken infantry that way. If I'd a pistol I might have blown your bloody head off."

"Good you didn't have one."

Ryan began telling Fincham what had happened and started over again when Wimberly came in combing his hair. Ryan waited silently for Wimberly to put away his comb before continuing.

"You think this Major Hampton chap gave you pukka gen?" Fincham demanded when Ryan finished. "Why would they send a Yank when Monty's in charge of the do?"

"Administrative error, probably," Ryan said with an irony lost on Fincham. "What makes you think he might be giving me a bum steer, other than the fact he's not English?"

"Oh, I suppose he's from HQ right enough. But what do those HQ wallahs know of our situation? They're sitting on their fat bums in cushy offices drinking pink gins, and we're here. I say wait for our chaps in the bloody hills as planned."

"And ignore top-level orders? Which incidentally seem to make damn good sense?"

Wimberly looked from one to the other and, unfortunately, let his gaze linger too long on Fincham.

"Look," Fincham said, "Wimberly agrees with me."

Ryan looked at Wimberly, who flinched.

"You're not here for a consultation, gentlemen," Ryan said. "You're here to receive instructions. Major Hampton gave me mine, I'm giving you yours. Everybody sits tight."

It was light outside and the camp was beginning to stir. The officer awakened by Hampton had spread the news of a mysterious visitor and soon the porches and center court were full of whispering men. Rather than permit rumor and speculation to upset them further, Ryan called an immediate formation in the center court. The men fell out half-clad and unwashed but for once Ryan overlooked it.

"Early this morning I had a visitor from Allied headquarters," he said. "Headquarters is aware of our situation and is keeping a close watch on P. G. 202. Plans are already in operation for our evacuation within three days."

He waited for the cheering to die down.

"The Germans are pulling out. As soon as the area is clear our paratroopers will move in with food and supplies. Meanwhile we're to carry on as before and keep the walls manned in Italian uniform to keep the Krauts from catching on. Any man who tries to leave for any reason whatsoever will be considered a deserter in the face of the enemy. You know the penalty for that in time of war. I'm depending on you men not to jeopardize the safety of your friends and fellow officers."

"Bit sticky with them, weren't you?" Fincham asked when the formation was dismissed.

"I meant it."

"I don't doubt that, more's the pity. I hope you know what you're about."

Battaglia was greatly relieved when Ryan told him of the instructions from Allied headquarters.

"It has been a heavy responsibility," Battaglia said. "A too heavy responsibility. To protect you when I had not the means to protect. I am please-ed the Tedeschi are in flight. Perhaps there is yet hope for my country."

"We don't know how far they'll be pulling back," Ryan said. "Only that it's north of here. What do you plan to do after P. G. 202 is evacuated?"

"Perhaps in my turn I am prigionero, Colonnello," Battaglia said with a sad smile.

"Not if I can help it, Colonel."

"Thank you, Colonnello Ry-an. But I accept the soldier's fate whatever it may be. I would prefer . . . I would prefer to be permitted to take up arms against the Tedeschi. They have done much harm to my country."

Beresford was waiting for Ryan when he returned to the compound. Ryan's visits to Battaglia had become so commonplace Orde was the only other officer at the barricade.

"I say, sir," Beresford said. "Now there's no need to conserve our stores . . ."

"It's all yours, Captain. You have a free hand with the parcels."

"Wizard, sir," Beresford said, showing his yellow teeth in the first smile Ryan had seen on his face. "Smashing. I'll lay on a bang-up lunch. Cold, I expect, though. We'll need the fires for dinner. Well, sir, I must get cracking. Thank you, sir."

He went to the kitchen at a gallop.

Hampton spent most of the morning sleeping. He awakened long enough for Stein to tend his hand and wash the burnt cork from his face and then went back to bed. All morning men filed by Ryan's quarters to peer in at their link with freedom and be assured there actually was such a person. Ryan did not discourage them.

Ryan took Hampton to lunch with him.

"You eat like this all the time?" Hampton asked, looking at

the spread of kippers, corned beef, cheese, and food paste. "I haven't had it this good since I left the States."

"That's about a week's ration you've got there," Ryan said. "We've started making up for lost time."

"I picked a good time to drop in," Hampton said, cramming a heavily laden British biscuit into his mouth.

Throughout the meal men crowded around Hampton asking questions. He answered cheerfully though he had to plead ignorance of the exact details of evacuation and what was to follow.

"I'm afraid that's not my department," he said. "All I know for sure is they know what you've been through and intend to take good care of you. I'm just a messenger boy."

Not all the questions had to do with the immediate situation. Officers wanted to know baseball and cricket scores, Hollywood gossip, names of new books, and if it were true there was a man shortage in the United States and all the girls were eager. Ryan had to call a halt to the inquisition so Hampton could finish his lunch.

After lunch Hampton informed Ryan he would have to leave as soon as it was dark enough to do so unobserved.

"I've got to make a rendezvous with my team in a field about three miles from here," he explained. "A light plane is picking me up to take back my report. My men will stay on and keep the camp under surveillance. Colonel, is there any personal message you want me to take back? For your wife?"

"Have all next of kin notified all P. G. 202 personnel are safe and in good health, Major," Ryan said. "And tell headquarters if there is any change in plans we damn well want to know about it without delay."

Hampton slipped over the rear wall a half-hour after dark, leaving Ryan an almost full pack of American cigarettes.

"These should hold you until the troops get here, sir," he said.

"Tell them not to drag their feet, Major. I'm a heavy smoker."

To Eunace Smith's chagrin, Ryan excused the men from calisthenics the next day, substituting a rigid personal inspection. The men stood in open rank formation for two hours while

Ryan passed slowly among them checking haircuts, shaves, and uniforms.

"I intend for us to leave P. G. 202 looking like officers and gentlemen," he announced. "Some of you look pretty raunchy. Personnel who have not cut their hair in the last seven days will do so without delay. If you have holes in your uniforms they will be mended neatly. Items of uniform which are not salvageable will be replaced on request by the quartermaster. You will shave every morning. You will clean your shoes every morning. You will replace broken shoelaces and missing buttons. The canteen will provide shoelaces and buttons without charge. You may expect a personal inspection every morning until your return to Allied control. As you know, if Allied intelligence is correct, that will be no later than day after tomorrow."

"Knock on wood when you say that, Von Ryan," a voice cried out.

Ryan bent down gravely and rapped his knuckles against the stool on which he was standing.

That day and the next the prisoners cut their hair, shaved, showered, sewed on buttons, mended shirts, worked on their fingernails, and stuffed themselves on three meals a day plus afternoon tea and late evening brew. They moved their stools to the upstairs porches and sat there by the hour waiting for the first sight of friendly troops, vacillating constantly between euphoric anticipation and tense impatience.

There was spirited competition for duty on the wall, particularly on the section that commanded a view of the road. Orde somehow managed to get on the roof and, when ordered down by Ryan, had to be helped from his precarious perch.

Costanzo began holding mass in one of the mess halls after breakfast, attended by as many non-Catholics as Catholics, including Stein. Ryan paid a courtesy visit the first morning and Costanzo came to him after mass.

"This is a surprise, Cuhnel," he said.

"Don't get any ideas, Padre," Ryan said. "I also visit the

kitchen and taste the soup to make sure the officer in charge is doing his job."

"And don't get any ideas about me, either," Stein said. "I'm not considering changing my affiliation. It's merely that I never had a chance to catch your act in full costume before."

"Any reason's a good reason," Costanzo said.

The third morning after Major Hampton slipped over the wall of P. G. 202, the profane shouts of the ORs who rose early to prepare morning brew brought Ryan and the others thronging into the courtyard. During the night, German paratroopers had quietly taken over the sentry boxes and surrounded the camp.

—XII—

The news spread with shocking speed. The men crowded around Ryan, stunned and seeking reassurance. Their insistent questions grew into an unintelligible roar. Ryan looked into the agitated faces around him and for an instant withered inside though his stolid expression did not change.

Fincham, clad only in his drawers, pushed through the mob to Ryan's side, his face grim.

"Lovely sight, aren't they, Colonel?" he demanded, waving a hand at the wall. "Though not precisely the sort of paratroopers your bloody Major Hampton promised, I'd say."

"This is not the time for bickering, Colonel," Ryan said. "Lieutenant Petersen, bring my stool."

Petersen only stared, his face white, his eyes burning.

"You said they'd come for us!" Petersen croaked.

"Pull yourself together, Lieutenant!" Ryan ordered.

Petersen's voice rose hysterically.

"You said they'd come. You promised."

He was shouting now.

His hysteria had a deeply unsettling effect on the already agitated men.

"Somebody shut him up, for God's sake," a voice cried.

Bostick lunged forward and hit Petersen on the chin with a clublike fist. He caught the smaller man before he fell.

"Sorry, Billy," he said. "God damn you, Ryan."

Ryan took no notice of Bostick's insubordination.

"Get him to his bunk and keep him there, Captain," he said. "Captain Stein, go with them and see if you can snap him out of it."

He knifed through the crowd and ran up the stairs, followed by every eye.

"It won't help to get into a flap," he shouted, looking down into the agitated, resentful faces. "I'll find out what this is all about and let you know. It may be nothing. Kitchen crew, get to work and fix breakfast. The rest of you get back to your bays and get dressed."

"Here they come!" Orde shrieked.

The front gate had opened and Falvi had come in, followed by the men who had been stationed in the guard boxes. With them was a German soldier, his machine pistol slung carelessly from his shoulder. The German looked curiously at the scene in the courtyard, hitched his weapon to a more comfortable position, and went out, closing the gate behind him. Falvi hurried for the porch as the men converged on the newcomers.

Ryan counted the group quickly. They were all there. No one had been harmed in the takeover. Falvi, breathing heavily, reached his side.

"Colonnello," he gasped. "They came in the night."

"How many?"

"I could do nothing, Colonnello. I was alone."

"Nobody's blaming you, Lieutenant. How many?"

"One hundred, perhaps. Heavily armed."

"Does Colonel Battaglia know about this?"

"He is in his office, sir. He requests you come at once. A German officer is with him. A tenente colonnello. Colonnello, what is to be done?"

"That's what I hope to find out, Lieutenant."

Among the prisoners returned to the compound was Carter, the lieutenant Ryan had sent to the hospital his first day at P. G. 202.

Ryan called down to him.

"Lieutenant Carter, get up here."

Carter tore himself free of his interrogators and ran up the steps.

"Tell me what happened while I get dressed," Ryan said.

He listened while he washed and shaved. Falvi waited on the porch, answering questions shouted from the courtyard.

The officers in the guard boxes had been taken completely by surprise, with no chance to warn the men inside the camp. They had been kept under guard all night in the Italian barracks, fed a good breakfast, and returned to the compound.

"You understand German, Lieutenant?" Ryan asked.

"No, sir."

"Did you see anything that might give a clue to their intentions?"

"No, sir. They acted friendly, though. They thought it was a big joke, us wearing Ite uniforms."

"Did you see any signs of transport they might be able to move us in?"

"No, sir. Not even a truck. I think they must have come in on foot. I didn't hear a thing."

"That's encouraging."

Ryan dressed and joined Falvi on the porch. Fincham was with him, asking angry questions.

"Get off his back, Colonel," Ryan said. "There's nothing he could have done. I'm on my way to Colonel Battaglia to see the Kraut commander. I'll get back with the poop as soon as I can. Get the troops calmed down."

"You think I'm a bloody magician? They've got the wind up and I can't say I blame them."

"You're Senior British Officer, Colonel. Behave like it."

Battaglia's face bore signs of worry and a sleepless night. The German officer with him was prematurely bald, his scalp as deeply tanned as his seamed face. His big crooked nose divided his face into unequal parts which looked as if they belonged to two different persons. He sprang to his feet and saluted when Ryan entered the office.

"Colonnello Ry-an," Battaglia said unhappily. "Tenente Colonnello Spoetzl. Colonnello Spoetzl desires to speak with you."

"What's the meaning of this, Colonel?" Ryan demanded, not troubling to acknowledge the introduction. "Aren't you aware under terms of the Italian surrender prisoners of war are not to be molested?"

"The Wehrmacht did not surrender, Herr Oberst," Spoetzl replied, stiffly respectful. "Only our Italian allies."

His English was excellent.

"I regret the necessity of placing your troops under guard," he continued. "It is a necessary measure. Do you not agree it is unsound to permit so large a group of unfriendly troops to move freely behind one's lines?"

"We weren't moving anywhere, Colonel. And we are unarmed. It's ridiculous to say we represent a threat to you. I demand you withdraw your men immediately."

"I am sorry, sir. It is not possible. We will remain only a day or two. Until we withdraw to the north."

"What happens to us when you withdraw?"

"You will remain where you are, sir. We have scarcely enough transport for our own troops. I regret the disturbance the presence of my troops has created. I request permission to enter the compound and assure your men we will remain only so long as security requires."

"What if I refuse permission?"

"I would be disappointed, sir. But I would not question your authority to do so."

"Request denied."

"Have I the colonel's assurance there are no arms in the compound and your men will remain quietly within?"

"There are no arms in the compound. As for remaining quietly, as long as you hold my men under guard they are still prisoners of war and it is a prisoner's duty to attempt escape. I refuse to promise they will not try."

"I understand, sir. I must inform you anyone attempting escape will be shot if necessary to prevent it."

"That goes without saying, Colonel. Have you got anything else on your mind?"

"No, Herr Oberst. Sir, I am fortunate enough to have several bottles of excellent brandy. May I send a bottle in to you?"

"Is it big enough for a thousand men?"

"I understand, Herr Oberst."

"Thanks anyway, Colonel. I'll be getting back now."

Spoetzl came to attention and saluted. Battaglia walked outside with Ryan.

"Can I believe him, Colonel?" Ryan asked.

Battaglia shrugged.

"One is never able to believe the Tedeschi," he said. "But he has brought no transport."

"How many men does he have?"

"One hundred thirty. Heavily armed. You are not considering . . . ?"

"No. It would be a slaughter."

"Colonnello Ry-an. There is only myself and Tenente Falvi. But if any way we are able to assist . . ."

"Thanks, Colonel. See if you can find out if Spoetzl was telling the truth. Have Falvi keep me informed."

The German soldiers saluted respectfully when Ryan approached but he took no comfort from it. He found himself looking back on the emotional, undisciplined Italian troops almost with affection.

It was not necessary to call a formation when he returned to the compound. The men were waiting in the courtyard, Fincham at their head.

"The Kraut CO claims we won't be moved," Ryan said in a low voice. "I'll give you a full briefing after I've passed that along. How's Lieutenant Petersen?"

"Captain Stein says bitter but in control," Fincham replied.

"That could describe most of us," Ryan said. "I can't understand him cracking up like that."

"I expect he's disappointed in you, old boy," Fincham said. "As much as anything."

Ryan stifled a sigh and went to the center of the courtyard where the men gathered around him, mute and tightly packed as roe.

"Gentlemen," he said, "the German CO has just informed me the presence here of German troops is strictly a precautionary measure. They are here to see that we stay put until the Germans have completed their withdrawal. He says they do not intend to move us."

Ryan felt the men's sharply released breath on his cheek like a fetid breeze. Then they cheered and broke into small, excited groups. An air of reprieve hung over them.

"Bloody fools," Fincham grunted at his elbow.

Ryan looked at him.

"You may be right," he said quietly. "Come on to my quarters."

Inside, he told Fincham what he had seen and heard.

"The Kraut may have been telling the truth as he knew it and he may not," Ryan said. "And if he was telling the truth, it doesn't necessarily mean the situation couldn't change without warning. The fact remains that now they've got us under guard they could do any damn thing they wanted with us."

"So that's occurred to you, has it?" Fincham demanded bitterly. "I'd like my two hands on that bloody Major Hampton of yours and those bloody HQ wallahs who sent him."

"They were acting according to their best information."

"While sitting safely on their rosy bums and sticking little pins in their bloody maps. If we don't get out of here straightaway we've had it. You say there are only a hundred thirty of the buggers. We're almost a thousand. If we could take them by surprise . . ."

"Nobody's taking these troops by surprise. They'd drop us like flies."

"What's the odds? We're bloody lambs for the slaughter in any case. And I've my own idea about the Judas goat."

"We'll get the tunnel going again. We should be able to get beyond the wall by day after tomorrow. If we're lucky we can get everybody out. Spoetzl will play hell trying to round us up with only a hundred and thirty men."

"Digging a bloody tunnel when we could as well have walked out the bloody gate and been safely in the hills."

"That's ancient history now, Colonel. You and Wimberly have your company commanders furnish the Escape Committee with all the men they can use. And don't sound too grim about it when you tell them. I don't want the men in another flap like the one this morning."

"How do you propose I manage that, Ryan? Tell them they're digging for bloody treasure?"

"Tell them we're completing the tunnel so we can get a man out to contact Major Hampton's team and get word about the situation back to Allied headquarters. Which isn't a bad idea at that. I wish to hell Hampton had told me who he's got in Domira."

The diggers resumed work that afternoon. The Germans on guard inside the compound were incurious and so inexperienced at prison guard duty that the lookouts seldom were required to give the warnings that suspended operations. The dirt was passed back in Klim cans and hidden under the kitchen woodpile. When darkness fell, the men spread the dirt around the compound, tamping it with their feet so that the fresh earth would not be too obvious next morning.

By the next afternoon the tunnel was thirteen feet from the wall. Though the ground was like stone and the tools were inadequate, the head of the Escape Committee estimated that by nightfall the next day the tunnel would be far enough beyond the wall to open up.

"If the Krauts are still here by then we'll go out," Ryan told Fincham. "We'll send out commandos first in case Spoetzl's posted men outside the wall. Have you got people who can do the job quietly?"

"Quietly and with pleasure."

At four that morning the sound of a shot awakened Ryan. It had not seemed near but he was not sure. He ran barefoot to the porch and looked into the courtyard. The camp was silent. The shot had not been fired inside the walls. Or perhaps he had dreamed it. From his vantage point on the porch Ryan saw the kitchen door ajar with a figure silhouetted in the opening. He ran the length of the porch and called down to the man in the doorway.

"Get that door closed!" he ordered in a low voice. "You want the Krauts on your neck?"

"We thought we heard a shot, sir."

"I heard it, too. But it's outside somewhere. Close that door and get back to work."

"Yes, sir," the man said, closing the door behind him.

Ryan waited on the porch a few minutes, listening. When he heard nothing, he returned to his bunk.

Fifteen minutes later a squad of German soldiers led by Oberstleutnant Spoetzl crept through the front gate and took up stations in the courtyard. The tunnel crew was discovered almost immediately by paratroopers who fanned out around the courtyard and surprised the sleepy lookout. The diggers were taken quietly into custody and held under guard in the kitchen.

When his men were in position, Spoetzl climbed quietly to Ryan's quarters, awakened him, and told Ryan it was his duty to inform him the prisoners must be ready to leave P. G. 202 in two hours.

Ryan clenched his fists in the darkness.

"Where are we going?" he demanded.

"I am not permitted to say."

"Germany, isn't it, you bastard? Congratulations, Colonel Spoetzl. You lied magnificently."

"One does one's duty," Spoetzl said stiffly. "You are a soldier. You should understand that."

Ryan slid from his bunk.

"I could kill you where you stand if I wanted to," he said quietly.

Spoetzl stepped quickly back against the wall, reaching for his holstered pistol. Before he could draw it, Ryan was there, his fingers biting into Spoetzl's wrist, a muscular forearm across Spoetzl's chest grinding him into the wall.

"I could," Ryan whispered. "But I'm not that stupid. Now get out of my quarters."

He released the German and turned his back in a deliberate gesture of contempt. Spoetzl's breathing was tortured as the German struggled for control. Ryan knew he was as close to death as he had ever been but somehow it did not seem important. Not now. When Spoetzl rushed out the door Ryan felt neither relief nor triumph.

The lights came on while he was dressing. He went to the porch. Spoetzl was standing in the center of the courtyard, an amplified megaphone in his hand.

The paratroopers stationed at the entrance to each bay darted inside and ran down the center aisles shouting, "'Raus! 'Raus!" then stood at the back of the bays, their Schmeissers held ready, and shrugged off all questions with a shake of the head or a muttered, "Nichts versteh'."

"Officers and men of P. G. 202," Spoetzl boomed from the courtyard. "You will dress yourselves and assemble for an announcement of importance."

The men were close to panic, cursing and trying to pull on clothes with hands that seemed to have lost co-ordination. Fincham came bursting out of his room, his body saffron in the weak light of the bulb over his door. He looked across the courtyard and saw Ryan on the opposite porch.

"What the bloody hell is going on, Ryan?" he bellowed.

"Look for yourself," Ryan called back.

A paratrooper rushed to Fincham and ordered him inside. Fincham ignored him.

"This is your doing, you bloody headmaster!" he cried.

The German prodded him with his Schmeisser. Fincham glared at him, his fists knotted.

"It's not your bloody arse I want, Jerry," he said, and went inside.

The men poured into the courtyard with shoes unlaced and shirttails dangling. Ryan, having been forewarned, was the first man down. Spoetzl came to him and the men collected around them in a growing mass.

"Herr Oberst," Spoetzl said, "I will require your assistance in obtaining order."

"This is your party, Colonel. I wouldn't think of butting in."

"In less than two hours you will move," Spoetzl said. "Regardless of your state of readiness. If you wish to waste the little time you have it is your concern, not mine."

"That's a good point, Colonel," Ryan said. "Brigade, fall in!" he shouted.

His command was lost in the uproar.

"Hand me that bullhorn," he said, reaching for the megaphone.

Spoetzl gave it to him.

"Fall in," Ryan said, his words echoing. "The sooner you do the sooner you'll know what this is all about. Fall in, fall in, fall in."

He continued repeating the order. The men, as if mesmerized by the insistent command, slowly regrouped around the courtyard in a ragged formation.

"It's all yours," Ryan said, handing back the megaphone.

"Thank you, Herr Oberst," Spoetzl said, resolutely correct.

"It was wrong of me to lay hands on you, Colonel," Ryan said. "I shouldn't have touched you unless I really intended to kill you."

"I accept the Herr Oberst's apology."

"It wasn't an apology, Colonel. Just a little self-criticism."

Spoetzl raised the megaphone to his lips. Before he could speak, the front gate opened and Oriani appeared in a pool of light.

"Oriani's back!" Orde shrieked.

Falvi was with the major, his face tear-stained and distraught. Oriani was smiling. The men watched his approach in silence. Spoetzl, seeing he had lost their attention for the moment, let the megaphone drop to his side. Oriani joined him.

"Good morning, gentlemen," Oriani said.

There was a stirring all along the ranks, and prisoners seemed poised to hurl themselves at him. At a nod from Spoetzl the paratroopers stepped forward and raised their Schmeissers. A long sigh coursed the formation and the prisoners fell back the few inches they had pressed forward.

"Thank you for your welcome," Oriani said.

"Colonel Spoetzl," Ryan said coldly. "You are permitting this man to waste our time. Get on with it."

Oriani smiled at Ryan.

"I see you have not changed, Colonel Ryan," he said.

Falvi, who had been standing tense and silent in the background, rushed suddenly to Ryan's side. Fresh tears sprang into his eyes as he spoke.

"Colonnello," he said brokenly. "Colonel Battaglia is dead."

"What! Did they . . ."

"By his own hand. When he learned what the Tedeschi proposed."

"I'm sorry, Lieutenant. What do they propose?"

He glanced around him at the men straining to catch every word.

"Never mind," he said. "I want to see you in my room."

"Now who is wasting your time, Herr Oberst?" Spoetzl demanded.

"Carry on, Colonel," said Ryan.

"Officers and men," Spoetzl said, "out of regard for your continued safety I am ordered to remove you from the path of anticipated military actions."

A rolling swell of groans and protests filled the air. Spoetzl waited until it subsided.

"Breakfast is to be prepared as quickly as possible. You will then assemble your kits and await further instructions. Orders are to be obeyed promptly. That is all."

"All right, knock it off," Ryan shouted above the din following the announcement. "I've got something to say."

The men booed him.

"Colonel Spoetzl has told you we're being moved for our own safety," Ryan continued patiently. "Which may or may not be true. But it won't help to get into a flap. We must be disciplined and resolute."

The men booed again.

"The kitchen crew will report at once and prepare breakfast," Ryan cried. "Double rations. Major Hawkins, arrange to distribute all remaining Red Cross parcels among the men right after breakfast. Now get back to your quarters and start packing."

The boos grew louder.

"Get going!" Ryan ordered. "It's your own time you're wasting. Dismissed."

Turning to Falvi, he said, "Come with me."

"You will remain," Oriani said to the lieutenant.

Falvi stared at the major, his face no longer boyish but ancient with hate. Without answering, he turned to follow Ryan.

"Shoot that man," Oriani said in Italian to the nearest paratrooper.

The soldier did not understand.

"Oberst Spoetzl, order your man to shoot that swine," Oriani demanded in English.

Spoetzl eyed him coldly.

"Italians do not give the orders here," he said.

"Your superiors will hear of this," Oriani spat. "I am not without influence."

Spoetzl turned his back. Oriani hesitated, seemed ready to hurl himself at the German, then whirled and strode from the compound.

Falvi continued behind Ryan.

In his room, Ryan said, "Now, Lieutenant, tell me exactly

what happened," and began stowing his belongings in a Red Cross carton.

There were no tears in Falvi's eyes now.

"Do not concern yourself with Maggiore Oriani," he said in a hard voice. "Colonnello Ryan, you have my promise I will kill him. He has joined the Tedeschi."

"That won't help, Lieutenant."

"But for him the Tedeschi would not be here and Colonnello Battaglia would not be dead."

Ryan put down the carton and gave Falvi his undivided attention.

"Oriani returned last night. I was prevented from informing you. He boasted he encouraged the soldati to desert and informed the Tedeschi the prisoners were unguarded. And that the Tedeschi would remove all to Germania."

Ryan sighed.

"I thought so," he said. "I should have moved the men out when I had the chance."

"It is not the colonnello's doing," Falvi said sympathetically. "You were trick-ed."

"Tricked," Ryan corrected absently. "I wasn't tricked. I was under orders from Allied headquarters."

"Colonnello, there were no orders from Allied headquarters." Ryan stared.

"Major 'ampton is not of your forces. Major 'ampton is of the enemy."

"What?"

"He was sent by the Tedeschi. When Oriani informed them of conditions."

"He was American," Ryan said. "I'd swear to it."

Falvi shook his head.

"The Tedesco is clever, Colonnello."

Ryan sat on the bottom rail of his bunk, head in hands.

"God," he said heavily. "How I've been had."

He jumped to his feet and hit the bunk with his fist.

"God damn it to hell!" he groaned.

Falvi looked on incredulously, as if he could not believe Ryan capable of human weakness. Ryan saw the look.

"Sorry, Lieutenant," he said wryly. "I didn't intend to bore you with my problems. Tell me what happened to Colonel Battaglia."

"When he learned you were to be transported he attempted to come to you. The Tedeschi imprisoned him in his office. In his desk was a pistol . . . He will be avenged."

"Listen to me," Ryan said, his voice again full of authority. "You won't help us or yourself by going off half-cocked. Oriani is just one man. If you really want to help us, get word to Allied intelligence about what's happened to us. And then get into the hills and fight."

"But Oriani goes unpunished."

"Being on the losing side is punishment enough for a man like Oriani. And he's on a sinking ship. Can you understand that, Lieutenant?"

Falvi pondered what Ryan had said.

"Yes, Colonnello," he said. "I think so. I will go now. Ask Padre Costanzo to pray for me."

Ryan held out his hand and Falvi shook it.

"You've been a good friend to us, Lieutenant," Ryan said.

"Thank you, sir. Arrivederci, colonnello. And good luck."

After Falvi left, Ryan looked down from the porch before going to breakfast. Prisoners were moving toward the mess hall. When they passed beneath him they stared up at the silent figure on the porch, their faces cold and accusing.

XIII

Two wooden desks were brought into the courtyard and set facing each other six feet apart. The prisoners, laden with their belongings and an unopened Red Cross parcel each, assembled beyond the desks in roll call formation. They were counted by paratroopers under the direction of Oriani. Despite the language difficulty, the count went smoothly until the final tally, when a man was found to be missing from Settore I. Spoetzl sent men to search the bays and in a few minutes one of them returned prodding Petersen ahead of him with his Schmeisser. He had found Petersen hiding under a bunk. Petersen refused to look at Ryan when he walked past the colonel to get to his place in formation.

"Now we are all here," Oriani said comfortably.

He sat down at one of the desks and took the camp roster from a drawer.

"You will make a single line and proceed between the desks," Spoetzl said. "Name and rank will be stated before proceeding beyond the desks. You will then re-form and remain in place until further instructions."

He walked to Ryan and said, "We will not depart for some minutes yet, Herr Oberst. Perhaps you and the Herr Oberstleutnant might wish to wait more comfortably in my office."

"I'll stay with the group," Ryan said. "And I'm sure Colonel Fincham will do the same."

"As you wish, Herr Oberst."

Ryan and Fincham, as the Senior American and British Officers, were checked off first.

"Have a pleasant journey, my dear Colonel," Oriani said as Ryan passed between the desks.

Ryan ignored him but Fincham paused, resting his knuckles on the desk top and leaning close to Oriani.

"Take care of yourself, Oriani," he said conversationally. "I'm depending on you to survive the war. I'll be coming back for you."

"Excellent, Colonel Fincham," Oriani replied. "I shall look forward to a jolly reunion."

Ryan waited for Fincham to join him but the Englishman walked past without acknowledgment and took a stand a dozen yards away. The prisoners, except those who stared at him with undisguised antagonism, also ignored Ryan as they passed into the forecourt to form new lines.

Costanzo stopped long enough to say gently, "Maybe this is the Lord's way of showing no man is infallible, Cuhnel. If you've learned humility you've gained something from it."

"Padre," said Ryan, "in your profession humility may be strength. In mine it's weakness."

Stein, too, had a word for Ryan.

"I speak pretty fair German if you need an interpreter, Colonel," he said. "If I can just do it with the accent I learned in college and not the one I learned at home."

"I may take you up on that, Captain," Ryan said, aware that Stein had spoken not so much to offer assistance as to assure him he did not share the harsh judgment of the others.

When the last man was checked off the prisoners were marched outside the gate, where rickety coke-burning Italian trucks were lined along the road in a motley convoy. Far across a stony field a hundred or so residents of Domira had gathered, drawn by the spectacle.

A rumor that they were to be moved only a few miles swept the men. The trucks obviously were incapable of moving them farther.

"Bloody fools," Fincham snorted. "If we don't ride we'll bloody well have to walk."

"We do not require officers to walk," Spoetzl said. "You will find we are reasonable men, we Germans."

"Ballocks," said Fincham.

Spoetzl kept Ryan and Fincham with him while the other prisoners were wedged tightly into the waiting trucks.

"You will ride with me in my sedan," he said when loading was completed.

"I'll ride with my friends," Fincham said curtly. "I'm rather particular about the company I keep."

"I do not understand," Spoetzl said, offended. "We are soldiers doing as we are ordered, you and I."

"It isn't you I mean," Fincham said.

He left them and climbed into the nearest truck.

Oriani strolled up to join Spoetzl and Ryan.

"Good-by, my dear Colonel Ryan," he said. "It has been a most interesting association."

"You're out of a job now, aren't you, Major?" Ryan said. "With no more prisoners to guard. And you're not fit for any other kind of duty."

Spoetzl smiled, showing strong yellow teeth.

Oriani was unabashed.

"Perhaps you are right," he said. "But I would say I did it rather better than you bargained for, wouldn't you, my dear Colonel?"

"You have a point, Major," Ryan admitted.

"You lose well," Oriani replied, holding out his hand.

Ryan looked at it.

"Kiss my ass," he said.

Some of the civilians across the field waved handkerchiefs as the convoy pulled out. Oriani stood at the side of the road with his hands on his hips, smiling, and waved a mocking goodby to Ryan.

"Schwein," said Spoetzl.

"He's your ally, Colonel, not mine," Ryan said.

The convoy passed through Domira, a poor village of stark stone houses. The road was deserted but faces peered out from every window. Beyond the village the road passed between fields of scrubby olives and sparse vines, with here and there a meadow where a few sheep or a bony cow grazed. Peasants looked up as the convoy passed, then bent quickly to their work again as if afraid their interest would displease the Germans.

The Americans rode in stolid silence but the British began singing a ribald song. Ryan sat next to Spoetzl in the back of a small black Fiat, staring straight ahead and refusing Spoetzl's offer of a cigarette.

They had been on the road a quarter-hour when the sharp ripping sound of a machine pistol back in the convoy caused Spoetzl to bark an order to his driver and thrust his arm out the window to signal a halt. Spoetzl leaped from the car and hurried toward the sound with Ryan at his heels. The prisoners were calling out from truck to truck.

"Somebody made a break for it," someone shouted. "Poor bastard."

A hundred yards back, in a sere brown stubble field, a paratrooper was running toward a sprawled figure. Costanzo and Stein jumped from their truck and started toward the downed man.

"It's the chaplain and the doctor," Ryan said to Spoetzl. "Tell your men not to shoot."

"If they had intended to fire they would have done so already," Spoetzl replied. "They will answer to me for not doing so."

A low wall of loose stones separated the field from the road. The prisoner was lying face down thirty or forty yards beyond it near a small plot of meager tobacco plants. Beyond the plot was a square stone hut, its wooden plank roof held on with

field stones. Just outside the sagging leather-hinged door was an
unkempt woman of undiscernible age and figure wearing a straggling garment of stained rough cloth. A small, dirty child, clad
only in a torn shirt too scanty to conceal the fact he was a boy,
clung to her legs, his enormous black eyes wide in an expression
more of curiosity than fear.

Stein reached the prisoner a few strides ahead of the others.
He dropped to one knee, turned the man over and felt his pulse.
Ryan pushed past Spoetzl and rushed to his side.

The man on the ground was Billy Petersen.

His eyes were staring, his face drained of blood, and his
mouth open in a grotesque death grin. The Schmeisser burst
had caught him in the back as he ran and there were no wounds
visible on his upturned chest, only flecks of blood on the stubble
around him, no more than might have come from a badly cut
finger, glistening like crimson dew in the morning sun.

"I'm afraid he's dead, sir," Stein said.

Ryan looked down at the dead man, a boy, really, his own
face gone stiff and white as Petersen's. Costanzo had crossed
himself and kneeled beside the body. Now he looked up at
Ryan.

"Don't blame yourself, Cuhnel," he said. "It's God's will."

"Regrettable," Spoetzl said without pity. "He was a fool to
attempt escape across an open field."

"Shut up!" Ryan snapped.

"I will not be spoken to in such a manner," Spoetzl began
angrily, checking himself when he saw the pain in Ryan's face.
"Come," he continued less harshly, "we must not delay. I will
send someone back for the body."

Out on the road someone yelled, "Petersen's bought it!"

The news spread quickly through the convoy.

The paratrooper who pursued Petersen had gone into the
tobacco patch and was stripping off the leaves and stuffing them
into the big pockets of his jacket. The woman began screaming at him and the child, frightened now, started wailing. The
woman picked the child up and continued to scream at the

German. Spoetzl looked at her, his mood changing to amusement.

"Who can smoke such tobacco?" he said. "Schrecklich. Terrible."

Costanzo went to the woman and tried to calm her.

"Stop that man!" he shouted over his shoulder. "This is all she has."

Spoetzl shrugged and gave an order. The paratrooper shoved the last of what he had plucked into his pocket and trotted back to his station.

"Padre Costanzo," Ryan said. "When she's calmed down find out if there's a church anywhere near."

"There is no time," Spoetzl said. "Come."

Ryan did not move.

The woman stopped crying and kissed Costanzo's hand when he told her he was a priest. It embarrassed him.

"She says there's a church over that hill," he said, pointing to a knoll a quarter-mile away. "Not too far from here."

"We'll take Petersen there," Ryan said.

"You do not seem to understand, Herr Oberst," Spoetzl said impatiently. "I will send men back for that. Now I must insist we return."

"Captain Stein," said Ryan, "help me take that door down. Padre, tell her we'll put it back when we're through with it. We'll carry Petersen on it."

"Herr Oberst," Spoetzl said coldly. "If you do not come at once I will have you shot."

"All right," Ryan said calmly. "I'm sure those men out there in the trucks would consider it a favor."

"He means it, Cuhnel," said Costanzo.

"So do I," Ryan said. "Colonel Spoetzl, I intend to leave the lieutenant where he'll have a decent burial. If you want to shoot me for that, get on with it."

"I had not expected such softness, Herr Oberst," Spoetzl said. "Not from you. But I suppose under the circumstances . . ."

Spoetzl summoned a pair of soldiers from the convoy while

Ryan and Stein took down the door and placed Petersen's body upon it. The soldiers picked up the door at either end and walked toward the hill, Costanzo walking beside the body and the others following.

The church was small, with an ancient graveyard nearby bordered by gnarled olives. As the group neared the church, an old priest came out and crossed himself with hands as gnarled as the olive trees. Costanzo spoke with him in a low voice.

"He says he'll give Petersen a Christian burial in the grave-yard," Costanzo says.

They carried Petersen into the little church, which smelled of age and generations of unwashed peasants. The sunlight pouring through the small windows shimmered with dust and divided the gloomy interior into bands of light and shadow which alternately illuminated and shrouded the body as it was carried down the narrow aisle.

Padre Costanzo had closed Petersen's eyes and wiped the grin from his face so that now he looked like a boy asleep. The soldiers set their burden down before the altar and Ryan and Costanzo came forward to lift the body from the door which served as a bier. The old priest left them and returned with a blanket, which he spread over the body.

"Padre," Ryan said, "will you say the necessary words? Colonel Spoetzl, call your men to attention."

Spoetzl gave an order and the two soldiers came to attention. When Ryan and Stein removed their caps, Spoetzl did likewise.

Costanzo spoke briefly in English, paraphrasing the military service for the dead. The old priest droned behind him in Latin. When it was over and the priests and one of the soldiers had crossed themselves, Spoetzl put his cap on and said briskly, "So it is done. Let us return."

"I'll catch up with you, Colonel," said Ryan. "Stein, see that these men put the door back the way it was."

"You may remain a moment if you wish but I must remain with you," Spoetzl said.

"I prefer to be alone. You have my word I won't try to escape."

"In that case . . ." Spoetzl said.

He saluted and left with the others.

When everyone had gone except the old priest, Ryan squatted by Petersen's body and lifted the blanket from his face. Petersen looked as he had when Ryan first saw him in the courtyard at P. G. 202, little more than a boy. He closed his eyes and saw the young face grotesque in death amid the stubble and then the image was replaced by another, a training plane spinning down and down to blossom on the desert in smoke and flame. It was an image which had not haunted him for many years.

Suddenly, face in hands, he was crying. He had killed Petersen as surely as he had killed his instructor and friend, Vic Runson. If he had not let the spurious Major Hampton mislead him Petersen would not be dead. The tears were hot and unfamiliar on his face but he could not check them. A hand fell on his shoulder.

"Figlio mio," said the tired old voice of the priest.

The tears stopped at once. Ryan rose and wiped his face with his forearm, composed.

"Scusate, Padre," he said, using the little Italian he had picked up in his weeks at P. G. 202. "I thought I was alone. Solo. Thank you for everything. Grazie."

"Pace, figlio mio," said the old man. "Pace."

Ryan hurried after the others, angry with himself for his sudden weakness and hoping his face would not betray it. The paratroopers were rehanging the door on its leather hinges and the child was eating a chocolate bar which Stein had given him.

The prisoners booed Ryan as he passed the line of trucks with Spoetzl. He looked straight ahead, expressionless. Costanzo's angry voice rose above the jeers.

"Is this how you mourn Billy Petersen?" he cried.

The booing stopped but the ensuing silence was no less accusing.

In another half-hour the convoy reached a siding where a

long string of boxcars waited, shimmering in the morning heat. A groan went up from the prisoners. German soldiers were perched on the tracks like ungainly gray birds. They leaped to attention at Spoetzl's approach.

A fat face wearing steel-rimmed spectacles appeared in the door of the boxcar second from the locomotive, and a moment later its owner was scrambling, broad rump first, to the ground. He was a short, obese man, stuffed to bursting into the uniform of a Wehrmacht major. He stood stiffly at attention, his upper lip leaking sweat, while Spoetzl dressed him down for the appearance of his troops. The major scrambled back into the boxcar and reappeared wearing a cap.

Spoetzl barked an order and his paratroopers formed a line across the road from the train. The prisoners were hemmed in between the road and the boxcars. Another order from Spoetzl sent the major's troops scrambling to the other side of the train where each soldier took up a position behind a boxcar.

Fincham, Costanzo, and Stein were called from the trucks to join Ryan, and the others were formed into four lines with their bundles and boxes piled at their feet. A sergeant went down the line dividing them into groups of forty-four. As each group was counted off, the prisoners shouldered their possessions and were marched to a boxcar by two paratroopers who slid the door shut behind them and returned for the next group. On the other side of the train, the soldiers slung their rifles and climbed steel rungs to the top of each car as it was loaded and sat on their folded greatcoats with their legs dangling over the end.

As the length of the line diminished, the men remaining grew more desolate. The unthinkable was reality. Freedom had been snatched from them and they were heading for a deeper captivity than they had known before. The slide and clang of every shutting boxcar door sounded a knell to any hope of deliverance. Even the ribald British grew silent.

Only Ryan, Fincham, Costanzo, and Stein were left standing in the road when all but the two cars next to the engine had been loaded and locked.

"Now, if you will come with me . . ." said Spoetzl.

The four prisoners and the fat major followed him toward the head of the train. A young soldier in shirt sleeves with a pencil behind his ear came to the door of the second car and looked contemptuously at the prisoners. Ryan made as if to climb into the car and was head and shoulders inside it when the young soldier pushed him back, shouting, "Nein! Nein!"

Spoetzl transfixed the soldier with a look and said, "Not this car, Herr Oberst. The first."

"My mistake," said Ryan.

"Do you intend for me to occupy the same car as Colonel Ryan?" Fincham demanded.

"But of course," Spoetzl replied. "You are next in rank. I have arranged more comfortable accommodations for Oberst Ryan and you. Also the chaplain and doctor. You will find we Germans are reasonable men."

"That's what you said when we left P. G. 202," said Fincham. "But Lieutenant Petersen didn't find you so reasonable."

"He attempted to escape. If he were your prisoner you would have done the same."

"Gnattering about it won't bring him back," Fincham said. "Look here, Spoetzl, I want you to put me in with the last lot. I'll not occupy the same car as Ryan."

"I do not understand," Spoetzl said.

"Maybe this will help you then. You know what the men call him? Von Ryan. Because they think he's more your sort than theirs. And we don't like your bloody sort."

Spoetzl looked at Ryan as if expecting him to reprimand Fincham for such insubordination. Ryan stared straight ahead, remote and uncaring.

"I regret you do not find the arrangements suitable, Herr Oberstleutnant," Spoetzl said when he saw that Ryan did not intend to pursue the matter. "But you must make the best of it."

"Pity you clots are on opposite sides," Fincham said. "You've so much in common."

"Thank you," Spoetzl said quite seriously, bringing his heels together and bowing slightly. "I am flattered."

The fat major threw back the sliding door of the first car and stood aside.

"Please enter," said Spoetzl.

Ryan climbed in without a word, followed by Costanzo, Stein, and Fincham. Spoetzl stuck his head in the door.

"This is as far as I accompany you, Herr Oberst. I return to the fighting. You will find honorable treatment at your destination."

"I hope you find a bullet up the arse at yours, Herr Spittle," Fincham growled. "And die harder than Petersen."

"Carry on, Colonel," Ryan said absently.

Spoetzl saluted and was gone. Two German soldiers, the last of the group which had been waiting for the convoy, climbed into the boxcar and took stations at either end. Four narrow wooden benches, set crossways and bolted to the floor, occupied the front half of the boxcar. The other end was empty except for a portable toilet. High up on each side of the car was a small window covered with heavy wire mesh.

The fat major scrambled into the car, groaning with the effort, and stood peeking out the door until Spoetzl's sedan was on its way. His furtively hunched shoulders straightened. He walked cockily to the center of the boxcar, assumed a stern expression, and faced the four prisoners, jutting his high, round stomach at them. Fincham looked at him with unconcealed distaste, Costanzo and Stein waited attentively, and Ryan did not seem even to notice his presence.

"I am Major Hubertus von Klement," the major announced.

"I assume the 'von' is honorary, you bloody storekeeper," Fincham said.

Klement's English was limited but Fincham's tone was obviously insulting. He grew instantly scarlet and pulled his head down between his shoulders. The fat above his collar compressed into thick ridges extending into the hairline.

"I am Kommandant here," he shouted. "Over alles."

Fincham shoved his hands in his pockets and stretched his legs out straight in front of him.

"Hear, hear," he said.

Klement's eyes bulged and he made a choking sound, as if something nasty were lodged in his throat.

"Cut it out, Finch," Stein whispered. "Is-thay aracter-cay is paranoiac."

"Ja wohl, Herr Kommandant," Costanzo said quickly. "Wir verstehen."

Klement turned his attention to Costanzo.

"Ah, Sie Deutsch sprechen," he said.

He addressed himself to Costanzo, shouting and gesturing and filling the air between them with saliva.

"Bitte, Herr Kommandant," said Costanzo. "Langsam."

Klement spoke more slowly but no less vehemently.

"He says he is in absolute charge of this train," Costanzo translated. "Responsible to no one except the Fuehrer himself. He has the Fuehrer's complete confidence. He is not soft with Allied gangsters, like Herr Oberstleutnant Spoetzl."

"A likely bit of bumpf," Fincham said.

"He will not tolerate insolence," Costanzo continued, Klement's almost hysterical words ludicrously softened by his southern accent. "Spoetzl may have permitted it but we will find him a different kind of soldier. And anyone attempting to escape will be shot. Also nine other men in his car."

"Who does he expect to believe that rot?" Fincham demanded.

"He's not bluffing," Stein whispered. "He's scared out of his drawers we'll try something. And trying to prove he's tougher than we are."

"Cuhnel Ryan," Costanzo said, "don't you think we better make sure the others know about it? About shooting ten men for every man who tries to escape?"

"And play the fat sod's game?" Fincham protested.

"All right," Ryan said. "You tell 'em."

The reply was so indifferent and so uncharacteristic of him

the other three prisoners stared at each other. Klement agreed with a smile of smug triumph when Costanzo asked permission to pass along his announcement. He motioned Costanzo out of the boxcar and followed with drawn pistol, locking the door behind them.

Ryan, Fincham, and Stein sat on their benches in silence. The guards leaned stolidly against the wall of the car at either end. One was so tall and cadaverous his uniform appeared hung on a rack instead of a human form. His tunic struck him inches above his thick, hairy wrists. His rifle, though the regulation German weapon, seemed no longer than an Italian carbine in his long arms. The other guard, a corporal, was shorter and more solidly built. He had the round, dark head and rosy cheeks of a Bavarian. He was sucking on his lower lip and kicking a heavy heel monotonously against the side of the boxcar, sweating in the heat.

"Come off it, for God's sake," Fincham growled at him.

The guard's half-closed eyes opened, as if he had been awakened from some reverie, and he pointed his rifle wordlessly at Fincham. It was not so much a threatening gesture as a reflexive one.

"He's seen a bit of action, that one," Fincham said to Stein. "Best not get too tricky with him."

"Thanks," Stein said wryly. "I don't intend getting tricky with any of them. Not with H on my dog tags."

"You didn't get rid of the bloody things when Jerry nipped us?" Fincham demanded.

Stein grinned in embarrassment.

"I just couldn't bring myself to do it," he said. "But Padre C. gave me a Christopher medal to wear with 'em. Supposed to protect the traveler. Four Aryan grandparents would be better but he couldn't swing that."

"What a bloody tart you are," Fincham said approvingly.

After fifteen minutes or so the car door slid open and Costanzo sprawled on the floor, pushed from behind by Klement. Fincham sprang to his feet.

"You bloody bag of suet!" he cried.

The thickset guard raised his rifle without changing position, his finger curving around the trigger. Fincham sat down.

"You'd love to give it me between the eyes, wouldn't you, Jerry?" Fincham asked conversationally.

The German betrayed not a flicker of interest. When he saw Fincham was seated again he lapsed back into somnolence.

Klement thrust his head into the car.

"I am Kommandant!" he cried. "Versteh'?"

He slammed the door shut and locked it without waiting for an answer.

"They're like cattle in those boxcars," Costanzo said, brushing himself off. "Jammed in there with their gear without room to move around. And it's stifling in there. I asked Klement to move a few in with us and he said they were lucky, I should see the way they transport Russians. We wouldn't even have this many cars if they weren't needed in Germany."

"He's worse than Oriani," Fincham said. "Oriani was a nasty bugger but he had style."

"I've heard everything," said Stein. "Oriani'd have a heart attack if he knew you said that."

He sighed.

"The poor kid," he said quietly.

They knew he was thinking of Petersen.

"Bloody useless, that," Fincham said. "He should have waited for a better crack at it."

He looked pointedly at Ryan.

"But I expect he'd too much of a bellyful to stand it any longer," he said. "Since his bloody headmaster failed to measure up."

"Don't," said Costanzo.

Ryan ignored them both.

There was silence again for a while, broken only by the monotonous sound of the corporal's heel against the wall. A train pounded by on the next track, shaking the car. The silence was heavier after it passed.

"Do they intend keeping us here on our bums for bloody ever?" Fincham demanded impatiently.

"I'm in no hurry to get to Germany, personally," Stein said.

Ryan had folded one of his blankets into a pillow and now lay stretched out on his bench, staring at the ceiling. The corporal called out to his companion, then sat on the floor with his back against the wall and went to sleep. Costanzo walked to Ryan's bench and crouched beside it.

"Cuhnel," he said in a low voice. "It wasn't your fault. Petersen or any of it."

"I'm aware of that, Padre," Ryan said. "While you were outside, did you notice if there was a guard on top of our car?"

"Sir? Ah don't think so. No. There wasn't."

"How about the one behind us? Klement's car?"

"Yes, sir."

"Thanks, Padre."

Ryan returned to his contemplation of the ceiling and Costanzo knew he was dismissed.

Late in the morning, the train started with a jerk. The car shook as the engine slowly gathered speed. Then they were moving easily on the main track.

"We're on our bloody way," Fincham said heavily.

Ryan said nothing. It did not appear to matter to him that with every passing second the train was rushing him and a thousand men farther from freedom, toward Germany.

XIV

It was an unusual train for that time and place. In the confusion and movement that followed the invasion of the mainland and Italy's capitulation, trains were assembled hastily and the cars were a mixture of the obsolete and new, their freight a random grouping of troops, war matériel, and civilian goods owing their place to expediency or influence. But the twenty-four boxcars of the prison train were uniform. They were all new and strong and the prisoners were locked inside them as securely as in the cells of a dungeon, a dungeon capable of moving along at sixty miles an hour.

Ryan had been correct in assuming the Germans had no transport to spare for hauling prisoners but he had not anticipated they would make it available at the expense of other pressing needs for so valuable a prize as a thousand Allied officers, nor that such rolling stock would be made available because it was wanted in the Fatherland as much as the prisoners themselves.

The boxcars, though narrower and almost eight feet shorter than those in America, were among the largest and finest available in southern Italy. Each had on both sides a sliding loading door which locked from without. The doors on the right-hand side of each boxcar had been wired shut. The steel mesh covering the small rectangular openings near the roof of the cars was riveted in place.

It was a long train but the engine pulled it along at high speed without strain. The men in the cars and their small possessions were a load of only a hundred tons or so. It was almost like pulling a load of empties for the locomotive, which was new and powerful with high-grade coal heaped in its tender.

Ryan and his companions were in the car next to the tender and behind it was Klement's car. There were thirty-five prisoners in the car behind Klement's and forty-four in each of the other twenty-one cars. On top of each car except Ryan's a guard sat on his folded greatcoat, legs dangling over the back, facing the rear of the train and watching the right of way and the door of the boxcar behind him. It was an uncomfortable perch but not nearly so uncomfortable as the jammed, noisome interior of the cars.

The train's six hundred-mile route to the Brenner Pass would follow the long spine of Italy from the stony fields and sharp hills of the Abruzzi to the mountains and plunging valleys of the Trentino, through Rome, Florence, Bologna, Verona, and Bolzano, a journey two-thirds the length of Italy for men whose chief and burning concern was in not making it.

The twisting journey began with a rush of speed but halted at a small station in less than an hour. Rail traffic was heavy and the prison train, despite the value of its cargo, had no priority. It would be obliged to make frequent stops in sidings for more important trains to overtake and pass it.

As soon as the train stopped rolling the prisoners in the packed boxcars began pounding on the walls and demanding to be let out. The clamor was clearly audible in Ryan's car.

"They've got to go," Costanzo said. "All they've got in their cars is one bucket in the corner. For forty-four men. And some of them have dysentery."

"It'll be a lot worse before this trip is over," Stein said. "Can you do something about it, Colonel? They'll be running out of water soon, too."

"It won't kill them," Ryan said. "I don't want to get Klement stirred up this early in the game."

"Packed in, have you?" Fincham demanded. "Washing your hands of the whole bloody mess."

He began pounding on the door, shouting, "Klement, you bloody swine, open up!"

The corporal reached him in four easy strides and hit him behind the ear with his rifle butt. He returned to his position against the wall without giving Fincham's sprawled body another glance.

"Ich bin Arzt," Stein said.

When he rose and went to Fincham the corporal made no move to interfere.

"Seems okay," Stein said. "Pulse regular. Skin's not even broken. The man's an artist with that rifle butt."

Costanzo crossed himself at that.

"Sie sind katholisch?" the cadaverous guard asked.

"Ich bin Pfarrer," said Costanzo.

"Ach, so," the guard said respectfully.

"Bist Du denn katholisch?" Costanzo asked.

"Jawohl, Vater."

Fincham began stirring. Stein helped him sit up. Fincham put the heel of his hand to the spot where he had been struck.

"I'll not bleed to death at any rate," he said, examining his hand.

He looked at the chunky guard.

"I'll not forget that, you bastard," he said cordially.

He got up and sat down on a bench. Ryan had not moved from his seat throughout the entire affair.

At a stop early in the afternoon the door was flung open and a German soldier slid two cans of meat and a wedge of bread across the floor to the corporal. The other guard came forward to get his share and waited while the corporal cut the bread in half with his bayonet. Ryan watched from his bench. The guards opened the tins with bayonets and sat down to eat. Fincham, Costanzo, and Stein spread food on one of the benches and ate together. Ryan refused Costanzo's invitation to join them though after a while he ate a small tin of English cheese and a few English biscuits on his own bench.

In midafternoon, after some minutes of creeping motion, the train halted and the hiss and throb of the engine stopped. In a little while the door was thrown back and Klement thrust his round, satisfied face into the car.

"Out," he ordered. "I give you walk for limbs."

The four prisoners jumped down from the car followed closely by their guards. They were in a busy, cavernous depot with row after row of tracks and platforms lined with trains. Civilians and uniformed Italians and Germans stared at them from a passenger train on the next track.

"Rome," said Costanzo.

"Rome?" Fincham echoed. "After six hours?"

"I'm in no hurry," said Stein.

"Komm," Klement ordered. "Spazier. Walk."

He strutted ahead of them, leading them along the passenger train. Back in the locked cars the prisoners were pounding the walls and cursing.

"Let us out, you stinking Krautheads!" sounded clearly above the din.

Klement flushed but gave no further acknowledgment of the clamor.

"Why this sudden display of concern for the four of us?" Fincham demanded.

Stein nodded toward the passenger train.

"He's showing us off," he said. "Look at him preen himself. Like he wants to convince 'em he captured us personally."

"Cuhnel, the men," said Costanzo. "They've been packed in there the last six hours."

"I know, Padre," said Ryan.

Ryan drew alongside Klement.

"Herr Kommandant," he said politely.

Klement swelled a little at Ryan's use of the title.

"Yes?" he replied.

"Those people on the train. Don't you realize what a poor impression they're getting of you?"

"Bitte?"

"Padre, ask him if he doesn't realize those civilians can hear the prisoners complaining. Doesn't make him look very good, keeping them locked up. And for all they know, he may have Italians in there."

Klement looked at the faces in the passenger train and saw disapproval instead of the admiration he had sought. He bit his lower lip and spoke to Costanzo.

"He'll let them out for five minutes," Costanzo translated. "For every man who tries to escape he will shoot ten when we get away from the station."

"Better pass that along, Padre," said Ryan. "But first ask him about water. Is he supposed to get us to Germany dead or alive?"

Klement agreed to let five men from each car go to the station under guard to fill canteens and water bottles for their companions.

"Thank you, Herr Kommandant," Ryan said.

"You smarmy bastard," Fincham said under his breath. "Next you'll be having the clot in for tea."

Costanzo and Stein went with the guards to warn the prisoners of Klement's threat. The prisoners stumbled out of the cars, stiff and rebellious. At the sight of the prisoners the passengers in the train at the next track crowded to the windows to examine them. Girls smiled and some of the men made V signs. The prisoners yelled and whistled and returned the sign. Klement began screaming at the guards, who quickly hustled the prisoners to the other side of their train.

There they dropped their trousers and squatted, their pale bare bottoms in view of the passenger cars. Costanzo winced.

"You can't deny nature, Padre," Stein said.

"Ah know they can't help it," Costanzo replied. "But . . ." He sighed.

"The ladies seem to be turning their heads the other way," he said hopefully.

The British built fires of scraps of paper and bits of Red Cross boxes and began heating hoarded water for tea. Before the water was hot they were herded back into the cars with the others, protesting bitterly. When the water-bearers returned and were locked in, Ryan and his companions had to get back in their car as well.

Fincham sat close to Ryan.

"Ryan," he said in a low voice, "I'm no more fond of you than you are of me but if we're to get out of this bloody car we've got to work together."

Ryan said nothing.

"We've got to do it before we're too far north ever to get back to our lines," Fincham said.

Interpreting Ryan's silence as agreement, Fincham continued.

"I had a look at the lock on the door. A bit of metal from a tin in the proper place will stop it engaging. When it's dark we can prang the guards and jump. Piece of cake."

"What about the others back there?" Ryan asked.

"By the time they've stopped the train and come after us we'll be well on our way."

"I don't mean the other guards," said Ryan. "I mean the other prisoners."

"They've their wits about them," Fincham said. "They've no doubt a few plans of their own."

"All of them?"

"I shouldn't wonder," Fincham replied, shrugging. "In any case it's no affair of mine."

"It is of mine. And what about Klement? He said he'd shoot ten for every one who made a break."

"Rot."

"Maybe. But if it isn't, it'll be the ones left behind whose necks will be sticking out."

"You really have chucked in, haven't you?" said Fincham. "I

hadn't expected that of you, Ryan. You're a dozen kinds of bloody fool but I thought you had more bottom."

"Shut up and listen," Ryan said.

"Now that has a familiar ring," Fincham said, sitting up attentively.

"If we go, everybody goes."

"Everybody? How do you propose to manage that, pray?"

"Take the train."

"Take the train!"

"Keep your voice down, Colonel," Ryan ordered. "These Krauts may know more English than they let on."

He studied the guards through half-closed eyes. The corporal was looking at them, as if wondering what they could be whispering about.

"I don't suppose you'd have anything like a deck of cards," Ryan said.

Fincham stared.

"Cards?" he demanded.

"The Obergefreiter looks suspicious," Ryan explained. "He's starting to wonder why we've got our heads together."

"Oh. A diversion. As a matter of fact, I do have cards. My poker school entrusted them to me as the senior member."

"Get 'em out and we'll play."

Fincham rummaged in his pack and found a deck of badly abused cards, greasy and freckled with grime. He faced Ryan on the bench, both of them straddling it.

"Deal the tickets," Ryan said. "Poker."

"A two-man poker school? Be a bit more convincing if we brought in Padre and Hank."

"No. At this stage it's just between the two of us."

Fincham dealt a hand.

"These are readers," said Ryan.

"Beg pardon?"

"You can tell what they are from the back."

"Some," Fincham admitted. "They're rather the worse for wear."

Ryan held up a card with the top left corner missing.

"What's this?" he asked.

"I don't . . ." Fincham began, grinning, and adding, "Queen of clubs or five of diamonds."

"Five of diamonds," said Ryan. "I've been doing some thinking."

"That's why you were so quiet, is that it? I thought you were sulking."

"With a few breaks we might be able to bring it off. I open for a hundred."

"Pounds or dollars?" Fincham asked, lowering his voice to add challengingly, "Now, Ryan, what's the drill? What makes you fancy we can bring it off?"

The "we" was not lost on Ryan. If the plan appealed to Fincham, the truculent Englishman would swallow his resentment and join him, take his orders.

They continued betting, drawing cards and dealing new hands while Ryan went over the plan he had been devising as he lay on his bench in seeming torpor.

"We start with our two guards and work back," Ryan said. "We get into their uniforms and then we take Klement at the first opportunity."

"What if the clot's got a car full of relief troops?"

"He hasn't. I had a good look in it when we got on this morning."

"Oh, yes. When that Hitler Youth type got in such a flap."

"Klement's got it fixed up like a home away from home. The young guy must be the radio operator. There's a transmitter in there. And two other soldiers with Schmeissers. And that's all."

"Didn't miss a great deal when you had your head in there, did you?" Fincham said.

"I've got two eyes, like anybody else."

"It wasn't by chance you blundered into the wrong car, was it?" Fincham asked with grudging admiration.

"We'll want Klement and the radio operator in one piece. We've got to know just how this train operates in case we run into problems before we've got it completely under control. What our schedule is. What's the routine at stops. Whether Klement files regular position reports or gets instructions on that radio. And if so, to and from whom. And when this set of guards is due for relief. That's what we've got to find out before we make the first move. Once we take over this car we're committed. We've got to keep going until we take the whole train. If they change guards before we control the train we've had it."

The train was moving now and the car rocked as they moved slowly from the station. Costanzo was talking quietly with the tall guard and Stein was standing on a Red Cross parcel, looking out the mesh-covered window. The corporal no longer displayed any interest in the conversation between Ryan and Fincham.

"P'raps Klement's got his relief troops in a separate car," Fincham said. "We could lock them in."

"Negative," said Ryan. "I checked the train out when we loaded this morning. Exactly twenty-four boxcars. Except for this car and Klement's they're all loaded with prisoners. There's a guard sitting on top of every car except this one and there's one in the cab of the locomotive."

"We could have taken on a troop car in Rome."

"I counted the cars before we got back in. Still twenty-four."

"They might have added a car after we were inside."

"We'd have felt the jolt."

"We might not have noticed."

"I would have. I was waiting for it."

Ryan turned and called to Costanzo.

"Can you come here a minute, Padre?" he said. "I want you to take a look at this hand."

When Costanzo reached him Ryan said, "Pretend to be interested in the game. After a couple of minutes go back and talk to the guard again. Find out when he expects to be relieved and where. And tell Stein to keep looking out the window and keep his eyes open for town names. And remember what time we pass 'em."

Costanzo watched a little, then spoke briefly to Stein and resumed his conversation with the cadaverous guard.

"Granted we take this car and Klement's without causing a flap, how do we get at the Jerries on top?" Fincham demanded. "Sticky business, that."

"We'll have Klement call down the one on his car. Once we have him, it's routine. I'll take his place and get the Kraut on the next car. They face the back and I can sneak up on him. Then you get into the act. After we knock off a guard we'll lower him into the car below and replace him with our own man. We do that until we've got all our own men up there. Then we open all the car doors and start bailing out. No telling how long the train will go on up the line before anybody catches on that it's empty."

"Why don't we simply have the chaps leave directly we take a car?" Fincham asked. "Means some of them will get away that much sooner and if Jerry gets on to us before we're done at least he'll not have the whole lot."

"Lots of reasons," Ryan said with uncharacteristic patience. "One. We have to get the front guards first and anybody jumping out of a front car will practically pass in review for the guards on the rear cars as the train moves along. Two. Some of 'em might get picked up right away and Jerry could put two and two together and have a reception committee waiting for us at the next stop."

"Three," Fincham said. "You're keen on getting the whole lot out of Jerry's clutches. Just part of the lot won't satisfy you."

"Right, Colonel. Just part of the lot won't satisfy me."

They continued playing cards, waiting for Costanzo's report. After a while Costanzo returned and watched in silence.

"Ah know how Judas felt," he said at last. "Cuhnel, you're putting my soul in jeopardy."

When he spoke, he smiled for the first time since Petersen's death.

"I'll try and look after your body, Padre," Ryan replied. "But

I'm afraid I can't accept responsibility for your soul. What did you find out?"

"His sergeant told him he'd be on duty at least eighteen hours."

Ryan gave Fincham a swift, significant look.

"All the time we need," he said.

"His name is Julius Schnitzler and he has six children he hasn't seen in three years," Costanzo went on quietly. "What will happen to him?"

"That's no concern of yours, Padre."

"Ah think it is, Cuhnel. He confided in me because Ah'm a priest."

"It wasn't the confessional, Padre. Whatever happens to him won't be your fault. And don't forget you're wearing a uniform, not a habit."

"That doesn't change the man underneath, Cuhnel."

Ryan looked at him soberly.

"I think it does, Padre," he said. "If you accept the responsibilities that go with it."

Costanzo left them to sit on the back bench with his pocket Testament.

"We'll get ours the first chance we have after about six," Ryan says. "Unless we get a chance too good to pass up before that. We'll have to wait until after dark to start operating outside. That's around seven-thirty."

Fincham pulled on his mustache and eyed Ryan.

"You'll not find me wanting, Ryan," he said. "But don't imagine I'm any fonder of your company. We'd be going the other direction if you'd known what you were about or listened to those who did. I'm with you in this do but once we're clear we go our separate ways."

"As long as your personal feelings don't interfere with your performance I don't care what they are, Colonel," Ryan said. "We've got a few minutes before we can get moving. I'm going to take a short nap. I suggest you do the same. We're likely to be up all night."

He swept the cards together and squared the deck.

"You owe me a million pounds," he said. "I'll give you a chance to win it back later."

He lay down between the benches and in minutes was sleeping. He had been asleep only a short while when the slowing of the train awakened him.

"Orte," Stein said from his window. "We're stopping."

Ryan looked at his watch. Five after six. Fincham was snoring on the other side of the bench. Ryan reached over and touched him on the shoulder. Fincham sat up with a jerk and hit his head on the bench. He began swearing with more vehemence than originality. A strange, low guttural sound came from the corporal. Fincham stopped swearing and looked at him. The German was laughing, his upper lip curled back over square teeth with one incisor missing.

"Amuses you, does it, Jerry?" Fincham demanded. "P'raps you'd like something else to laugh about."

"Don't antagonize him," Ryan said.

The corporal stopped laughing and leaned back against the wall.

"You're getting a great collection of bumps on that thick skull, Finch," said Stein. "Give a phrenologist a bad time."

"How about another hand of poker?" Ryan said. "Maybe you can win back your million."

"Right," Fincham said.

"Don't straddle the bench," Ryan said in a low voice. "Keep both feet on the Obergefreiter's side."

He dealt the cards and studied his hand.

"The Obergefreiter keeps looking at his watch," he said. "Must be time for chow. At noon, Schnitzler came back to get his rations. If he does the same thing again, that's the best time to jump 'em. When they're together."

"I want the Obergefreiter. I didn't much care for the way he pranged me with that bloody rifle."

"Okay. You've picked the roughest one, though. As soon as they're out of commission . . ."

"Precisely what do you mean by out of commission?"

Ryan looked into Fincham's eyes.

"Dead," he said succinctly.

"Merely wanted to be certain," Fincham replied.

"As soon as they're out of commission we'll slip into their uniforms. You take the Obergefreiter's. You're close to the same build. I'll take Schnitzler's. His tunic's short on him so it shouldn't be too bad on me."

"If it's a proper fit you'd be rather conspicuous, old boy," Fincham said. "Did you notice the uniforms on those troops when we drove up?"

Fincham was cheerful now, almost ebullient, at the prospect of action.

"We'll stow them between the benches under the blankets. Like they're us, taking a nap."

"And then?"

"We wait. We'll have to hit Klement's car just before we pull out. We can't do it if there's a bunch of roof guards milling around on the ground."

Someone fumbled at the door.

"This may be the rations," Ryan said. "Remember, when Schnitzler comes back to get his. When I touch your knee, it means go."

Fincham nodded, his eyes bright.

The door was flung back and a soldier shoved two cans, bread, and a wedge of cheese inside. The corporal spoke angrily. Ryan looked inquiringly at Costanzo.

"The Obergefreiter's chewing him out for putting the bread on the floor," Costanzo said. "He says next time hand it to him or he'll spend the rest of the war on the Russian front."

The soldier slid the door closed. The corporal called to Schnitzler, who slung his rifle over his shoulder and shambled back to pick up the rations. He divided the bread and cheese with a pocketknife and the corporal, holding his rifle loosely in his left hand, took a step toward him with his free hand outstretched. Schnitzler handed the corporal his share of the rations.

Ryan touched Fincham's knee.

—XV—

Ryan and Fincham charged off the bench like football linemen on a power play, taking the guards completely by surprise. The corporal's rifle and the two cans of meat clattered on the floor of the boxcar. One can rolled under the benches and stopped against Stein's foot. He did not notice it. He and Costanzo were transfixed by the suddenness and fury of the attack.

Ryan jammed a fist into Schnitzler's spine just above the belt and arched the tall man backward with a forearm hooked under his chin. Fincham came up low, driving the corporal back against the wall with a thick forearm across the German's throat. The German's head smashed the wall with a sound like a cracked gong being struck. The forearm blow crushed his larynx and he was already unconscious when he hit the wall. His body was suspended from Fincham's arm, legs flaccid, like a man hanging.

Schnitzler struggled, his long arms flailing, but in vain. Ryan forced him into a tighter arc, his crooked arm holding the German's neck in a vise of sinew. Schnitzler's resistance lessened, then ceased entirely. Ryan continued the pressure on his throat, just as Fincham was doing with the corporal. There was silence in the car except for the heavy breathing of Ryan and Fincham and Costanzo's whispered prayers. Stein had not moved or said a word.

Ryan eased Schnitzler's body to the floor and breathed deeply. Fincham was still holding the corporal pinned upright by the throat. Ryan gripped his shoulder.

"That's enough, Colonel," he said. "He's had it."

Fincham stepped away at once.

The German's body flowed to the floor and sprawled there in a heap. Ryan tried to think of Petersen lying dead in an Italian stubble field but it did not help. Stein went quickly to the bodies and felt the pulses in turn.

"Dead," he said, looking up at Ryan, his hand on the corporal's wrist. "Both dead."

"Good show," said Fincham.

"Did you have to kill them?" Costanzo asked. "Schnitzler had six children."

"I didn't enjoy it, Padre," Ryan said angrily.

Costanzo sighed.

"Ah know it," he said. "Ah'm sorry Ah said it."

"I'm afraid I wasn't much help," Stein said sheepishly. "I couldn't move a muscle. I never saw a man killed that . . . well, that personally before."

"It's not your kind of work, Captain," Ryan said hoarsely. "Mine, either. I never killed a man that personally before."

Of the four officers, only Fincham was unmoved.

"Piece of cake," he said briskly. "No noise, no blood. No fuss, no muss, as you Yanks say."

"We're wasting valuable time," said Ryan. "We'll get into their uniforms and stretch 'em out between the benches."

Stein began stripping the dead men without being told while Ryan and Fincham got out of their uniforms. The two men dressed quickly.

"Bit tight across the shoulders but otherwise a rather decent fit," Fincham said.

His eyes bulged when he turned to Ryan.

"Great God!" he blurted. "If the Fuehrer saw you he'd have you on a bloody postal stamp."

With his hard, flat-planed face and closely cropped blond hair, Ryan looked like a Nazi propaganda poster in the German uniform. The trousers were large in the waist and so long Ryan had to tuck them up but the tunic fit fairly well.

"Let's get these men out of the way," he said. "And be sure the blankets cover them completely."

"Jawohl, Herr Oberst von Ryan," said Fincham.

"There's nothing funny in this, Colonel," said Ryan.

"No fault of mine you sort out to a smashing Jerry. What now, Herr Oberst?"

"Six twenty-five," said Ryan. "We've got about an hour before dark. Stein, what's doing out there?"

"Nothing," Stein called from the window. "As far as I can see. I can only see straight out."

"I'll just slide the door back a crack and take a look," said Ryan. "If there's nobody around we'll pay a little courtesy call on Klement."

The door was locked.

"Damn!" said Ryan. "We're stuck until somebody opens up."

The train started moving. Ryan came back and sat down.

"We can't do anything until the next stop," he said. "I hope it's not one of those long ones when the guards climb down and roam all over the place. Next time we slow down, you take one side of the door and I'll take the other. We'll clobber the first man who sticks his head inside and if the coast's clear we'll rush Klement's car."

"What if there's Jerries about?" Fincham said.

"Then you won't have to worry about the million pounds you owe me, Colonel."

They rode in silence for twenty minutes.

"It'll be dark in half an hour or less," Ryan said. "That's in our favor."

Fincham chuckled.

"When Klement sees you he'll be that jealous he'll wet himself," he said. "The clot would give his ballocks to look as Nordic as you. If he has any."

It was almost dark in the boxcar when the train slowed, though the opening at which Stein watched still formed a rectangle of light in the side of the car. The train ground to a halt.

"Attigliano," said Stein. "Looks like it'll be dark before long."

"Any activity?" said Ryan.

"None that I can see. I can hear the guards calling on the roofs. Doesn't sound like they're getting down."

"Good," said Ryan. "Now, if somebody will just open that door."

He took a position on one side of the door and posted Fincham at the other.

"We'll wait for the door to open," he said. "If it's one man, I'll get him. If it's two, take the one nearest you and I'll get the other."

"And if there's three?"

"We've had it," Ryan said flatly.

They stood on either side of the door, their ears pressed against the wall. There was movement and the sound of German voices outside.

"The guards have climbed down," Stein whispered.

Footsteps approached. Ryan and Fincham tensed. The footsteps continued by. Nothing happened. Nothing at all.

"Sounds like they're coming back," Stein said after a few minutes.

The only sound was the quiet chugging of the idling locomotive. A train roared by on another track, filling the car with a blast of sound and setting it to rocking.

Someone banged on the door and called out. Ryan and Fincham stiffened.

"Padre," Ryan said in a low voice, "what's he saying?"

"We're ready to pull out," Costanzo replied. "He wants to know if everything is all right. What shall Ah tell him?"

"With that Southern accent? Don't say anything."

"Ah can manage the right accent if Ah go slow and pick my words, Cuhnel."

"Not a word," said Ryan. "Don't anybody open his mouth."

The voice outside grew insistent.

"Someone'd best answer or the sod'll have the whole lot about our ears," Fincham whispered.

"Not a word," Ryan said again.

It was completely dark in the car now and the window was less definable. There was a fumbling at the door. The door slid back and a German soldier stood outlined in the dusk.

"Was ist los?" he demanded.

He leaned inside for a better look. Ryan brought his rifle butt crashing down on the German's head. Almost simultaneously Fincham bent forward and pulled the man into the car. Ryan slid the door shut quickly but carefully, making sure the lock did not engage.

"This one's had it," Fincham whispered from his position beside the body.

"Stein, put him back with the others," Ryan said. "Fincham, take the other side of the door."

Ryan slid the door open a crack and stood with his eye pressed to the opening. A train whistle blew. Feet pattered by the car and an anxious voice called, "Heinz! Heinz! Wo bist Du, Du Esel? Heinz?"

The caller ran past and back again. No one breathed.

"Obergefreiter," the voice said, "hast Du den elenden Heinz gesehen?"

Ryan slide the door open a foot. The German reached out to open it wider. Ryan brought his heavy shoe down on the man's neck where it joined his shoulder. The soldier gasped and reeled back. Ryan shoved back the door with his shoulder and, leaning out of the car, grabbed the German by his tunic and dragged the floundering man inside. Fincham smashed the German's skull with his rifle butt.

"That's four of the perishers," he said with satisfaction.

"We're in luck," Ryan said. "They must be from Klement's car. The others must be at their stations waiting to pull out."

"If they're Klement's two, I'd say he'll be screaming his bloody head off for them any moment," Fincham said.

"Captain Stein, close the door behind us but be damn sure it doesn't lock," Ryan said. "Sit tight and don't open it for anybody except Fincham or me. Understand?"

"What if something happens to you?" Stein asked quietly.

"You'll know. If you hear shots, it'll mean they've tumbled to us. You and Padre take off in a hurry. Fincham, remember we've got to have Klement in one piece. The radio operator, too, if we can. Let's go."

Ryan leaped to the ground with Fincham at his heels. They ran quietly to Klement's car in the thickening dusk. No one in the little station gave them a second glance. Klement was standing in the door of his car, looking out. He called angrily to the running men, thinking they were his soldiers. He did not recognize Ryan until the colonel was quite close. He shrank back and his mouth opened to cry for help but Ryan's fist in the groin crumpled the fat little man in his tracks and cut off his shout. The radio operator was sitting in front of his transmitter, studying a manual. He turned toward the commotion at the door. Recognizing Ryan immediately, he sprang from his folding stool and darted for a rifle leaning in the corner. Ryan vaulted into the car and went after him. He reached the German just as the young soldier got his hands on the rifle. Ryan hit him a leaping, clubbing blow on the temple which sent the German bouncing off the wall to slide to the floor, stunned.

The car creaked. The train was starting to move.

"Fincham!" Ryan cried. "Get Padre Costanzo here on the double! Tell Stein to sit tight!"

Fincham did not wait to ask questions. The car moved forward with ponderous inevitability. Klement writhed on the floor gasping and sweating, his face smeared with vomit. The radio operator lay motionless. Ryan checked the radio and was relieved to discover it was not turned on. The car moved a little faster and he went to the door. Fincham and Costanzo came pounding back. Fincham threw the smaller man in bodily and scrambled in behind him, Ryan helping with a hand at his belt. As soon as they were inside, Ryan slid the door gently to, saw it had an inside handle, and shut it all the way.

Behind him, Fincham was helping Costanzo to his feet and brushing the priest off.

"Sorry if I was a bit rough, Padre," he said. "Couldn't miss our train, you know. Might not be another for hours."

"Are they . . . ?" Costanzo asked, nodding at the Germans on the floor, one still writhing in agony, the other inert.

"They'll be okay," Ryan said. "Fincham, Klement's got some."

"What?" Fincham demanded.

"Ballocks."

Fincham looked down at Klement, still rolling on the floor, and smiled cruelly.

"At the moment he wishes he hadn't, I expect," he said.

"Put him in his sack until he snaps out of it," Ryan said. "Get his pistol. Padre, see what you can do for the boy."

Fincham grabbed Klement by the collar and dragged him across the floor to a narrow but substantial bed in the corner.

"Silk sheets, no less," he said.

Costanzo knelt by the radio operator, chafing his wrists and patting his face. After a moment the young soldier groaned and opened his eyes. One side of his face was puffy and starting to discolor. He looked blankly at Costanzo. Awareness dawned in his eyes when he saw Ryan, and he stared at the American with undisguised hate.

Ryan surveyed the car. It was brightly illuminated by two electric lights strung to the ceiling, a wire leading from them to a portable generator chugging near the center of the car. A pot bubbled on a gasoline stove against the side of the car. Near it was a folding table spread with a heavily embroidered cloth and set with heavy silver and fine china and crystal. There were two bottles of wine on the table, a salver heaped with wedges of cheese, sliced meats, olives, and green onions, and a cut-glass dish of anchovy fillets.

The back quarter of the car was heaped with a jumble of goods—boxes, cartons, whole cheeses, paintings in ornate frames, sausages the size of a man's arm, small pieces of statuary, an accordion, books in gilt-leather bindings, rolled tapestries, bolts of cloth, and a tall, richly carved clock. Strings of onions, garlic, and dried mushrooms hung from the walls, held in place by strips of adhesive tape.

Next to Klement's bed was a deep leather chair with a matching hassock over which was flung a soft lap robe of blue and gold mohair. Beside the hassock was a pair of wine-colored slippers.

The radio transmitter and receiver were on a steel folding desk against the wired-up far door. A small folding table alongside held pencils, a notebook, radio handbooks, a pad of message forms, and a map.

At the opposite end of the car from Klement and his loot were the guards' knapsacks and rations, a toilet partially surrounded by a carved wooden screen, and the radio operator's sleeping bag.

Ryan bent over the map. A heavy line was drawn from their starting point in the Abruzzi through Rome to Innsbruck, with Rome, Florence, Bologna, Verona, Trento, and Bolzano circled in red. Verona was further marked with a bold X.

He turned back to the two Germans. Klement had stopped writhing and begun moaning monotonously with every breath. The radio operator appeared fully recovered.

"On your feet," said Ryan.

The youth did not move.

"Tell him to get up, Padre," Ryan said.

The German shook off Costanzo's hand when the priest tried to help him to his feet. He got up and leaned against the wall, hate-filled and unafraid.

"One of those," Fincham said. "Believes all their bloody rot."

"Tell him you're a priest, Padre," Ryan said. "You'll see he's not harmed if he co-operates."

The youth listened, stony-faced, then spat on the floor at Costanzo's feet.

"Thought as much," said Fincham. "Best finish him now, Ryan. Or he'll queer the do for us."

"We may need him."

"You know he'll be no help to us. No stomach for it, Colonel? I'll take care of it."

Costanzo pleaded silently with his eyes.

"Tie him up," Ryan said.

Fincham started to complain, shrugged, and began tearing strips from Klement's silk sheets. He trussed the German and propped him in the corner against the bales and boxes. Returning to Klement, who was quiet now, he reached inside the major's tunic and took out a small folder.

"What are you doing?" Ryan demanded.

Fincham flipped open the folder without answering, then laughed triumphantly.

"How was that for reading his bloody character?" he demanded, pleased with himself. "The clot's identity card. No bloody Von to his name. Hubertus Ignatius Klement."

Klement looked up at Fincham, his lower lip trembling with rage and humiliation.

"Feeling better, Major?" Ryan asked solicitously.

Klement sat up and put his hand to his face. He stared with disgust at the vomit on his palm.

"For this you die," he said.

"That's a possibility," Ryan answered agreeably. "But if we go, you go. Padre, tell him that in German."

"I understand," Klement said. "You have no chance. You surrender now, I show mercy. If no . . ."

He held a pudgy forefinger to his temple as if it were a pistol barrel.

Costanzo brought him a towel and a water bottle. Klement took them without thanks and began cleaning his face. Ryan waited until he finished. Fincham went prowling around the boxcar and stopped to lean over the bubbling pot.

"Lovely," he said rapturously. "I do believe it's chicken."

He turned to Klement, who scowled at him.

"I'll say this much for you, Von Ignatz," Fincham said, "you do know how to do yourself well. Your invitation to dinner is accepted."

"That can wait," said Ryan.

He carried the folding stool to Klement's bedside and sat down facing the major.

"Major Klement," he said, "I'm going to tell you how you can stay alive."

"I do not fear," Klement said.

"Padre, translate for me. I want to be sure he knows exactly what I'm telling him."

"Yes, Cuhnel," said Costanzo.

He had been pale and quiet since the killings.

"Major Klement," Ryan said carefully, "four of your men are lying dead in the boxcar up ahead. Nothing we do from now on could possibly make things worse for us. Nothing. Do you understand?"

Klement nodded curtly when Costanzo translated.

"You're going to stay alive only as long as you answer my questions and do exactly as I tell you," Ryan said.

Klement squared his plump shoulders defiantly.

"First question," said Ryan. "Why are those cities circled on the route?"

Klement clenched his teeth stubbornly when Costanzo translated the question. Ryan reached out deliberately and hooked a forefinger in Klement's collar. He gave a twist, tightening the collar around Klement's throat. The major clawed ineffectually at Ryan's arm, his eyes popping. Costanzo looked on in helpless disapproval. Ryan released his hold and Klement gasped for air.

"Once more, Major," Ryan said relentlessly. "What do they mean?"

Klement licked his lips. His eyes roved as if searching for a way out.

"Next time I'll choke you until you're unconscious," Ryan said. "Then I'll revive you and start over again."

Klement rubbed his throat and spoke.

"That's where the train stops for instructions," Costanzo translated. "He and the engineer get orders telling them where the train has to clear the track and for how long."

"What's the X at Verona for?"

Klement hesitated, then spoke up when he saw Ryan setting himself to reach out.

"The train changes guards there," Costanzo said.

"That appears to confirm what Schnitzler told you," Ryan said. "But I've got to be certain. That's a hell of a long way to expect a soldier to bounce around on top of a boxcar. Tell him I think he's lying."

Klement spoke earnestly, gesturing with his pudgy hands.

Costanzo smiled faintly when he translated.

"These are times when German soldiers must be willing to make sacrifices for the Fatherland," Costanzo said. "This is why he accepted an assignment to command a prison train when what he really wanted was to go south and join the fighting. And you must understand the reason he's kept the men locked in the cars is because he has so few troops to control them. Actually he is very sympathetic to us. We are all soldiers doing our duty."

"I'll buy the Verona part," Ryan said. "What's the radio for? Does he get instructions on it, or file reports? If so, from whom and to whom?"

Klement's instructions came only from dispatchers in the circled stations. The radio, he said, was for emergency use only. If there was trouble en route he was to radio ahead to the next station. Thus far it had not been used.

"I'll buy that," said Ryan. "Nothing but blank message forms on the radio man's table. How long do we stop at the next station? Chiusi?"

Klement said he was not sure. The engineer had the schedule.

He thought it was fourteen minutes. They were due there a little after 8 P.M. Ryan looked at his watch.

"That means we'll hit Chiusi in ten or fifteen minutes," he said. "Major Klement, when we get there I want you to order the guards to stay at their posts. Tell 'em they'll get a break at the next stop. I'll tell you what else to do after we get there. And if I as much as suspect you're trying to tip 'em off I'll kill you in your tracks. Make sure he understands that, Padre."

Fincham had been rummaging around in Klement's loot while Ryan interrogated him. He set three places at the table and sliced a round dark loaf with a bayonet, munching a mouthful as he worked, then ladled the steaming chicken onto plates and poured white wine into stemmed glasses.

"Grub up," he announced.

"We haven't got time," Ryan said. "We're due in a station in about ten minutes."

"There's always time to eat," Fincham said. "When the train starts slowing we'll have bags of time to make ready for whatever you propose doing there."

He plucked a chicken wing from his plate, licked off the sauce, and began eating.

"All right," said Ryan. "It may be a while before we get another chance."

"I'm not hungry," Costanzo said.

"Drink a little wine, Padre," said Ryan. "You look like you could use it."

Fincham handed Costanzo a glass. Costanzo took a few sips and set the glass down.

"That's no vino at all," Fincham said. "Toss it down."

"That's fine, thank you," said Costanzo. "Ah'm fine."

There was color in his face now and his voice was firmer.

"Never thought you'd get the wind up, Padre," Fincham said. "Not you."

"Don't be stupid, Fincham," Ryan said. "Captain Costanzo's being called on to do things a chaplain shouldn't have to do. I'm sorry, Padre. It can't be avoided."

"Ah know, Cuhnel," Costanzo said with a sigh. "You can count on me for whatever Ah have to do."

Ryan filled a plate and gave it to Klement.

"Fincham, when you get through feed the radio operator," Ryan said.

"Feed him?" Fincham demanded. "Am I his bloody nanny?"

"It's that or untie him and tie him up again."

"I'll feed the little swine," Fincham said.

"You better eat a little something, Padre," Ryan said. "Before you start I want you to slip into the radio operator's uniform. You'll have to come outside with Klement and me to make sure he tells the guards what he's supposed to."

"Ah'm a noncombatant, Cuhnel," Costanzo said quietly.

"I'm not asking you to kill anybody, Padre. Just to take a chance on getting yourself killed."

"That's different, Cuhnel," Costanzo said with a grin. "Ah'll be right with you."

"Fincham, get the radio operator's uniform for the padre," said Ryan. "You can handle him better."

"What a bloody bore," Fincham said. "First I'm to feed the bugger, now I'm to get him ready for beddie-byes."

The German's long drawers were soaking wet in the crotch. His face was stiff with anger and embarrassment.

"Nanny's babykins should have told nanny he needed to make pottykins," Fincham scolded.

The German gritted his teeth.

Costanzo retired behind the screen concealing the toilet and Fincham brought the uniform to him.

The locomotive whistle blew and the train lost speed.

"Get a move on, Padre," said Ryan. "We're almost there. Fincham, get a gag on that Hitler Youth."

"Blast!" said Fincham. "I haven't half finished my bloody dinner."

XVI

The train stopped with a sudden jerk and Costanzo came tumbling from behind the screen, the German trousers around his knees. He pulled them up quickly and buttoned himself.

"I say, Padre," Fincham said, studying his slight frame. "I wish Jerry had more of your sort. Be a bloody short war."

"Tell Klement when we step out of the car I'll be right behind him with a Schmeisser in his back," said Ryan. "He'll tell the guard on this car to stay at his post and pass the order on down the line. If a guard has to relieve himself he's to climb down and do it by his car and climb right back up. That stands until further orders. Then we get back inside the car. Make sure he's got it. And Fincham, you stay inside and keep an eye on your little friend. While you're resting dig up Klement's razor and shave that mustache."

"What!" Fincham bellowed, outraged.

"You couldn't show your face outside this car with that brush," Ryan said. "It's a dead giveaway. That's an order."

Ryan opened the door and looked out into a blacked-out and almost empty station. He jumped lightly to the ground and looked along the train. The guards were already starting to climb down from their stations.

"Get Klement out here quick!" he said. "Tell him to order the guards back to their posts."

Klement scrambled out with Costanzo behind him.

"Don't get too close, Padre," Ryan warned. "They'll know you're not one of their buddies."

Klement shouted an order and the men on the first cars began climbing back reluctantly. Ryan stood where none of them could see his face.

Down at the end, some of the guards were already on the ground. Ryan could not see them in the darkness but their complaining voices were clearly audible.

"Yell at 'em!" Ryan ordered. "Tell the men at this end to pass it along and be quick about it."

Costanzo translated the order but Klement hesitated. Ryan nudged him in the neck with his Schmeisser. Klement began shouting. The prisoners in the cars set up their usual clamor.

"Give 'em hell, Major," Ryan said. "Threaten to shoot 'em if they don't shut up!"

He talked directly to Klement with Costanzo translating as he spoke.

Klement yelled at the prisoners and they shouted back insults.

"Sounds normal, wouldn't you say, Padre?" Ryan whispered. "I'm taking Klement back in the car. You slip up front to our car and tell Captain Stein to come back here with us. But to put on a Kraut uniform first."

Fincham had found a razor and was stirring lather in a cup. He did not look happy. Ryan waited at the door for Costanzo. He opened it just wide enough for Costanzo to climb in.

"Hank'll be along in a minute," Costanzo said.

Ryan resumed his vigil at the door. He could hear the prisoners beating on the walls of their boxcars and cursing the Germans. In a few minutes Stein whispered at the door and Ryan let him in.

"Am I glad to see you guys!" Stein said. "It was lonesome up there with those . . ."

"Help yourself to some chicken, Captain," said Ryan. "But easy on the wine."

Stein stared at the laden table.

"Good Lord," he said. "I didn't know this train had a dining car."

"What now, Cuhnel?" Costanzo asked.

"We wait a few minutes."

Fincham was busy with his mustache, his back to Ryan. After a while he turned around. Instead of shaving the mustache completely he had left a Hitlerian brush and smoothed his hair down across his forehead.

"Now who's the better bloody Jerry?" he demanded.

"You look like a night club comedian," said Ryan. "Comb your hair right."

"Jealousy doesn't become you, Ryan," Fincham said, pushing his hair back in place.

Ryan looked at his watch.

"We should be moving out in a few minutes," he said. "Major Klement, stick your head out the door and tell the guard on this car you want to see him. Stein, throw that spread over our friend in the corner. Be sure he's covered. Fincham, when the Kraut gets to the door I'll pull him in. You know what to do."

Ryan pulled back the door and Klement called up to the guard. Inside the car they could hear the soldier's boots on the steel rungs. Ryan motioned Klement back from the door and stood concealed behind it. When the guard put his hands on the floor of the car to climb inside, Ryan reached down and pulled him in with a jerk, like landing a fish. The German was still on his hands and knees when Fincham broke his neck with a neat thrust of his rifle butt.

"Five of the buggers," Fincham said.

Klement stared down at the body, his eyes glazed and sick.

"Shouldn't wonder if it isn't the first Jerry corpse he's seen," Fincham said.

"I'll get on top just before we pull out," Ryan said. "Can't take a chance on the next guard getting a close look at me. After we start rolling I'll get him. When you hear a rap on the door, open up."

"I should prang the bugger," Fincham protested. "I've a bit more experience at this sort of thing."

"I'm giving this party," Ryan said. "Have Stein and the padre tear up Klement's sheets and make a stout rope. We'll need it. If you hear shooting, it'll mean I missed and the game's over. So bail out. If not, just wait for my knock."

He tore a yard-long strip from Klement's silk sheet and stuffed it inside his tunic. He waited at the door until the locomotive whistle signaled departure.

"See you later, gentlemen," he said, and jumped down.

He climbed quickly to the top of the car as the train started rolling. It was cold and he knew it would grow colder. Not wanting to be encumbered, he had not taken the dead guard's greatcoat. He stretched his arms and felt a moment of freedom and exhilaration which vanished quickly when he looked along the line of rattling boxcars stretching behind him in the night. Though he could not see them in the darkness he visualized them clearly. Twenty-two boxcars, and each with an armed man on it who must be killed.

Ryan took the strip of silk from his tunic, crouched, and leaped silently to the car behind. He lost his balance when he landed on the swaying roof but steadied himself with a quick thrust of his palms. He waited, listening. The only sound was that of clicking rails, creaking cars, rushing air. He knew the train seemed to be moving much faster than it actually was because of his unprotected position. The next station was Terontola, twenty miles away. He had at least thirty minutes.

Ryan lay flat on his belly and inched toward the guard at the far end of the car, a formless shadow in the darkness thirty feet away. The wind tore at him and stopped his ears with sound. He welcomed that. The same rush of air would muffle his approach.

Midway along the car he stopped to wind an end of his silken garrot around each fist before resuming his stealthy crawl toward the guard. When he grew close he heard a sound above the train noises. The guard was singing to himself. The man was hunched forward, his head drawn down into the upturned collar of his greatcoat. It would be difficult to slip the garrot around his neck.

Ryan hugged the top of the car and studied the guard's back and the tilt of his head. Could he get the twist of silk beneath the German's chin on the first try? There would be no second. Perhaps he could stun him first with a blow at the base of the skull. The German's neck was concealed in his collar. He might miss the mark. Ryan felt a gnawing urgency.

He raised himself silently to his knees, adjusted himself to the swaying of the car and raised his flexed arms, his hands as far apart as the twist of silk permitted.

"Pst," he hissed.

The guard jerked erect. Ryan slipped the garrot over his head and jerked it tight before the man could turn. The German's arms flailed, sending his rifle flying into the darkness, and his feet drummed against the car. The ends of the silk bit into Ryan's palms but he did not slacken his grip.

The German stopped kicking. Ryan held on a moment longer, every faculty straining for a sign he had been heard by the guard on the next car. Nothing. He stuffed the garrot in his tunic and dragged the body forward to the end of the car. He studied the gap between the cars a moment, then reached down and took the body by belt and collar. He swung the body in increasingly longer arcs and, putting all the strength of his arms, back and bent legs into the effort, heaved it across to the next car and leaped after it.

The body slid toward the edge. Ryan threw himself across it, pinning it to the top of the car. He lay there a moment to catch his breath, conscious of his macabre couch, then dragged the German to the middle of the car. He arranged the body crosswise so it would not roll with the swaying of the car. Crawling to the edge, he hung over the side of the car as far as he dared. Holding the edge with one hand, he banged on the door with the other. The door slid open almost immediately in a burst of light and Fincham was looking into his face from only a few inches away. Ryan blinked his dazzled eyes.

"Somebody get the light!" he ordered.

It went out at once.

"Mission accomplished?" Fincham asked.

"I'll swing him down," Ryan whispered. "You grab him and pull him in."

"Good show," said Fincham.

Ryan grabbed the German by the ankles and slid the upper part of the body over the edge. Fincham was waiting. He seized the arms and jerked. Ryan was almost dislodged from his perch. He fought desperately to regain his balance, clawing with his cold hands and grinding the sides of his heavy shoes against the roof. One knee slid over the edge and he clamped it inside the car, one hand grasping the edge and the other scrabbling desperately for a handhold on the smooth roof. The wind pulled at him and he teetered on the edge of the car.

The car swayed, throwing him back. Taking advantage of the momentum he unhooked his knee and threw himself toward the middle of the car. He lay on his back, panting and regathering his strength. The sky was black and immense, pierced with starlight. For a moment Ryan had the illusion he was not looking up into the sky but down from it at a city far below, lit with coruscating brilliance.

"I say," Fincham called anxiously. "Are you all right?"

Ryan rolled over on his stomach.

"I'm okay," he said. "Is somebody watching Klement?"

"Stein. I gave him Klement's Luger."

"Have Padre take off the Kraut's uniform and roll it up in his greatcoat. Then hand me the end of the rope they made out of the sheets. I'll haul you up."

"Right," said Fincham.

"They can turn the light back on after they close the door behind you," Ryan said. "But tell Stein to keep Klement down.

Don't let him out of his sack. When the train stops they're not to open the door except for one of us. Got that?"

"Right," Fincham said again.

After a couple of minutes he said "Here we are" and handed up the German uniform balled in a greatcoat. Ryan held it against the car with his body and reached down for the silken rope. When he had it, he shifted to a sitting position on the uniform and hauled away. Fincham helped by pulling himself up with his powerful arms. When he was half on the roof, Ryan grabbed his belt and pulled him the rest of the way. Fincham rolled over and sat up.

"Lovely view," he said. "But bloody cold."

"Come on," said Ryan. "Bring the uniform with you."

He ran lightly toward the rear of the car, by now accustomed to the swaying motion.

"Half a mo'," Fincham called in a low voice. "I'm no bloody gazelle."

Ryan waited for him to catch up and walked with him to the next car.

"Sit down where the guard's supposed to be and wait for me," he whispered. "I'll be back in a minute."

"You're having yourself another Jerry, aren't you?" Fincham demanded. "Should be mine, you know. Fair's fair."

"You'll have all the Krauts you want before the night's over," Ryan said. "If we're lucky."

The guard on the next car was lying on his back, his arms folded across his rifle. Ryan could not tell if the German were asleep or awake. He rolled painstakingly over on his back and inched feet first toward the guard. The man grunted and stirred. Ryan froze. The German was still again.

Ryan continued his stealthy approach until he was so near he could almost touch the guard with his drawn-back foot. He straightened his leg with a snap and kicked the German in the head. Pain ran from his heel up his calf. The soldier, only dazed, struggled to sit up. Ryan clamped his forearm across the German's throat. He died more quietly than his comrade before him. Ryan dragged the body back to the middle of the car and rejoined Fincham.

"Here's the drill," he said. "I want to hang over the side and open the car door. Think you can hang on to me?"

"Despite the temptation, yes," said Fincham.

"All right. I'll tie the rope around my waist and when I go over you anchor me. Okay?"

"Okay."

Ryan folded himself down against the side of the car and reached for the door handle, the cold wind plucking at him. The handle was more than a foot out of his reach. He worked himself down until only his legs were still on the roof and he hung suspended by the rope around his waist. He pressed both palms against the door to keep the wind from spinning him. The rope bit into his sides but now the handle was within his grasp. He pushed down on it and the lock disengaged but he did not have enough leverage to slide back the door. He banged a stiff hand against the door.

"Open up," he called.

The door slid open and he was dangling head down, looking into fetid darkness smelling of sweat, urine, and excrement and broken here and there by the red glow of a cigarette. A face thrust close to his and a startled voice cried out.

"My God! It's Von Ryan!"

"Pull me in," Ryan ordered.

No one moved.

"Somebody pull me in!" Ryan snapped urgently.

The prisoners nearest the door reached for him. The doorway was full of groping hands. They slid over his face and plucked at his arms and shoulders, then pulled him inside. Fincham, thinking Ryan was slipping, hauled back on the rope. For a moment there was a tug of war, with the rope tightening around Ryan's waist.

"Let go, damn it!" Ryan barked.

Everyone did, simultaneously, Fincham as well as the men in the car. Ryan's upper torso was inside the car, deep in a wall of flesh. The lower part of his body plummeted toward the rushing ground. Ryan, face up, reached into the mass of bodies and grabbed a double armful with desperate strength, his face pressed into someone's acrid crotch. The prisoners drew back in a reflexive movement, pulling Ryan far enough that his buttocks hit the floor just inside the car. The men behind Ryan's armful surged forward against the pressure. For a moment Ryan and the men he hung onto were poised delicately in the door, then the men behind them came to life and took hold of them. Ryan was hauled inside to sprawl on his back in a welter of bodies and limbs.

Fincham's head came poking over the edge of the roof.

"Where's Ryan?" he cried.

"Hold it down," Ryan answered. "I'm okay."

He struggled to his feet, pushing against bodies which moved aside with the mute resentfulness of feeding cattle. He was standing on someone's leg. When he moved, his feet encountered more legs. He twisted as if digging into loose sand and the tangle opened enough for him to plant his feet on the floor, then enveloped his legs to the calf.

Suddenly everyone was shouting questions.

"Quiet!" Ryan yelled.

The shouting stopped abruptly.

"I haven't got much time so don't ask questions," he said. "Just listen. Colonel Fincham and I are taking over this train. The whole train. Nobody's leaving until we've got it. Then we all leave. I need two of you men to get into Kraut uniforms and replace the roof guards. You should know if you're caught in a German uniform you'll be shot."

"Why don't you do it, Von Ryan?" Bostick's high voice demanded. "It's the kind you ought to be wearing anyway."

Ryan made room with his elbows and lit a match. He held it high above his head. Eyeballs gleamed in the wavering light.

"Looka that!" a voice said incredulously. "Ain't he the Jerriest looking Jerry you ever saw?"

"I'll put one on," Bostick said, unabashed.

"Thanks, but you're too big," Ryan said. "I need a man about five-eight, hundred forty-five, and one about five-eleven, hundred sixty."

"I'll take the little one, Colonel," Frankie Orde called from the darkness.

"You stay put, Lieutenant," Ryan said.

He turned and called up to Fincham.

"Lob that uniform in here, then ease the Kraut down."

The German uniform came sailing into the car and the prisoners began fighting for it.

"Knock it off," Ryan ordered. "That's the small one. The nearest one to it the right size gets it. The rest of you quit shoving."

The body of the German came dangling down from the roof and a dozen hands pulled it into the car.

"Strip him and hide the body under your gear," Ryan said. "Get into those uniforms fast. Sing out when you're ready and we'll pull you up."

He thrust the free end of the rope up to Fincham.

"Going up," Fincham murmured, hauling away.

Together they pulled the other two men to the roof.

"You'll have to give one of 'em your rifle," Ryan said to Fincham. "I lost one over the side."

"Should've let me handle it," Fincham growled.

Ryan turned to the two prisoners.

"You're replacing the guards on the commander's car and your own car," he explained. "We've got the commander. Padre Costanzo and Captain Stein are in there with him. There's nobody on the next car at the moment but from there on back there's a Kraut on every car. So if and when we stop, stay where I put you. Don't talk to anybody, including me, and try not to let any of the guards get a good look at you. Got that?"

Both nodded, plainly nervous.

"Takes guts to be up here," Ryan said reassuringly. "I appreciate your help. Just sit tight. Colonel Fincham and I'll do the rest."

When he had posted the men, Ryan crawled back to the next car with Fincham. Fincham sat in the guard's position and Ryan climbed down between the cars.

"Twenty guards to go," he said. "Plus the one in the cab. I make it about fifty, sixty miles to Florence. We go through at least four stations before we get there. One of 'em should be coming up any minute. We'll knock off until we pass it."

Ryan remained close to the ground when the train stopped in the next station, Terontola, ready to dash to Klement's car if the guards left their posts. The train paused only briefly and none of them did, though the Germans called out to each other from car to car, complaining as soldiers do. When they were moving again, Ryan climbed back up, his head even with the top of the car.

"We'll alternate from here on out," he said. "One can fill in for the guard and keep his eyes peeled for stations while the other one works."

"I believe it's my turn at the wicket," Fincham said.

Ryan offered Fincham his length of silk. Fincham shook his head.

"Shan't need it," he said.

"They hunch over," Ryan warned. "To get out of the wind. And the last one was sleeping flat on his back."

"I'll cope, Herr Oberst," Fincham said cheerily.

He crawled back toward the next guard. Ryan replaced him on the end of the car and watched him go. When Fincham was half a car-length away his body lost its distinguishable outline in the darkness but was nevertheless visible. If the guard looked around he would know someone was on the car with him. The guard himself was discernible but only as a lump of thickened darkness.

Ryan watched attentively as the lump which was Fincham merged with that which was the guard. This was what the German on the next car would also be able to see if he chanced to look around. Ryan heard no sounds of struggle, only the familiar rush of wind and creak and click of metal.

In a moment Fincham came crawling back, dragging a limp body.

"Piece of cake," he murmured. "Neck like a bloody chicken's."

"Let's get him down," Ryan said. "I'll congratulate you later."

They worked smoothly together this time, getting the car door open and the body inside without difficulty. Ryan chose Lieutenant Carter to get into the German uniform.

"You've already had a dry run as an Ite," he said.

The train churned through the night, now speeding along in the level valleys, now slowing as it climbed or skirted foothills of the Apennines, pausing at sidings as faster trains sped by, stopping at times for ten or fifteen minutes. At the longer stops the guards climbed down but, obeying the orders Klement had given them at Chiusi, remained close to their stations.

Alternating as lookout and executioner, they had disposed of five more guards and Ryan was in a boxcar with the body of the latest victim when Fincham thrust his head down into the car and said, "We're amongst buildings of some sort."

"Damn," said Ryan. "I didn't expect Florence quite so soon."

The dead guard's uniform had been removed but the man who was to put it on was still in his underwear.

"Get on top quick!" Ryan ordered. "Don't try to get dressed. Slip on the greatcoat and take the uniform with you. Fincham, get between the cars. I'll stay here until we know what's going on."

He boosted the prisoner to the roof and pulled the door almost shut, blocking it with his foot. The train was creeping now past outlines of low buildings, smokestacks, and strings of boxcars broken by an occasional open space. It made a jolting stop alongside a string of boxcars. Ryan was out of the door and running after sliding the door shut behind him. He did not trust the prisoners to remain inside.

It was quiet outside and dark except for a sprinkle of yellow lights close to the ground. There was no sign of human activity among the dark shapes of the boxcars on the next siding. Ryan rapped on the door of the commander's car.

"It's me, Colonel Ryan," he said in a low voice.

The door slid open and Costanzo's voice whispered, "Am Ah glad to see you!"

"Everything okay in there?" he asked.

"Fine," Stein's voice called from the darkness. "Where are we?"

"Florence, maybe. The outskirts. I'm not sure."

Ryan climbed into the car and slid the door shut.

"You can turn the lights on now," he said.

Klement was lying in his bed, his face sullen, his pudgy arms folded across his stomach. Stein was sitting at the table, his chin propped on one hand. The other held Klement's pistol. The radio operator was stretched out on the boxes, covered to the chin with the lap robe, a pillow under his head. His face was wooden but his burning eyes betrayed his hatred.

"How's it going out there, Colonel?" Stein asked.

"We've got nine of ours on the cars now," Ryan answered. "Fourteen to go. Had any trouble?"

"Private Pleschke's been giving the major a hard time," Stein said, nodding toward the radio operator. "Called him a traitor and a coward and some other things I never learned in college German. No way for an enlisted man to address a field grade officer. I don't know what the Wehrmacht is coming to."

Klement, understanding much of what Stein said, took it seriously and sat up.

"You have heard," he said stiffly. "This schwein . . ."

He pointed angrily at his radio operator.

"You permit this, Herr Oberst?"

"I haven't got time for your troubles, Major," said Ryan. "We've got a lot to do."

He knew that he could no longer keep the guards confined to their stations when the train reached Florence. But he could not permit them to mingle with the prisoners in German uniform nor to get too close a look at Klement's constant escort. The station would be blacked out but none of the false guards could stand close inspection.

"How long have your men been together?" he demanded of Klement.

"Since last night," Costanzo translated. "They were pulled out of different headquarters units for this detail."

"Good," Ryan said. "That helps some. But we still can't let 'em roam around at will."

He gave instructions swiftly. Klement was to walk along the train giving his men their orders for Florence. Klement's sergeant should be doing this, Ryan knew, but the sergeant had been among the first four Germans killed.

The prisoners in German uniforms, on the first nine cars, were to descend immediately to the offside of the train. The fourteen surviving Germans were to descend on the other side, thus keeping the train between the real and the pretended.

Stein was to accompany Ryan and Klement to make sure Klement told his men only what he had been ordered. Costanzo was to remain in the boxcar until Fincham came back with further instructions.

Outside, Ryan climbed to the top of each car with his own man on it and whispered his instructions to them. Klement grew pale when he heard the guard on his car speak English. Ryan sent Fincham back to pick up Costanzo and go forward to the locomotive.

"Get the guard out of sight of the engineer and knock him off," Ryan whispered. "Then have Padre find out where we are and how long we're supposed to be here. Get the Kraut's uniform and hide him in the front car with the others."

Fincham trotted forward to the commander's car while Ryan walked on with Klement. He and Stein remained close to the cars, out of sight of the Germans sitting on top.

Fincham and Costanzo joined him as he was returning to the commander's car. Fincham had a uniform under his arm.

"This place is just a few miles outside of Florence," said Costanzo. "We'll be here another ten minutes. We're waiting to let a train by. We'll pull out as soon as it does."

"Let's get back to the car and go over what we've got to do in Florence," Ryan said.

Fincham walked ahead and slid the door open. He froze in the act of vaulting in.

"He's gone!" he cried.

"What!" Ryan demanded, pushing by him.

The spot where Private Pleschke had lain was empty except for a twisted strip of silk.

XVII

Ryan's consternation lasted only an instant. He stared
at the twist of silk, his mind racing. Only one strip meant the
German had not freed himself completely of his bonds. Since
he was gone, it meant his feet were freed. The German had not
waited to untie his hands and thus handicapped he would be
slowed down. Pleschke could not have run along the train in
either direction without encountering either himself or Fincham.
The German could only have crawled under the boxcar and
away or slipped under the cars on the next siding. When a man
was in a tearing hurry his instinct was to move in a straight line.
Pleschke would have jumped out the door and kept going. He
would have crawled under the cars on the next siding.

"Stein," Ryan snapped, "get Klement inside and keep him
there. Padre, get up there with the engineer. Fincham, come
with me."

With Fincham at his heels, he crawled under the string of
boxcars and found himself facing a long, low building.

"That way," he said, nudging Fincham to his left. "Check
the doors. If they're locked, check the back of the building. I'll
go the other way."

Ryan ran along the building, trying doors. All locked. A high
mesh fence topped with barbed wire extended from the end of
the building. If Pleschke had come this way he could not have

climbed the fence with his hands tied and must be somewhere among the boxcars. Fincham came running up behind Ryan.

"There's a bloody great fence," he said. "The bugger must still be about."

"Check the cars from here on back," Ryan said. "I'll go the other way."

Ryan moved slowly along the boxcars, crouching to peer beneath them. If Pleschke had climbed inside one of them they would never find him before the prison train moved on. He heard a train in the distance. It must be the one for which they were waiting, he thought. He had to find Pleschke before it went by and the prison train had a clear track.

A smear of white on the ground caught his eye. He ran to it. A twist of silk from Klement's sheet. Pleschke had come this way. Ryan peered into the surrounding night trying to pierce the darkness by sheer force of will. He saw nothing but the outline of the fence on one side and the bulky shapes of boxcars on the other. Pleschke was somewhere up ahead, either hiding among the cars or looking along the fence for a way out.

The train on the main track was close now and moving fast. Ryan increased his pace to a trot. The boxcars shook with the passage of the train on the main line. The train sped by with a long, diminishing rush of sound. The boxcars creaked for a moment after the train passed, and the siding was still again. Ryan strained to hear breathing or scraping feet. Back at the prison train a voice called out in German, followed by a cackle of laughter. One of the guards had made a wry soldier's joke.

Pebbles rattled a car-length ahead. Ryan tensed. The noise was not repeated. Ryan walked toward the noise and went beyond its point of origin before he stopped, deliberately offering his back to anyone who might be lurking in the shadows. He waited.

Pebbles rattled, then came a quick patter of feet. Ryan crouched and whirled just in time to avoid the downward smash of a heavy stick. Pleschke, wraithlike in his long white underwear, jerked the club back to launch another blow. Before it could descend Ryan hurled himself shoulder first against the slighter man. Pleschke was dashed back against a boxcar. Without waiting to see the effect of the impact, Ryan was upon him, his thumbs digging into the German's throat. Pleschke tore at his wrists with frenzied hands.

Ryan pressed harder and beat the German's head against the car. The locomotive whistle signaled imminent departure. Pleschke was limp now, his eyes protruding. Fincham came pounding up.

"The bloody train's . . ." he cried. "Oh. Good show."

"Slide the car door open," Ryan said quickly.

He tossed Pleschke's body inside and Fincham slid the door shut again. Together they raced for the slowly moving prison train.

"Get back to your car!" Ryan panted. "Come to Klement's car as soon as we stop rolling in Florence."

They separated, Ryan running for the commander's car. Stein was standing in the door. He stretched a hand to Ryan as Ryan ran alongside. Ryan's feet dragged along the roadbed. With Stein's help he pulled himself inside and lay face down, gasping for air.

"You had me worried," said Stein. "Did you get him?"

Ryan sat up and nodded.

"Tell Klement that," he said.

Klement took the news of his radio operator's death with mixed emotions. Ryan was not surprised. Klement believed he would be killed if the train were retaken. And Pleschke's death not only punished the young soldier for his insults but also removed the only eyewitness to Klement's abject submission.

Ryan put Klement in a chair and sat facing him, almost knee to knee, Stein at his side to translate.

"I want you to pay careful attention, Major," Ryan said. "Your life depends on whether you do exactly as I say. When we reach Florence you will go wherever you have to go as if everything is normal. I'll be right there with you. If you make a false move I'll kill you. I'll have nothing to lose by doing it. If you co-operate, you live. You have my word for that. It's as simple as that. Co-operate, you live. Don't, you die. Is that clear?"

Klement watched Ryan's face earnestly as he spoke, then watched Stein just as earnestly as Stein translated. When Stein finished, Klement nodded.

"Versteh'," he said eagerly.

"You're a wise man, Major Klement," Ryan said. "You may live to a ripe old age yet."

The car clacked slowly over the rails. After a while it stopped completely, then moved in the opposite direction.

"We're backing in," said Ryan.

He looked at his watch. It was ten minutes after eleven.

"Getting sleepy, Captain?" he asked.

Stein shook his head.

"I'm too scared to get sleepy," he said.

When the train stopped Ryan cracked the door and looked out into semi-darkness glowing with purplish blackout lights.

"Stein, go get Padre Costanzo," Ryan said. "Talk German to him."

Stein left at a trot as Fincham came up to join Ryan.

"As soon as the padre gets here I'm taking Klement into the station to pick up his schedule," Ryan said. "You stay here and keep an eye on things."

"I don't like it," said Fincham. "Not half. What's to keep him from turning you in?"

"Got a better suggestion, Colonel?"

Fincham shrugged.

Stein returned with Costanzo and Ryan ordered Klement from the car. The guards had all climbed down. Following Klement's orders, those on the last fourteen cars had climbed down on one side, those on the first nine on the other. The prisoners in the rear cars were kicking the sides and shouting. Those in the front cars, knowing the situation, remained silent. The contrast spelled danger. The guards might wonder why some of the prisoners were behaving themselves. Ryan sent Stein along the cars to warn them to join in the clamor. The din increased all along the train. Klement looked inquiringly at Ryan.

"What is to do, Herr Oberst?" he asked.

"Keep 'em in," said Ryan.

"They've been locked in since Rome," Costanzo protested. "It must be awful in those cars by now."

"Can't help it, Padre. We can't open the doors just yet. If somebody decided to make a break for it we'd have security troops all over our necks."

The clamor was attracting attention all over the station. Ryan could hear Italian and German voices raised in inquiry.

"Damn," he said. "They'll have the SS on our necks one way or another. Klement . . ."

Before he could complete the sentence an Italian officer came hurrying up to them. He spoke angrily to Klement, gesticulating. Klement shook his head. He did not speak Italian. Costanzo interpreted for both. The word "Italiani" kept recurring. Ryan knew the Italian officer was demanding to know if there were Italians locked in the boxcars. Costanzo summoned a grin from somewhere and motioned the officer to draw closer to a car and listen. The officer listened to the unmistakably American voices and, with a final disapproving gesture, left them.

"Good going, Padre," said Ryan. "And Klement, you played it smart. Keep it up and you won't get hurt. Tell the troops on this side of the train they can take a fifteen-minute break to find themselves something hot to drink."

The Germans slung their rifles and trooped off into the gloom, delighted with Klement's unexpected and uncharacteristic solicitude. As soon as they were gone Ryan slid open the door of the first carload of prisoners.

"You can hold it down now, men," he said. "But you're going to have to stick it out inside a few more hours."

The men fell silent, grumbling. They still harbored deep resentment against Ryan but realized they were completely dependent upon him.

"Anybody here speak Italian?" Ryan asked.

Several voices replied in the affirmative.

"One of you slip back to the commander's car and tell Colonel Fincham I sent you to put on a Kraut uniform and get up to the cab."

Ryan climbed to the top of the next car and called in a low voice through the mesh-covered window, ordering the men to quiet down and telling them they would have to remain locked in a few hours longer. He went from car to car with the same instructions until he reached the first not under prisoner control.

"You men in there," he said. "Listen. This is Colonel Ryan."

"Hey, guys!" a startled voice cried. "Did you hear that? Von Ryan's loose!"

"Hold it down," Ryan snapped. "You want to advertise it all over Florence? Shut up and listen. There's no time for questions. Colonel Fincham and I are taking the train. When we've got all the Krauts we're all bailing out."

The men broke into excited babble.

"I said hold it down!" Ryan whispered sharply. "After we get going, open up when you hear a rap on the door. I'll have unlocked it. Pull in the Kraut we hand down and get somebody into his uniform. We'll pull him up and tell him what to do. You'll be locked in here a few more hours so make the best of it."

When he had visited every car he trotted back to rejoin Klement and Costanzo. The guards were drifting back in twos and threes. Ryan kept his back to them until they reached their posts farther down the train. He took a deep breath.

"Well, Padre," he said. "We can't put it off any longer. Let's go to the dispatcher's office and get it over with."

"It's called the Ufficio Movimento," Costanzo said. "The engineer told me. We got right cozy."

They walked across the crowded station, detouring around passenger trains and freight cars in which sat German troops with their legs dangling out the open doorways. The Italians in the passenger cars stared at them with impassive faces.

Costanzo walked abreast of Klement, with Ryan a pace behind. Uniformed Germans and Italians mingled with civilians on the main platform. None favored the approaching trio with more than a casual glance. Nevertheless, Ryan knew that if Klement summoned up his courage and moved quickly enough he could slip away in the crowd before he could be restrained. Ryan called a halt.

"Padre," he whispered. "Remind Klement that I'm desperate. I'll shoot first and ask questions afterward."

When Costanzo translated Ryan's message Klement looked back at the colonel in mixed fear and malevolence.

"Don't look at me again!" Ryan grated.

Costanzo walked just ahead of Klement, blocking his path while appearing deferentially to be clearing a way for him, with Ryan just behind, his Schmeisser slung from his shoulder but clamped between side and elbow, ready for action. A Luftwaffe captain inspected them as they brushed past, smiling with proprietary pride at Ryan's soldierly bearing and Teutonic visage.

Costanzo asked a uniformed Italian the location of the Ufficio Movimento. The Italian looked at him a moment before answering and Ryan tensed. The Italian was not suspicious, however. He pointed out the way with such poor grace it was obvious he merely did not like Germans.

A German soldier inside the door of the office came briskly to attention and saluted when Klement entered. The major was stiff and noticeably ill at ease. Sweat was beginning to form on his upper lip. He was so intent on avoiding any action which Ryan might interpret as an attempt to give the alarm that he brushed by the soldier without acknowledging the salute.

A large wall diagram behind the counter marked the position and movements of trains in the station with electric lights. Klement approached a dispatcher already conferring with an Italian in a trainman's uniform. Costanzo turned to Ryan, pointing surreptitiously at the Italian and then at himself. At the same time his lips soundlessly formed the words, "Our engineer." Ryan caught enough of Costanzo's meaning to understand.

The engineer smiled when he saw Costanzo and called out a

greeting. He was a pleasantly ugly man of middle age with a pitted bulbous nose. Costanzo chatted with him while the dispatcher checked his traffic control chart and filled out a form, which he gave the engineer. Costanzo spoke to the engineer, who said something to the dispatcher. The dispatcher made a copy of the order and gave it to Klement. While they were so engaged, Ryan turned around to inspect the German soldier. The German smiled and spoke. Ryan looked quickly at Costanzo. Costanzo raised one shoulder a trifle in a gesture which told Ryan there was nothing to worry about.

Klement and the engineer checked their watches with the clock on the wall. Ryan checked his, too. Two minutes slow. He pulled back his sleeve to set it. When he looked up, the engineer and the German soldier were staring. His flyer's chronometer was not the sort of watch a German soldier would be wearing. Costanzo understood the situation at once. He nudged the engineer in the ribs and nodded toward Ryan, grinning.

"Americane," he said.

He extended a finger as if shooting.

"Bim," he said.

"Multi bene," the engineer said, holding thumb and forefinger together in a circle of admiration.

The soldier furtively worked a worn billfold from a tunic pocket and thumbed it open to show a wad of lira notes.

"Vier tausend," he said under his breath.

Ryan shook his head.

"Funf," the soldier said.

Klement turned and looked at the soldier. The soldier folded the wallet, thrust it into his tunic, and looked away quickly. Klement and the dispatcher exchanged Fascist salutes. The engineer shook hands with the dispatcher and Costanzo and left.

As Klement turned to follow, an involuntary deep, agonized sigh escaped him. The German soldier looked at him with renewed interest. Something he saw made him stiffen. Ryan slipped his finger inside the trigger guard of his Schmeisser and glanced from the soldier to Klement following the soldier's line of sight. Klement was perfectly still, not making a signal of any kind. The soldier was staring at his vomit-stained blouse.

Ryan moved close to Costanzo and spoke with his lips scarcely moving.

"Tell Klement to ask the soldier what he's staring at. And eat him out for leaving that tunic pocket unbuttoned. He better make it good."

Costanzo whispered to Klement with a show of deference.

Klement squared his shoulders and snapped at the soldier. The soldier pulled his feet together with a thump and stood at attention, his eyes fixed straight ahead. Shielded by Klement's thick body, Ryan nudged the major toward the door. It was like touching an inflated balloon. As they went out, Ryan turned and winked conspiratorially at the soldier. The soldier returned the wink and raised a thumb in a derisive gesture at Klement's departing back.

Fincham and Stein were waiting anxiously in the commander's car.

"You actually brought it off," Fincham said. "How did you manage it?"

"Klement was a perfect little gentleman," Ryan said. "And Padre here is the slickest opportunist you ever saw."

"Why must we Jesuits always be burdened with that slander?" Costanzo asked wryly.

"Padre, tell Klement to get into a clean uniform. The one he's got on almost gave us away. Then go over the schedule with Colonel Fincham and me."

Ryan and Fincham leaned over the table with the map and the dispatcher's form between them. They were scheduled to leave at twenty after twelve, Costanzo said. It was then eleven after. They were to make two stops before Bologna, Costanzo continued, both only a few miles north of Florence, and then have a straight run in. They were due at Bologna at two forty-five. Ryan measured the distance on the map.

"That's a straight run of about fifty miles from Prato to

Bologna," he said. "And if we're not due until two forty-five we won't be making too many knots. If we can get all the Krauts before Bologna we'll bail out, right after we pull out for Verona."

"What about your chap in the locomotive?" Fincham demanded.

"I'll trade places with him at Bologna. At the first stop after that I'll just walk off and not come back."

"Suppose Jerry learns we've all buggered off before you've the opportunity?"

"Does the prospect disturb you, Colonel?"

"I shouldn't have expected so," Fincham said thoughtfully, "but as a matter of fact it does. It would seem a pity if you brought this off and then lost your own chance."

"You won't get an argument from me over that," said Ryan.

"We'll draw straws for the honor of being the last man to leave," Fincham said.

"We'll cross that bridge when we come to it. But thanks for the offer, Colonel."

Ryan sent Costanzo to the cab to replace the man he had posted there earlier. When the locomotive whistle sounded its signal for departure and the guards, both real and pretended, had mounted to their perches, Ryan left Stein to guard Klement and led Fincham and the new man back along the train. He posted the new man on the car Fincham had occupied and had Fincham stand on the coupling between it and the car ahead.

"I'll be between the next two back," he said. "I'll wait for you there until we get out of the station."

Fincham joined him as soon as the train cleared the station.

"We've got less than two and a half hours minus stops to get fourteen Krauts," Ryan said. "Let's get going."

"As I recall, it's my turn," Fincham replied.

"Look, Colonel, do you consider this a game?" Ryan demanded. "We're not trying to run up scores. Is that clear?"

"Pity you're such a perishing ass personally," Fincham replied blithely. "When you're such jolly good company in a do."

They moved about their task with deadly precision, needing to exchange few words as they stole from car to car killing Germans and substituting prisoners for them. It went more quickly now that the prisoners inside the cars already knew what was expected of them. At one-thirty the train was deep in the Apennines, toiling up steep grades in the chill darkness. The guards, huddled in their greatcoats, had been easy prey. Eight remained, and with an hour and fifteen minutes to go Ryan hoped to get them before Bologna.

He felt an enormous weariness which did not come entirely from sheer exertion and lack of sleep. There was a horrible and enervating monotony in what he was doing, killing one unwary human being after another and handling their bodies like so much baggage. It appeared to bother Fincham not at all. If anything, he grew more vigorous and jaunty as the toll of guards mounted.

It was one forty-five and there were six guards remaining as Ryan pulled himself painfully along the top of a car, his elbows, knees, and ankles chafed and burning from hours of scraping. A tunic button grated on the cartop. Twenty feet away the guard, who had been dozing, jerked awake and looked back. Ryan flattened himself against the roof, not breathing. The guard was on his feet now, crouched and swaying, his rifle leveled from a hip.

"Wer ist da?" he called nervously.

Ryan did not move. He could see the guard outlined against the darkness. Could the guard see him?

"Wer ist da?" the guard called again, taking a step toward Ryan.

Ryan realized the guard could see him. The name "Heinz" came to him from what seemed the dim recesses of memory though he knew he had heard it only a few hours before when he was locked inside.

"Heinz," he said, getting slowly to his feet.

"Heinz?" the German repeated, puzzled and suspicious.

He did not lower his rifle.

"Komm her," he ordered, craning his head forward in an attempt to make out Ryan's face in the darkness.

Ryan advanced slowly, his head down, tensed to attack as soon as he drew close enough.

"Halt!" the guard ordered.

Ryan stopped in his tracks. The guard moved warily toward him. Ryan launched himself at the German, sweeping aside the rifle with his forearm and ramming the top of his head into the guard's face. The guard's rifle clattered to the roof as Ryan seized the front of his greatcoat to keep him from reeling backward. He dragged the German down and gripped his throat.

"Was ist los?" the guard on the next car called.

Ryan did not answer.

"Was ist los?" the guard called more anxiously.

He began moving forward toward Ryan and the downed guard. When Ryan was sure the downed German was dead, he picked up the man's rifle and waited for the other guard, his head pulled as far as possible into his upturned tunic collar as if against the cold. When the guard reached the end of his car Ryan pointed silently at the sprawled figure and motioned for the guard to join him. With a cry, the German leaped across to Ryan's car and bent over the body. Ryan broke his neck with a chop of the rifle butt.

The guards on the last cars were calling out to each other. They had heard the second man's nervous challenge. Fincham came scuttling back on his hands and knees.

"Run into a bit of trouble, old boy?" he whispered. "I say, two of the perishers. Good show."

"The guards are in a flap," Ryan said. "I better get back there before they start nosing around."

He ran back to the next car and sat down on the end with his feet dangling. The guard on the car in back had started forward to investigate. When he saw the post was manned he stopped and called out. Ryan raised his hand in a gesture of reassurance and the guard returned to his station.

After a few minutes Fincham joined Ryan.

"Four of the buggers left," he said. "How much time have we?"

"About forty-five minutes," Ryan whispered back.

"Let's finish the lot."

Ryan shook his head.

"They're too jittery," he said. "We've got to let 'em calm down a little. And it'll take us ten, fifteen minutes to get the two we've got into the cars. If we try to get the rest it'll cut it too fine. We'd never get 'em out of sight before Bologna."

"We could chuck them off instead of putting them inside. And bugger off before Bologna."

"It'd be like blazing a trail. We'll just have to wait."

The train entered a tunnel as they were lowering the first guard into a boxcar. The smoke was choking and they had to wait for a few minutes to clear their lungs and eyes before disposing of the second. When they had their own men atop the cars they crawled back to the coupling at the end of the commander's car to await their arrival in Bologna.

They pulled into the station at two forty-seven with Germans still mounting guard on the last four cars.

—XVIII—

Ryan was on the ground before the train stopped rolling. He hustled Klement to the rear cars with Stein translating his instructions as they hurried along. The four Germans were to be ordered down to guard the offside of the train. The prisoners in German uniform were already following instructions and climbing down on the platform side. Klement grew increasingly subdued as their number mounted. When he realized only four of his twenty-nine soldiers survived he licked his lips and looked imploringly at Ryan.

When the guards had been posted, Ryan joined Fincham in the commander's car and sent Stein for Costanzo. He studied Klement carefully. There seemed to be more danger that Klement would betray them by folding completely than by any act of will. The major was pale and dry-lipped and his eyes would not remain still.

"Pull yourself together, Major," Ryan said reassuringly. "You're doing fine."

When Costanzo arrived he had the priest repeat his words in German. A little color returned to Klement's face but he was still shaky. Ryan gave him a tumbler of wine which Klement tossed off gratefully. His eyes stopped their roving.

"This will be the last time I'll need your help, Major," Ryan said, keeping all hint of threat from his voice. "If you just get us out of Bologna you haven't got a thing in the world to worry about."

The engineer was with the dispatcher when they reached the crowded Ufficio Movimento. They were arguing. When Klement and Costanzo joined them the dispatcher spoke to Klement in German, jabbing his finger emphatically at a clipboard on the counter. The engineer was furious. He threw his cap down on the counter, scowling, and turned to Costanzo as if for sympathy. A look of hastily concealed relief and triumph crossed Klement's face. Costanzo turned to Ryan with an expression of dismay, shrugging his shoulders helplessly, unable to give Ryan an explanation on the spot.

When they were outside he explained.

"We're being held here until morning," he said. "The line's been sabotaged up north and traffic's backed up all over the place."

"We can't afford to stay overnight," Ryan said. "It would mean a daylight run all the way to the Brenner. Isn't there an alternate route?"

"That's what the engineer was so sore about. He's supposed to go off duty at Verona. That's where he lives. And the dispatcher told him the alternate routes were all jammed."

"We've got to get out of here," Ryan said. "That's all there is to it."

Back in the commander's car he explained the situation to Fincham.

"I don't know what you're in such a flap about," Fincham said. "We'll have Von Ignatz send his men into town for the night and then we'll simply open the doors and slip off silently into the night by twos and threes like wogs folding their bloody tents. Piece of cake."

"A thousand men? In a busy station?"

"Have you a better notion, Colonel?"

"Let's have a look at that map," said Ryan.

He studied it a moment.

"We can't go north but maybe we can go east or west," he

said. "We've got to get back on the road where we can finish the guards and take off."

He pointed at the rail line running northwest through Modena and Parma.

"Why don't we ask to be routed this way? They can switch us north when the traffic thins down."

"The dispatcher's already turned us down on that, Cuhnel," said Costanzo. "Traffic's moving fine through Parma all the way to Milan but he wouldn't give the engineer a thing going north anywhere along the line."

Ryan rubbed his chin thoughtfully and bent over the map again.

"Why not?" he murmured, as if to himself. "We'll have him route us to Milan," he said in a louder voice.

"Milan?" Fincham cried. "Are you around the bend?"

"One way or another we've got to get rolling. It doesn't matter if it's toward Verona or where. Just so we can get out into open country and bail out before dawn."

"They'd never permit a train bound for Verona to alter for Milan," Fincham protested. "It's the wrong bloody direction. They'd not be so stupid."

"They might if we had the right story," Ryan said. "Between the capitulation and the German take-over and the general confusion they hardly know if they're coming or going. Padre, how's your written German?"

"Fine, if Ah can print. My script's nothing to brag about."

"This will be printed. I want you to write what I tell you on one of those radio message forms, only express it in German construction."

Costanzo sat down at the folding table while Ryan paced back and forth, hands behind his back.

"You are instructed to proceed to Milan without delay," he said.

He waited while Costanzo translated his words into German on the message form.

"At Milan you will take on twelve Allied officer prisoners and fresh security troops," he continued, "and receive special instructions regarding a consignment from Gruppenfuehrer . . . Padre, what's a good German name, reasonably common but not too?"

"Dietrich?"

"That'll do. . . . regarding a consignment from Gruppenfuehrer Dietrich to be delivered personally by you immediately upon arrival in Innsbruck en route to originally planned destination. When you've got that down, sign it Obergruppenfuehrer something-or-other, SS, Rome. Not too legibly, in case somebody takes a close look."

Costanzo handed the message form to Ryan when he finished.

"Looks official enough to me," said Ryan. "I hope the dispatcher doesn't know any more about this kind of thing than I do."

"Seems a bit thin to me," Fincham said doubtfully.

"You'd be surprised what you can get by with when things are in a flap and you act like you know what you're doing," Ryan said. "And the worst that can happen is that they turn us down."

Ryan sat Klement down with Costanzo and began coaching him in his role. Klement shook his head doggedly when it was first explained to him.

"He says it's impossible," Costanzo translated, "and you'll blame him when it fails."

"Everything will be fine if you do exactly as I say," Ryan said. His voice took on an edge. "You've just got to go into it with confidence. Remember how you racked us back when we first got on this train? That's the way you're to talk to the dispatcher. Understand?"

Klement nodded unhappily, anything but confident. Ryan nodded toward the wine bottle and Fincham poured a drink. Klement drank it down and held out the empty glass for another filling. Fincham looked at Ryan. Ryan nodded. Klement drank the second glass more slowly.

"Now," said Ryan. "Pretend I'm the dispatcher."

Klement stared blankly when Costanzo translated.

"Pretend I'm the dispatcher," Ryan ordered again. "And you're the Kommandant. Over all. Responsible only to the Fuehrer. Remember?"

"I am Kommandant," Klement said unconvincingly. "Over all."

"You'll have to do better than that," Ryan said.

Klement looked wistfully at the wine bottle.

"He'll make himself tiddly," Fincham said.

"When we get back from the Ufficio Movimento, Herr Kommandant," Ryan said. "Now, once again."

He drilled Klement in what he was to do and say until the major acquired a degree of confidence. Klement was to tell the dispatcher he had radioed his headquarters in Rome to advise his superiors of the delay and that the matter had been referred to Schutzstaffel headquarters, resulting in new orders from the Obergruppenfuehrer. He was to hint strongly that the real reason for the rerouting was to pick up the personal consignment from Gruppenfuehrer Dietrich.

"And remember," Ryan said. "If the dispatcher gives you any lip, rack him back. He's an Italian civilian and you're a major in the glorious Wehrmacht."

Klement nodded vigorously when it was translated for him. Though he was not tipsy, the wine had relaxed him.

"Mind the store 'til we get back, Colonel," Ryan told Fincham.

The engine had already been detached from the train when Ryan climbed down from the boxcar with Klement and Costanzo. Unless they could get another they were helplessly immobile. Though he might be able to avert a change of guards in Bologna, Ryan knew it would be impossible to free the prisoners even if he and Fincham managed to eliminate the remaining four Germans in the station. The prisoners could leave the train only in open country and under cover of darkness.

The dispatcher shook his head when Klement presented his radioed order. Klement jutted his chin and insisted, browbeating the dispatcher. In the midst of his harangue he shot a quick look at Ryan, seeking approval. The dispatcher was intimidated by Klement's attack but instead of complying with his request spread his hands helplessly and picked up a telephone. He spoke rapidly, gesturing as if speaking face to face with the party on the other end. Ryan looked to Costanzo for a clue. Costanzo raised one shoulder a quarter-inch and crossed his fingers behind the concealment of his leg.

They waited.

There was constant movement in and out of the Ufficio Movimento—trainmen, other civilians, Italian and German military. Ryan studied every newcomer intently. Who had the dispatcher called and what was the subject of the conversation? The dispatcher could not have suspected anything was wrong or Costanzo would have known it and signaled a warning.

They waited for five agonizing minutes, Klement's confidence gradually oozing away. He was sweating lightly now, and his eyes began roving. The dispatcher looked up and beckoned when a middle-aged Italian civilian with a Fascist party button in his lapel entered with a short, well-knit German colonel. Ryan came immediately to attention, though holding his Schmeisser so that a slight movement would bring it to bear on Klement.

The colonel looked up approvingly at Ryan and said something to the Italian, who looked at Ryan and nodded agreement. Klement appeared confused, almost dazed, when the two joined him and he hesitated a moment before returning their Fascist salutes. The colonel spoke to him and Klement muttered an answer. Ryan was watching Costanzo's face. When it did not change expression Ryan knew that nothing damaging had been said. From the colonel's manner, it appeared he had merely been inquiring about Klement's health. Anyone not knowing the circumstances might assume Klement was ill. He looked it.

The Italian held out his hand and the dispatcher gave him the radio message form. The Italian read it quickly, shook his head, and gave it to the colonel. Ryan's hand stole to the trigger of the Schmeisser as the colonel read the message. The colonel said, "Gruppenfuehrer Dietrich?", shrugged, and returned the message form to the Italian. The Italian shook his head again and said something to Klement. Ryan understood enough to know the Italian did not want to honor the request. The colonel appeared unconcerned. The authenticity of the message apparently was not being questioned. Klement's eyes roved nervously to Ryan. Ryan tilted his Schmeisser significantly. Klement wet his lips and spoke insistently to the Italian. The Italian lost his temper and began berating Klement.

The colonel's manner underwent an abrupt change. He silenced the Italian with a curt word and began speaking coldly and emphatically. He took the message form from the resentful Italian, scrawled something on it, and thrust it at the dispatcher. The dispatcher looked at the Italian civilian, who nodded reluctantly, then whirled and stalked angrily from the office. The colonel smiled and shook hands with Klement. Klement, breathing easier now, managed a wan smile.

When the colonel turned to leave, Klement's hand rose in an involuntary gesture of appeal which he halted abruptly with a fearful look at Ryan when he realized what he had done. The colonel did not notice it, however. He was smiling at Ryan with the same proprietary pride the Luftwaffe captain had displayed in the station at Florence.

The colonel stopped in front of Ryan and spoke to him. Ryan came to attention again. The colonel had asked him a question. Ryan caught the word "wo." He knew it meant "where." The colonel must have asked where he was from. The colonel was waiting for an answer.

"Hamburg, Herr Oberst," Ryan said, pronouncing the words carefully.

Costanzo blanched at his words and the colonel's jaw dropped. He stared at Ryan a moment, then suddenly threw back his shoulders and roared with laughter. Wiping the tears from his eyes, he spoke a few words and patted Ryan on the back before leaving. Ryan looked to Costanzo for an explanation. Costanzo wagged his head slowly from side to side.

Klement and Costanzo conferred with the dispatcher, who was checking traffic reports and making phone calls. When, at last, he handed Klement his orders, Costanzo turned to Ryan with a look of dismay.

When they were safely outside he said, "It's bad, Cuhnel. They're routing us to Milan but things are so jammed up they can't give us an engine and crew until after five."

"We've got to have it sooner," Ryan said. "It's light by six and we'd never finish the job by then."

"Ah'm afraid that's it, Cuhnel," said Costanzo. "He tried but that's the best he could do."

"We'll try to work out something when we get back to the car," Ryan said. "Padre, what was that all about when the colonel talked to me back there?"

"Ah thought we'd had it for sure. He asked you where a magnificent German soldier like you would like to serve, in Italy or on the Eastern front. And you said Hamburg."

"I had to say something," Ryan said sheepishly. "What was that he said at the last?"

"If the Third Reich had ten thousand like you in Italy we would drive the enemy into the sea," Costanzo answered, grinning.

When they reached the train, Fincham demanded, "Well, did they laugh you out of the bloody office?"

"We're moving out," Ryan said. "To Milan."

Fincham stared incredulously.

"Only one catch to it," Ryan said. "Not until after five."

"Then we're no better off than before," Fincham said. "If we can't bugger off before dawn we've had it. We could get the last four while we're waiting and leave the train directly we're clear of Bologna."

"That's what I've been thinking," Ryan said. "And we've got to give the men in the cars a break to get the kinks out. I hadn't counted on 'em being locked in this long."

Stein, who was listening closely, yawned. Then they were all yawning except Klement, who was in his bed with a bottle of wine.

"Can you finish out the night, Fincham?" Ryan asked.

"I've gone thirty-six hours without a bloody wink in my time," Fincham replied, affronted.

"How about you, Padre? Stein?"

They nodded.

"First thing we'll do is let the men out to go to the latrine and to fill their water bottles," Ryan said. "Three cars at a time. We'll send the Krauts with 'em. If their own buddies are guarding 'em they might be tempted to wander off and foul up the whole deal. Soon's they're locked back in we'll go to work on the Krauts. Klement can order them in here one at a time and we'll do the rest. It's still going to cut it mighty fine. But I guess it can't be helped."

Klement was pried loose from his wine bottle and led outside to order his four surviving guards to escort groups of prisoners for water. The officers in German uniforms were sent out beyond the ends of the train as if to form a corridor against escape. By four-fifteen the prisoners were locked in their cars again and Ryan was ready to eliminate the last guards. Klement was snoring in his bed.

"Padre, wake him up and tell him to call one of his men in here," Ryan said.

Costanzo touched Klement's shoulder. The German did not move. Costanzo shook him, with no more effect. Ryan went to the bed and raised Klement to a sitting position by the front of his tunic. Klement was limp, his head lolling.

"Look here, Cuhnel," Costanzo said, raking two empty wine bottles from beneath the bed.

"Passed out!" said Ryan. "Stein, see what you can do with him."

Stein slapped Klement's face smartly, then lifted his eyelids and peered into his eyes.

"Plastered," he said. "Is there any coffee?"

"Must be," Ryan said. "He's got a year's supply of everything else."

Costanzo found some coffee and brewed it. He poured a cup for everyone. Ryan drank gratefully.

" 'Tisn't tea," Fincham said, "but it's better than nothing."

Stein raised Klement with an arm behind his back and held the cup to his lips. The coffee dripped down Klement's chin.

"He's *really* plastered," said Stein, "medically speaking."

"Do you think he's putting on?" Ryan demanded.

"No. He's out like a light."

Ryan looked at his watch.

"Four-thirty," he said. "We've got to get moving. Padre, do you think you could get the guards in here without tipping your hand?"

"Cuhnel, you're asking me to send men to their death," Costanzo said quietly.

"We've got twenty-four dead Germans stowed away in this train," Ryan answered just as quietly. "If we're caught, every one of us in German uniform will be shot. Possibly the whole trainload of us. Who would you prefer to send to his death?"

Costanzo sighed deeply.

"Ah think Ah could do it, Cuhnel," he said. "If Ah don't have to say too much."

"Thanks, Padre. I know it's not easy for you. Call the first one in."

Costanzo went out and, standing between two cars, summoned one of the guards who had returned to his post on the offside of the train. Fincham broke the German's neck as he was climbing into the car.

"Stein, take his uniform down to the fourth car from the end and get a man in it," Ryan ordered. "On your way back tell Padre to call another one."

Stein still had not returned when a jolt sent Ryan and Fincham sprawling. An engine had coupled onto the first boxcar. Costanzo thrust his head in the door.

"Looks like we'll be leaving before we thought," he said. "What now, Cuhnel?"

"Tell the men to get to their posts," Ryan ordered. "Then get up there with the engineer. Soon as Stein gets back Fincham and I'll get out between the cars."

Leaving Stein to guard the snoring Klement, Ryan and Fincham went to the rear of the train and mounted the couplings between cars. The train was motionless for several minutes, then it moved backward. After more minutes of backward motion, it stopped for a while, then moved forward, only to stop again. Then more minutes of backing, stopping, moving forward. It was five twenty-five before the train was out of the station at last and moving into open country.

Ryan and Fincham met on top of the fifth car from the end.

"We'll never get the men off before dawn," Ryan said. "Let's try to get the last three Krauts while it's still dark and we'll at least have the whole train."

When they had killed the guard on the third car from the end and replaced him with a prisoner, Ryan no longer needed to look at his watch to know that dawn was near. A narrow edge of gray, so faint that it merged with the surrounding darkness if stared at too intently, suffused the eastern horizon.

"In a few minutes it'll be light enough to see," Ryan said. "We'll have to get the last two without stopping to get one into a car. And hope we can get 'em inside before we hit a town. Keep right behind me. As soon as I get the next one, you go on by and knock off the last man. Let's go."

Before Ryan's man had stopped struggling Fincham crept by in a crouch. Ryan arranged the body so it would not roll from the car and crawled after Fincham. When he reached Fincham, the last guard was already sprawled at his feet, his head tilted at a sharp, grotesque angle.

Fincham leaped into the air and clicked his heels.

"Finito!" he cried exultantly.

Ryan had to grab him to keep him from toppling from the car when his foot struck the brake wheel. They shook hands solemnly. The guards were all dead now. Every one. They controlled the train.

The edge of gray on the horizon was broader now and no longer elusive. The countryside emerged slowly, taking form like a photographic negative in its bath of developer. Here and there spectral wisps of mist hung over low places. The train moved along easily through flat country, swaying with a lulling, cradle-like motion.

Ryan stood erect and stretched, for the first time realizing how utterly fatigued he was and how great had been the tension of the past hours. Except for the train noises there was only peace and stillness. Ryan had once parachuted from a burning B-25 and floated down from twelve thousand feet. His sensation now was the same blending of detachment, calm, and timelessness.

"What's the drill now?" Fincham demanded at his elbow.

Ryan was abruptly thrust back into awareness of time and place, of urgency.

"We've got to get our own men on the cars before we hit a town," he said.

Fincham yawned and stretched, then stiffened.

"May take a bit of doing," he said. "There's a town yonder."

—XIX—

Far up ahead a slender column glistened like a white thread dangling from the rim of the sky. Around it, at that distance and in that light little more than a smudge on the face of the pale morning, was a sprawling huddle of indistinct buildings among which the first tentative rays of the sun struck fire on window glass.

"Modena!" Ryan exclaimed. "We really made time."

He bent suddenly and pitched the dead German from the train.

"What the devil!" Fincham cried.

"See you later," Ryan called back over his shoulder, running forward toward the engine.

He pounded over the cars, leaping from one to the other without breaking stride. He began shouting to Costanzo when he reached the third car from the locomotive. Costanzo could not hear him above the roar of the engine. It was only when Ryan leaped to the tender, still shouting, that he was heard in the cab. Costanzo, the engineer and the fireman all turned and stared.

"Halt! Halt!" Ryan cried, gesturing violently toward the rear. "Mein Kamerad . . . gefallen!"

Costanzo, responding quickly, told the engineer to stop the train. The Italian, who knew no more German than Ryan, un-

derstood Ryan's words and gestures without translation and
was already bringing the train to a halt. Ryan pitched forward
to his aching knees. Regaining his balance, he leaped from the
tender with a jarring thud and motioned Costanzo to join him.

"We've run into a little trouble," he said in a low voice. "Nothing serious. Tell the engineer to back up, one of the guards
fell off. When you see my signal, tell him to stop. And then
get him away from the window so he can't see what's going on."

Costanzo nodded and climbed back into the cab. Fincham
was running forward on top of the cars and Ryan trotted to meet
him. When the train started rolling he swung aboard a car, holding on to the rungs.

"Get on back and when we stop shove the last Kraut off," he
told Fincham when the Englishman reached his car. "Then get
down fast and get both of 'em inside cars. I want our men on
top of those cars in a hurry. Come on back to the commander's
car after they're in place."

Ryan hung on the side of the car, facing the rear. When the
end of the train neared the body of the German he had thrown
from the car he turned and signaled to Costanzo. The train
stopped almost immediately. Moments later a body came tumbling to the ground, making a sound like a belch when it hit.
Fincham scrambled down after it. He slid over the door of the
next to last car and tossed the body inside.

"Ticket to Blighty," he said cheerfully.

He did the same at the last car with the remaining body.

Ryan went back to the locomotive. Costanzo was standing
in the window of the cab, the engineer was leaning against the
tender, and the fireman was sitting with his legs dangling out of
the other side of the cab. Both the Italians were smoking.

"He gelikes Englosen cigaretten," Costanzo said with a nod
toward the engineer. "Ich getold him wir from der Englosen
getooken dem."

"Mein Deutsch ist better getten," Ryan said. "Ich Du geun-
derstanden."

The engineer held up a cardboard box of Players cigarettes.

"Molto bene," he said.

He offered a cigarette to Ryan. The eagerness with which Ryan accepted was not feigned. He had not smoked a cigarette since before the death of the first guard. He took a huge, grateful drag and looked back along the train. After a minute or so a man jumped from the next to last car and climbed to the roof and shortly thereafter a man climbed to the roof of the last car. There was now a prisoner on every car. Fincham was approaching the head of the train.

"How ist our Kamerad?" Ryan called.

Fincham was startled.

"Is he alles right?" Ryan asked.

Fincham understood at last.

"Kaput," he called.

Ryan sighed and shook his head.

"Mein Kamerad is kaput," he said heavily.

There was no need for Costanzo to translate the pidgin German. Kaput was a familiar word to the engineer. He clucked his tongue and crossed himself. Costanzo crossed himself, too. An expression of pleased surprise lit the engineer's face.

"Cattolico?" he asked.

"Si," Costanzo replied.

"Bene."

Motioning Costanzo to follow, Ryan dropped to the ground. Fincham was waiting at the door of the commander's car.

"They're all ours now, Padre," Ryan said, looking back along the train.

Costanzo looked at the long file of men sitting motionless atop the cars.

"Madonnini," he murmured.

"What did you say?" Ryan asked.

"That's what the Italians call the man who sits on top of a boxcar. Madonnina. Little Madonna. When it's cold and they wrap up in blankets they look like sacred statues. The engineer told me."

"Now they're ours instead of theirs, I rather fancy the notion," said Fincham.

"We don't stop long in Modena, do we?" Ryan asked.

"Not unless the engineer wants to report the . . . accident," Costanzo said.

"Get back in the cab with him and tell him we're radioing ahead to find out what to do. He needn't bother. And find out as much as you can about how the Ites run their railroads. Never know when it might come in handy."

Costanzo went back to the engine and Ryan and Fincham climbed into the commander's car. Klement was on his back, snoring, his lower lip dribbling moisture. Stein sat wearily at the table, bleary eyed and stubble-chinned. He pointed the pistol at the opening door and put it back on the table when he saw Ryan.

"We got 'em all," Ryan said.

Stein gave a deep sigh of mingled weariness and relief.

"I never really thought you would, Colonel," he said.

"Piece of cake," said Fincham.

The whistle blew and the train began moving. Ryan sat down at the table, closing his eyes and propping his forehead on his hands. When he opened his eyes again Stein had placed a steaming cup of coffee before him.

"I don't suppose there's tea?" Fincham asked.

Stein shook his head and poured another cup of coffee.

"Pity," said Fincham.

He and Ryan hunched wearily over their cups. The train moved easily and swiftly among the wheat fields and orchards of the Emilia. The car swayed slowly in a sort of half-time rhythm to the clicking of the rail joints.

"Well, Colonel, we've the bloody train at last," Fincham said, breaking the silence. "What now?"

"I'm thinking," said Ryan.

"Are you now?" Fincham said. "I hope the results are as interesting as the last time."

Ryan studied the map and the route order Costanzo had given him at Bologna.

"We check in at Parma," he said. "At the rate we're going it shouldn't take more than forty minutes or so. Stein, can you have Klement functioning by then? I may need him."

"He seems to be breathing normally now, Colonel," Stein replied. "I can have him on his feet but it's anybody's guess whether he'll be coherent or not."

"Do your best, Captain."

He turned to Fincham.

"Not getting that last Kraut before dawn has got us in a bind," he said. "We can't possibly leave the train before dark."

Fincham nodded.

"The problem is, at the rate we're moving we'll be in Milan in three, four hours, even with stops. That means we'll be heading back for Verona and the Brenner Pass with lots of daylight left. And the Krauts may still be holding those relief troops in Verona to take over."

"Bit sticky, that," Fincham said soberly.

"But supposing we got orders to lay over somewhere and not get to Milan before dark?" Ryan continued.

"Another wireless chit?"

"It worked once. No reason it won't again. All we need's a halfway plausible reason for the lay over. The Ites don't seem to give much of a damn about this train as long as it doesn't foul up traffic."

"It's worth a go. Then we could leave the train before it reaches Milan."

Fincham studied the map and reached for the mustache tip which was no longer there. He tugged at his chin instead.

"It's bloody deep in Italy, isn't it," he said thoughtfully. "We'll have our work cut out for us making our way back to our own chaps."

"That's what I was thinking," Ryan said.

Something in his tone made Fincham eye him speculatively.

"Supposing we did manage to leave the train without being

detected right away," Ryan said. "That means almost a thousand British and American officers right in the big middle of Italy. Leaving behind a couple of dozen dead Germans. The civilian population might be friendly enough but the country's swarming with Krauts. We couldn't expect much help from the Italians. Not on any large scale."

"Agreed," said Fincham.

"Chances are the bulk of the men would be killed or recaptured. And if the Krauts could tie 'em in with this train they might not bother shipping 'em to a prison camp."

"Agreed," Fincham said again. "But there's nothing else for it. We've no choice but to bugger off as soon as we can."

"There's one other possibility," Ryan said.

"And that is . . . ?" Fincham demanded.

Ryan traced a line on the map with his forefinger.

"Switzerland?" Fincham exclaimed incredulously.

"Train and all," Ryan said calmly.

"You're quite mad, you know," Fincham said.

"We took the train and we got ourselves routed to Milan when we were supposed to go the other way, didn't we? All we need is a little bluff and bluster. And a lot of luck. The Ites don't know if they're still in the war or not, the Krauts are in a flap, communications are all fouled up; between bombing and sabotage and nobody being sure just what's going on rail traffic must be all screwed up, too. When we reach Milan the Ufficio Movimento won't know what the hell we're supposed to be doing except what we tell 'em. Our order from Bologna just clears us to there. It doesn't say what for. The radio message tells that. We can put anything we want to in another one. We know military orders from Rome override civilian dispatchers in the stations if you're German and push hard enough."

Fincham's scowl of disapproval began to fade and he hitched his chair closer to Ryan's.

"They're expecting us in Verona," he said, not voicing an objection so much as asking Ryan how he intended getting around the fact.

"They don't have an ETA for us. All they know is the train was held up at Bologna and rerouted. Until they hear from Milan they won't know when to expect us. It's a hundred fifty kilometers from Milan to Verona. A hundred sixty to Tirano, where we cross."

"You don't simply take a train where you please, like a bloody automobile. They've schedules and switches and all that nonsense."

"True, Colonel. But by the same token, when you see a train coming down the track you assume it's supposed to be there. Or it wouldn't be. The only real problem will be at the point where we're supposed to head one way but go the other. If we can get past that we'll have it licked. Until we get to Tirano."

"I was on the point of mentioning that, Colonel."

"Tirano's a relatively obscure crossing point. They can't have too much of an operation up there. We'll slow down as if for inspection then bust on through before they know what's going on."

"What a strange, icy mind you have, Ryan," Fincham said. "You know, actually I was like Hank Stein. I never really expected we'd bring it off. Taking the whole bloody train. But I thought it worth a try. And we did it. I think this is worth a try, too."

"Good," said Ryan. "Then it's settled. We're going to Switzerland."

"One thing," Fincham interposed.

Ryan waited patiently for Fincham's objection.

"I needn't remind you if we don't bring it off we may all very well end against a wall. I think we should tell the other chaps what we propose and allow those who don't want to risk it to leave the train."

"Negative," Ryan said firmly. "We've already been over that. One man picked up in the wrong place at the wrong time could blow the whistle on the rest of us. When the time comes I'm willing to tell the men what we plan to do but I'm not giving them any choice about taking it or leaving it. If necessary, I'll keep 'em locked in the cars."

"The way you kept them locked in P. G. 202?"

"A decision had to be made and I was the man to make it," Ryan said coldly. "Subsequent events showed I made the wrong decision. That doesn't alter the fact that another decision has to be made now and I'm still the man to make it. If you're looking for apologies for past decisions or reassurance for future ones you've come to the wrong place."

"I'd have kept my mouth shut if I'd known I was bringing on a bloody sermon," Fincham said ruefully. "I'd no idea you were so thin-skinned on the subject. With all that headmaster self-righteousness of yours."

"The thickness of my hide is not the subject under discussion, Colonel. We were talking about a trip to Switzerland. Are you still with me?"

"I'm with you, right enough," Fincham growled. "You're bloody difficult at times but you're an absolute smasher when there's work to be done."

"Exactly my sentiments about you, Colonel Fincham. We'll just keep busy and get along."

While they talked, Stein had been working with Klement and now had the major walking around. Klement's face had the vacant stare of a jowly infant and when Stein let go of his arm he reeled.

"He's never going to make it by Parma," Stein said.

"We'll have to check in with the dispatcher without him," Ryan said. "They'll be speaking Italian anyhow and Padre shouldn't have any trouble. It's only a routine stop. But keep working on him. We never know when we may need him in a hurry."

"Yes, sir," Stein replied, stifling a yawn.

"You can get some sleep when we leave Parma," Ryan promised. "We all need it. Fincham, we'd better all shave. It won't do to look too raunchy. Somebody might start wondering why."

Ryan, because he would be visiting the Ufficio Movimento

at Parma with Costanzo, shaved first. Klement's shaving mug was silver, engraved with his name, including the gratuitous "von," and an equally spurious coat of arms. His wash basin was of silver as well, a finely chased ewer which looked as if it had been stolen from a museum.

Fincham busied himself getting together a staggering breakfast of bread, cheese, and salami. Klement did not want to eat but Stein forced him to while dosing him with three cups of strong black coffee. They were still eating when the train reached Parma. Fincham went immediately to the front car and returned with a packet of tea, his own shaving gear and everyone's toothbrush. Costanzo joined him on the way back to the commander's car.

Ryan had Costanzo shave his heavy whiskers, telling him of his decision to go to Switzerland as the priest did so.

Costanzo turned and looked at him, his fatigue-smudged eyes dark in a mask of white lather.

"You think it's possible, Cuhnel?" he asked.

"I wouldn't try it if I didn't, Padre. It's no milk run but we've got a fighting chance. I'll need your help in the tight places. You're the only one who speaks both good German and good Italian."

"Ah'll do my best, Cuhnel."

Fincham went out again to have the men on top of the cars pass along Ryan's instructions to remain at their posts and to tell the men inside the cars they would have to remain locked in a while longer. Stein had Klement talking coherently now but the major was wretchedly ill.

By the time Costanzo finished shaving Ryan had told him what was wanted from the Parma dispatcher. They prepared a new radio message form instructing them not to arrive in Milan before eight that night.

"We don't want to start our final approach until after dark," Ryan explained. "And we can't risk sitting around in the station at Milan all day waiting for nightfall."

The message further instructed them to make their delay en

route at some point away from main stations and heavily popu-
lated areas to minimize the risk of the prisoners communicating
with the civilian population and where their guards would have
an unobstructed view of the surrounding countryside.

Costanzo was to explain to the dispatcher that they were
scheduled to pick up more prisoners in Milan and that the new
prisoners would not reach the station until after seven. He was
to add, in strict confidence, the real reason was that a personal
shipment from a high SS officer would not be ready until then.

"It worked once and it'll work again," Ryan said.

"Cuhnel, as long as we're writing our own ticket why don't
we just give ourselves orders right through to Tirano?" Costanzo
asked.

"I'm afraid that would be a little harder to explain," Ryan
answered. "And once we did that, this train would just drop
out of the traffic schedule for Verona. We can't afford to drop
out of sight until the last possible minute. Add one more item
to that message, Padre. We're to keep the body of our dead
comrade aboard and turn it over to the proper authorities at
Innsbruck."

The engineer was waiting for them in the Ufficio Movimento.
He greeted Costanzo warmly although it had been only half an
hour since they had last been together. One of Costanzo's English cigarettes was dangling comfortably from his lower lip. He
had already received instructions as far as Piacenza, a major rail
junction a little less than half the distance to Milan, but when
Costanzo presented his radio message to the dispatcher and explained his commander's needs, the engineer supported him
with enthusiasm. Costanzo was obliged to do nothing more than
stand aside and wait while the engineer and dispatcher worked
out a new schedule for the prison train.

"I had no idea you were so cozy with the engineer," Ryan said
when they were returning to the train with orders permitting
them to make a nine-hour halt before Piacenza. "I don't know
if I'm too happy with an engineer that friendly to the Krauts."

Costanzo grinned.

"Maurizio told me confidentially that he hasn't any use for most Tedeschi but I'm different. I'm more like an Italian than a German."

As soon as the train left the outskirts of Parma, Ryan opened the car door a foot or two. It was a fine, clear morning and the clean air swept the reek of Klement's wine and vomit from the car.

"Makes me feel guilty about the guys locked in back there," said Stein, filling his lungs.

"They'll all be out in the open in a few minutes," Ryan said. "When we get to the siding I'm going to let everybody out for a few hours. Fincham, before I do we've got to be damn sure they know exactly what's expected of them."

Together they worked out the details of the stop. They would first summon all the men in German uniform to a formation beside the commander's car where they would be given instructions. Each was to open the car he guarded and let the men out after warning them to remain together beside their cars until Ryan came along with further instructions. The guards who had been up most of the night would go inside their cars and change uniforms with men who had been locked inside. Every man in German uniform was to shave and make himself as presentable as possible. Some of those in German uniform would then be posted to form a perimeter and the men allowed to move away from the train, though still in carload groups. Other men in German uniform would supervise the digging of latrines by prisoners and escort groups of their comrades to the nearest source of water to fill canteens and water bottles.

"When we've got things organized Costanzo and Stein can get some sleep," Ryan said. "You and I'll have to spell each other. I don't want both of us sleeping at the same time."

"I'm not sleepy," Fincham said.

"You better get some sleep while you can," Ryan said. "We've got a long day and night ahead of us."

—XX—

The siding into which the train backed twenty minutes later was but a single dead-end track, rusty with disuse, beside the rectangular outline of a concrete block foundation
where once a warehouse or factory had stood. Across the main
line, to the west, was a long, sloping meadow broken by a clump
of trees and bounded a quarter mile away by a highway sprin-
kled with traffic. Half a mile beyond the siding a small village
clamped the highway like a vise.

The fireman was uncoupling the tender from the first car and
Costanzo was on his way back to the commander's car when
Ryan dropped to the ground.

"What's going on?" Ryan demanded in a low voice.

Fincham was at the door, looking out.

"What the devil?" he demanded.

"The locomotive's leaving us," Costanzo said, addressing both
men. "The engineer said they can't let a locomotive sit here idle
all day. Another one from Piacenza is supposed to pick us up at
five-thirty."

"Hadn't planned on that, had you, Ryan?" Fincham asked.

"I don't know that it matters," Ryan said. "Unless there's a
foul-up and we're stuck here. In that case . . ."

He gazed along the two-hundred-fifty-yard stretch of laden

boxcars from which twenty-three anxious men looked at him expectantly, awaiting orders.

"In that case we'll have to go back to our original plan and head for the hills," he continued. "And lose too many of those men back there. But we'll cross that bridge when we come to it. Colonel, go down the line and tell the men on the cars to get down and form up outside our car."

While Fincham was doing that, Ryan thrust his head inside the car. Klement was in his bed with a wet cloth on his forehead and Stein was shaving.

"He'll live, Colonel," Stein said over his shoulder. "But I had a heck of a time convincing him it was worth it."

"Good. When he can face himself in a mirror have him shave and spruce up. I want him presentable. Then you can get some sleep."

Turning back to Costanzo, he said, "Padre, I'm afraid you'll have to put off sleeping a while longer. When I've got the men briefed I want you to take a party up to that village and locate water and digging tools."

The men from the cartops gathered around Fincham and Costanzo asking questions. They were less resentful of Ryan than they had been at the beginning of their journey but it was to the other two men they turned in excited camaraderie.

"At ease, gentlemen," Ryan said after allowing them a moment to stretch their legs and ease their tensions in talk. "The sooner we get this over with the sooner the others can get out of those cars."

The men fell silent and waited for him to continue.

"It took real courage for you to put on German uniforms and sit up there on those cars," Ryan said. "I commend you."

He gave them the instructions he had discussed earlier with Fincham and deployed them along the train, a man to each car. At his signal they slid back the doors. The men spewed out, cramped and stiff from their hours of crowded confinement, to stretch and blink in the sun. They stood in yawning, groaning clusters, scratching and gazing around at the meadow and the sky as if newly fledged and seeing the world outside their box-cars for the first time. Many, unable to wait by the cars as in-structed, hurried across the tracks to the meadow but returned to their places as soon as they relieved themselves. Some of the British had to be restrained by their companions from starting brew fires immediately.

With Fincham at his side, Ryan addressed the first two car-loads. They listened attentively with mixed resentment, curios-ity, and grudging respect.

"We're fifty or sixty miles from Milan," he said. "We're stop-ping here for the day so we can get there after dark. You will take food and what articles you'll need for the next few hours into the field with you. You will conduct yourselves as if still un-der guard by Germans who will shoot without hesitation. You men in German uniform will conduct yourselves as if you were disciplined German soldiers. Don't forget that for one second. You will not fraternize with the others in any way.

"You will remain together in your boxcar groups. Fires are permitted if you can find fuel in your immediate area but there will be no straggling away from your groups. Padre Costanzo will be taking a detail to the village up ahead for spades and wa-ter. A latrine will be dug for common use. When you're settled in, eat well and get some rest."

"When do we take off?" Bostick demanded. "From the train, I mean?"

"We're not," Ryan said calmly. "We're taking the train with us."

"Taking it with us? Where to?"

"Switzerland."

"Switzerland?"

A dozen voices echoed the word and it raced from car to car along the entire train.

"Hold it down!" Ryan snapped. "Or we may not be going anywhere except in front of a wall."

The men nodded agreement as he explained the necessity for

the change in plans though some of them muttered they would prefer trying it on their own.

"We stay together," Ryan said. "We can't risk having a few endangering the lives of the whole group."

"Like at P. G. 202?" Bostick demanded.

Ryan looked at him without emotion.

"Like at P. G. 202," he said.

Ryan went from car to car repeating his message. His instructions to the first cars preceded him so he was quickly done. As each group was dismissed the men went back into their cars for Red Cross parcels, packs, and water bottles and raced out into the field, whooping. Ryan did not object. After their hours in the boxcars they would have behaved no differently if the guards were actually Germans. With Fincham he checked every car to be sure the bodies of the German guards were well-concealed. The stench of too-crowded occupancy was appalling.

"After they've gotten a little rest we'll have 'em clean up the cars," he told Fincham.

Within an hour latrines had been dug and men from each boxcar had gone into the village to fill water bottles and canteens for their companions. The men spread out across the meadow, maintaining several yards distance between groups. They sprawled on the ground, eating and smoking, enjoying the luxury of space and clean air. The British, as usual, brewed tea over little fires of twigs, grass stalks, and bits of Red Cross boxes.

When he was satisfied the men were comfortably settled, Ryan went back to the commander's car. Stein was asleep in Klement's bed and Fincham was snoring in the leather armchair. Klement and Costanzo sat at the table, Klement with his head in his hands. Klement looked up when Ryan arrived.

"What do you do with me?" he demanded. "You have the train."

"You'll be all right, Major," Ryan said. "Just keep on co-operating. Padre, why don't you get a little sack time? I'll keep my eye on things."

"Ah'm all right, Cuhnel. Why don't you take a nap? You've had a busy night."

"Maybe I will."

He had just stretched out on Pleschke's sleeping bag when a shout from the meadow brought him to his feet. He looked out the car door to see a band of civilians approaching the train from the direction of the village.

He awakened Fincham to stand guard on Klement and motioned Costanzo to follow him.

"Find out what they're up to," he told Costanzo as they hurried to meet the Italians before they reached the prisoners.

An old man with a wrinkled, leathery face walked at the head of the group. He held a net bag of grapes in one hand and a long, thin green bottle in the other. Behind him was a crowd of other old men, children and women of all ages from budding girls to crones. Each carried something—a bottle of wine, a wedge of bread or cheese, olives, onions, fruit. They stopped when Costanzo hailed them in Italian.

They stared wooden-faced at the men in German uniforms, except for the younger children, who gazed at them with unabashed curiosity. The old man stepped forward and Costanzo spoke with him. Unlike so many of the Italians Ryan had encountered, the old man did not gesticulate. He spoke in a tired, firm voice and as he did so the Italians behind him nodded in confirmation. Costanzo came back to Ryan and spoke in a low voice.

"They have food and wine for the prisoners," he said.

"They must think we're a load of Italians," Ryan said. "Did you tell him the prisoners are British and American?"

"He knows that. He saw them when we went for water."

"Tell him they can't come any farther. They can leave what they've got here. I can't afford to have 'em mingling with the men."

"That's hardly the way to respond to their generosity, Cuhnel," Costanzo chided.

"We're supposed to be Krauts," Ryan said. "They expect us

to behave that way. I can't understand it, Padre. These people
are obviously hard up and they're bringing presents to men who
were their enemies up until a few days ago."

"I find it easy to understand," Costanzo said quietly.

"You should, Padre. It's your line of work."

The old man only motioned to his people and resumed his
slow walk toward the train when Costanzo ordered him to come
no closer. The men in the field were on their feet now, watching. Ryan stepped in front of the old man and barred his way
with a Schmeisser across his chest. The old man looked fearlessly into his eyes but the people behind him halted in confusion and shrank back. Indicating the old man was not to move,
Ryan stepped back a few paces and summoned Costanzo.

"Get Klement out here," he whispered. "The old boy may
try to push his luck and we'd be in trouble no matter what we
did. Tell Klement to order these people to stop and call in a detail of guards from the field to enforce it. Stein can get out there
on the double and tell three or four of 'em what Klement's telling 'em to do."

Costanzo ran back to the commander's car. The old man
started forward again, regarding Ryan steadily. Ryan scowled
and again barred his way. Klement jumped from the car, groaning and grumbling, and Fincham came to the door stifling a
yawn. His eyes fell on a plump, red-lipped young woman in
the van of the group behind the old man.

"By God!" he exclaimed. "Frippet!"

Ryan shot him a look of angry warning, reminding him he was
a German. Fincham reddened and felt his mustache but continued his inspection of the girl. She looked away angrily.

Klement pushed out his stomach and shouted. The Italians
turned to go but the old man stopped them with a gesture, facing Klement as fearlessly as he had faced Ryan. Klement grew
genuinely angry and, forgetting for the moment he was himself
a prisoner, began shrieking orders at the three men in German
uniform hurrying up with Stein. The men in the field jeered
him and called to the Italians in English and Italian.

"Bella ragazza," Orde's piercing voice shouted, and the plump young woman turned toward the source of the compliment with a dazzling smile.

The other men began whistling and waving their caps and handkerchiefs. An old woman next to the girl jerked at her arm and scolded her. The girl lowered her eyes demurely. Ryan longed to be able to shout "Knock it off!"

The three men in German uniform, taking their cue from Ryan, flanked him elbow to elbow, their rifles forming a barrier. The men were dangerously boisterous now and the Italians hesitated in frightened confusion, wanting to retreat but unwilling to leave the old man to face the Germans alone. Costanzo resolved their dilemma and Ryan's.

"Io sono cattolico," he told the old man in preamble to earnest conversation.

The old man listened in silence, then nodded. Turning, he spoke to the nervous throng behind him. They came forward and deposited their gifts in a neat row by the first boxcar. While they were so engaged, Orde came forward carrying a Red Cross box of tea, chocolate, soap, and sugar, a gift to the Italians from his companions. Ryan pretended to bar his way. When Costanzo interceded, after a show of reluctance Ryan permitted Orde to present the box to the old man. The old man kissed the embarrassed lieutenant on both cheeks.

"For the bella ragazza," Orde said gallantly, producing from his pants pocket a bar of scented soap someone had received in a personal parcel and offering it to the pretty girl.

She came forward, giggling and took it from him. She put the soap to her nose and wriggled, an expression of rapture on her face.

"I'll scrub your back for you if you want," the donor called from the fields.

The men began laughing and shoving him forward. When he saw Ryan's expression he stepped back into the group.

The other groups sent their own representatives forward with gifts and the old man embraced each in turn, tears flowing unashamedly down his seamed cheeks. Costanzo wiped a furtive tear from his own eye and gave a guilty start when he saw the gesture had not escaped Ryan. He raised a hand to bless the old man but caught himself in time.

The Italians left at last, more burdened than when they came. The buxom girl kept looking back over her shoulder at her large, appreciative audience, stumbling when the old woman who had scolded her earlier tugged at her arm.

When they were gone, Ryan and Costanzo added the food in Klement's hoard to the pile and divided it into twenty-two equal portions. The wine he held back and placed inside the car.

"Gonna drink it yourself, Von Ryan?" Bostick cried from across the tracks.

Ryan walked swiftly across the field to where Bostick waited, hands truculently on hips.

"Captain," he grated, "you're no ordinary fool. You're a dangerous fool. You want the world to know what's going on here? The next time you pull a stunt like that and endanger these other men I'm going to give you a rifle butt in the teeth."

He returned to the train without another word. After the food had been distributed he climbed inside the commander's car to find Costanzo and Stein asleep and Fincham wakeful.

"Take over, Colonel," he said. "If anything comes up, wake me."

He stretched out on Pleschke's sleeping bag again and was asleep within minutes. After lunch, Fincham lay down and Ryan remained awake. Costanzo and Stein slept on. Klement, who had overcome his hang-over but was growing increasingly apprehensive, tried to talk to Ryan, picking his words with painstaking care. Ryan was taking too many chances, he complained, permitting the men to remain in the field. If someone learned the train was no longer in German hands and it was retaken Ryan would blame him although it would not be his fault. And when was Ryan going to take his men off and let him go free?

"Don't worry," Ryan said reassuringly. "Nothing's going to

happen to you unless you bring it on yourself. And I'll let you know when you can go."

Until early afternoon the men were content to eat, smoke, and rest. They napped, shaved, washed their feet and mended socks or sat together in small groups talking and brewing coffee and tea.

Cars would stop on the highway occasionally and their Italian occupants would inquire about the presence of the men in the field. The men in German uniforms, following instructions, waved them away.

Around two o'clock the men became restless. They spread out until there was no clearly defined separation between the car groups and the more adventurous began edging toward the road and the far end of the meadow where they were turned back by their companions in German uniform after low-voiced arguments. Some of the men began questioning the wisdom of Ryan's plan and urging their friends to join them in leaving the train as soon as darkness fell. The first flush of gratitude to Ryan for capturing the train had worn off and now they reminded one another how he had permitted them to be taken at P. G. 202 and asking if it could not happen a second time.

When Ryan awakened he saw at once that the men were growing impatient and sent a dozen from each boxcar to empty their toilet buckets into the latrine, sweep out the cars with bunches of meadow grass, and restack their boxes and knapsacks in the smallest possible area. Those remaining in the field he ordered back to their areas.

At three he awakened Costanzo and called him into conference with himself and Fincham.

"We've got to brief Klement on what to say at Milan," Ryan said. "Once we're past Milan we should be able to make it to Tirano before Verona starts worrying."

"Ah'm afraid it won't be that easy, Cuhnel," Costanzo said. "Ah talked with the engineer like you asked. We can't go north out of Milan without orders. The switching is centrally controlled and the train goes the way they throw the switch at the control board."

"Don't they have manually controlled switches, too?" Ryan demanded.

"Ah don't know but it wouldn't matter if they did," Costanzo replied. "You saw that diagram with all the lights in the Bologna Ufficio Movimento. The dispatcher can follow every train that goes in and out of his station on that board. We've got to go the way the order says."

"Let's have a look at that map again," said Ryan.

He studied it a moment.

"Look here," he said. "Here's Monza, just north of Milan. Seven, eight miles. If we had an excuse to go there we'd have to go on a little further to this junction, Carnate, to head back for the Verona line through Bergamo. They must have manual switches at a little station like Carnate. Supposing we kept going on the main line out of Carnate instead of heading back toward Bergamo?"

"They'd still know at Milan, Cuhnel. When a train passes a station the dispatcher reports it to the station before and the one after."

"How?"

"By telegraph."

"I say," Fincham put in, "you certainly pumped the bugger, didn't you?"

"He was right proud to have such a fascinated audience," Costanzo said, smiling.

"In that case, if we can just bluff our way to Monza I don't think there'll be any problem," Ryan said. "At least not about getting on the northbound line."

Before he could say more he was interrupted by Orde's breathless arrival at the car door.

"Colonel Ryan," he said, gasping for air, "there's two Jerries heading this way. They drove up in a car and stopped on the road."

Ryan sprang to the door. Two Germans were walking across

the meadow, picking their way through the throng of prisoners.

"Padre, tell Klement to get rid of 'em as quick as he can," Ryan ordered. "If they ask questions, the prisoners are on their way to Milan to work in the factories and are being held here until he gets word they'll have transportation for 'em when he gets there."

"I think we should simply prang the buggers," Fincham said. "Then there'd be no chance of a ballocks."

"Someone might come looking for them," said Ryan.

"Think they smell something, Cuhnel?" Costanzo asked.

Ryan shook his head.

"If they did you could be damn sure there'd be more than two of 'em."

One of the Germans was a first lieutenant, the other a sergeant. The lieutenant was a thick-necked young man with a well-placed dueling scar on his heavy face. He wore a single ribbon on his tunic. The sergeant was older, with deep wrinkles around his eyes and an air of cynical weariness. He wore an Iron Cross and rows of ribbons.

The lieutenant's face brightened when he saw Ryan's classic Nordic features and he seemed on the verge of speaking when he realized he was in the presence of a major. He saluted Klement briskly, thrusting out his arm and heiling Hitler. The sergeant did the same, though not so briskly. Ryan and Fincham saluted the newcomers, followed by Costanzo and Stein, who had been awakened from a sound sleep and was still puffy-eyed.

Klement, afraid something might go wrong, was nervous and abrupt with the lieutenant. Fincham removed himself by sitting down at the radio and pretending to be working on it, though keeping his Schmeisser close at hand. Ryan stood a little behind Klement and to one side, as if in deferential attendance. Stein busied himself among Klement's boxes. Seeing everyone else engaged, the sergeant struck up a conversation with Costanzo while the officers talked. Costanzo, not trusting his pronunciation, answered with grunts and monosyllables until the sergeant gave up the attempt at conversation and transferred his attention to the front of the car, where Klement's loot was piled.

The lieutenant could not take his eyes off the treasures, either, and despite Klement's growing impatience did not seem inclined to leave. Ryan's scanty German was enough for him to understand the lieutenant was hinting to be invited to have a glass of wine with the major. Klement ignored the hint, afraid if he encouraged the lieutenant to linger Ryan would question his motives.

The sergeant had grown bored with his survey of Klement's loot and now his eyes roved instinctively in the manner of a soldier accustomed to knowing his surroundings intimately. His eyes stopped roving and narrowed when they reached Stein.

"Soldat," he said.

Stein looked at him.

"Ja, Sie," the sergeant said.

He pointed at Stein's shoes. They were brown American army shoes. Ryan and the others had on black English boots issued at P. G. 202, not easily distinguishable from German shoes.

Stein looked down at his shoes as if surprised to see them. Fincham half turned and put his hand on the Schmeisser, looking to Ryan for a signal. Klement grew pale and licked his lips. The lieutenant stared at his sergeant in annoyance, then followed his gaze to Stein's brown shoes. His brow wrinkled.

"Amerikanische," Costanzo said with a grin.

He held up his foot.

"Englische," he said.

Reaching into Stein's tunic pocket he took out a packet of Players and offered the sergeant a cigarette, saying, "Auch Englische."

The sergeant took a cigarette and said something in reply. Though Ryan did not understand the words the sergeant's manner left no doubt that he had made a cutting remark about how soft some men had it while others were fighting a war. Ryan had heard Americans express the identical sentiment too many times to be mistaken.

Costanzo turned to Klement.

"Jawohl, Herr Kommandant," he said, as if in reply to an unspoken order.

He plucked two bottles of wine from the pile at the front of the car and put them on the table.

"Genug, Herr Kommandant?" he asked.

Klement knit his brow, then suddenly understanding what was expected of him, blurted, "Ja, ja. Gut. Gut."

He motioned to the lieutenant to take the wine.

"Danke, Herr Major," the lieutenant said enthusiastically. "Ich trinke auf ihre Gesundheit."

He ordered the sergeant to take the bottles and the two left after a round of Nazi salutes and "Heil Hitlers," in which Ryan and his companions joined. Stein blew out a long breath.

"Bit near, that," Fincham said.

Ryan said nothing. He stood in the door and watched the Germans until they crossed the field, climbed into their automobile, and drove away. Then he turned to Costanzo.

"Padre," he said, "if you weren't a priest you'd be one hell of a con artist."

"Ah've been studying under a master lately," Costanzo replied.

"Thank you, Padre," Ryan said dryly.

"Ah'm not sure Ah intended it as a compliment," Costanzo said with equal dryness.

—XXI—

Ryan and Costanzo sat down to work out a radio order to present to the Milan Ufficio Movimento.

"This time instead of a pickup we'll say we're making a delivery," Ryan said. "Putting off a personal consignment for Gruppenfuehrer Dietrich at Monza."

"I'm getting rather fond of Gruppenfuehrer Dietrich," said Fincham. "Decent sort, for a Jerry."

They were interrupted once when Beresford, the messing officer, came to the door escorted by one of the men in German uniform.

"I thought if I had Dickie bring me along it mightn't be improper for me to come to you," he explained. "Colonel Ryan, I was wondering . . . The chaps haven't had a proper meal since yesterday morning. With a few kettles from the village and a nice fire I could have a hot dish for them with no trouble at all. Tinned M and V from the parcels would be simple to do and quite tasty."

"I appreciate your concern, Captain," Ryan said, "but it won't be necessary. We'll have to get along on cold food a while longer."

Beresford sighed.

"Very well, sir," he said unhappily.

It was after four when Ryan finished working out the details

of the radio message and drilling Klement in his duties at
Milan. The major had not fully recovered from the tensions of
the two Germans' visit and his responses were halting.

"You're doing fine, Herr Kommandant," Ryan said sooth-
ingly, "but you can do better. We'll work on it some more after
we get rolling."

Outside in the meadow, the men were restless again and inclined to wander aimlessly from group to group. The men in
German uniform were finding it increasingly difficult to keep
them under control. Traffic on the road was heavier now and
creeping along as the passengers stared at the curious spectacle
of a field swarming with strange uniforms.

"We better get 'em back inside," Ryan said. "The locomotive'll be here in another hour."

"If the bloody Ites haven't simply forgotten us," Fincham
said.

"Not much chance of that, Colonel. Go on out and re-form
the men. I've got a few things I want to go over with Costanzo.
Have the guards count 'em. I want to be sure every man is where
he belongs. And Colonel, see if you can find me a good radio
man who understands German and an engineer who's had experience cutting wire."

Fincham returned twenty minutes later, his face perturbed.

"What's the matter?" Ryan demanded.

"There's a man missing."

"A man missing! Do you know who it is?"

"Yes. Goon Bostick."

"Bostick!"

Ryan swore.

"I should have known that thick-headed idiot would . . ."

He looked at his watch.

"We've got forty-five minutes to find him," he said. "Colonel,
get the men in the cars and keep them there. Did you get my
radio man and an engineer?"

"Right."

"Get a Jerry uniform out of the front car and get the radio

man into it and into this car. Get the engineer into a German uniform and put him on top of this car. Padre, you come with me. I'll want another man who speaks a little Italian, too."

"Leftenant Hedley knows a bit of Ite," Fincham said. "And he's already in uniform."

"Let's get going," Ryan said.

He went out into the field where Bostick's group waited apprehensively.

"All right, you men," he said softly. "You must have known when Bostick took off. When did he leave and which way did he go?"

No one answered. They looked sullenly at the ground in mingled shame and truculence.

"We're not playing games, gentlemen," Ryan said. "The locomotive will be here in forty minutes and if we have to leave without him he'll be a constant threat to the rest of us. If any of you know where to find Bostick and withhold the information you'll share Bostick's responsibility for whatever happens to us if we're caught. If we leave without him and we don't make it we may never know if it was because of him. But we'll wonder. We'll always wonder. Well, men, I'm waiting."

The prisoners remained silent but Orde shifted uncomfortably. Ryan transfixed him with a narrow-eyed stare.

"Lieutenant Orde, you look like you're trying to tell me something. Are you?"

Orde's good eye studied the ground, Ryan, the men around him, and the ground again.

"We haven't got all day, Lieutenant," Ryan said implacably. Orde cleared his throat.

"He left when those two Jerries were in your car, sir," he said in a voice so low Ryan could scarcely hear him.

"Did he say where he intended to go?"

The other prisoners were murmuring and glaring balefully at Orde. Orde hesitated.

"That's enough!" Ryan snapped. "Stand at attention, you men. All right, Orde, you've got nothing to worry about from these schoolboys. I'm the only one you have to worry about. Did he say where he intended to go?"

"He said to that little town up there. He got the idea when they acted so friendly. He figured they'd hide him until dark."

"You're off the hook, Lieutenant," Ryan said. "But don't expect me to pat you on the back for doing what you should have done when there was still time to stop Bostick. As for the rest of you men, you're a disgrace to your uniforms and I'm sorry I have to take you with the rest of us. Colonel Fincham, start them moving to the cars and lock 'em in."

He turned on his heel and left them standing in shamefaced but resentful silence.

"Get cracking, you bloody clots," Fincham said.

With Costanzo and Lieutenant Hedley, a yellow-haired young officer with a rosy English complexion, Ryan hurried across the meadow toward the village, stopping to accost the man in German uniform stationed in his path.

"What's your name?" he demanded.

"Albert Logan, sir. Lieutenant."

"Lieutenant Logan, you permitted a man to leave. Get back to your car and change uniforms with a man I can trust."

"But, sir . . ."

"I gave you an order. Consider yourself lucky I'm in no position to have you court-martialed."

As they moved quickly through the meadow Ryan issued instructions.

"When we get there, we've got to be rough," he said. "They'll expect it. We're supposed to be Krauts. If I have to talk to you I'll do it in phoney German. But only if there's no getting around it."

"We'll never find him if they're set on hiding him, Colonel," said Hedley. "It would take a full company to comb that rabbit warren."

"We'll have to try. Padre, if there's a church handy you can sound out the priest. If necessary you may have to tell him ho we really are. I don't think a priest would give us away."

"Ah'm deeply flattered, Cuhnel," said Costanzo.

There was no sign of life in the village except for a small boy playing in the dirt. He scrambled to his feet and trotted off when the three men approached.

"He may be a lookout," Ryan said. "Don't lose him."

They trotted after the boy who, looking back over his shoulder, suddenly darted inside a door.

"Come on!" Ryan ordered, breaking into a run.

He raced toward the door through which the boy had disappeared and, kicking it open, burst inside with his Schmeisser ready. The boy was nowhere to be seen. The only occupant was the old man who had led the villagers to the train. He was sitting placidly in a wooden chair. He looked at Ryan without moving. Costanzo and Hedley crowded in behind the colonel. The room was dim and, except for a few poor sticks of furniture and a holy picture, bare.

Ryan pointed the Schmeisser at the old man's head and motioned Costanzo forward. The old man shook his head when Costanzo questioned him. Ryan grabbed him by his coatfront and jerked him to his feet.

"Der gefangener!" he demanded.

The old man pressed his lips tightly together. Ryan shook him. "Der gefangener!"

Costanzo tapped Ryan on the shoulder and indicated he wanted a word with him. With a muttered oath, Ryan threw the Italian back into the chair. It collapsed and the old man went sprawling on the stone floor. At that an old woman came flying out of a back room, screaming, to throw herself down beside the man. He spoke to her and she grew silent.

"Maybe you should try telling him who we are," Costanzo whispered. "Seeing as how he's on our side, not the Germans'."

"Can't take that chance."

"Even if he knows where to find Bostick he won't tell us," Costanzo argued. "He'd die first."

The old woman, thinking her husband's fate was being decided, began to rock back and forth on her knees, moaning. The old man silenced her again with an angry word.

"We'll search the place," Ryan said. "There can't be too many places to hide a man the size of Bostick in this little house."

Leaving Costanzo on guard, he ran through the house with Hedley, kicking over furniture in the two small rooms and poking under the bed. There was no place a man might hide, or even a child as small as the one who had run in the front door and who obviously was no longer in the house. There was a rear window, however, and it was open.

"Heinz!" Ryan shouted. "Komm."

Costanzo came running.

"If he was here he had to leave by the window," Ryan said. "Come on."

They climbed out and found themselves in a foul-smelling narrow lane facing another row of forlorn houses. The doors and windows were all tightly closed and there was no sign of human occupancy except on the second floor of one house where a tattered curtain fell back against a sill, as if released by someone who had been peering from behind it.

"Try there," Ryan ordered, pointing at the house.

Before Costanzo and Hedley could obey there was a sharp hiss from the end of the row of houses and a head covered with a blue-black shock of tangled curly hair was thrust cautiously around the corner. Its owner was a young man with a thin, pale face and thick eyebrows. When he saw he had their attention he motioned for them to approach and drew back around the corner.

Leaving Hedley to cover the house from which they had been watched, Ryan took Costanzo around the corner with him. The man was short and wiry. His eyes moved restlessly, as if he feared someone were spying on him. He wore broken shoes and his stained white shirt was buttoned to the neck, though tieless.

"Parlate italiano?" he asked.

Costanzo replied in Italian and the young man talked rapidly in a low voice, pausing to look back apprehensively over his shoulder. Costanzo nodded and drew Ryan aside.

"He says he knows where the American is," Costanzo said. "He wants to know if there's a reward."

Ryan stepped quickly to the Italian and cuffed him with an impersonal backhand blow, driving him cowering against the wall, then moved back as if studying him.

"Tell him his reward is performing a service to the Fuehrer," Ryan whispered to Costanzo. "It is his duty to lead us to the American."

Costanzo spoke to the young man, who leaned against the wall clutching his face and looking fearfully at Ryan. He answered with an eager rush of words, his eyes not leaving Ryan as he talked or when Costanzo stepped back for another conference.

"He'll tell us where the American is but he can't lead us there," Costanzo said. "He's afraid the others will kill him if he does. He's been hiding here himself. He's a deserter from the Italian army and wants to help his German comrades."

"That idiot, Bostick," Ryan said. "Imagine what would happen if real Krauts found this man instead of us. Find out where Bostick's hiding and then tell him to take off before I decide to punish his insolence for asking for a reward."

The Italian nodded and gestured violently toward the narrow lane as he spoke. He took off at a dead run after a last frightened look at Ryan.

"There's a little place down at the end of the row where they sell wine," Costanzo said. "Bostick's hiding in the cellar."

Rejoining Hedley, Ryan led the way down the rutted lane. He could feel the fear and tension gripping the little village though there was still no sign of human occupancy.

The wineshop was a sour-smelling little cubicle with two broken cement steps leading to a scarred door. Ryan kicked the door open and stepped inside, thrusting his Schmeisser ahead of him. Three old men were sitting on boxes near a round iron stove in which no fire was burning. Another man, somewhat younger, leaned on a low, rough counter on which lay two small casks with spigots jutting from them. On a shelf behind him was a collection of dusty unmatched tumblers.

The middle-aged man at the counter tugged at the handkerchief knotted around his throat and, with a forced smile, said, "Vino, signore?"

The three old men stared into their wineglasses and resolutely ignored Ryan. They did not look up when he was joined by Costanzo and Hedley. At a sign from Ryan, Costanzo began questioning the proprietor, who shook his head and shrugged. While they talked, Ryan looked around the dark little room. There was a clean rectangle the dimensions of the counter in the otherwise dirt-scaled floor.

With a sudden movement, Ryan swept the kegs from the counter and kicked it over. One of the kegs broke and wine spilled over the floor like blood. No one was looking at the wine. Every eye was turned on what the counter had concealed, a narrow door set in the stone flagging, with an iron ring in its center.

The proprietor shrank back against the wall, his grizzled face pinched with terror, and the other old men huddled together in mute panic. Ryan motioned Costanzo to raise the door and, taking the flashlight Hedley had hanging from his belt, climbed down frail steps which creaked and bent under his weight, shining the light ahead of him.

The cellar was the same size as the room above. The sour, acrid smell of bad wine was overpowering. Half a dozen small kegs were stacked on their ends in one corner. In another corner was a sodden heap of coarse brown sacks.

Ryan knelt by the sacks and spoke in a virulent whisper.

"Listen to me, you dim-witted bastard! I know you're in there. You're going to get up and come with me. And not say a word that'll tip those people off I'm not a German."

The pile of sacks heaved and Bostick sat up, blinking in the flashlight's glare.

"You can go to hell, Von Ryan," he said defiantly. "I'm not

getting back on that train and be picked off like we were in P. G. 202."

Ryan was standing over Bostick now, looking down at him. "On your feet," he said. "Those people up there expect me to knock you off and I'm tempted not to disappoint them."

"You wouldn't shoot me and you know it. You just trot on back to that train and let me alone. I can take care of myself."

"The locomotive's picking us up any minute," Ryan said with icy control. "When it leaves you're going to be on that train."

He bent down and dragged the big man to his feet. Bostick jerked away and raised his fists.

"Who's gonna make me, Von Ryan?" he whispered.

Ryan hit him.

The Schmeisser slid down Ryan's arm on its sling and clattered to the floor. Bostick stumbled back a step from the force of Ryan's blow but did not go down. He recovered his balance, shook his head, and charged. The onslaught drove Ryan back against the wall and sent the flashlight spinning to the floor. It rolled to the wall, making an erratic pattern in the dim cellar as it spun across the floor, then went out. The only light came from the trap door at the top of the ladder.

Bostick's huge arms were around Ryan now, squeezing. One of Ryan's arms was trapped, the other free. Ryan pressed his thumb into the soft flesh under Bostick's chin and forced the big man's head back. Bostick released him to get away from the agonizing pressure. Ryan hit him three times before Bostick could get his hands up, driving him to the middle of the cellar. Still Bostick did not go down. He stepped back to get punching room but before he could launch a blow Ryan kicked him in the kneecap and he fell to the floor with a yell of pain.

Costanzo's anxious face appeared in the square of light at the head of the ladder.

"Alles under control ist," Ryan gasped.

He picked up the Schmeisser and turned to Bostick, who was sitting up clutching his knee.

"I'll try to explain the spot you're in," Ryan said. "I know it's hard for you to get it through that thick skull but try. There're two more of us up there in German uniforms. The Ites know we've found you. We either take you back or knock you off. Or it's all over for everybody on that train."

"They wouldn't tell," Bostick said. "They want us to get away."

"There's an informer in this village, you dumb bastard. How do you think we found you? Now come on. I haven't got time to argue."

Bostick rose painfully to his feet and pulled himself up the ladder, favoring his bad knee. When he reached the top Ryan gave him a shove which sent him sprawling on the floor at the feet of the Italians. They pressed back against the wall, afraid even to breathe. Ryan jerked Bostick to his feet, cuffed him for the benefit of the Italians, and shoved him back toward Hedley, who covered him with his rifle.

Then Ryan methodically kicked in the head of the undamaged wine cask, kicked the counter into kindling, swept the glasses to the floor with his Schmeisser, and kicked the stove from its moorings. The proprietor watched the destruction of his wineshop in helpless terror. When Ryan had stamped the stove into scrap metal he leveled his Schmeisser at the Italian. The proprietor hunched his shoulders and braced himself, resigned. Ryan lowered the Schmeisser with a contemptuous snort and, motioning to Costanzo and Hedley to follow him, shoved Bostick out the door.

There was a flurry of movement in doors and windows when they stepped into the street, then all was empty again. Ryan looked at his watch. Five thirty-two.

"Hurry it up," he said. "The locomotive should be there by now. Hedley, keep an eye on our rear. They might get some harebrained idea about saving this clown from us."

"Not bloody likely, sir," said Hedley. "Naught but women and old men about."

They hurried along in silence, Bostick limping, until they were outside the village. Up ahead, a locomotive was just coupling onto the train.

"Well, we made it," said Ryan.

"Did you have to do that, Cuhnel?" Costanzo asked. "Wreck the man's wineshop?"

"Would you rather I shot him, Padre?" Ryan demanded. "To those people we were Krauts. I did what a Kraut would have done. A soft-hearted Kraut."

"Sorry, Cuhnel," said Costanzo. "You were right."

Bostick was quiet as they crossed the field toward the train, his face troubled.

"Padre," he said at last, "was there really an informer in that town?"

"Yes, Emil," Costanzo said. "He wanted a reward for telling where you were."

"They'd have caught me, wouldn't they?" Bostick asked quietly.

Costanzo nodded.

"And maybe the rest of us, Emil," he said.

Bostick flushed and turned to Ryan as if to speak. The harsh contempt he saw there stopped him. He limped on with his head down.

Fincham was waiting for them with a sharp-faced little Italian in a trainman's uniform. He had a narrow head and a Hitler mustache. There was a black mourning band on his arm. When Ryan and his group drew near the Italian gave a Fascist salute and cried, "Heil Hitler!"

Ryan had scarcely returned the salute when the engineer began berating him in Italian.

"Sprechen Sie Deutsch?" Costanzo asked.

The Italian shook his head.

"He ist Du eaten out for late commen," Costanzo said.

"Getellen him wir ein gefangener ketchen," Ryan said. "Und nix mit ein Deutscher to freshen get."

The Italian was servilely apologetic when Costanzo translated.

He approached Bostick and stopped a foot away to look up into the American's battered face, smiling cruelly. Suddenly he gave Bostick a ringing slap. Bostick twitched, as if to strike back.

"Nein," Ryan shouted, raising his Schmeisser.

Bostick relaxed.

Ryan slapped the Italian on the back, rocking the little man.

"Du bist ein miserable little cur," he said, laughing as if in approval of what the Italian had done.

The engineer said something to Costanzo and left them.

"We're leaving in five minutes," Costanzo said. "We're cleared through to Milan."

Ryan sent Hedley to the locomotive and ordered Bostick into the commander's car.

"You're staying where I can keep my eye on you, Captain," he said.

"I won't pull that again, Colonel," Bostick said.

"I don't trust you," Ryan snapped.

Fincham looked at Bostick with approval.

"Knocked you about a bit, did they?" he said. "Served you bloody well right."

A man in German uniform was tinkering with the radio.

"Lieutenant Heinke," Fincham said. "One of yours."

The man turned to face Ryan.

"Gus Heinke, sir," he said.

"How's your German, Lieutenant?" Ryan demanded.

"Good, sir. We spoke it at home."

"Where's home?"

"New Braunfels, sir. Texas."

"I know the place, Lieutenant. From my Randolph days. Would a Kraut think you're German?"

"I doubt it, sir. I'm third generation. I guess the way we speak it's a little different from in the Old Country."

"You know how to operate that radio? Just the receiver, I mean?"

"I'm figuring it out, sir. It's not much different from ours."

"When you get it figured, see what you can pick up. Let me

know if there's anything about us. There won't be any reason there should be for a while but keep listening out anyhow."

"It'll be like looking for a needle in a haystack, Colonel. Trying to find the frequency they'd be operating on."

"I know, Lieutenant. But if you stumble over any German communications out of Verona, lock on to that frequency."

"Verona. Yes, sir."

Ryan turned to Fincham.

"You got that engineer on our car, Colonel?"

"A sapper," Fincham said. "One of mine. OR. But a wizard at his job. Only one drawback."

"Yes?"

"He's a Welshman," Fincham said, grinning. "Doesn't understand Yank as well as he might."

The train backed into Milan at eight-fifteen after delays at Piacenza and a smaller station, at neither of which, however, had it been necessary to visit the dispatcher. Klement was dangerously close to collapse at the prospect of having to visit the Milan Ufficio Movimento with Ryan.

"Do you think another medicinal dose of vino would do any good, Captain?" Ryan asked Stein.

"Watch Von Ignatz doesn't get himself tiddly again," Fincham warned.

"Don't worry, Finch," Stein replied. "I'll be careful with the dosage."

Two glasses of wine helped Klement somewhat but he was still far from confident. Ryan refused his plea for a third glass.

"Better nervous than drunk," he said. "Padre, you better do the talking in there. Tell the dispatcher the Herr Kommandant isn't feeling well."

"Why fetch him along at all?" Fincham asked.

"If the dispatcher gets salty about routing us through Monza a couple of enlisted men might have a hard time changing his mind."

"Put Padre in his uniform."

"Wouldn't fit him and Padre couldn't pass for a Kraut very

long if we ran into another German officer the way we did at Bologna. We've got to have Klement along as insurance."

Directly across from the commander's car was a long line of German soldiers being served hot soup from a steaming kettle presided over by two virile-looking women wearing Fascist party arm bands. When Ryan climbed out with Klement and Costanzo the soldiers were inviting the men on top of the boxcars to join them. When the pretended Germans did not answer, some of the men in line grew insistent. Ryan had Klement order his men to remain at their posts. They did not understand Klement's words but it did not matter because they had Ryan's instructions not to move until he told them to.

"Tell Klement to order those soldiers to keep away from the train," Ryan told Costanzo. "He can tell 'em it's loaded with prisoners taken down south and he'll have anybody who tries to get near 'em shot."

The German soldiers cheered at the news and called to Ryan and Costanzo for more details. They shrugged, as if fearful Klement would not approve of them entering into conversation. At Costanzo's whispered command, Klement led them across the rows of tracks and platforms to the station offices.

The Ufficio Movimento was teeming with activity and they had to wait for a dispatcher. The feisty little engineer was in a friendly mood and chatted volubly with Costanzo while they waited.

"If there's time he'd like to hit the big American some more," Costanzo said out of the corner of his mouth. "And show him the Germans and the Italians stand shoulder to shoulder against the barbaric Americani."

"I'd like to pinch his head off," Ryan replied. "We get rid of him here, don't we?"

"No. He's going all the way to Verona with us, he says."

"I don't like that. Be a whole lot better if we had a sympathetic type like the last one. Guess it can't be helped."

What little poise Klement had brought to the Ufficio Movimento was steadily draining away. He was noticeably pale and kept wetting his lips. When a dispatcher was free, Ryan had Costanzo present the radio message and request to be routed to Monza as ordered by SS headquarters in Rome. The dispatcher read the message without changing expression, his lips moving. He stopped once to ask Costanzo to translate a word into Italian. Then he nodded and consulted his traffic schedules. After a few minutes' study, he wrote out a train order and shoved it at Klement. Klement stared at the piece of paper as if powerless to touch it. Costanzo took it from the dispatcher and handed it to Klement.

"Alles ist in Ordnung, Herr Kommandant," he said, stepping back to salute.

Klement nodded vaguely.

The dispatcher and engineer looked at each other, then at Costanzo.

"Malato," Costanzo said with a deferential nod at the major.

The engineer shook his head and clucked sympathetically. Costanzo retrieved the order from Klement's hand, studied it, and gave it to the engineer. The engineer read it, shoved it in his pocket, and left them. Ryan moved Klement toward the door, as if helping him.

"That was almost too easy," Ryan said when they were outside. "I didn't think Klement was going to make it."

"We'll be here another hour and a half, Cuhnel," Costanzo said. "What does that do to us?"

"It's only nine," Ryan said. "That'll give us over seven hours to make it to Tirano before dawn and Tirano's only a hundred miles. Time's not the problem. The problem's getting to Tirano before we're missed. Let's get Klement back to his bed before he faints on us."

Ryan took Klement's arm and was guiding him across the busy platform when, from a few feet ahead of them, a voice cried, "Hubertus!"

Klement looked up, shaken from his stupor, as a smiling officer in the black uniform of an SS Obersturmfuehrer stepped toward him, a hand outstretched in greeting. Klement took one step to meet him, then froze. He cast a terrified look over his shoulder at Ryan. Shielded by Klement's body, Ryan pushed him toward the SS man with his Schmeisser, holding the weapon against Klement's back and concealing the action from passers-by with his own body. Klement reached out and clasped the outstretched hand and gave it one quick, limp shake. The smile died on the SS officer's face.

"Hubertus," he said anxiously, peering into Klement's face, "was ist los? Bist Du krank?"

Costanzo looked helplessly at Ryan.

Klement began trembling.

"Was ist los, Hubertus?" the SS officer said more sharply. "Was machst Du hier im Norden?"

Klement's lips moved but no sound came out. The SS man took Klement by the arm and turned his attention to Ryan, speaking with quick, demanding authority. Unable to understand or to answer, Ryan took refuge in coming to attention. The German, not satisfied with this, pressed him for an answer. Costanzo came to his rescue, speaking very carefully, and economically. Ryan knew from the few words he understood that Costanzo was telling the SS officer the Herr Kommandant was ill.

The Obersturmfuehrer appeared satisfied with the explanation but Ryan saw that as the German listened to Costanzo he was studying him. The German's eyes lingered for a moment on Costanzo's ill-fitting uniform then quickly, too quickly, looked away and, with feigned disinterest, gave Ryan the same careful scrutiny.

"Ach, so," he said with a sigh. "Gute Besserung, Hubertus."

He took Klement's flaccid hand, gave it a shake, and left them, walking slowly.

"That was close," Costanzo said, exhaling.

"Take Klement back to the train," Ryan said urgently. "I'll be there as quick as I can."

Falling in behind a knot of passers-by, he hurried after the black-clad officer. He did not like the way the SS man walked with such elaborate casualness, not even looking back at his sick friend. Far down the platform, dimly visible in the eerie glow of a purplish blackout light, was a German soldier with the silver breastplate of a military policeman dangling from his neck. It was toward this soldier Klement's friend seemed to be making his too casual way.

Ryan stayed as close to the officer as he dared, his eyes searching restlessly for a place where he might be able to stop the German without attracting attention. The platform was hopelessly crowded. Klement's friend would have only to cry out.

The officer approached a long rank of racks holding row upon row of storage batteries. As he drew almost abreast of an opening between the racks, Ryan hurried forward and reached him just as he arrived at the opening. With a sudden lunge, Ryan shouldered him into the opening. The SS man gave a cry of surprise and annoyance and struggled to regain his balance. He turned as he stumbled back between the racks, opening his mouth to cry out when he saw Ryan, but the barrel of Ryan's Schmeisser was already crashing against his neck. The German fell to his knees with a gasp. Stooping, Ryan bundled him farther back among the racks and, putting aside his machine pistol, quietly strangled him.

He crouched over the body a moment, breathing heavily, then shot a quick look back between the racks, toward the platform. He looked directly into the startled face of an Italian civilian, clearly defined against the lesser dimness of the platform beyond the racks. The Italian, graying and well-groomed, remained perfectly still. Ryan could not tell if it were from choice or shock. If the man chose to move there was nothing he could do to stop him. He had put his Schmeisser aside and was in no position to take the Italian by surprise with a sudden spring.

Ryan stared mutely at the Italian, who seemed more curious now than shocked. Still in a squatting position, Ryan carefully rotated on the balls of his feet, avoiding any sudden movement, until he faced the Italian. The Italian stepped back a pace, wary but unafraid. Ryan continued staring into his eyes, looking for some clue to his intentions. The Italian seemed to be studying him in precisely the same manner. It was a stalemate.

"I'm an American," Ryan said quietly. "Prigioniero di guerra."

The Italian's eyes widened in the only indication of his surprise. Still keeping his eyes on Ryan he reached inside his coat. Ryan tensed. If the Italian had a pistol he would have to take a chance on jumping him, regardless of the odds against success. Instead of a pistol the Italian produced a pack of cigarettes. He lit one calmly and ground the match under a narrow, well-polished shoe without looking down at it. Then his left eyelid dropped in a wink and, holding his hand against his chest, made a V sign. Without a word, he turned and sauntered away.

Ryan grabbed his Schmeisser and leaped to his feet. The Italian was strolling toward a string of passenger coaches. Ryan followed him. The Italian did not look back. But neither had the SS officer. The wink and the V sign could have been only a trick. The Italian climbed into one of the coaches and after a moment appeared in a compartment and took a seat by a window. He unfolded a newspaper but before turning to it looked out at the busy platform. His gaze swept past Ryan with no sign of recognition. Then he began reading his paper.

Ryan went back to the battery racks and dragged the body as far back among them as he could. The black uniform was almost invisible in the darkness. No one would find the body without stumbling over it.

Fincham and Costanzo were waiting anxiously at the door of the commander's car.

"We thought you'd had it for fair," said Fincham. "What kept you?"

"What happened?" Costanzo asked.

"That friend of Klement's," Ryan said. "He smelled something. I killed him."

"Good show," Fincham cried.

"When will it end, Cuhnel?" Costanzo said wearily.

"Before the night's over, Padre. If we're lucky."

The men in the cars grew impatient and began banging on

the walls and calling out as they had when the train was still
under German control. The clamor was clearly audible in the
commander's car.

"It's almost an hour to go," Costanzo said. "Couldn't you let
them out for a while, Cuhnel?"

"By morning they'll be out for good, Padre. I'm not going to
take a chance on any of them pulling a Bostick."

Bostick, who was sitting on the sleeping bag with his legs
drawn up under his chin, looked up at the mention of his name,
flushed, and looked down again.

Heinke worked tirelessly at the radio, without results.

"There's a lot of radio traffic, Colonel," he said. "Most of it
coded. If I do stumble onto Verona I might not know what I'm
getting."

"You picking up anything out of Rome?" Ryan asked.

"Plenty, sir. Voice and code both."

"Any of it in the clear?"

"Some, sir. Nothing that amounts to anything, though."

"Keep doodling around with those Rome frequencies," Ryan
said. "Try to figure what net they're in. If Verona starts hunting
for us they're sure to report in to some headquarters in Rome."

Ryan put Stein to work lettering "Dietrich, W. E., Gruppenfuehrer, SS," on half a dozen of Klement's boxes. Klement, who
had been lying in his bed staring at the ceiling, sat up and
watched him. He turned to Ryan.

"For why?" he asked, showing more spirit than he had since
Parma.

"You can read, can't you?" Ryan said.

"There is no Gruppenfuehrer Dietrich," Klement said.

"These boxes say there is," Ryan answered.

"I do not understand," Klement protested.

"You don't have to," Ryan said. "You just have to hope I
know what I'm doing."

"We all hope that, Ryan," Fincham said. "If you don't . . ."

The train left Milan at ten thirty-five and fourteen minutes
later was in Monza.

"What's your man's name?" Ryan asked Fincham. "The one on our car?"

"Evans," said Fincham. "All Welshmen are named Evans, if they're not Morgans."

Ryan climbed to the top of the car and ordered Evans to get down on the off-side and cut the telegraph lines a quarter-mile ahead.

"You've got ten minutes," he said. "Can you make it that fast?"

"Aye, Colonel," said Evans.

He was a short, knotty man with the build of a coal miner.

Returning to the car, Ryan had Fincham and Heinke help him unload the six boxes for Gruppenfuehrer Dietrich and then, with Costanzo's assistance, found an Italian station man to take them in charge. Costanzo, at Ryan's instructions, told the Italian Gruppenfuehrer Dietrich would send for his shipment in the morning and demanded a receipt, which the Italian gave him grudgingly.

"If Monza reports us back to Milan it'll confirm the radio message that got us routed here," Ryan said. "If not, we'll at least have redistributed a little of Klement's loot."

"He sure didn't want to part with it, did he, Cuhnel?"

"Either way, we're in the clear with Milan until we pass Carnate," Ryan continued. "That's where we leave the pattern."

Evans was back at his post when Ryan returned. Ryan summoned him down.

"Everything go okay?" Ryan asked.

Evans nodded.

"Good work. Know anything about railroad switches?"

Evans nodded again.

"When we stop at the next station climb down and cut the wires from the station control. Can you do it with your bayonet?"

"Aye, sir."

"Set the switch manually to take us north if it's not already that way. Then get up ahead and cut the telegraph lines and get back here on the double. Got that?"

"On the double, sir?"

"Quick time."

"Right, sir. Bit of a lark this, ain't it, sir?"

"Glad you think so, Corporal. Wish I did."

Back inside the car, he ordered Fincham to keep an eye on Klement and Bostick, and Heinke to keep working the Rome frequencies.

"Don't let Klement get plastered again," he told Stein. "We may not need him any more but if we do we'll need him bad. Padre, you come with me. We're going to the cab."

He sent the cab guard back to join Fincham in the commander's car and climbed up behind Costanzo. The engineer was glad to see Costanzo but puzzled at the presence of two Germans in his cab. He wanted Ryan to leave, Costanzo explained in pidgin German. Ryan ignored his protests and the engineer lapsed into resentful silence. The fireman, a balding, roundheaded man, said nothing. He merely leaned on his shovel and gazed into the firebox, indifferent to all else.

It was eleven-sixteen when they reached the junction at Carnate. The station was dark and appeared deserted except for a bored and solitary German soldier who tried to start a conversation with the men on the cartops. When no one answered he shrugged and resumed his leisurely patrol of the empty platform.

A door opened with a burst of light and an Italian civilian came out to the engine. He talked for a while with the engineer and Costanzo before going back inside the station. Ryan waited, listening. When he heard Evans returning on the offside of the train he dropped from the cab and caught up with him at the commander's car.

"Okay?" he asked.

"Done, sir."

Ryan crawled over the coupling and opened the door to the commander's car.

"Fincham," he said, keeping his voice too low for the German on the platform to hear, "we're ready to switch north. When we leave the station get down and get on the last car. We'll be stopping right after that. Throw the switch back the other way so if anybody looks they'll think we switched for Bergamo. Then hang on until we stop again a few miles up the line. I'll meet you at our car."

He returned to the cab to find the engineer chatting amiably with Costanzo.

"Tell him we're going north, Padre," Ryan said. "If he does as he's ordered he won't get hurt."

Costanzo was startled by Ryan's use of English. The engineer was dumfounded. The fireman looked up from his shovel, his dull, pleasant face creased in a puzzled frown.

"You can talk English now, Padre," Ryan said. "We're making our move. He's got to know who we are."

"Ah guess he does at that," Costanzo replied.

The engineer stared from one to the other, trying desperately to understand what they were saying. When Costanzo told him what Ryan had said, his incredulity changed to defiance. He folded his arms, spat on the floor, and shook his head violently. Ryan slapped him with his open hand, knocking him back against the tender. The fireman shrank back against the far side of the cab, as far from Ryan as he could get. Ryan bent quickly and jerked the engineer to his feet, pinning him against the tender with a hand at his throat.

"Tell him again, Padre," he said. "Tell him he's got thirty seconds to make up his mind whether he wants to live or die."

The engineer nodded reluctantly when Costanzo translated and Ryan released him.

"Tell the fireman not to worry," Ryan said. "Just keep shoveling that coal."

The fireman bobbed his head eagerly at Costanzo's reassuring words.

"Tell the engineer to start rolling," Ryan said. "When the last car's past the switch, stop."

"His name's Marco," Costanzo said, absently.

"What's eating you, Padre?" Ryan demanded.

"He said he thought Ah was his friend and Ah betrayed him."

"Forget it. He's a miserable Fascist who'd like to see us all on our way to a German prison compound or worse."

"He's a human being."

"I don't intend harming him, if that's any consolation to you, Padre."

"But you'll kill him if you think it's necessary, won't you? Like you did the Germans?"

"Naturally. And make sure he knows that, too."

The train rolled forward a few hundred yards and stopped. Ryan leaned out the cab and looked back. A brief stab of light from Fincham's German flashlight told him the switch was thrown.

"Start him rolling again," Ryan said.

They rode in silence for a few minutes.

"What was all that talk about back at Carnate?" Ryan asked suddenly. "I meant to ask you."

"The dispatcher wanted to know if we saw anything suspicious back down the line. His line to Milan was out. He thought it might be sabotage."

"Did he say there was much of that sort of thing up this way?"

"Ah didn't ask. Sorry."

After ten minutes Ryan said, "This is far enough. Tell him to stop."

The train slowed to a halt.

"I'm leaving you in charge a few minutes, Padre," Ryan said. "You'll have to forget you're a priest and remember you're a soldier. There's a thousand lives at stake."

"Ah'm a priest and Ah can't forget it, Cuhnel. But Ah'll see Marco behaves."

"You'll shoot if you have to?"

"Yes," Costanzo said reluctantly.

Ryan waited for Fincham outside the commander's car.

"What's the drill, Herr Oberst?" Fincham asked.

"Help me get the men off the cars and back inside. I want everybody out of German uniform except Evans and the men in our car."

"Off the cars?" Fincham demanded.

"As of now we're not a prison train any more, Colonel. We're a string of empties heading for Sondrio to pick up freight."

"What sort of bloody freight would call for twenty-four cars?"

"That's a question I hope we don't get asked, Colonel."

"I think we should have the chaps in the Jerry uniforms. Might prove useful."

"If we don't make it everybody in Kraut uniform will have had it. There's just a bare chance the others won't be shot. I want as many men as possible to get that chance."

The men inside the boxcars demanded to be let out when the doors were opened but Ryan refused.

"We've got two or three more hours to go," he said at every car. "You'll just have to stick it out the best you can."

The men's resentment against Ryan had renewed and burgeoned with their apprehension and his brusque orders evoked angry rebuttal. The occupants of a number of cars said they had taken a vote and wanted to leave the train and try for Switzerland individually on foot. Ryan did not bother to argue. He merely locked every door after the man from the roof was inside.

"They're going to be frightfully displeased with you if you don't bring them through this, old cock," Fincham said.

"When they're not displeased with me is when I start worrying, Colonel," Ryan replied.

"I've just had a ghastly thought," Fincham said suddenly as they were walking back toward the head of the train.

"Just one?"

"Since Monza there's been only one bloody track. And we've not been cleared this way. What if we should meet a train coming the other way?"

"One hell of a crash, Colonel. But judging from what I've seen at the stations there isn't much doing up this way this time of night. We'll see what Padre can find out at Lecco."

They rolled into Lecco, on the shore of Lake Como, at twenty minutes after twelve. The little town was dark and silent and no one was at the station except the usual cold and bored German sentry. Ryan let the train go through without stopping.

"There can't be much traffic expected through if there's nobody on duty," Ryan told Costanzo. "We'll just have to take our chances on a clear track."

"If there's something up ahead there'll be a red signal light down along the track, Cuhnel," Costanzo said. "Ah'll be looking."

The air grew colder as the train burrowed deeper into the night and the high country, pinned between Como on one side and the towering Grigne on the other. The engineer maintained a righteous silence, staring straight ahead into the narrow beam of light escaping from an opening in the blue-coated headlight, turning occasionally to glance at Costanzo in bitter reproach.

Ryan studied the map in the beam of his flashlight.

"We hit Lecco just about the time we were due at Bergamo," he told Costanzo. "If Bergamo knows we're coming they may start asking questions. If not, we've got nothing to worry about except meeting another train until we crash the border. Bergamo's farther from Verona than we are from Tirano. So far it still holds that we can make it to Tirano before they miss us at Verona. Cross your fingers, Padre."

"Ah'll cross my whole self, Cuhnel."

Ryan leaned back against the side of the cab and huddled into his German greatcoat. His back was cold but he was warm in front from the heat of the firebox. From now until they reached Tirano it was just a pleasant train ride through the mountains, with plenty of fresh air. He closed his eyes in brief surrender to fatigue.

A cry from Costanzo jarred him to full wakefulness.

"Cuhnel! There's a flare up ahead!"

—XXIII—

Up ahead the night was pierced by a wavering red glow.

"Railblock!" Ryan said. "Tell him to stop the train!"

The engineer hit the brakes and the train began sliding, metal gripping against metal.

"Run back and have Fincham bring Klement up here, if he's fit to meet the public!" Ryan snapped.

Costanzo leaped from the cab as the train stopped sliding.

Fincham came running up with Klement, who was buttoning his tunic over his paunch and protesting with unexpected vigor. He had regained his confidence in the belief that Ryan could no longer hold him responsible for the fate of the train.

"What's up?" Fincham demanded. "Padre didn't say. Oh. I see. What do you think that signifies?"

"Looks like a railblock," Ryan said. "Maybe they're on to us. Take Evans with you and unlock all the doors. Tell the men to sit tight. If they hear a Schmeisser burst, bail out and head into the mountains. Every man for himself. But if they don't hear any shots, sit tight."

"So near and yet so far, eh, Ryan?" Fincham said.

"Too early to tell. Soon's you get back to our car give me a signal with your flashlight."

"Right."

Fincham pounded back into the darkness. Costanzo had returned to the cab while Ryan was giving Fincham his orders.

"Padre," said Ryan, "tell Klement if he's questioned he's on his way to Sondrio to pick up a special shipment. He's under orders not to divulge what it is because it would jeopardize Swiss neutrality. If they ask for orders, he's to say they're back in the command car and he'll send you for them. You start back, then take off like a bird."

"What will you do, Cuhnel?"

"Depends on the situation. But that's no concern of yours. You just take off with the others. That's an order."

The dozen minutes before Fincham's signal flashed from the commander's car were agonizing. The menacing red glow up ahead persisted.

"Tell the engineer to get moving," Ryan said. "Slow. As soon as we're close enough to see what that is up there, stop. We want as much distance between us and the railblock as we can get."

The train crept toward the flare. The splash of red deepened and expanded as they approached, spilling out over the nearby waters of the lake in a shadow-edged pool of blood. Ryan looked intently along the constricted beam of the headlight, his finger curved around the trigger of his Schmeisser. The ray pierced the darkness only a short distance, but as they approached, a bulky mass took shape astride the tracks, bathed in red by the glow of the flare.

"Panzer!" Klement grunted.

"Stop!" Ryan cried.

The train stopped.

The barrel of the tank's 88-millimeter gun was clearly outlined against the crimson light. The turret was facing almost directly down the tracks. Two helmeted figures detached themselves from the shadow of the tank and ran toward the engine.

"Tell Klement if we get in trouble the signal is a machine pistol burst," Ryan said to Costanzo. "And if I have to give it it'll be into his back."

He pushed the snout of the Schmeisser into Klement's back and waited.

The soldiers shouted as they ran. When they neared the locomotive the engineer made a sudden movement and called out. Ryan whirled, the Schmeisser at shoulder level. The short barrel caught the Italian across the bridge of the nose and he fell to the floor of the cab and lay there moaning. Without another look at him, Ryan pressed the Schmeisser into Klement's back again. The fireman leaned on his shovel and said nothing.

"The soldiers don't speak Italian," Costanzo whispered. "They're asking what he said."

"Tell Klement to ask them what they want. He knows what he's supposed to say if they ask questions."

The Germans were at the engine now, looking up into the crowded cab. They were hard-faced, alert men. The taller of the pair shouted with harsh urgency. When he saw he was in the presence of an officer he snapped to attention and saluted, followed by his companion. When he spoke again it was with more respect but no less urgency.

"What's he saying?" Ryan whispered. "Is he asking for our orders?"

"No," Costanzo whispered. "He says there's a dangerous crossing up ahead. Italian bandits tried to blow up the road and railway bridges."

"Have Klement find out if the tracks are usable."

Costanzo was standing back in the cab, visible from the ground but partially concealed by Klement. He could whisper to the German without being overheard on the ground.

"The track's not damaged," Costanzo reported after Klement's inquiry. "But they're afraid the trestle won't hold the weight of the train. They want us to go back to Lecco until it's checked and repaired."

"Have Klement tell 'em the train's empty and should be light enough to make it. We've got an important pickup in Sondrio. And they better be damn sure to have the trestle repaired by the time we come back loaded in the morning. And shove your handkerchief in Marco's mouth. They might hear his moaning down there."

The soldier listened respectfully to Klement, then sent his companion running back to the tank. He returned with a sergeant. Klement was obliged to repeat his demands. The three Germans walked a few feet away and went into a conference. The sergeant returned alone.

"He says it's too dangerous," Costanzo translated. "But if the major insists he must obey the orders of a superior officer. If the major insists on taking the train across the bridge he respectfully asks for something in writing to show he halted the train and informed us of the situation. In case there is an inquiry later."

"Tell Klement to give it to him. You write it and have Klement sign it."

"I haven't got pencil and paper."

"Get it from Klement."

Costanzo whispered to the major.

"He doesn't either," he told Ryan.

"There's paper and pencil in the commander's car," Ryan said. "Get back there and get it fast. But tell Klement not to open his mouth. If the sergeant says anything to him he's to shake his head."

Costanzo ran back to the commander's car. When he returned, Fincham sauntered after him, to lounge carelessly against the back of the tender, his Schmeisser dangling from his hand.

Costanzo scrawled a note acknowledging they had been warned of the condition of the bridge and gave it to Klement to sign.

"You hand it to the Feldwebel, Padre," Ryan said. "And be damn sure Klement didn't write anything on it but his name."

Costanzo handed down the note. The sergeant read it in the beam of his flashlight, saluted and barked an order. The soldiers saluted him and ran back to the tank.

"Hold him a minute, Padre," Ryan said. "Find out how he

knew we were coming and if he knows if there's anything coming south up ahead."

Costanzo passed the question through Klement.

"He didn't know we were coming," Costanzo said when the sergeant had explained. "They blocked the tracks to be on the safe side when they couldn't get through to Lecco. He thinks the same bandits who tried to blow up the bridges must have cut the telegraph lines to Lecco."

"What about southbound traffic?"

"Nothing between here and Colico, wherever that is."

"It's about twenty-five miles north of Lecco. Where we head east for Tirano."

"He doesn't have any information beyond Colico. Any train coming south would get the word there about the bad bridge."

"That leaves us with a forty-, forty-five-mile blank between Colico and Tirano," Ryan said. "I'll worry about that when we get across the bridge."

The sergeant saluted again and returned to the tank. The two soldiers had already climbed inside and now started backing the tank from the tracks under his supervision. Fincham sauntered to the cab and handed a cigarette up to Ryan.

"Bloody near one, that," he said in a low voice. "For a moment I thought we were in for a bit of a do."

"Could be worse. We found out they think Italians cut the Lecco wire. And there's clear track ahead. Has Heinke come up with anything?"

"Sweet Fanny Adams. But he's identified SS headquarters transmissions from Rome."

"In the clear?"

"Some coded, some not."

"If he hears anything I ought to know, shine your light up toward the cab."

"Righty ho."

"Soon's the Feldwebel gives the go-ahead we're moving on."

"Risky business, that railway bridge."

"The whole thing's a risky business. You can get out and walk across if you're nervous."

"Are you walking across, Colonel?"

"No."

"Thought not. Shall I take Von Ignatz back to his private car now?"

"Do that. We're ready to go."

"Cheers, Colonel," said Fincham, reaching up for Klement. "Come along, Iggy."

Costanzo had propped the engineer against the tender in a sitting position and was wiping the blood from his face. Both the Italian's eyes were beginning to puff. The fireman had continued his slow, mechanical stoking. His frequent stealthy looks at the engineer revealed he was not so unconcerned as he pretended to be.

The engineer tried to pull away from Costanzo's solicitous hands but Costanzo persisted until the Italian's face was clean. His nose had stopped bleeding.

"He may have a broken nose but he won't die from it, Padre," Ryan said. "Get him on his feet and tell him to move us out. Tell him to take it slow and if he feels the bridge going to throw her into reverse. Then you get back to the front of the second car and stand by to uncouple if it looks like the bridge's going. You know how to uncouple a boxcar?"

"No."

"Ask the fireman. Then let's get moving."

The train moved forward. The sergeant waved as the engine went by and Ryan returned the gesture.

"Good luck, Cuhnel," Costanzo said as he prepared to crawl back along the tender.

"I didn't know you believed in luck, Padre. I thought you were strictly a praying man."

"Sometimes you need a little luck for your prayers to be answered, Cuhnel."

There was a soldier standing guard on the trestle when they reached it, a mile up the track. He held up a round reflector on a long handle as they approached but did not try to flag them down. He called out something as the train edged by but Ryan merely waved in reply.

The locomotive inched onto the trestle. The span seemed sturdy enough but it creaked and groaned and when it took the full weight of the heavy engine gave off sharp, cracking sounds like pistol shots. Though the engineer had not understood the conversation about the bridge, the situation was obvious to him. He held his breath and nursed the lumbering engine along the trestle as if leading a kitten by a string. The span sagged noticeably when they reached the center and the fireman looked up from the firebox in panic. Past the center, the trestle seemed firmer.

Then they were on solid ground again. The fireman crossed himself. The boxcars, much lighter than the engine, rolled across without incident. The middle cars were still on the trestle when Costanzo came crawling back to the cab.

"Have a good pray, Padre?" Ryan asked.

"Couldn't you tell from the results, Cuhnel?"

Ryan looked at the luminous dial of his watch.

"How we doing for time, Cuhnel?" asked Costanzo.

"No problem. I make us about twelve, fifteen miles from Colico. Another forty-five or less to Tirano. It's one-thirteen now, which ought to put us at Tirano by three at the latest. Gives us a three-hour spread before dawn. More than enough. Not a thing to worry about, Padre. Except blown bridges, another train, and crashing the border. And Verona getting in a flap and trying to locate us."

When they were a mile or so past the bridge, Ryan had Costanzo tell the engineer to stop the train.

"Get on back and tell Fincham to lock the men in again," Ryan said. "Some of 'em may start getting a wild hair."

When Costanzo returned he said, "Gus Heinke picked up something that ought to interest you, Cuhnel. SS headquarters in Milan just radioed Rome about the brutal murder of an Obersturmfuehrer Aschenhof in the station."

"So they found Klement's friend. Anything to tie us to it?"

"Not as far as Gus knows. They didn't give any details."

"That sounds like the frequency we want. Is he staying on it?"

"Yes, sir."

The locomotive rolled on between Como and the Grigne, now moving easily, now toiling up the shoulder of a slope leaning down toward the lake. The settlements through which they passed were dark, the stations deserted.

"That's a good sign," Ryan said. "Seems like they'd have somebody on duty if there was any traffic."

The grade sloped down now.

"We must be getting close to Colico," Ryan said. "The junction's beyond it. One line goes north to Chiavenna. We want the other one. Have the engineer stop the train as soon as we spot the junction up ahead."

Colico was dark and silent like the villages before it and the train rolled through without stopping. Ryan had the engineer slow the train to a crawl to they would not overrun the junction. Ryan and Costanzo spied the dividing tracks almost simultaneously. When the train stopped Ryan sent Costanzo back to the commander's car.

"Send Evans up ahead to make sure the Sondrio switch is open for us. And tell Colonel Fincham to get up here."

In a moment Evans trotted by the engine and Fincham came hurrying along behind him.

"What's the drill?" he asked.

"We're on our final approach," Ryan said. "About forty miles to go."

"Just what do you propose doing at Tirano?" Fincham said. "Jerry may get a bit sticky about letting us by."

"That's what I wanted to see you about. I doubt if the Krauts will have much at the station the time of the morning we'll be getting there. A man or two at the most. We'll stop at the station and have Klement call 'em to his car. Then we'll cut the lines in and out of the station before we go on. Tirano's not right on the border but I can't tell exactly how far from my map."

"There's no doubt a checkpoint at the border."

"They'll figure we've been cleared through at Tirano. We'll slow down as if we're stopping, then barrel on across before they can get a railblock up."

Evans returned from the junction to report the track to Sondrio was open.

"We'll be moving on, then," said Ryan. "If there's any static at Sondrio I'll be back for Klement. How's he holding up?"

"The bloody bugger's sleeping like a baby. What'll we do with him after Tirano?"

"Shove him out with the engineer."

"Let the bloody bag of suet go free? Not bloody likely. I'll take care of Von Ignatz."

"No. I promised him he wouldn't be harmed if he got us through."

"A promise to a Jerry's worth no more than a promise from a Jerry. Or have you forgotten Herr Oberstleutnant Spoetzl so quickly?"

"I haven't forgotten. And I'm not Spoetzl. We're letting Klement go unharmed."

"I'm that shocked, old boy. Von Ryan gone soft."

"Wish you'd tell that to Padre Costanzo. I think he's worried about my soul."

"Gritty little bugger, isn't he? Bloody fine soldier if he weren't a priest."

"He's a bloody fine soldier, period. We couldn't have made it without a man who spoke both German and Italian."

"Unusual in a Yank, you know. Most of you can't even speak English properly."

"You better get on back. Keep Heinke monitoring that SS net and let me know the minute he hears anything that might affect us."

"Needn't fret on that count, Ryan. He won't even leave the bloody wireless to empty his bladder."

Costanzo returned from the commander's car and the train moved on. They ran smoothly between the highway and the river Adda in the broad valley of the Valtellina.

"Emil Bostick's in the dumps, Cuhnel," Costanzo said. "He knows he was wrong leaving the train. He said not to tell you that but Ah think you ought to know."

"I don't need Bostick to tell me it was wrong, Padre."

"That's not what Ah meant, Cuhnel. And you know it. Ah think he deserves credit for admitting he did wrong."

"By your accounting system, Padre. Not mine. Look. We don't know a thing about the setup at Tirano. See if Marco knows this part of the country. Find out what the station's like, how far it is to the border, and what kind of checkpoint the Krauts have there."

The engineer, whose eyes were blackening, refused to answer Costanzo's questions.

"Guess he's a little sore at me," said Ryan.

"He's more angry with me than you, Cuhnel. You only broke his nose. He thought Ah was his friend."

"Tell him you're a priest."

"He wouldn't believe it. Not after the way he's seen me act."

"Don't you carry some kind of credentials or something, Padre?"

"Just my shining faith," Costanzo said with a hint of a smile. "Anyhow, Ah think he'd be more disappointed than ever in me if he knew Ah was a priest. Italians expect their priests to act a little more . . ."

"Priestly?" Ryan put in.

"That's the word."

"Maybe you're right. This guy's not as easy to scare as Klement. But he knows I mean business. Look. Pretend to argue with me. Then tell him I want to kill him now that we don't need him any more but you don't want me to. Tell him to please co-operate with me so the blood of a fellow Catholic won't be on your hands."

Ryan and Costanzo argued hotly about the relative merits

of Big Ten and Southern football, then Costanzo turned to the engineer. At first the engineer would not even look at him but then, with a baleful glance at Ryan, he responded.

"He says the tracks out of Tirano have been torn up," Costanzo said. "And the border's sealed and heavily guarded."

"He's lying," said Ryan. "If the tracks were torn up there'd be no reason for a heavy guard."

"What if he's not?"

"We'll stop before we reach Tirano and I'll run a reccy. We've got time. It's only two-ten. I expect it'll be three or later before Verona starts wondering."

"What about other trains on this track?"

"So far all the signs seem to indicate nothing's moving."

"Don't you ever have any doubts about anything, Cuhnel?"

"I try never to have doubts, Padre. Only alternatives."

It was three-forty when they reached the outskirts of Sondrio. Minutes later they glided through the station. The town was completely dark and the station appeared shut down for the night with only the now familiar guard on duty. Ryan waved to him as they passed. Then they were in open vineyard country again in the narrowing, steepening valley.

"We'll be in Tirano in half an hour," Ryan said. "We'll stop the train before we get in and I'll sneak up ahead for a look."

The engineer began singing to himself in a raspy, nasal voice.

"What's he so cheerful about all of a sudden?" Ryan demanded. "A few minutes ago he was so mad he was tripping over his lower lip."

"Ah don't know," said Costanzo. "Maybe he's decided Switzerland might not be so bad."

"I don't like it. He doesn't want to see us make it. Maybe he wasn't lying about the tracks out of Tirano."

Ryan looked from the map to his watch and back again.

"Verona'll be checking with Milan after a while," he said. "Then Milan will start checking along the route. When they find out we didn't make it to Bergamo they'll start wondering. Unless they suspect we left the scheduled route my guess is they'll have people make an eyeball check of the rails between Monza and Bergamo. By the time they tumble we're not stalled somewhere along the way we'll have made our final move. If Milan keeps SS headquarters read in on what they're doing Heinke'll hear it."

The engineer kept singing. Once he turned to stare at Ryan with a curiously smug expression on his battered face.

"I don't like it," Ryan said again. "He knows something we don't. And I wish to hell I knew what it was. Pump him, Padre."

The engineer responded freely. Too freely, Ryan thought. He admitted to Costanzo he knew nothing about Tirano. He had never before been beyond Sondrio, where the state railway system ended and a privately operated line took over. For all he knew, the line went directly to St. Moritz and in a few hours the Americani and Inglesi would be skiing and stuffing themselves with chocolates.

"He's ribbing us," Ryan said. "Where's he getting all that confidence?"

The steady throb of the engine stopped and the train lost speed.

"What's going on?" Ryan demanded, seizing the engineer by the arm.

The engineer said nothing.

"Padre, find out why the engine's stopped. And tell him to start it up again."

The train was coasting and steadily losing speed. With no engine noises, the clicking of wheels over rail joints was clearly audible.

The engineer pointed at the water gauge as he answered Costanzo. There was no water level.

"He says the boiler'll crack if he does," Costanzo said. "We're out of water."

"We can't be," Ryan cried.

He spun the engineer around to face him.

"We must have had enough to take us to Verona," Ryan said. "And we haven't come any farther than that. Tell him I know he's stalling and if he knows what's good for him he'll come off it and get moving."

The engineer unleashed a spate of words, his voice full of triumph.

"He's been releasing water since Colico," Costanzo said. "Something about priming the injectors, as near as Ah can make out."

"There's got to be water in the tender. Tell him to transfer it."

"He says the tender's empty," Costanzo said. "He's run it all out."

"I don't believe it. Tell the fireman to check."

The fireman checked a valve and reluctantly confirmed what the engineer had said. Ryan transferred his grip from the engineer's shoulder to the front of his jacket and pulled him close.

"You're not going to harm him, Cuhnel?" Costanzo said.

"Too late for that, Padre," Ryan said, releasing the Italian.

The train slowed to a halt, hung poised a moment on the grade, then began rolling back.

"Tell him to hit the brakes!" Ryan ordered.

The engineer did so before he was told.

"Kill the light!" said Ryan.

The weak beam of the painted-over headlight went out.

The train was enveloped in chill darkness and a tense, penetrating silence, the locomotive and its twenty-four cars pinned to the long grade by its brakes, like a worm rigid in death on a mounting board. To the north was the Swiss border and refuge, as inaccessible behind its bastion of mountains as if it were a continent away. To the south lay all of Italy, a vast enemy camp. Soon men would be probing the main lines and sidings, searching for the missing train. But ten miles ahead rails pierced the mountains. Ten miles away lay freedom, receding with every minute that passed.

And the train lay motionless, groaning as its metal contracted in the deepening cold.

"*What do we do now, Cuhnel?*" Costanzo asked quietly. "Start walking?"

Before Ryan could answer, Fincham came running up.

"What's up?" he demanded. "Why've we stopped here?"

"We're out of water," said Ryan.

"What?"

"Marco here. He ran us out of water. The machine is non functione."

"What the bloody hell are we waiting for, in that case?" Fincham said. "Let's finish the bugger and get cracking for the border."

"Let's not go off half-cocked, Colonel. Come on back to the car, where it's warm. Padre, tell Marco and the fireman to come along."

Klement was sleeping and Stein, Bostick, and Evans were sitting at the table drinking coffee. Heinke was at the radio. They all looked at Ryan when he got into the car.

Evans sprang to his feet, embarrassed to be found sitting down with officers. Stein's eyes were bleary from lack of sleep and he needed a shave. Bostick had a black eye and a swollen lip. There was a bruise on one cheek.

"Anything wrong, Colonel?" Stein asked.

"The engineer ran us out of water," Ryan said.

"Then we're in big trouble, aren't we?"

"That's what I'm back here to figure out, Captain. You men clear the table so we can spread out the map."

He sent the fireman and engineer to sit on Klement's boxes and then bent over the map with Fincham.

"I make us about here," Ryan said, pointing to a spot three miles east of Sondrio. "That puts us about five, six miles from the nearest border point. About twelve from Tirano."

"It's only 0300 hours," Fincham said, studying the map. "If we got cracking now we could reach the border here well before dawn."

"Not with the mountains we'd have to climb. And with a thousand men on the move, the Krauts would spot us before we got near the border."

"In that case we'll simply spread out and try for the border in small groups."

"Spread out where, Colonel? We're in a funnel. Mountains to the south and mountains to the north and the valley getting narrower and narrower up ahead. And if we go back we're that much farther away from the border."

"What else is there, Ryan?" Fincham demanded.

Klement sat up and rubbed his eyes. His jaw dropped when he saw the engineer.

"Why we are stilled?" he asked.

He frowned petulantly when no one answered.

"Tirano's still our only real chance," Ryan said. "We're close to Sondrio. I'm going back there and try to steal a water truck."

"That leaves the lot of us in rather an awkward position, don't it, Ryan?" Fincham said. "What with Jerry likely to start wondering what's become of us any moment now."

"I'm taking Padre with me," Ryan said, as if Fincham had not spoken. "I may need an interpreter. Send Evans a quarter-mile back and Captain Stein the same distance ahead. If they hear a train coming they can flag it down before it rams into us. If they spot a Kraut patrol they're to get back here on the double. Either way, I want you to let the men out of the cars and start 'em for the border. Or if I'm not back in an hour. Until then, keep 'em locked in. But you better go back along the train and tell 'em to keep quiet. Bostick, can I trust you to keep Klement and the Italians out of mischief?"

"Yes, sir," Bostick said stonily.

"And Lieutenant Heinke, you keep listening out on that SS frequency," Ryan said. "If you hear anything that sounds like they're on to us tell Colonel Fincham immediately. He'll know what to do."

Heinke, who had slipped off one earphone to listen, nodded and put it back.

"One more thing, Colonel," Ryan said. "If you have to leave the train, try to hide the dead Krauts somewhere before you take off. Be a lot better for us if the Germans don't find 'em right away."

"Roger," said Fincham. "That's the proper Yank reply, isn't it?"

"Come on, Padre," Ryan said. "Let's get a move on."

Fincham thrust out his hand.

"Good luck," he said quietly.

"Thanks," Ryan replied.

They shook hands.

Though he was bone-tired and ached in every joint, and the stiff material of the German uniform chafed his raw elbows and knees, Ryan maintained such a rapid pace that Costanzo had to trot to keep up with him.

"What if you can't find a tank truck with the key in it?" Costanzo said, panting. "Or have you stolen cars before?"

"I know how to short an ignition," Ryan said. "That's the least of our problems."

They had been walking only a few minutes when a figure stepped from the darkness alongside the tracks and confronted them.

"Buon giorno, amici," the newcomer said pleasantly. "Dove andate?"

Ryan covered him immediately with his Schmeisser and motioned Costanzo to approach the man. The Italian answered Costanzo's questions readily. Ryan summoned Costanzo back a few steps, still keeping his machine pistol pointed at the stranger.

"What's he doing out here this time of night?" Ryan whispered. "What's he want with us?"

"He lives near here," Costanzo said. "He said he heard the train stop and came to see if he could be of service to his German comrades. He wants to know what's on the train."

"Tell him none of his business. And then stand clear. We can't have him running around loose."

Costanzo spoke to the Italian but before he could step aside the Italian whistled and a dozen men came running out of the darkness to surround them. Ryan made an involuntary movement with the Schmeisser, then lowered it. He could not possibly get them all. The Italian thrust his face in Ryan's, no longer deferential and pleasant but harshly demanding. He was inches shorter than Ryan, clean shaven but in need of a haircut. His breath smelled of garlic and Ryan suddenly was reminded of the carabinieri who had captured him. He pushed the Italian away and stared at him with grim defiance. The armed men raised their rifles menacingly.

"He's taking us back to the train to see for himself," Costanzo whispered. "If we try to warn our comrades he'll kill us."

"It doesn't figure," Ryan whispered back. "He's not acting like a friend of the Krauts."

The Italian had been listening closely. His face grew puzzled.

"Voi non siete tedeschi," he said. "Chi siete?"

"I hope he's not," Costanzo said. "He knows we're not German."

"Inglesi!" the Italian blurted, showing his teeth in an incredulous grin.

"Americani," Ryan said calmly.

The Italian grabbed his hand and pumped it, then embraced Costanzo.

"Amico," he said. "Fren'."

His companions began talking excitedly while he engaged Costanzo in conversation. Costanzo looked to Ryan for instructions.

"He wants to know what we're doing way up here in German uniforms," he said.

"Give him the whole story," Ryan said. "And find out what he's up to."

The Italian was impressed when he learned Ryan was a colonel. He turned and saluted before continuing with his account.

"Some of his men are from around here and some slipped back over the border after the capitulation," Costanzo explained. "They're operating against the Fascists and Germans up here until they decide whether to work their way south or go on over to the Brenner area. Everything's too unsettled now. They need weapons and explosives. And a radio."

"Are they the ones who tried to blow up the bridge out of Lecco?"

The Italian nodded when Costanzo asked him.

"He's very sorry he failed," Costanzo said. "He didn't have the proper charge."

"I'm damn glad he didn't," said Ryan.

"They were on their way to attack our train when he saw us," Costanzo continued.

"Find out if he can get us some water and if he knows the Tirano area. He must, if he's been operating around here."

The Italian had two trucks and twenty-one more men just off the highway. He would send men back to Sondrio to steal a tank truck.

"He can tell you whatever you want to know about Tirano," Costanzo said. "He knows it very well."

"Tell him to come on back to the train with us," Ryan said. "We can talk it over there. I want Fincham to know we've got water coming."

The Italian gave an order and his men faded into the night.

"Ask him what chance he thinks we'd have of working our way south with him to guide us," Ryan said when they were walking back toward the train.

"Impossible," Costanzo said, after a conference. "He says it'll be hard enough just getting his own men through if he decides to take them south."

"Could we hide out in the mountains and try it later?" Ryan asked.

"He says no," Costanzo replied. "There're too many of us. Not enough food, not enough cover. And it'd draw so many troops here he couldn't operate himself. Why you asking, Cuhnel?"

"Just exploring the alternatives, Padre. Looks like it's still Switzerland or nothing."

When they neared the train a figure rose out of the darkness and lifted a rifle. It was Evans, who had been posted there at Ryan's instructions.

"Halt," he called. "Stand and be recognized."

"It's Colonel Ryan," Ryan snapped. "Don't you know better than to stand there in plain sight, soldier? And to talk English? Get down and if somebody comes along make sure you know who it is before you start sounding off. If it's a Kraut, get on back to the train without letting him hear you."

"Yes, sir," Evans said, abashed.

The train was dark. As they walked by the cars they could hear a low murmur of voices inside them.

"Back so soon?" Fincham demanded when Ryan's face appeared in the car door. "You can't have done the job already."

Ryan climbed in, followed by Costanzo and the Italian.

"We found a friend," Ryan said.

The Italian looked quickly around the room, scowling when he saw the engineer and fireman. He pointed at them and the other occupants of the car, asking questions.

"He wants to know if the Italians are with us or against us," Costanzo said. "And if everyone in German uniform is American."

When Costanzo identified the occupants to the Italian, the newcomer said something short and bitter to the engineer. The engineer flushed and looked away defiantly.

The Italian moved to the radio and fondled it. His eyes lingered on the rifles Fincham had stacked at one end of the car, and then on Klement's boxes and bundles.

"He wants the radio and the rifles and whatever else his men can use against the Fascists," Costanzo translated.

"Everything but the radio," Ryan said.

The Italian nodded in agreement and stepped back from the radio with a last reluctant pat. He joined Ryan, Fincham, and Costanzo at the table, where the map was spread out.

"Tell him what we intend to do," Ryan said.

The Italian spoke rapidly, making stabbing gestures at Tirano. Costanzo's face grew somber.

"Ah'm afraid it's bad news, Cuhnel," he said. "The tracks don't go right through Tirano. It's what he calls a head-in station. You go in and then have to back out and switch onto a different track for the border."

"We'll work something out," Ryan said. "Find out how far it is to the border and whether they keep it blocked."

It was five uphill kilometers to the border-crossing at Campo Cologno, which had a well-guarded checkpoint but no fixed barricade. It could, however, be quickly blocked if the guards wanted to stop a train from going through.

Ryan rubbed his chin.

"Ask him if he thinks he could take the checkpoint and hold it ten minutes," Ryan said.

The Italian said he could.

"But it'll have to be before dawn," Costanzo said. "And if the Tedeschi call in a tank he'll have to pull out. The Germans have a couple tanks up here and some armored cars."

"It's three-forty now," Ryan said. "That gives us over two hours of darkness. Find out how long he thinks it'll be before his men get back with the water."

Before Costanzo could ask, Heinke said, "Colonel!" and held up his hand.

Everyone turned to look at him. Heinke was listening intently, his brow wrinkled in concentration.

"Milan just told SS headquarters we've been reported overdue at Verona," he said. "Milan's checking all stations along the route. SS headquarters is trying to contact us."

"They checking north of Carnate?"

"No way of knowing, sir. They're checking by telegraph. All I can get is what Milan SS headquarters reports to Rome by radio."

"That tears it," said Fincham.

"Not necessarily," Ryan said. "We're in the clear to Carnate. If they check the switch there they'll think we headed back toward Bergamo. They've got no reason to suspect trouble. Unless somebody starts asking questions about Gruppenfuehrer Dietrich. And examining the radio orders that diverted us to Milan."

"Ah hung on to them, Cuhnel," Costanzo said quietly.

"Good. Then that just leaves Gruppenfuehrer Dietrich to worry about."

Ryan smacked a fist into his palm.

"And that sergeant at the bridge," he said. "He's got a piece of paper with Klement's name on it. If it turns up in the wrong place it'll place us north of Lecco."

"Jolly prospect," said Fincham.

"Keep me posted, Lieutenant," Ryan ordered. "How about that water, Padre?"

"He says very soon," Costanzo replied. "His men are expert."

"All right," said Ryan. "Say we're moving by four. That still gives us two hours of darkness."

He pondered a moment.

"Here's what we'll do. You translate it for our friend while I tell Colonel Fincham. When we roll into Tirano they won't be expecting us or know who we are. Unless Rome has alerted 'em by radio. In that case we've had it. We'll know when we get there. We head into the station as if we intend to stop and report in. We'll have a man in German uniform hanging on the end of the last car. The minute we roll past the switch to the outbound track he'll signal us with his flashlight and drop off. Soon's he's thrown it he'll give us another signal. Then we start backing out.

"That's when we tip our hand. We should be out of the depot before they can stop us. But from then on, everything they've got will be alerted. Including the checkpoint."

Fincham nodded. So did the Italian when Costanzo translated.

"This is where timing becomes important," Ryan continued. "If our friends hit the checkpoint before we reach Tirano, there's always the chance the Krauts there will have time to alert the Krauts at Tirano something's up. If we make our break from Tirano before they hit the checkpoint it'll be the other way around and their Krauts would have their guard up."

"Si, colonnello," the Italian said, nodding his head vigorously.

He said something to Costanzo.

"He likes the way you operate, Cuhnel," Costanzo said.

"We'll have to work out a signal," Ryan said. "Ask him if he's got any flares."

The Italian shook his head regretfully.

"We have, Colonel Ryan," Bostick said. "There's a whole box of 'em. And a flare pistol."

"Thanks, Captain," Ryan said curtly. "He'll take red and green flares with him. When we enter the depot we'll give him two short blasts on the whistle. That's his signal to move. Soon's he has the checkpoint secured he gives us a green flare. If they're beaten off, he'll fire a red. If he gives us a red, we'll abandon the train and start scrambling. We'll unlock all the doors before we pull out of here."

Fincham touched his mustache with a knuckle.

"Seems sound enough," he said.

"All right," said Ryan. "Padre and I'll ride in the cab. Everybody else except the man on the last car gets back into his own uniform. Fincham, tell Evans to get Captain Stein and report back here. Then go down the line and tell every car we're on the last leg and nobody's to make a move unless they hear one long blast of the whistle. And to be damn sure they don't move on two short ones. If they get the long blast, they're to take off and scatter. And Colonel, I want every dead German moved into the car behind the engine."

Fincham shot him a questioning look.

"We're not going into a neutral country with a load of dead Krauts," Ryan said. "We'll send the car back with the engine."

"I'm on my way," said Fincham.

He jumped out and slid the door shut behind him.

"Anything new, Lieutenant?" Ryan asked Heinke.

"Milan's told SS headquarters we dropped out of sight after Monza. Just a minute, sir."

He broke off and listened.

"SS headquarters in Rome just said they have no record of any Gruppenfuehrer Dietrich. For Milan to check with Monza and see what they have on him."

"Looks like they're breathing down our necks, Cuhnel," Costanzo said soberly.

"Doesn't mean they suspect we've come north," Ryan said. "Even if they do know something's fishy. Stay with it, Lieutenant."

Bostick cleared his throat.

"Colonel Ryan," he said.

"Yes, Captain?"

"Sir, I'd like to be the man to throw the switch. At Tirano." Ryan studied him.

"On your record you're hardly the man for that job, Captain." Bostick's face was stiff.

"You never did have much use for me, did you, Colonel?" he said.

"You never gave me any cause to, Captain."

"How does a man get a chance to do that once he's on your

list, Colonel?" Bostick said bitterly. "Or don't you ever change your mind once it's made up?"

Ryan regarded him in silence. Bostick stood his scrutiny without flinching.

"You'll never fit into one of those Kraut uniforms," Ryan said at last. "You'll have to get by with my greatcoat. It's the biggest one we've got."

Bostick opened his mouth to say something but Ryan cut him off.

"This may be a point in your favor at your court-martial, Captain," he said evenly. "Don't expect it to outweigh the bad ones."

Klement had been sitting quietly on his bed listening with agonized concentration to everything that had gone on since Ryan's return to the car. Now that Ryan seemed free for a moment he suddenly spoke up.

"Well, Ah'll be . . ." Costanzo exclaimed. "Cuhnel, he wants to go with us. He says he's tired of fighting."

"Tired of fighting?" Ryan demanded. "He's never done any. Tell him there'll be no sandbagging on this trip."

"Sandbagging?" Costanzo said.

"That's when a pilot comes along just to get flying time," Ryan said. "Tell him Tirano's as far as he goes."

Klement argued with Costanzo.

"He says if you take him along you can have everything," Costanzo said, nodding toward Klement's loot.

"Tell him it's not his to give, Padre. Our friend here will see that it's redistributed where it'll do the most good."

Klement protested bitterly when Costanzo translated but lapsed into brooding silence when the Italian, for whom Costanzo also translated Ryan's words, made a slicing motion with his palm upturned, a gesture of unmistakable menace.

He did not want the larger art treasures, the Italian said. They would only be a burden to men obliged to travel light. He would take only such necessities as food, military supplies, clothing, and whatever valuables might be readily bartered for them.

"What about the wine?" Ryan asked.

The Italian seemed surprised by the question.

"He said he wanted the necessities," Costanzo said with a smile. "Obviously that includes the wine."

When Stein and Evans returned to the car Ryan told them to change into their own uniforms.

"I'm going outside to wait for the tank truck," Ryan said. "If Heinke picks up anything, let me know. And when Colonel Fincham comes back send him up to the engine."

He took Costanzo and the Italian forward. He stood with his hands in his pockets and looked back along the train, all but the first few cars hidden by the night. But he knew they were there, twenty-four of them, and that inside them were German corpses and almost a thousand men waiting in painful silence, woven together in a ragged tapestry of arms and legs, breathing foul air, knowing the next hour would bring freedom or death but helpless to influence the outcome. Ryan shivered involuntarily.

"Cold, Cuhnel?" Costanzo asked.

"No," said Ryan.

At five after four Fincham came running out of the darkness.

"Heard a vehicle coming our way," he said. "Think it's our bowser?"

"It's due," said Ryan.

Then they could all hear the grinding sound of a heavy vehicle running slowly and a pair of dim bluish lights nicked the darkness like the eyes of some monstrous cat. A tank truck marked with a swastika lurched to a halt abreast of the locomotive. Two grinning Italians climbed from the cab. They shook hands all around, then one unlimbered the hose while the other prepared the tender to receive it.

"Tell them they don't have to fill it," Ryan said. "Just enough to let us roll. And tell 'em to snap it up. We haven't got all day."

Costanzo spoke to the man who seemed to be directing the operation, then turned a stricken face toward Ryan.

"Cuhnel," he said. "He says it'll take an hour to get up steam again."

—XXV—

Ryan's face stiffened into impassivity. When he spoke there was nothing in his voice to indicate the gravity of the situation.

"That complicates things a little, doesn't it, Padre?" he said.

"That's one way of putting it," Fincham said. "I'd say we've bloody well had it. I'll be getting back to tell the chaps we're abandoning the train."

Ryan stopped him with a gesture.

"Ask them if they can't beat that, Padre?" he said.

Only by a few minutes at the most, was the reply.

Ryan looked at his watch.

"Four-ten," he said. "Yesterday morning dawn was at six-six. Up here it'll be four or five minutes later. If we can get up steam by five-ten we'll still have about an hour before dawn. We're not dead yet. Let's get back inside."

Inside the commander's car, Stein and Evans had already changed uniform and Heinke was buttoning a khaki shirt, the headset still clamped to his ears.

"What's the latest, Lieutenant?" Ryan asked.

"They couldn't find any Gruppenfuehrer Dietrich. Just a Hauptmann Diederich. Now they think the diversion to Monza was some personal business of Major Klement's. They opened the boxes and found 'em full of loot. He's in big trouble with the SS."

Klement looked up at the mention of his name.

"That's a break," said Ryan. "But what about the train?"

"They think we must be stalled somewhere between Carnate and Bergamo, sir. They've got patrols out checking the line."

Ryan looked at the map.

"Something under thirty kilometers of track," he said. "Should keep 'em busy a half-hour or so. When did they start the search?"

"Just ordered 'em out, Colonel. Almost when you were coming in the door."

Something about Stein appeared strange. Ryan stared at him.

"I had to put on Padre's uniform, Colonel," he said. "I left mine in our old car and . . . I couldn't get to it. The bodies. Doesn't fit so good, does it?"

"I'll overlook that under the circumstances," Ryan said dryly. "We've got bigger problems. We've got bigger problems. We're stuck here another hour."

Despite the shock of the announcement, Ryan's apparent unconcern had a steadying effect and Stein and the others took it well.

"Here we are at the bloody conference table again," Fincham said impatiently. "What's the drill?"

"We assume departure time's five-ten," Ryan said. "We can make it to Tirano in under twenty minutes. We'll lose maybe four, five minutes there unless something goes wrong. Then another six, eight minutes to the checkpoint. Thirty-five minutes at the outside. That'll leave our friends a good fifteen minutes or more of darkness to cover their pullout. Ask him if that's enough, Padre."

The Italian shrugged and spread his hands when he answered.

"He says it's not much time," Costanzo said. "But he'll do it."

"Ask him if he can post a man down the track from both ends of the train until we pull out," Ryan said. "We don't want anybody coming on us without warning."

The Italian went to the door and whistled. A man appeared moments later and went scampering off again into the darkness.

"I'm going to take a walk along the train," Ryan said. "Fincham, send Evans if Lieutenant Heinke picks up anything hot."

Ryan walked the length of the train, rapping on every door for attention. He gave the same message at each.

"This is Colonel Ryan," he said. "There'll be a short delay while we get up steam. It looks like we'll make it okay but the doors will be open in the event there's a foul-up. Remember. Disregard two short blasts of the whistle. Your signal to abandon is one long one. I don't expect you'll be hearing it. You won't hear from me again until you're in Switzerland. Good luck."

It was four forty-two when he returned to the commander's car and got Fincham, Costanzo, and the Italian. The patrols from Bergamo and the Carnate area had met between the two points and reported no sign of the train to SS headquarters.

"Milan's checking the main line to Como now," said Heinke. "That consignment for Gruppenfuehrer Dietrich's got 'em wondering what Klement's up to."

"When they don't locate us on the Como line they may try Lecco," Ryan said. "But Lecco was shut down when we went through. They'll have to send somebody to ask the guard if anything went through. Padre, let's get to the engine and see how our steam's coming."

One of the Italians took them into the cab and showed them a gauge.

"He says fifteen to twenty minutes, Cuhnel," Costanzo said, pointing at the gauge and continuing, "When the indicator gets here we're ready to go."

"Then let's get our friends started for the checkpoint," Ryan said. "They'll need more time than we do. They've got to work their way in close and get set to jump the Krauts while we're on our way."

The Italian leader agreed. He brought his trucks up and his

men quickly loaded on the German weapons and supplies and whatever loot of Klement's could be easily handled. Klement seemed on the verge of tears when he saw his treasures disappearing.

Ryan held back a Schmeisser for himself and Klement's pistol for Fincham but the Italian looked at both so longingly that he exchanged them for rifles.

"It's ten to five," Ryan said. "We'll be on our way in another fifteen minutes. Padre, tell him if he doesn't get our signal by five-forty it'll mean we got held up and he won't have time to pull out before first light. And he'd better not wait any longer. Tell him to set his watch by mine."

The Italian held up a bare wrist.

"You've got to have a watch," said Ryan.

He looked at the men around him.

"Captain Stein," he said, "it looks like you're elected."

Stein slipped off his wrist watch with a mock sigh.

"My folks gave it to me when I graduated from medical school," he said. "To time pulses with. Never did like the damn thing. Now I can tell them I sacrificed it for my country."

"They've wizard watches in Switzerland," said Fincham.

"This is Swiss," said Stein.

"Then I suggest you get another make, Captain," Ryan said.

The Italian said something to Costanzo which caused him to hesitate before translating it.

"What is it, Padre?" Ryan demanded.

"He wants Klement and the engineer. You won't turn them over to him, will you, Cuhnel? He'll kill them."

"No, Padre. Tell him we need the engineer to run the locomotive. And we may need Klement to get us through Tirano. I don't want to hurt our friend's feelings after he's been so cooperative."

The Italian agreed reluctantly, then pointed at the radio.

"He'd sure like to have it," Costanzo said.

"Negative," said Ryan. "Explain to him it's the only way we have of knowing if Tirano's going to be laying for us."

The Italian nodded, then said something and gestured toward the radio again.

"He says you could throw it off the train on the way to the checkpoint and he could pick it up," Costanzo said.

"Doesn't he know that would bust it all up?" Ryan demanded. His eyes fell on Klement's bed.

"Just a minute," he said. "Captain Stein, as soon as we start backing out of the station, you and Evans bundle up the radio in Klement's mattress and button it in that sleeping bag. Then drop it out the door when we get close to the crossing. Maybe it won't get too banged up."

"Grazie, colonnello, mille grazie," the Italian said when it was translated for him.

He shook Ryan's hand, saluted and kissed him on both cheeks before departing.

"Pair of bloody lovebirds, you are," Fincham said.

After Bostick squeezed into the German greatcoat and put on a German cap, Ryan sent him to the back of the train and then took Klement, the engineer, the fireman, and Costanzo to the cab. He ordered Klement to sit on the floor. Klement did so, groaning.

Then Ryan watched the gauge. The indicator crept toward the mark with excruciating slowness. Fifteen minutes had passed since he had been told steam would be up in no more than twenty minutes and the indicator still had not reached the point where the Italian had said it must before they could leave. Ryan looked from his watch to the gauge. Four minutes passed in silence. Then, with a twitch, the indicator reached the mark.

"Let's roll," Ryan cried.

The engineer backed against the tender and crossed his arms. He stared doggedly at his feet when Costanzo gave him Ryan's orders, then raised his head and spoke defiantly.

"He says he won't do it," Costanzo said. "He won't help us if you kill him for it."

"We'll see about that," Ryan said, reaching out for the engineer.

Costanzo put a hand on his arm.

"Ah think Ah can run the engine, Cuhnel," he said.

"You can run it?"

"Ah've been watching how they run an engine since yesterday. There's not that much to it."

"Are you sure, Padre?"

"Yes, sir."

"All right. I'm taking Marco back to our car for safekeeping.
Here's my rifle. Keep your eye on Klement."

Ryan hustled the engineer back to the commander's car and
instructed Fincham to push him out when they got outside the
station at Tirano. He was returning to the engine when Fincham
called him back.

"Milan's got through to Lecco," Fincham said. "Lecco told
Milan about the bridge. Said nothing could have gone past it.
They've a party out having a shufty from Lecco to the bridge."

"If our sergeant's still there he'll give 'em the note," Ryan
said. "But maybe they won't think to jump all the way up here
hunting us. If Milan starts a station-by-station check we should
be past Tirano before they hear anything there."

"Our luck can't hold forever, Ryan," said Fincham.

"I don't ask for forever, Colonel. I'll settle for thirty more
minutes."

Costanzo was looking back anxiously from the cab.

"Ah was wondering what was keeping you, Cuhnel," he said.

"Had some poop on the radio," Ryan said as he mounted to
the cab. "They're starting to trace us north. But they still
haven't . . . Where's the fireman!" he demanded.

The fireman was gone, his shovel left propped against the
side of the cab.

"He was here just now," Costanzo cried. "He must have . . .
When Ah looked back for you. Cuhnel, Ah'm sorry."

Ryan looked at his watch. Five-sixteen.

"Nothing we can do about it now, Padre," he said. "Get her
rolling. I'll fire."

The train edged forward, gathering speed as the great drive

"Start her back toward Tirano and bail out, Padre," Ryan ordered.

Then the throng of men was upon him. Still cheering, they raised him to their shoulders and bore him back along the train. At every car exultant men called out his name and pressed around him to shake his hand.

The snowy peaks were clearly defined in the first light now, and the darkness faded as Ryan's bearers made their interrupted way toward the end of the train. Orde jittered along behind, his good eye aglitter and his voice hoarse from yelling. Bostick was busy at the last car. He had found a bucket of paint and a brush by an unfinished shed and was slopping hasty letters on the side of the car.

When Ryan reached the end of the train Bostick was standing back to admire his work. Ryan climbed down from the clutching hands and looked at the boxcar.

He threw back his head and laughed.

The sign said, "Von Ryan's Express."

"Look at Von Ryan!" Orde shrieked. "He's laughing!"

The news raced back along the seething ranks.

Von Ryan was laughing out loud.

The cheering swelled to a great roar.

"God damn it, Colonel!" Bostick yelled. "You did it! God damn! God damn!"

Fincham came running back with Stein and Costanzo and pushed through the mob to Ryan's side.

"Congratulations, gentlemen," Ryan said. "And thanks. And Bostick, maybe I was right in not washing you out."

Bostick grinned.

Ryan stood back and surveyed the dripping letters on the boxcar again, his hands clasped behind him in the old, familiar manner. Suddenly his expression changed.

"Captain," he snapped. "You know better than to deface government issue. You've got exactly five minutes to police up that mess."

wheels took hold. Ryan shoveled coal into the firebox. It was not demanding work but he was weary.

When they were pounding along at full throttle, Costanzo spoke out above the engine's roar.

"Cuhnel," he said, "do you think he'll . . ."

Ryan straightened and eased his shoulders.

"The fireman? He just wanted to get away, Padre. Even if he wanted to turn us in there wouldn't be time. We'll be out of Tirano by the time he could walk to Sondrio and give the alarm."

"You're saying that for my benefit. Ah appreciate it, Cuhnel."

"Padre, just because it can't hurt us doesn't excuse your negligence. It happens that this isn't the time or the place to give you the eating out you deserve."

"Cuhnel," said Costanzo. "You have no idea how much better it makes me feel when you talk like that."

"Just keep your eye on Klement," Ryan said. "If he tries to get up sing out."

After fifteen minutes Ryan ordered Costanzo to ease back on the throttles.

"We must be getting close now," he said. "We can't go barreling into the station."

It was five thirty-four when they were close enough to recognize the outlines of the town against the dark sky and five thirty-eight when they began creeping into the station. Up ahead on the platform two German soldiers with rifles slung over their shoulders watched them approach. After a quick glance told him they were displaying no more than casual interest, Ryan looked back along the train. A short flash of light cleaved the darkness.

"Two blasts on the whistle, Padre!" Ryan said urgently.

It was five thirty-nine.

The soldiers stared at the engine, perplexed at the strident sound. Ryan was looking back. The light gleamed a second time.

"That's it!" Ryan cried. "Pour the coal to her!"

The train stopped with a grinding shudder, poised motionless for a moment, then crept backward. The soldiers watched indecisively, then began walking toward the train. A civilian burst out of the station house, waving his arms and shouting. The German soldiers looked back over their shoulders at him without stopping. As the train increased speed, so did they. From far up the slope came the sound of gunfire and a heavy explosion.

One of the Germans was only a dozen yards away now, the other a few steps behind him.

"Halt!" shouted the first soldier, almost to the engine now.

He stopped and raised his rifle to his shoulder as the other caught up with him. Ryan could see the man's determined face and leveled rifle in the thin glow of the headlight. He took careful aim and shot the German in the head. The other soldier threw himself to the ground and began firing. His bullets clanged against the steel side of the engine and ricocheted with a penetrating whine.

"Kill the headlight!" Ryan cried.

The narrow beam seemed to hang in the air for an instant, then darkness was complete. The train was moving as fast as a fat man could run now and the German soldier had stopped firing and run to the fallen man.

"Let's jettison Klement," Ryan said. "He can't hurt us now."

He pulled Klement to his feet. The major began pleading in a high, sweaty voice.

"Over you go," said Ryan, pushing him from the cab.

Klement hit and rolled like a ball, almost colliding with the engineer, who had just come tumbling out of the commander's car. The engineer rolled once and sprang to his feet, shaking his fist. Then Klement was on his feet, too, and running after the locomotive, shouting. When he saw he could not catch up he stopped and looked forlornly after it.

And now the train was pushing laboriously up a long grade. Far up ahead the snowclad tops of mountains were whitening in the refracted rays of a sun still far below the horizon, making a faint smear in the darkness like a single drop of milk in black coffee. The gunfire at the checkpoint had diminished to sporadic bursts. And still there was no signal flare.

Off to the left of the center cars a burst of red and yellow fire bloomed in the night and the air reverberated with thunder as concussion sent a wave of shock rippling along the train. Ryan looked back toward the road from Sondrio to see a flash of light as a second explosion shook the train.

"Tank!" he cried.

"Cuhnel!" Costanzo yelled.

Up ahead a green flare hung in the air a moment, then arched toward the ground.

Shells were exploding ahead of the front cars now.

"They're trying to hit the tracks," Ryan said.

A stream of tracers lobbed at the locomotive with illusory slowness from the darkness behind them and bullets ripped the tender.

"Armored car!" Ryan cried. "Gaining on us! Firewall her, Padre!"

"We're going as fast as we can," Costanzo said huskily.

A flickering, candlelike light arced through the air a hundred yards behind them and suddenly the armored car was sharply visible, painted in fire. An explosion sent flames spurting from its ports and it fell on its side, one blazing tire spinning in a circle of fire.

"Molotov cocktail!" Ryan cried. "He had a man covering our rear."

"Good show!" Fincham bellowed from the open door of the commander's car, almost as if in answer to Ryan's words.

"He'll never get his radio now," said Ryan. "Not with that tank back there cutting down on us."

"How can you think of that at a time like this?" Costanzo demanded.

A bundle flew out of the commander's car to roll along the right of way.

"Fincham thought of it, too," Ryan said. "Too bad he won't get it after all he's done for us."

A truck loomed out of the lessening darkness.

"He's coming after it!" Ryan cried in admiration. "The crazy bastard!"

As the truck passed the engine the Italian leaned half out of the cab, his fingers held in the victory sign.

"Arrivederci, amico!" he bawled. "Buona fortuna."

The first cars were crossing into Switzerland now and Bostick was signaling wildly from the foremost with his flashlight. The truck stopped and a man jumped off the back and threw the radio into it. The tank stopped firing at the tracks and was after the engine. The shells fell close. One of them sent a shower of dirt and stones over the cab.

"You all right, Padre?" Ryan yelled anxiously.

Costanzo answered with a dirt-streaked grin.

And then they were across the border.

Costanzo set the brakes and the train slid over the smooth rails. The tank had stopped firing and the last echoes died away in the surrounding hills to leave a plangent silence.

The car doors popped open and men came spilling out as if poured from buckets to roll on the ground, jump to their feet and shout, leaping into the air and beating each other on the back and shoulders. Some of them kneeled and kissed the earth. The Swiss border guards came from their posts to look on incredulously. Prisoners engulfed them and shook their hands in an orgy of friendship, as if the Swiss were instrumental in their deliverance.

Ryan gave a long sigh and climbed down stiffly from the cab. His body was a lump of aches and his mind was blurred with fatigue. He wanted to lie down in his tracks and sleep. A band of cheering prisoners rushed toward him. He pulled himself erect and faced them, as straight and controlled as the day he walked into P. G. 202.

Fincham had uncoupled the car behind the engine and was calling out above the din.